To my babes that love to be called a good girl but crave to be called a dirty slut. You're in good hands with Camden Hunter.

Playlist

Daylight - Taylor Swift
Blue - Zach Bryan
I'm Yours (sped up) - Isabel LaRosa
Don't Blame Me - Taylor Swift
Fall Into Me - Forest Blakk
Hate To Be Lame - Lizzy McAlpine and FINNEAS
Glitch - Taylor Swift
Moodswings - 5 Seconds of Summer
My Bed - Leah Kate
Chance With You - Mehro
Burning Bridges - Bea Miller
I F*cking Love You - Zolita
Much Better - Jonas Brothers
Love Me Harder - Ariana Grande and The Weeknd
Perfectly Wrong - Shawn Mendes
Going Home - The Aces
Be More - Stephen Sanchez

Author's Note

Tempt Our Fate is a small-town, billionaire, enemies-to-lovers romance. It is full of banter, sweet moments, and scenes that'll have you blushing. I hope that you love Camden and Pippa as much as I do. This is the second book in a series of interconnected stand-alones set in Sutten Mountain.

Tempt Our Fate contains mature content that may not be suitable for all audiences. Please go to <u>authorkatsingleton.com/content-warnings</u> for a list of content warnings for the book.

Chapter 1
PIPPA

THE MOST ANNOYING THING ABOUT MEN IS THEY ALWAYS ASSUME that you actually give a damn what they're talking about. I stand at the register, nodding to the customer on the other side of the counter in hopes that by pretending to care, he'll order quicker.

His suit looks expensive, even if it is a little too large on him. Judging by his arrogance and the way he carries himself, coupled with the fact that this is a small town and I don't recognize his face, my guess is that he isn't from around here.

"It's just, I think you should really consider sourcing your coffee beans from somewhere else," he continues, pushing me past my breaking point.

I give him a sickeningly sweet smile. "I don't remember asking for your advice. Remind me what you'd like to order again?"

His mouth falls open in shock. "I know this amazing coffee shop in New York that—"

I clap my hands together. "Great, you can get your coffee from there, then!" I look around him, motioning for the next person in line. "Next," I state, trying to get rid of the guy standing in front of me.

The dude in a suit narrows his bushy eyebrows. "Excuse me," he argues, turning around to the customer behind him. "I'm not done ordering yet."

I roll my eyes. We're packed, and I'm down an employee today due to a stomach bug. The last thing I need is for some tourist to lecture me on where I get my beans from. I'm proud of the relationship I've built with my supplier. I'm not in the least bit interested in getting a new one.

My coffee shop and bakery are my pride and joy. Emphasis on *my*. Wake and Bake is my baby. I've poured my heart and soul into this business, and I have no desire to let some stranger tell me how to run it.

My nostrils flare as I take a deep breath. Being rude to customers is not something I enjoy, but I'm tired, and there's a line of people behind him that I need to attend to. Once I get the chance to step away from the register, I also need to put a new batch of cupcakes in the oven and begin prepping all of the pastries for tomorrow.

There are a thousand things on my to-do list, and none of them involve looking for new coffee beans.

"What can I get you?" I ask, my voice dejected.

His lips purse. I brace for him to bring up the topic again, but he doesn't. "I'll take a water, please."

I fight the urge to tell him we have multiple water stations set up around the shop. At this point, I'll do whatever it takes to get him out of the line so I can help the next person. "One water. Got it. Name, please?"

"Peter."

I nod, writing his name on the hot pink cup. "Peter," I repeat. He *looks* like a Peter.

I set his cup in the line of drinks that need to be made. I have one of my employees, Lexi, still here with me today, but she's on lunch, so I'm left taking orders and making the drinks.

Time flies as we get through the afternoon rush of customers. Thankfully, Lexi knows what she's doing, and upon her return, we were able to get through all of the orders in a somewhat timely manner. Wake and Bake has kind of taken off in the past few months, and I've been considering hiring a new employee or two, especially before ski season starts back up and thousands of tourists descend on Sutten Mountain for their winter vacations.

I'm glad it's been busy recently. It helps dull the sting of losing my mom unexpectedly a few months ago. Losing her was the worst pain I've ever been through, and I handled her death the only way I knew how—by throwing myself into work.

I wipe my hands on my bright pink apron, the vibrant color the same as the far wall. "That was crazy." I sigh, leaning against the counter to rest for a minute.

Lexi nods, pushing pieces of her red hair out of her face. "I think I blacked out. That was *way* busier than normal."

"I wonder why," I muse, taking a sip of my own iced coffee. The ice has melted, and it doesn't taste as strong as when I first made it, but I need a coffee IV at this point to keep me on my feet, so I slurp it down anyway.

"Someone told me that there's a large group of people in town looking at the Richardsons' gallery next door."

My heart sinks. "Looking at it?"

Lexi shrugs. "Since Barb passed, the space has been left vacant. With no one to run it, and apparently no one local renting it, I think it went to auction. At least that's what my dad said."

I stare at her for a few moments, wondering if Peter from earlier is part of that group. Why would people from New York be looking at the space? I've asked about renting the place for months to help expand Wake and Bake, and I've always been told it wasn't for rent—or for sale.

I hum under my breath, annoyed. Typically, the Livingston Real Estate group handles all sales in Sutten, but for some reason, our entire block is owned by some other company from out of town. Maybe all along, that space was available; it just wasn't an option for *me*.

Reaching underneath the counter, I pull out one of the pastry to-go boxes. I open it, laying out the classic pink doily we put on the bottom of each order.

"Do we still have catering orders?" Lexi asks, confused. There's panic in her eyes. Probably because we're just now dying down, and we're both finally getting the opportunity to take a breath.

"We sure don't," I answer, continuing my task. "But if there is something going on next door, I feel like I need to welcome them the only way I know how—with treats."

Lexi smirks as she shakes her head at me. "So you're taking treats over there, but you're really going over there to snoop?"

I snap the tongs between us. "That's *exactly* what I'm doing." Our most popular croissant sold out this morning, but I pick out a few other customer favorites that we still have left to include.

Once I have a dozen different options in the box, hoping that's enough for whatever kind of crowd is gathering next door, I close it and even add a cute Wake and Bake sticker to seal it shut.

"We might have new neighbors to welcome, Lexi. This is the nice thing to do." I wink at her, setting the box on the counter so I can adjust the claw clip in my hair.

I probably look like a wreck after the long morning and afternoon that I've had, but I don't care about my appearance too much. I'm not trying to impress these tourist businessmen—I'm just trying to get information on why the space next door is suddenly available for sale when I've been told multiple times otherwise.

I wrap the long tendrils of my dark hair in a twist, pinching the sides of the clip together and securing it in my hair. My hair is too messy to even try to wear down, but I do pull out a few pieces in the front to attempt to style the updo a little more.

"How do you still look so good after an afternoon like that?" Lexi comments, looking down at her coffee-stained apron. We accidentally collided at one point during the chaos, sloshing a fresh espresso shot onto both of us. Luckily for me, her apron took most of the damage.

I roll my eyes at her. The only thing I did this morning was put on mascara and a little bit of blush. I didn't have time to do anything else before I had to race to the shop to get things started for the day. I wouldn't describe myself as put together, but it'll do. I don't care about impressing anyone with my looks, but I wouldn't mind if they loved my treats. Maybe if I can impress one of the owners before the sale is final, they'll reconsider and sell it to me instead.

I'm about to head out the door when Lexi rushes forward, pulling at the string of my apron. "Wait!" she calls, tugging at the neck loop. "Maybe take this off first?"

I laugh, looking at the abundance of flour and icing covering the fabric. "Yeah, probably should."

The apron makes a soft thud as I toss it onto one of the counters behind us. "This T-shirt probably isn't the most professional attire either," I note, kind of wishing I'd worn something else this morning.

Lexi shakes her head at me. "It works. It's better than the apron. Plus, I think the Wake and Bake merch is cute. Own it, Pippa."

My shoulders straighten as I flash her a wink. "You're totally right. Time for me to go make some friends."

Chapter 2
PIPPA

THERE ARE MULTIPLE SUVs LINED UP IN FRONT OF THE GALLERY. A man in yet another suit stands outside the front door. He presses a phone to his ear, not even noticing me walking toward him.

"I just don't see your vision for this. Who would want to come here to look at art?"

He sighs at whatever is said on the other line. He scowls, creating a crease on his already wrinkled forehead. "No, I'm not questioning you, sir. It's just that—"

Whatever is said on the other line can't be good because he pulls the phone away from his ear slightly.

My cowboy boots scuff against the pavement as I come to a stop. The sound catches the guy's attention. His eyes travel up and down my body. He grunts at whatever is said on the other line. "See you in a bit," he clips before tapping something on the screen. His eyes focus on the box in my grasp.

"Are you looking at the space?" I ask, nodding toward the building.

His eyes follow mine. He scratches at his chin awkwardly. "Did you need something?"

I smile when he focuses on me again. *Yes, sir. You could help me by telling me why the hell the owners will sell to you and not me.*

I hold up the box of pastries, giving it a gentle shake. "I own the cafe right next door and wanted to introduce myself. I wasn't sure if you were just looking or if you owned it. But I wanted to give you guys a warm welcome either way..."

My attempt at fishing for more information doesn't work. He does give me the slightest of smiles. Hooking a thumb over his shoulder, he takes a step toward the Richardsons' old gallery. Their custom sign and awnings still hang on the building, but I wonder how long it'll last. Judging by the guy's demeanor, my hopes of renting this space are dwindling.

It seems like it's already been sold, but I follow him inside just to scope things out. My feet come to a halt when I see the inside of the building. I used to frequent the Richardsons' shop. Al was one of the nicest humans I'd ever met, and he was so proud of the gallery he and his wife created. It was their pride and joy. They worked so hard to highlight the talent of local artists. My heart feels heavy as I look around the space. There used to be so many variations of different art pieces in here. There were paintings, sculptures, photographs, and pottery. It was filled with life.

Now, it feels void of life. The stark white walls contrast three men in dark suits. The men talk in a semicircle, one of them looking over at me midconversation.

"How can I help you, dear?"

I try not to scoff. I'm twenty-three years old. I'm not anyone's dear. I smile anyway because now I'm even more curious about who purchased the space. I want to know their intentions—and maybe part of me still wants to know if they'd want to sell it again to someone else...to me.

"She runs the restaurant next door," the guy from outside pipes up, "and brought some food to welcome us."

"Technically, it's a bakery and coffee shop," I add. "And I brought pastries."

Their eyes light up, the three men making their way toward me. I open the pink box for them, loving how distracted they are by the treats inside. The guy from outside joins them, and they all pick something to eat. A satisfied smirk crosses my lips as they take a bite, and I relish their sighs of approval.

"I was excited to hear we might have new neighbors." I wasn't in the slightest, but they don't need to know that. "I wasn't aware this space was for sale."

One of them nods, opening his mouth to talk despite his mouthful of food. "Sure was. The deal went through last week."

Shit. Those out-of-state assholes really did sell the space to someone else, despite my inquiries.

"Interesting," I squeak, plastering a fake smile on my face when one of them narrows their eyes on me. "So happy to have you here," I add for pleasantries.

"We're only here to oversee the grand opening," he explains.

Before I can get a word in, the guy from outside joins the conversation. "Yeah, here to tell Mr. Hunter that there's no way this is going to work. People here don't have good taste." His eyes bulge, like he halfway feels sorry for the insult he just threw out. "No offense," he adds.

"None taken," I snap, quickly shutting the box. "Because your opinion is wrong."

The air gets thick with tension—and not the good kind. The asshat from outside clears his throat uncomfortably. "It's not that. I just meant—"

"Oh, I know what you meant." I begin to back up. There's no use for me to stay here and listen to these guys from the city who don't know a thing about this town and the people in it. "It's just that you're very, very wrong, but that's okay. We can't always be right, can we?"

His mouth flops open. He looks like the fish in the big tanks at an aquarium I once visited as a kid. His mouth opens and closes as if he's blowing bubbles into the water.

"Maybe this town isn't for you," I say, backing up toward the door—taking my pastries with me because they do not deserve even the smallest bites of my creations. "In fact, maybe this town isn't for you and whoever this Mr. Hunter is. Maybe you could pass that info to—"

All of a sudden, I collide with something—or rather a some*one* than a some*thing*.

I let out a yelp, trying to keep hold of the box in my hands so I don't spill the remaining pastries all over the ground.

Turning around, I almost drop the box again when I see who is standing in front of me. He's tall, nearly having to duck to get through the low doorframe. He smirks, but it doesn't reach his eyes. "I'm really tired of us meeting like this," he declares, his voice low but smooth. I hate the shiver that runs through my body at his cold but gravelly voice.

Now I'm the one who looks like a fish because I'm speechless that somehow, fate hates me enough to bring this guy into my life again.

And it only gets worse when he opens his mouth and says, "Pass what info to me, shortcake?"

Chapter 3
CAMDEN

IT'S BEEN A LONG TIME SINCE I'VE HAD A WOMAN GLARE AT ME THE way this local is staring at me right now. If looks could actually kill, she'd have me lying dead on the floor.

"I know it isn't my charm that rendered you speechless," I chide, wondering what kind of planets aligned to put her tragically back into my life once again. At least this time, she didn't spill something all over me, unlike our previous two encounters. The first time we met was at my best friend Beck's bachelor party, when she spilled beer all over me in some godforsaken local dive bar. The second was at Beck's wedding, when I wound up covered in cupcake frosting. I could have gone my entire life without a third encounter.

"You're Mr. Hunter?" she squeaks. Now that she's gained her composure, she scurries away from me, putting a good chunk of distance between us. "Please don't tell me you're the one who bought this place," she pleads.

"Please don't tell me that me buying this gallery means I have to put up with you," I retort.

Her eyes roll. Any other time, I'd be bothered by someone having the nerve to roll their eyes at me, but not with her.

"Why do I have such shitty karma?" she mutters, looking briefly over her shoulder at my business associates.

"I was just asking myself the same thing." I let out a bored sigh, stepping around her and deeper into the gallery space. It doesn't look like a lot right now, but tomorrow, two of my designers from Manhattan will fly in to get this space ready for our grand opening next weekend. I'd been told by every single person I spoke with, most of all by my parents, that I shouldn't waste my time opening something in this town. It only made me want to make this work even more.

The last thing I expected was having to deal with the woman glaring up at me.

"Can you get on with what information you needed to pass on so I can go back to planning my opening?"

She thinks about her words for a moment, which catches me by surprise because she strikes me as someone who says exactly what they're thinking the instant it comes to their mind.

"One of your lovely friends was just saying how they thought people in Sutten didn't have taste. As someone who grew up here and knew the Richardsons and the art they featured *very* well, I firmly disagree."

"If I thought people didn't have taste in Sutten, I wouldn't be dumping money into opening a gallery at this location." It's a half-truth. When I first visited for Beck's wedding, I hated the town, but I couldn't deny the bustling tourism that I noticed. It didn't take long for me to learn that people with money preferred to vacation in a town like this. It's quieter than other ski destinations in Colorado, and the real estate is a gold mine for what you can get for your money. So I saw a new niche I could tap into by purchasing a gallery here. Unlike my gallery in New York, which relies heavily on exhibits of one artist's work, I want this one to showcase the best work from the most talented artists I know.

People spend money on vacation. They'll walk in here and feel sentimental about buying art because *everyone* has a good time on vacation.

I look toward Daly, someone I've known most of my life. He's a colleague of my parents, and the moment I wanted to open my own gallery, I knew I wanted his help. He has a good eye, despite his lackluster personality, but I don't appreciate him bad-mouthing this town to a local—even if it is to the bane of my existence.

"Apologize," I clip, my tone leaving no room for argument. At least, I thought it didn't leave any room for discussion, but apparently, Daly has decided to grow a pair today because he dares to open his mouth and disagree.

"I only meant it as—"

"You were very clear with what you meant. There's not much to misinterpret when you say an entire town doesn't have taste. Ever heard of a generalization?" she fires at him. Damn, she's mouthy.

I cough, attempting to hide a laugh at her sass. It's kind of funny when it isn't aimed my way. It doesn't make me dislike her any less, but it is mildly entertaining, at least.

"I don't listen to half the things that come out of his mouth anyway. He knows art. Everything else is debatable," I tell her.

She narrows her eyes, keeping them trained on me. Whatever's going through her mind doesn't soften her features at all. The tiniest of creases appears on her forehead, right between her dark eyebrows.

I let my gaze travel down her body, letting it focus on the box in her hands. Luckily for me, this time, the contents of the box aren't splattered all over my very expensive suit. "What's in the box, shortcake?"

She scoffs, rolling her eyes at me once again. Fuck. Why do I want to find another way to get her to roll them at me? "Ew, shortcake? My name is Pippa, not shortcake, but you don't even have to call me that. It's best if we just don't talk at all. How about that, Mr. Hunter?"

The smile on my lips isn't forced. "I don't care about your name, shortcake. I'll call you whatever I want to call you. The nickname fits." I look her up and down. "I've got to have at least a foot on her, and I think the little pair of pink cowboy boots she's wearing generously give her a few inches. The cake part is just for fun. It fits. Two of the three times I've had the displeasure of seeing her, she's had cake with her. The little cake embroidered on her T-shirt only sealed the deal for the nickname. "But for the record, Mr. Hunter is my father, and I'd much prefer not to talk about him. I'm Camden. Camden Hunter."

Daly clears his throat. He's never been comfortable with the way I speak about my dad, but I don't typically care about how people feel. Maybe I would've if my parents cared more about me, but they don't. So he can be uncomfortable. I'm sure it won't be long until he's reporting back to my father about everything that happened today anyway.

"I would much prefer calling you a raging asshole. Or douchebag if I'm feeling frisky."

"Cute."

"No, what's cute is the damage I'll do to you if you call me shortcake again."

I roll my bottom lip between my teeth. "Don't tempt me."

She lets out a grunt of disgust. Leaving a huge amount of distance between us, she ambles around me and returns to the doorway once again, this time managing not to collide with me.

"Not going to share?" I nod toward the box in her hands.

A sarcastic laugh slips from her lips. "Absolutely not. I already regret giving it to your snooty friends and—"

"Colleagues," I interrupt.

She looks like she could hit me for interrupting her. "I don't think you'd enjoy them, not that any of you deserve my hard work anyway. Us townies don't have taste, remember?" This time, the scathing look isn't aimed my way; it's aimed at Daly. I look over my shoulder at him, laughing at the petrified look on his face.

Damn. She might scare him more than I do.

My hands find my pockets as I really look at the woman making her way out the door. "Hope to see you never, shortcake."

"The feeling is very mutual," she counters, pushing the door open. "However, if you do happen to come next door, know that the discount I used to give the Richardsons doesn't apply to you. You'll pay full price. Maybe double."

"I have no intentions of coming next door."

She lets out a long, frustrated sigh. If she's trying to hide how she's feeling, she's doing a terrible job at it. "Perfect. I had no intention of serving you anyway."

I shrug carelessly. "So it's settled."

She stares at me. I don't hate the way she takes her time looking at me from top to bottom before her hazel eyes come to a stop on my face. "It's settled."

"Goodbye, then, shortcake."

Her nostrils flare, but she doesn't say anything on her way out. At least, she doesn't use words. But the middle finger in the air as her footfalls hit the pavement tells me enough.

Her colliding into my life once again just made this new business endeavor a hell of a lot more interesting.

Chapter 4
PIPPA

I'm busy folding puff pastry dough for my sausage-and-cheddar pastries when the bell to the bakery door rings. Lexi is helping me open the cafe today, but I just got a text from her a few minutes ago telling me she was running late this morning. There's no way it should be her walking in, but we're also closed, so I don't know who could be walking through the door unless I accidentally left it unlocked.

I wipe my hands on my apron, hurriedly trying to finish folding the pastry before busting through the kitchen doors.

"I'm sorry, we're—" My feet come to a halt a few feet away from the counter when I see the person standing in front of the register.

"*You.*" The sweet tone I normally use with customers is gone. In its place is something much closer to a growl.

Camden tucks his hands into the pockets of his slacks. It's barely five in the morning, and he's dressed like he's about to go to some sort of fancy business meeting. "Good morning," he says, his voice sharp and cold.

"It's not a good morning if I have to see you before the sun has risen."

His lips twitch with humor. It's the only movement of his body; the rest of him stands as still as a statue. Except for his eyes—they travel over my body, coming to a stop on my face. "Trust me, you weren't my first choice. In fact, you were my last. But there's nothing open here that has coffee."

"There's a Starbucks about fifteen miles away. You should try it."

"I've had it every day since I've arrived. My assistant has run and got it for me, but she woke up with a fever this morning, and I don't have time to go there."

"What a bummer for you." I shrug. Caffeinating him is not my problem. He can figure it out. "We aren't open." I point to the giant pink neon sign that sits in the window. "In case you don't understand how it works, typically if a place is open, their sign is lit. The closed sign on the door is *also* a great indicator that, you know…" I gesture to the empty space around us. "We aren't open."

"Figured you could do a favor for a friend."

I choke on my own spit. Awkward sounds come from my throat as I try to regain my composure. I eventually get it together, able to finally swallow without causing another coughing fit. "I know you just didn't call me a *friend*."

He takes a step closer, his eyes training on the menu board behind me. "I did. It tasted vile coming from my mouth, but it was worth a shot."

I stare at him in shock. My mouth hangs open as I try to figure out what in the hell is going on. Am I still dreaming? It's been a few days since we last spoke next door. I thought we had an agreement—he stayed on his side of the boundary line, and I stayed on mine. He's come to enemy territory, and his air of superiority makes him so arrogant that he assumed I'd just welcome him in with open arms.

Hell no.

"Camden, leave," I demand. "I'm not serving you coffee."

All he does is glare at me. It makes me uncomfortable. His icy-blue eyes stare *too* deep. Men shouldn't be allowed to have hair so dark but eyes so light. It's like he can see right through me, and I hate it with every fiber of my being.

"Hello?" I press, trying to fill the silence. I want him out of my bakery and, quite frankly, out of this town, but that might be a little dramatic. Just sending him back to his own property will do for now. "I'm quite worried about your understanding of the word *never*. I vividly remember you saying you never wanted to see me again. The feeling was very mutual."

He lets out a small groan. It's so quiet I almost miss it. It's the first real emotion I've seen from him. The first time his rigid demeanor has fallen, at least for a moment. "Look, I said that thinking there'd be somewhere else to get a cup of coffee. But nothing is open, and I have a splitting headache that has made me resort to asking you. All you have to do is make it, and you'll never see me again. Trisha should be back on the mend tomorrow, and we'll pretend this never happened. Okay?" He pinches his perfectly straight nose between his thumb and pointer finger, massaging to ease the ache.

I chew on my lip. Camden doesn't seem like the kind of person to back down if he wants something. And I really do need to get back to baking to get everything ready before the store opens. I could just leave him here…

I sigh, knowing he'd have the audacity to follow me back there. The easiest choice is one I hate—I think I could get rid of him if I just make the damn cup of coffee.

"I'm only doing this because I want to get rid of you," I tell him, pinning him with a glare.

"I'm only here because I'm desperate." He smiles. Actually smiles. Why does it look so good? It seems unnatural for him to smile. He shouldn't look good doing it.

I spin on my heel immediately, not wanting to stare at him for a second longer. His teeth are too straight and perfect, and the long dimples that form on either side of his upturned lips are too deep—too enticing.

A man with dimples is my freaking weakness. They aren't supposed to look good on a man as ice-cold as Camden.

"How do you like your coffee?" I ask, speaking to the wall instead of looking at him.

He clears his throat. "Flat white. Hot. As big as you can make it with vanilla and oat milk."

I laugh, starting the espresso machine. I welcome the hissing of the machine as it rumbles to life because it fills the tension-filled silence between us.

"Something funny?" he asks once the shots start to trickle out.

I look up, making eye contact with him through the mirror on the wall. "Your order just wasn't what I was expecting."

"Something wrong with my order?"

"You strike me as a black coffee kind of guy. Maybe an Americano."

"I spent some time in France in my twenties. I do enjoy just an espresso shot every now and then."

I don't answer him. I want to ask him more about France, about what it was like. I've always wanted to go to France. It's on the top of my bucket list. I would geek out to go to a French pâtisserie. All of my dreams would come true just to be in the presence of pastry chefs with that much talent and finesse.

Neither one of us speaks as I finish making his coffee. At one point, he answers a call, but it doesn't last long. After a brief exchange, he's silent again.

Turning around, I set two large to-go cups in front of him. He looks from me to the coffee cups to me again. His dark eyebrows pull together on his forehead. "I only asked for *one* coffee." Reaching into his suit jacket, he pulls out a sleek black wallet. He hands me his credit card, and even his card feels expensive. It's heavy and metal and far more fancy than my creased, plastic card that I'm pretty sure expires in a few months.

"There's only one coffee," I answer, suddenly feeling self-conscious about the other drink I made him. It was more out of habit than anything, but it's too late to go back on it, so now I just have to own it.

"Okay," he drawls, dragging out the word like he's confused.

"One is the drink you ordered; the other is a tea. With chamomile, honey, and a couple of secret ingredients. I always had migraines, and my mom would make it for me. I figured it might help..." My words fall flat because now it seems ridiculous. This man has yelled at me multiple times for things that were a complete accident. I shouldn't be nice to him. I don't know what possessed me to make him the drink, but now I have regrets.

"That's, uhh..."

Clearly, neither one of us knows what to say about the gesture. I hurriedly swipe his card and pretty much toss it back to him, wanting to be done with him and this interaction. My mom didn't raise me to be rude to people. As someone who has suffered from many migraines, I just wanted to help.

Even if it was for him—the douchebag in a suit that tests every last ounce of my patience.

"I didn't want to listen to you complain," I rush out. "Couldn't let Mr. Fancy Art Gallery have a headache."

"Yeah." He studies me for a second. I look right back at him, even though my cheeks burn from embarrassment that I just might've extended an olive branch to enemy number one.

"Don't think too hard about it. You're already enough of an asshole. I didn't want anyone to have to deal with you if you had a headache as well."

He picks up both of the cups, handling them with care. The hot pink cups seem out of place in his large hands. I don't stick around to say anything else. Things are back to enemy-ing between us the way they should be. I blame the fact that it's too freaking early to be dealing with him.

I scurry back into the kitchen, taking comfort in being alone and doing the mindless task of folding out dough. The bell above the door dings a few moments later, and it's only then that I can take a deep breath.

Today is already weird, and the sun hasn't even risen yet.

It gets weirder when I greet Lexi later on in the morning and find a crisp hundred-dollar bill neatly placed in our tip jar.

Chapter 5
CAMDEN

"YOU'VE GOT TO BE FUCKING KIDDING ME." MY VOICE ECHOES through the space, the anger surrounding everyone in the room.

Daly takes a few steps backward until he's almost hiding behind a large gallery print. "Well, Mr. Hunter…"

I grunt, hating the sound of the name. My hand waves in the air dismissively as I look from him to Trisha.

"They really just canceled?"

She nods. Trisha is the one person who doesn't ever cower at my mood swings. It might be because she's old enough to be my mother and was the very first employee I ever hired. My raised tone doesn't seem to deter her in the slightest. "I've tried calling a few local places. There's not a ton of options, but I'll continue to try and find something, sir."

I take a deep breath, looking at the space around me. The gallery is pretty much completely ready for the opening tonight —except for the fact I don't have a goddamn caterer for the night.

"We've used them countless times. I don't understand why they're suddenly canceling now," I grit out, grasping for straws because everything tonight has to be *perfect*.

So many people I know have already flown in from New York for the night. Word spreads quickly, and the news of the opening tonight is spreading from one wealthy family to the next. I'm hoping even people who are vacationing here or close by come to see it.

It's all supposed to be perfect. And it's supposed to be a big fuck-you to my father, who told me this would be the worst career move of my life if I opened something here.

But I can't have a room full of bored, rich people and not have anything to serve them.

"What if we ran to the store and just bought stuff to serve? They wouldn't know any different," Daly offers, his tone cautious.

I shoot a scathing look in his direction. Tonight is supposed to be immaculate. I'm not serving store-bought vegetable trays and cheap meats, no matter how desperate of a situation I've found myself in. "Over my dead body," I growl, the idea preposterous.

In an hour, the first wave of people are set to arrive. Granted, it's some of the artists I've flown in to see the space, but I don't want to be trying to sort all of this out with them here.

I look back to Trisha. "Their flights were supposed to get in last night, so they had all day today to prepare. They're just now telling us?"

"Yes," Trisha answers.

"That's incredibly unprofessional," I snap.

"Something about how they got offered a different event. Much bigger, couldn't say no..."

My loud sigh tells her I've heard enough. They'll never be getting my business again, and I'll make damn sure that no one else I know in my social circle uses them either. This kind of professionalism is unacceptable in my book and won't be tolerated. I booked them the moment the sale went through, even going as far as to book their plane tickets and have Trisha set them up with everything they needed for this opening.

My footsteps are heavy as I bound through the gallery and to my small office space at the back of the building. The door cracks against the wall as I angrily shove it open.

Trisha follows me, leaving everyone else behind. Their ideas are useless anyway.

"We have to figure this out," I tell her, my voice softer now that it's just the two of us. It's not her fault they've suddenly canceled at the last minute. She did everything she was supposed to do. It wouldn't be fair to take my anger out on her.

"I think the answer is to find someone locally."

My fingers steeple underneath my chin. I haven't exactly gotten to explore the town since arriving last week. I've been at the gallery from early in the morning to late at night, surviving off whatever food Trisha forces me to eat. I don't know where to start on what to eat and how fast I can get it from them, but I don't really have many other options.

The opening is in four hours, and somehow, I have to start feeding people shortly after that. I don't have the luxury of time on my side.

"What about the little bakery next door?" Trisha offers. "You've had me grab your drinks there every morning. I'm sure we could get some finger foods to serve from them."

My eyes cut to her immediately. It was supposed to be our little secret that I've had her going next door instead of traveling to Starbucks. We've been busy, and I needed her here. It was just more convenient that way.

"I'm sure we have other options," I clip. My phone vibrates in my pocket, but I ignore it. Nothing is more important than dealing with this catering situation and figuring it out fast.

"Well, sure, but I don't know if anything is better than the cute shop next door. She seems to work so hard and always has a lot on hand. If you just went over and asked nicely, maybe…"

"Trisha, there has to be somewhere else. Isn't there another bakery here? Or a nice restaurant? Where do people eat?"

She stares at me for a long time, a slight frown to her lips. "There are other places to eat; I'm just not sure there are places that can make the elegant finger-type food we're looking for at this opening. The last thing people want to do while milling about and munching on snacks is have something messy. Little pastries would be perfect."

I groan, running my hands up and down my face. "The girl there hates me," I admit. "She hates everything that has to do with this gallery. I think she was friends with the previous owners. She doesn't seem like the type that likes the fact that we made the small little gallery more..."

"City?" Trisha finishes.

I nod. "Yeah. That."

"Then go to her and tell her that even though this isn't the gallery they're used to that you appreciate small businesses and would love to show off her delicious food at the opening."

Trisha crosses her arms over her chest, pinning me with a stare that doesn't leave a lot of room for arguing. She's right. Pippa's little bakery would be perfect for the mess I've found myself in, but I'd much prefer riding the god-awful mechanical bull at one of the bars in this town than asking her for help.

"She's too smart," I remark off-handedly. "There's not enough smoke I could blow up her ass to make her believe the whole small business speech. It's too last-minute. She'd be onto me immediately."

"How about I go ask her?" Trisha offers. "No one can say no to an old lady." She flutters her eyelashes, making me bark out a laugh.

"You're not old," I tell her, sitting up in my chair.

She smiles. "Good answer. I'm off to go lay on my old-lady charm anyway."

Trisha doesn't say anything else. She flutters out the door, and as I watch her leave, I already know what Pippa's answer will be. I just hope I'm wrong.

Chapter 6
PIPPA

"No," I tell the woman standing in front of me. She's been in here every morning recently, and now with her request to help Camden, I'm wondering if that sneaky asshole has been drinking my coffee.

"I think it could be really great exposure for you," she continues, seemingly unfazed by my answer.

I wipe at the table in front of me, trying to get all of the surfaces clean before closing up the cafe for the night. It was another busy day, and all I want to do is get home, take my shoes off, make some dinner, and sit on the couch for the rest of the night. There are multiple new episodes of some of my favorite TV shows tonight, and I've got a bottle of wine I've been dreaming about opening all day long.

"I'm sorry, I'm really not trying to be rude, but the answer is no," I tell her again. I'm often terrible at names, but I think she said her name was Trisha and she was the assistant to the owner of the gallery next door. Considering there's only one gallery next door and there's only one owner as far as I know, I'm pretty sure the sweet woman behind me has to work for Camden Hunter.

"Camden told me you'd say that," she says. This catches my attention. I look at her from over my shoulder, my interest piqued.

"He did?"

"Sure did. In fact, he told me not to come over here at all. But there's probably only one more person on this Earth more stubborn than him, and that's me." She shrugs, a grin playing on her lips. "So here I am."

"He seems like the kind of man who would fire an assistant for not following his requests."

This makes her laugh. A long, high-pitched laugh that takes me by surprise. I make eye contact with Bri, another one of my employees, trying to figure out what's happening here. "He truly comes off like a pompous asshole, I know. But he's not so bad. A lot of bark but very little bite."

"Now, I think that comment would really get you fired," I mutter under my breath.

Why does this woman seem to be so fond of him? Surely there are better people to work for.

The woman sighs, her eyes drifting around the room. We don't close for another hour, but we typically don't get many customers this late in the day. We'll get a few stragglers wanting to pick up bread to go with their dinners or a dessert for the night, but for the most part, we stay pretty empty once the late-afternoon fades into evening.

"We're really in a bind." Her voice gets softer, but there's still a hint of worry to it.

I set the rag on the table behind me, turning around with a large sigh. "Look, even if I wanted to help, there isn't enough time. I'm sorry."

She nods, already looking at the door with a sad look on her face. "I'll tell Mr. Hunter you're sorry."

"Oh, I'm not sorry for him. I'm just sorry you'll have to deal with him."

"He's really not so bad."

I laugh. "Yeah. He's worse."

"What if he came and asked you personally?"

"He wouldn't be caught in hell coming to ask me for help," I point out. I hardly know the man, but I've gathered that much from him. He seems like the kind of person that doesn't ask for help, let alone ask for it from someone he said he never wanted to see again.

"But if he did? If he came over here and begged for your help, would you help us then?"

I smirk, trying to get the mental picture of him in my head. It would be pretty nice to hear him beg and grovel. Maybe I could find a way to make it work if he just got down on his knees...

"Sure," I say, mostly as a joke. There's no way he'd come over here and beg. He's too good for it, but it gives me an excuse to not feel like I'm being rude to this nice woman. She reminds me of my mom in a way. There's a quiet kind of confidence to her. One that doesn't accept bullshit but is still one of the nicest people you know.

Trisha holds up one finger in the air as she begins to back up. "Don't move."

"Not going to hold my breath," I call after her. There's no way he's coming through the door, but I don't burst her bubble.

"He might just surprise you."

I try not to roll my eyes at her statement. Camden could never surprise me. What you see seems to be what you get. And what I see is an asshole.

With Trisha gone, I turn to face Bri. "Now with that over with, I'm going to go finish a few things in the back."

I'm busy preparing a tub of icing for tomorrow when the door to the kitchen is thrown open. "What the f—!" I yell, accidentally dropping a bottle of food coloring. It splatters on the floor, red dye exploding at my feet.

"I truly don't think I've met a messier human."

I scowl, giving him my dirtiest look. "What are you doing here?"

Camden looks at the floor. It looks like a murder scene with the amount of red dye all over the tile. It goes up my jeans, ruining the pair I just bought a few weeks ago. I groan, wondering if I'll be able to get the stains out. My size is always sold out online, and these fit my body better than any pair before.

"I'm here to ask for help."

"You would've been a lot more help if you hadn't ruined my brand-new pair of jeans."

"I'll buy you a new pair if you help me out tonight."

I wipe at the food coloring with a rag, but all it manages to do is further spread it everywhere.

"We have a deal?" he pushes.

I scoff, looking at the red splotches all over the light denim. "No, we don't have a deal. They take forever to come back in stock."

"I'm in a real fucking dilemma right now." He seethes, his voice tight and low, the grit to it sending shivers down my spine. "I'll find the jeans. I'll buy you ten. I just need food at this opening, and I need it now."

Camden Hunter sounds vulnerable.

What alternate universe am I in?

I sigh, slamming the rag on the counter. It used to be beige. Now it's almost red, truly looking like something they'd keep as evidence in a murder case. "What time is the opening?"

He clears his throat and looks down at an expensive watch on his wrist. It's so shiny it catches the light from the ceiling, almost blinding me when he turns his wrist a certain way.

"Technically, the artists are arriving within the hour. Guests will be here in a few."

"And what happened to your fancy caterers? Clearly, I wasn't your first choice."

He laughs. It seems a little less cold than the times I've heard him laugh before. "No, you weren't, shortcake. Yet here we are."

My eyebrows raise as I grab the edges of the counter. "I'm waiting."

"Waiting for what?"

"For you to tell me that maybe fancy, uppity choices aren't always the best option."

"Not going to happen."

I shrug, going back to my earlier task before he scared the shit out of me. "Then it seems like you don't need help that bad."

"I'm not going to stoop that low and tell you that until I at least know you have the time to create something suitable for the night."

"It isn't stooping low when it's the truth."

"Just because one business from New York has shitty business principles doesn't mean that everything here in this dingy town is better than Manhattan."

"Call Sutten dingy again and you'll get a knee to your manhood." I smile sweetly at him, remembering the second time we ever ran into each other—literally. I'd joked about his size and how it felt like he was overcompensating. He didn't take it well.

The look on his face tells me he may not take my threat very well now either.

He lets out a long, aggravated sigh, even going as far as to drag his fingers down his perfectly sculpted face.

It's really a shame he's such an asshole because he's easily one of the best-looking men I've ever seen. Everything about his features is perfectly proportional. Eyebrows are supposed to be sisters, not twins, yet his are clones of each other. Straight eyebrows with a slight arch at the ends frame the clearest, bluest eyes I've ever seen. To top it all off, the man has thick, dark eyelashes.

I hate him. For so many reasons. For being an asshole. For buying the space I wanted to expand my business. For ruining my jeans. For being blessed with such good looks when he has such a terrible personality.

"I don't have the time to go back and forth with you," he

confesses. He sounds agitated, but not necessarily at me for once. More like at the circumstances.

"Sounds like you don't have much time for anything, considering you might need to borrow an apron and cook some food up for your guests."

"That won't be necessary if you help me."

"Big emphasis on *if*. The shop closes soon, and I have a date with a bottle of wine and some reality TV."

"Whatever you want, I'll do it. Just say yes. Help me. I'm begging."

"Anything I want?" I ask, my mind filling with so many terrible things I could make him do if I agree to this.

One single piece of gelled hair falls into his face, making him seem a little more...normal.

"Yes, anything."

Chapter 7
CAMDEN

SHE BEAMS AT ME. HER SMILE IS SO WIDE AND VIBRANT THAT MY stomach drops at the sight of it.

It's probably because that smile can't be good for me. But I'm a desperate man. If she tells me no, I'm going to have to serve Lay's chips with sour cream dip because I have no other option. Or fucking hot wings from the dirty bar down the street.

I refuse to resort to either of those options. Which means all my eggs are in one basket—Pippa's basket. The woman who hates me—for good reason. The woman who irritates the hell out of me, but somehow, the one person I need right now. The only one who can get me out of my current dilemma.

It's ironic. She's the last person I want to have to be around in this town, and yet, she's the only one who can help me.

"So anything, anything?" Pippa prods. Her voice is giddy and full of amusement. This can't be good.

I clear my throat, trying to think if I have any other option than having to agree to whatever stupid, tragic idea is going through her head.

"Yes, anything. But please be professional."

"You said anything. You didn't say professional."

My groan ricochets through the small kitchen space. "Fine," I clip, growing more frustrated by the second. "But the offer expires in two seconds because I don't have the time to do this with you anymore. I need food, and I need it now."

She bites her plump bottom lip in excitement. I know by the glint in her eyes I'll despise whatever's about to come out of her mouth.

Feeling on edge, I pull out my wallet and open it up. "Why don't you just name your price? That seems more professional anyway."

A loud, dramatic snort comes from her mouth. She shakes her head, pieces of her hair falling into her eyes with the movement. She tucks one of the stray locks behind her ear, looking at me like I'm the funniest guy she knows. Which I know isn't the case because I'm not a particularly funny guy. Especially under circumstances like this.

"Care to tell me what's so funny?"

Her cheeks are flushed a perfect pink from her laughter. Even her nose gets pink. I avert my eyes, finding myself paying too close attention to the perfect shade spreading over her skin.

"I'm sorry," she wheezes, pressing her hand to her chest. She takes a shaky breath, trying to gain her composure. "It's just hilarious you think I want your damn money."

My eyes narrow. "Everyone has a price. What's funny is that you don't know that."

She puffs out her cheeks as she lets air out from the small opening of her pursed lips. "Not me."

"Respectfully, I don't believe you."

"Because you're a rich, entitled asshole," she answers, a little too chipper. "Disrespectfully."

I thumb through the hundred-dollar bills in my wallet, wondering if her seeing I'm good for it will change her mind.

It doesn't. She just stares at me with humor written all over her face.

I take a deep breath. Fuck, she knows how to wear out every ounce of my patience. Anyone else, I'd already be out the fucking door, not willing to put up with the antics. But I need her, so my feet stay planted.

"Showing me your money isn't going to change my mind. But there is one thing you can do to get me to agree to whip up some food for you tonight."

A glimmer of hope sparks deep in my chest. "What is it?"

"Give me a day."

"I don't have a day. I need food right now."

"No, you give me a day. Of your time. In this town. I think if you really spent some time in this community, you'd understand why I love it so much. It wouldn't be some dingy town to you anymore."

Words don't come to me. I just stare at her, trying to decide if she's serious. "That would involve us having to spend time together."

"I'll try not to kill you."

I have no desire to spend any more time in this town than I need to. I didn't buy the gallery to become a local. There's no reason for me to get to know the town. The gallery is to cater to people visiting the town, not living here. The artists are people I already know, none of whom live in Sutten.

"I don't see the reason for doing it." My voice gets sharper, but I can't help it. It sounds like a form of torture to spend an entire day with her. In this town.

When Beck and Margo got married here, they made me do all the touristy things with them. I didn't enjoy it. And I actually like Beck. I don't like Pippa. Not in the slightest.

She shrugs dismissively. No one has ever dismissed me the way she does. She goes right back to cleaning the tiny kitchen, totally pretending like I'm not standing right here.

My body is frozen as she begins to hum to herself. Holy shit. She's *serious*.

She turns around, letting out an annoyed sigh that I'm still in her presence. "Stop gawking. You'll get wrinkles."

I must be terrible at hiding my thoughts at the moment

because she opens her mouth to speak again. "Two can play this game, Camden. I don't see the reason in doing you a favor if you aren't even willing to give Sutten a chance. If you don't want to embrace this town, that's fine. But don't expect me to help you out. If you aren't willing to give me one day, then I hope this opening fails epically and you're forced to leave us alone."

This. Woman.

Typically, people don't have the nerve to speak to me the way she has, especially not a stranger. Maybe my friends, but even that's pushing it.

My mind races with my options. She's made her position clear as day. Now it's up to me to decide if I want to actually agree to her stupid, useless idea.

It really is just a day.

But one day of my time is worth a lot of money. Time is money, and every single one of my days is planned out in perfect precision. I like numbers. I like things neat. Order turns me on, and looking at the red-splattered Pippa reminds me of one thing: Pippa is anything but orderly. She's quite the opposite, and one day with her might drive me to the brink of insanity.

There's only one thing that'll drive me even further to the brink of insanity. This gallery failing. I won't let it happen.

And one way to make sure this business flourishes is a successful opening.

I need her, and she knows it. I'm at her mercy, and even though I fucking hate it, I have to agree to her silly request.

"Fine," I rasp, the word tasting like acid in my throat. "One day. It's yours."

Her large, round eyes go wide in shock. "Seriously?"

I give her a curt nod, tucking my hands in my pockets because I'm anxious about what the hell I just agreed to. I already regret it.

"How do I know that you won't bail on me? It seems unfair that I have to make everything tonight and you could just tell me to fuck off tomorrow."

Her words are insulting. I know she knows nothing about me, and I sure as hell haven't given her any reason to want to know me, but if I say I'm going to do something, I'm going to do it. "I'm a man of my word." I'm pissed she would think otherwise.

"I don't know if I believe you."

My body moves of its own accord, cornering her against her counter because of the frustration coursing through my veins. "Listen very closely here, shortcake."

Her chest heaves up and down as her breathing speeds up. "Stop calling me that."

"Staying true to my word is very important to me. I hate liars. I hate cop-outs. So, *shortcake*—" I draw out the nickname because it's fun to piss her off. "—I'll say this again, and then I won't ever repeat myself again. I'm a man of my word. You impress my guests with your baking tonight, and I'm yours for a day so you can fail at attempting to impress me with this town."

Neither one of us speaks. We're too busy staring daggers into each other's eyes. The air is lit with angry, sizzling electricity around us. If I leaned in any closer, each one of her exhales would push her chest against me.

"Shake on it, then," Pippa manages to get out. Her voice has lowered an octave, sounding too sultry for my liking. It sounded far too good coming out of her mouth. I imagine how she'd sound if I…

I shake my head, ridding myself of the mental image. *No, no, no.* That thought should've never crossed my mind. I despise her, and the feeling is very mutual. I have no business imagining what she'd sound like if I let my knuckles brush against her hard nipples, which fight against the fabric of her T-shirt.

Like a bat out of hell, I back away from her, needing the distance between us.

What the actual *fuck* just happened?

"You're really not a man of many words," Pippa notes, seemingly unfazed.

I clear my throat, trying to get my shit together. I've already been here far longer than I'd anticipated. Trisha made it sound like a done deal; I just had to come in and tell Pippa myself I needed help. But I should've known she'd put up more of a fight. "I've got to get back to the opening."

She nods, but as soon as I wonder if she's going to forget about her previous request, she holds out her hand between us, her pink-painted fingernails waggling in front of her. "Shake on it. Give me your word that you'll agree, and I'll blow the socks off all your entitled friends."

Not having any other options, I hold my hand out and wrap my fingers around hers. My hand dwarfs hers, but it welcomes the warmth. My skin is cold and dry against her soft, warm palm.

"So it's settled," she says, her voice breathy again.

"Yes," I clip, letting go so I don't have to feel her bare skin against mine for another second. My father always told me to never be the first to break a handshake, but desperate times call for desperate measures. I can't touch her—thoughts I shouldn't have fill my head, and I know I'd regret every single one rushing through my mind if I acted out on them. "Bring the food when it's ready. I'll also need your help serving it."

"Wait, what?" she questions, anger flashing in her eyes.

A grin pulls at my cheeks. "See you in a bit. Don't disappoint me."

"I hate you!" she calls out.

I chuckle, stopping in front of the door. "Not as much as I hate you, shortcake."

Chapter 8
PIPPA

"I don't know if I'm going to be able to feel my feet after this," Lexi whines from my side. I'd recruited her and Bri's help the moment Camden waltzed out of my kitchen, knowing I'd need more backup to execute my plan for the night. I hated asking Bri to stay past closing, but we needed the help, and she was excited for the extra money.

The two of us work at twisting dough into mini soft pretzels. The dough has been enriched with garlic and rosemary in a way that makes the baked goods seem more luxurious. Camden's gallery opening officially started an hour ago, but we've been serving a couple of different finger foods at a time to allow us to offer a variety of options.

So far, people seem to be enjoying the food, but I agree with Lexi. I'm exhausted.

"At least you had the day off," I counter, brushing butter mixed with rosemary on each of the shaped pretzels. "I've been on my feet since four this morning, and there's a great possibility that my feet will fall off."

Lexi laughs, grabbing a pan filled with precooked pretzels in each hand and walking them over to one of our ovens. We managed to call in help from two part time employees, Bri and Lauren as well, the two of them busy over at the gallery, serving the food and making sure it all goes smoothly there.

With the pretzels in the oven, I turn to the pesto mozzarella rolls I have cooling on a rack. I put my hand over them, satisfied with the temperature they've cooled to. "Okay, I'm going to go run these over," I tell Lexi. It's my turn to pass them out, even if I really don't want to go next door because I'm far too interested in watching Camden in his element than I should be. I can't help it. The guy is a raging asshole—probably the biggest one I've ever met. But damn, I don't know how he turns on the charm when working. It's intriguing to watch everyone in his vicinity gravitate toward him. They eat out of his palm. It's transfixing.

"Good luck over there. Those people are feral for the food," Lexi warns.

I can't help but laugh at her remark. The people at his opening are ravenous for everything we've made tonight. We're trying our best to keep up with their hunger, but damn, spending money apparently makes people starved.

Before I go, I look at my reflection in the stainless steel refrigerator. My cheeks are flushed from working so hard, and my smooth hair from earlier in the day is gone. Left in its wake is a frizzy mess. Sighing, I take two seconds to try and tame it. I attempt to pull it back in a chic, slicked-back bun. But it doesn't look as chic as I'd imagined it would.

"Would you rather me take this round?" Lexi asks from behind me.

"No." I sigh, wiping a bit of flour from my forehead. "This is just going to have to work."

"I think you look hot as hell. The bun looks good."

"I don't have to look hot. I just don't want to look like I just got electrocuted as I walk around a bunch of people with expensive blowouts."

"Honestly, they could look better. I feel bad for them if they're paying good money to have their hair look like that."

I laugh because she has a point. "I just wish I didn't look like I'm about to go to church in this outfit." Luckily, I keep an extra outfit at the shop just in case I have an event I forgot about. Unfortunately for me, I forgot that my spare outfit is a dress that does nothing to accentuate my body. It's tight around my boobs, and the fabric hugs me oddly in other places. It's like wearing an ill-fitting paper bag. Just another reason I feel severely out of place at Camden's stupid opening.

But the people there probably won't even spare me a second glance while I serve them, so it doesn't really matter. At least that's what I tell myself as I pick up a platter and rest it on my shoulder. Every single person at the event feels like they don't belong in this, and I hate it. I want the rooms to be filled with locals, people who could tell you who makes the best lasagna in town or who is sleeping with who despite being married to other people.

That's what it was like when the Richardsons still owned it. Sure, people vacationing would stop in. But it still felt like a little piece of Sutten. What Camden has created doesn't feel like home. Not in the slightest.

Lexi follows me out of the kitchen, holding the door open as I walk over to the gallery. The awning is black with boring block letters. It looks funny next to my bright pink awning. I've got greenery outside the front, vines crawling up the fixture to make the atmosphere feel even more cozy.

Next to me sits Ms. Lori's flower shop. It's also full of life and color. Camden's place sticks out next to our buildings like a sore thumb.

A rush of hot air hits me when I walk through the open door of the gallery. With all of the lights shining on the art and all of the people, it feels way warmer in here than it does outside. It's part of the reason I threw my hair up, needing it off my neck as I carry around the tray and serve people.

These rich people are hungry vultures. The moment they spot me with a tray of new food, they beeline for me, all of them picking the food off the tray before I even have a chance to tell them what it is.

"Are these gluten-free?" one of the women asks, eyeing the rolls like she's starved.

"Uh, no," I answer.

She pouts, jutting her bottom lip out so far that it leaves a lipstick stain in the cleft of her chin. "There should be gluten-free options here," she tells her friend. All her friend does is nod, her mouth too full of the mozzarella ball to say anything else.

I step away from them, hoping to leave the conversation behind. There are plenty of people who don't care what's in the food, and they take it without asking any questions.

I didn't know art could make people so hungry.

Stopping next to a large group of people who all want to take a roll, I let my eyes roam the space. It feels so...clean in here. The walls are white, the concrete has been painted white, and the only splashes of color are the art.

And even a lot of the art is void of color. It's charcoal or black and white paint. The little bit of color on the walls catches my eye. There's a section with three different paintings that are vivid. If I didn't have a swarm of people around me, I'd take a step closer and take a look. Not a single piece of art on the walls has caught my attention tonight except these.

Just then, I see a large figure step into my eyeline. He stands with two other people, the three of them staring at the same pieces I was just admiring from afar.

Camden is magnetic. I can't look away. I credit it to the fact he appears so different tonight. He seems actually charming. He speaks to a couple, but the woman looks like she wants nothing to do with the man standing next to her, despite his attempt to pull her closer to him by wrapping his arm around her.

She doesn't notice; she's hanging on to every single word Camden says as he looks at the art in front of him. He's passionate about art, that much I can tell. But this looks like something more. He seems to talk about the art the way I talk about Wake and Bake. Like he's put his heart and soul into it.

I hate it, but I can't help but think maybe he's different than what he seems. At least he is tonight. I'm sure around me, he'll go back to his true personality of being an asshole. Even though I can tell my tray is empty and I should go get another round of food, I can't tear my eyes away from him as I wonder…what is his true personality? Is it the raging asshole I've encountered a few times? Or is it this man tonight? The one who actually cracks a smile when the woman clearly asks something about the piece they're looking at.

I'll probably never know for sure. Our relationship has been established, but it's fun to wonder.

I'm so lost in watching him do his thing that I don't notice the three men who walk up to me.

"You're out of food," one man says, his tone rather rude. His voice takes me by surprise, making me jump and lose my grip on the tray for a moment.

"It appears I am." The tray is completely empty except for one sad mozzarella ball that's been unraveled, the pesto dripping out all over the tray.

"So are you going to get more, or are you just going to stand here looking clueless?"

My jaw snaps shut. Oh no he didn't.

The guy who I'm tempted to put into his place looks to his friends. He laughs, running a hand over his protruding gut. They laugh with him, even though it seems forced and they both appear rather uncomfortable with his harsh words.

"Hunter really needs to get himself better help, doesn't he?" the man continues.

"What was that?" My pulse angrily thrums through my veins. I can hear the thumping sound in my ears.

The man's beady eyes widen as he realizes that I'm not some meek human who will let him berate them without sticking up for themselves.

"I said, Hunter needs to get himself more competent help."

I let the tray slip from my hands with a wide smile on my face. It crashes to the ground with a loud smack to the concrete.

The lone mozzarella ball covered in pesto flies in the air and lands with a *plop* against the pompous asshole's shiny shoe.

He lets out an inaudible string of curses as he looks down at the mess on the floor.

"Stupid bitch. You did that on purpose."

We start to catch the attention of people around us, but I don't care if they're watching or not. I'm not going to let this man talk down to me because he thinks he's better than me. "No," I lie, sidestepping a bit until I grab two full champagne flutes from a nearby table. "But this is." And then I go against every moral my mom ever taught me, and I toss the champagne on the guy.

He screeches, the sound hilarious.

"You worthless little—"

"Leave," a voice commands from behind the guy. He steps aside, allowing Camden to come into view.

Even though he's soaking wet with champagne, the guy stands in place, looking from Camden to me. "You heard him. Leave." He has the audacity to feel smug. If I knew how to throw a punch, I'd knock him right in his terrible veneers.

A pit forms in my stomach because for a split second, I'd hoped Camden was better than these people. There's no way he didn't hear that asshole call me name after name, resorting me down to nothing. But he's one of them. Of course he'd tell me to go when he was the one who begged me to help to begin with.

I take a shaky breath due to the adrenaline running through my body. I look at Camden, shaking my head at him. "You're no better than him." I seethe with disgust. I take a step forward, hitting my shoulder with his as I make my way away from these people who don't deserve to be in this town.

A large hand grabs me by the bicep, strong fingers digging into my skin and making me come to an abrupt stop. Shocked, I look up and make eye contact with Camden, wondering why he has a viselike grip on me. I hate that I can't get out of the hold. I hate that he might be able to feel the shakiness of my arms and mistake it for fear instead of what it truly is—rage.

My attempt to make eye contact with him fails because he's looking over my shoulder at the terrible excuse of a man behind me. "No," Camden clips, his voice so calm and collected that it's almost scary. "She stays. *You* leave, Jason."

The guy makes a sputtering sound—or maybe it's from me. I don't truly know because voices begin to whisper around us. Maybe the onlookers are just as confused as I am.

"Now," Camden barks, his voice louder this time.

I try to pull my arm from his once again, but he holds on even tighter. This time, there's a sting from his fingertips pushing deep into my skin. My feet stay planted as Camden stares daggers over my head. Anger sizzles in the air between us as I try to wrap my head around the fact I think Camden—the man who has been an asshole to me from the moment we met—is sticking up for me.

Chapter 9
CAMDEN

Pippa tries to wiggle out of my grip, but I don't give her any leeway. She isn't leaving. But this sorry excuse of a human I regret ever inviting sure is.

"You can't be serious," Jason hisses, outstretching his hands to try and play it cool.

It isn't.

He just called Pippa stupid in multiple different ways, and he thinks everything is cool? Absolutely pathetic.

"Camden, it's fine," Pippa insists from my side. "I can go."

I don't even give an answer. There's no way in hell she's going anywhere when she's done nothing wrong.

"Jason, don't make any more of a scene than you already have. You can leave, or I can make you leave, which would make me very, very upset because I don't like drama or theatrics."

"You're going to defend a server over me? I've been friends with your father since before you were born."

I hate the feeling of all eyes on us. I've never been one who enjoys attention. It reminds me of when I was a child and my parents would parade me around to all of their friends—some of whom are in the room right now—and then discard me the moment the doors were shut. It made me hate the attention because I caught on at a young age that I was being used. I don't like being used.

"It's a great thing I don't give a shit about that." My jaw tenses. This conversation is already far longer than it was supposed to be. Tonight was supposed to be about the art, about bringing luxury art somewhere new. Jason's narcissism and egotistical personality fucked that up.

"But I'm not the one who—"

"Go," I interrupt, my voice booming because my patience is wearing thin.

He and I stare at one another. It's like he's trying to figure out if I'm being serious or not. It's a stupid mistake of his. He's been around all thirty-six years of my life. He should know by now that I mean what I say.

It's comical now that the men surrounding Jason all pretend they don't know him now. He looks to them for help, but they say nothing. They're all cowards. The only person here brave enough to speak for themselves is the woman trying to pull out of my grip.

"This is a mistake," Jason rants.

I click my tongue, cocking my head as I stare him down. "No, the mistake was inviting you."

He finally gains enough common sense to leave. But not without stomping his way out, acting far too childish for a man who has grandchildren.

The moment he's gone, I look at the guests around us. I fake a smile, even though my body hums with rage.

"Now that that's handled, let's get back to the reason you're here. The pieces are flying off the walls, so if you see something you're interested in, make sure to find an employee to help you purchase it."

The group of people milling around us begins to chatter, but I don't listen to them at all. I'm already busy pulling Pippa through the group of people until we're safely out of sight in my back office. The door slams behind me, shaking the walls of the old building.

The door is barely shut before I'm pushing Pippa against it, my eyes roaming over her body. "Did he hurt you?"

She shoves against my chest. "What? Get away from me, asshole."

My vision begins to clear as I regain a sense of reality and no longer see red. "Did he hurt you?" I repeat, backing away from her until I bump against my desk. I undo the button of my jacket, placing my hands safely in my pockets as I wait for her to answer.

"No, of course not. He was just being a demeaning prick."

"He's an asshole."

She laughs. "Tell me something I don't know."

"What happened?" I was busy selling one of Margo's— Beck's wife—pieces for the highest price one of her pieces has ever sold for when I heard the commotion from across the room.

Maybe costing me the sale, I left Jared Stingmore and his wife immediately to go see what was happening. I'd gotten close enough to hear Jason call Pippa a stupid bitch when I started to see red. When he called her worthless, I was moments away from grabbing onto his collar and dragging him out by his neck to prove who the worthless human in the scenario was.

Pippa glares at me as I stare at her right back. Her chest heaves with angry breaths. Mine does, too. The problem is she looks at me like I'm the one who's done something wrong.

"I didn't need your help. I had it handled," she snaps, completely ignoring my question.

I chuckle under my breath because while she was handling it, he wouldn't have left until I told him to. And even when I did, he argued. "Sure you did, shortcake."

A loud, aggravated noise comes from her throat. It's something between a growl and a shriek. "Stop calling me that!"

"What did he say to you?" I press, needing to know what the hell happened. I'll ask his dimwit little friends, too, but first, I want to hear it from her.

"It doesn't matter."

"It does to me."

"Why? So you can use the same insults as him against me?"

My jaw snaps shut. Damn. Her words hit deep. Because they aren't completely out of line. I've been a dick to her. Numerous times. Because she gets under my skin in a way I haven't experienced before.

Pippa rolls her eyes, reaching for the door.

"No," I hurriedly say, reaching out to stop her but thinking better of it. Maybe I should let her go. Jason is gone and surely not coming back. I really shouldn't care anymore what she has to say.

"I know I've been an asshole, but I'd never call you the help. Or worthless. Or stupid or anything that he said because they're all lies. You're none of that. You're—"

"I don't need you to tell me what I am, Camden. I know what I am. His words don't matter."

Her words cause me to pause because they weren't what I was expecting. Was she really not hurt by what he said? I blink, trying to figure her out. She's like staring at an abstract painting. Just when I think I can make out what she is, I notice something else that shifts my entire perspective.

"No, they don't matter. But I need to know."

I'm beginning to accept that she won't tell me and I'm going to have to get the story from someone else when she takes one hesitant step closer to me. "It all started because I ran out of food. He said you needed to hire new help, and, well, I won't let someone insult me. You know that *very* well."

I laugh because it's true. "I'm sorry he said those things."

Pippa's eyes search my face. I wonder what she sees in me. What she thinks of the man standing in front of her. I stuff my hands into my pockets to give them something to do.

"I never thought I'd hear those words come from your mouth," she teases. "Even if you were apologizing on somebody else's behalf instead of your own."

I'm about to open my mouth when her eyes catch on something in the corner. "What's this?" she asks, closing the distance to the small table with the sculpture on it.

"Oh, just a piece I'm debating about selling in the gallery," I answer, feigning nonchalance.

"Can I touch it?" she whispers, her eyes trained on the piece in front of her.

"I don't think the artist will mind."

Chapter 10
PIPPA

I DON'T KNOW IF I'VE EVER SEEN SOMETHING SO BEAUTIFUL THAT IT took my breath away. I'm speechless, allowing my finger to gently run over the carved curves of the statue.

It's of a couple, but only from their waist up. They clutch one another so delicately, so fiercely, that it's obvious they're in love. You look at them and it seems like something is trying to keep them apart, but they're clinging to each other so tightly, like they won't let anything come between them. The way her back arches, it appears as if some outside force you can't see is pulling her from him.

"This is stunning," I whisper, running my finger along their outstretched arms.

"You think?" Camden keeps his voice poised, but I can feel his gaze hot on me.

"Why isn't it on display out there? It would sell immediately."

"The artist doesn't want to sell it."

I look at him in shock. Who wouldn't want to sell this master-piece? I don't know anything about art, but it's so intricate I have to imagine so many people would want it. "Do you know why?"

Camden swallows, his eyes staying locked with mine. I don't know what's more perfect to look at, the slopes and planes of the statue or the slopes and planes of his face. His features are so perfect that they deserve to be forever carved in stone.

I forgot I'd even asked him a question, too focused on tracing his cheekbones with my gaze, when he speaks up. "No." He sighs, looking away from me to the statue in front of me. "I don't know why."

"Well, I think you should get them to change their mind."

His shoulder brushes against mine as he takes a step next to me. He smells different than any other man I've been around. It's expensive but earthy and warm. It's a smell that I don't think I could ever grow tired of. It's overpowering but in a good way. A way that slowly overwhelms your senses but not in the way where you'd get a headache.

"What about this makes you think it should be sold?"

I feel disarmed having him this close to me. Every other time he's been near, we've been in the middle of fighting. It feels off to have him so close and things be civil between us. At least as civil as things could ever be between me and him.

I look back at the statue, welcoming the reprieve of getting lost in the perfect proportions that are his face.

"The moment I saw this, I could feel the emotion between the two of them. I think the little details of the statue add up to depict this beautiful and tragic love story. At least that's what I gathered from it." I shrug, trying to act nonchalant. "But what do I know about art?"

He looks at me—and I mean really looks at me. He stares at me so intently that it makes me shift uncomfortably on my feet. It seems like time stops around us as we stare at one another. "That's exactly what I got from it."

I rip my gaze from his because it feels wrong to be so close to him, to not be fighting—for me to want to inch even closer to him. "From far away, you'd think the two of them are in love and are happy, but that doesn't seem to be the whole story once you get closer and start taking in all of the details."

I look at where, somehow on such a small scale, you can see the way the fingertips dig into skin. I marvel at the attention to detail of the artist. The way you can tell they cling to each other like their lives depend on it.

Camden is silent. So silent that my cheeks begin to flush because I wonder if I'm making any kind of sense at all. My skin feels hot as I push stray pieces of hair from my face, needing to give my body something to do once I realize I've been rambling.

"Sorry," I mumble, feeling embarrassed for the first time in my life. "I'm probably not making any sense."

"No." I wish I knew how he kept his voice so cool and collected. It's smooth like velvet, wrapping around me. "You make perfect sense. What makes you think that?"

"It's the desperate way they cling together. They grasp at one another too tightly to be fully happy. Something is ripping them apart. I wish I knew what..."

"What if the sculptor didn't want you to know what it was? Maybe they wanted you to come up with the answers yourself. Maybe they wanted to make you think about what things in life could rip you apart from someone you love so deeply."

An uninvited thought creeps into my mind. Has Camden ever loved somebody like this? Has anybody ever loved him? He doesn't seem like the type to get involved. He seems too selfish to love someone, but he's so breathtaking I could see why women could fall for him before he ever uttered a word to them—then they'd learn about his horrid personality, and hopefully, they'd run for the hills.

But has anyone gotten through his rough exterior?

"Tell me this isn't the time that you shut your mouth for once." His verbal jab brings me back to my senses. I'm thankful for the snarky tone to his voice, for things to go back to normal between us. I was too far deep in wondering why Camden is the way he is.

"Just when I think you *might* not be the biggest asshole I've ever met, you prove me wrong."

He gives me a wolfish grin. "Come to New York. You'll meet men far worse than me, shortcake."

"Yeah, I'll pass. You're a dick for no reason. I have no desire to meet anyone worse than you."

"What if I apologized?" His words come as a shock. I can't imagine him apologizing. I don't know if I want him apologizing. It's easier to hate him, to remind myself that even through the charm he sometimes shows me, deep down he's an asshole. At least, that's what I choose to believe.

"I wouldn't believe it."

He nods, looking back at the sculpture in front of us. "It's time I get back to my opening."

My eyes go wide because I'd totally forgotten why we were here in the first place. I'm supposed to be serving food. He's supposed to be selling art—even though the most stunning piece I've seen tonight is the one not for sale in front of us.

"Right." I rush to get out. In my attempts to scurry out of the office, I almost run right into him. We both move to the left at the same moment, our bodies narrowly colliding with one another.

Camden grabs me by the arms to steady me. He opens his mouth to say something, but I beat him to it.

"Before you say anything, that was *your* fault, not mine."

A chuckle rumbles deep in his chest. "I was going to say thank you for saving me tonight. People might be talking about the food more than the art."

The fact that he's not being a total jerk disarms me. "Yeah, of course." I fumble on my words, not knowing how to respond to him. I was expecting an insult, for him to comment on how I ran into him again.

I don't say anything else. I book it out of the room as my mind races about what just happened.

Did Camden Hunter just say something nice to me?

Chapter 11
CAMDEN

I TAKE A SECOND BEFORE GOING BACK TO THE EVENT. PIPPA WALKED out the door a few minutes ago, yet I haven't moved since she left. It still smells like her in my office, the scent of her surrounding me, even though I'd prefer it not to. I don't like how she smells unlike any woman I know. I'm used to the scent of a few different expensive perfumes. All women in my circle wear the same handful of fragrances. They're either way too flowery or way too overpowering.

Pippa doesn't smell like either. Everywhere she goes, she leaves the scent of vanilla and strawberries. I find myself taking a deep inhale, hating myself for wanting to get another waft of her.

I stare ahead of me at the statue in the corner of my office. It's something I almost didn't bring with me from Manhattan. It wasn't intended to be sold; there was no reason for me to bring it with me. But I couldn't help it.

And now after watching Pippa marvel at it, I'm wondering if maybe it has a chance to sell. Maybe I *should* give it a chance.

I'm so lost in thought that I don't even notice the door to my office opening. I don't see the person until he comes to a stop in front of me, softly clearing his throat to get my attention.

"Everything okay in here?" Beck asks, looking at me with concern.

My back straightens as I look up to make eye contact with him. He watches me warily, which I don't blame him for. He witnessed me kick out a man who is very prominent in our social circle and then disappear, pulling someone by the arm into my office. It probably doesn't add up to him.

I let out a slow breath. "Why wouldn't it be?"

He chuckles, running a hand over his mouth. I hate it, but he's known me almost my entire life. Beck can read me like a damn book, no matter how much I hate it. We've had the same friend group since we were in school, but he and I have always been the closest. He's my best friend. Which is great occasionally, but times like right now, it's rather inconvenient.

"Because you basically just told someone who spends a lot of money on art to fuck right off."

"I don't want his money," I snarl.

Beck's hands come up in front of him defensively. "Calm down." He laughs. "I gathered that by the way you basically shoved him out the door, no matter who was watching."

"He's an asshole."

"Everyone here is an asshole," Beck responds.

I throw a dirty look his way. I hate that he has a response for everything. Apparently, I need to find a friend who doesn't like to talk at all.

"I should probably go back out there and make money off the assholes."

"Probably should. Although I know Margo is doing a great job out there in your absence."

This makes me laugh. Margo is my most profitable artist. I wouldn't tell her this, but I also consider her one of my closest friends, even though we work together. Margo's hard to not like. Plus, she makes Beck happy. He'll always be an asshole in my mind, but he's a lot more tolerable to be around now that he finally has his girl and they're happily married.

"Maybe I'll just let Margo take over the gallery, and I'll ride off into the sunset."

Beck crosses his arms over his chest, the humor wiping straight from his face. "Not going to happen. She works too much for my liking anyway."

"Says the guy who is constantly working." Beck is the CEO and creator of Sintech Cyber Security. He doesn't fully know how to take a day off, even though he may tell you otherwise.

"Right back at you, Hunter. You wouldn't know what to do with yourself if you weren't always working."

I have ideas, but I don't say them out loud. There's no use. I know some things I could do if I wasn't always worrying about my galleries, but that'd never happen. It'd take a lot for me to let go of them. I started them to prove something. And I don't know if I'll ever feel like I proved enough to stop.

"How long could we hide in here until Margo comes looking for us?" I change the subject, trying to deny the inevitable. After the confrontation with Jason and my conversation with Pippa, I don't feel like going back out there. I want to be alone, but I don't have a choice. Despite Jason derailing things for a bit, I need to get everything back on track. I need to sell more art. And I need to prove that I can make a gallery profitable, no matter the location.

"She's too busy to—" His words stop when his wife comes into view.

Margo gives Beck a look, her dark eyebrows raised to her hairline. "You said you'd be *one* minute." Her voice goes up an octave at the one. Maybe she didn't have as much fun out there as he thought she would.

Beck shrugs, closing the distance and pulling her into his body. He plants a kiss on her lips. I'm worried they might start making out in front of me like a pair of horny teenagers, but Margo pulls away. "No, no, no," she scolds. "You don't get to kiss me and pretend that you didn't leave me talking to two dudes who kept asking me who my art tutor was as a kid so they could get their grandkids in with them."

"Did you have an art tutor?" I ask, fairly confident Margo

grew up in Iowa. Or was it Ohio? I don't remember what state it was, but I know it wasn't New York.

Margo laughs, shaking her head as her almost-black pieces of hair dance with her movement. "I had an art teacher, Mrs. Kiebler, and she was a saint. But my family couldn't afford an art tutor. They could barely afford the supplies I begged for."

"What'd you tell the men?" Beck asks. His fingertips stroke over the bare skin on her shoulder. I never thought I'd see the man so happy and in love. For a fraction of a second, I wonder what it's like to love someone as much as he loves Margo. What it's like to be loved the way she loves him. It's only a thought I humor for a moment before I rid it from my mind. I don't want to be in the position he's in. I remember the terrified phone call I got from him when he thought she'd ended their engagement.

To love is to be vulnerable. I've never been very good at being vulnerable.

I've been lost in my own world, not hearing a thing either one has said. I only catch the tail end of their conversation. One that has apparently reverted to me because they both stare at me expectantly.

"What?" I ask, stepping around them to finally leave this office and return to the event.

"I asked how you felt it was going." Margo's voice is cautious. I don't know why.

"Oh." I clear my throat, my fingers absentmindedly fiddling with one of my cufflinks. "I think it's going great—despite the one minor mishap. I haven't rung up all of the purchases, obviously, but it seems like a lot of it has sold. Last I checked, there was a bidding war going on over your newest piece."

Beck hums. "Maybe I need to put them all to shame and buy it for my own personal collection."

This makes Margo roll her eyes. She playfully swats at his abdomen. "Like you don't have enough already."

Beck's voice gets low as he mutters something against her

ear. It makes me want to throw up. I need space from the lovesick puppies, and I need it immediately.

"I'm leaving. The two of you aren't allowed to fuck in my office," I growl.

I hear Beck's laugh from behind me. "Maybe we already have, Hunter."

I don't enlighten him by reacting. But before I step through the small entrance to the hallway and join the party, I rattle off a text to one of my employees still in Manhattan despite the opening and tell him I need the entire art gallery cleaned. Immediately.

Chapter 12
PIPPA

"PIPPA, DARLING, WHO ARE YOU GETTING FREAKY WITH LATELY?"

I'd respond to the sweet old lady sitting in the salon chair next to me, but I'm too busy choking on the latte I'd been sucking down. I sputter, trying to swallow the iced coffee that'd gone down the wrong pipe.

"Stop wiggling," Rhonda chides, holding on tight to a chunk of my hair as I try not to die at the words from a lady who hosts her bible studies at Wake and Bake some mornings.

"What?" Rosemary asks innocently, like the question she asked me was completely normal conversation for a Saturday afternoon at the hair salon.

"You can't just go asking young ladies who they're boinking, Rosemary," Lenora chides from next to her friend. They're both old enough to be my grandmother. In fact, they both were very close with my Grandma Pat before she passed.

"Who uses the word *boinking*?" Rosemary fires back, her focus on the gossip magazine in front of her. I wish I was underneath one of the hair dryers so I could pretend this conversation wasn't happening. That might not even work, considering the both of them seem to be hearing things just fine, despite being under the hair dryers themselves. "The kids these days are using the term *getting freaky with it*."

If I wasn't attempting to melt into a puddle of embarrassment because two sweet old ladies are arguing over which terminology to use while discussing my sex life, I'd correct them that neither are relevant terms.

"Leave the girl alone," Rhonda demands, painting hair dye onto strands of my hair. It'd gotten a shade lighter than I prefer over the summer, so I've decided to spend my Saturday getting it touched up. Maybe I should've forgone the haircut and color. At least then I wouldn't have to talk about my nonexistent sex life with half the women of Sutten. But Camden had dropped off a large check for me and everyone who helped with his opening, and I wanted to treat myself after dealing with the people he'd invited. At first, I wanted to tell him not to bother. But it took a lot of ingredients and overtime from my staff. His payment was the right thing to do. I deserved to pamper myself. I just thought it'd be relaxing and I wouldn't be discussing my sex life with Rhonda and Rosemary on a Saturday afternoon. "Maybe Pippa isn't sleeping with anyone," Rhonda continues. "There's nothing wrong with waiting for the right person."

I groan, trying to slide down in the salon chair. Rhonda keeps a hold of my hair, pulling on it slightly, which I'm sure shouldn't be good practice for hairstylists. Isn't she supposed to be gentle with me?

"Can we have a new subject, please?" I beg.

Rosemary snickers. She knows exactly what she's doing. I'm never serving her again. "No, dear. You aren't getting any younger. Soon, someone will have to plant their seed in you."

Oh my god. It keeps getting worse. My cheeks heat. I'm sure my entire body is red with embarrassment. I want to disappear. Move away from this town forever so I never have to look at Rosemary again and remember her telling me that someone needs to plant their freaking seed in me.

"I didn't have my first baby until I was twenty-nine," Rhonda says from behind me, finally being somewhat gentle with me again. "Pippa has time."

"I had three kids by Pippa's age," Lenora adds.

That's great, Lenora. I've started a successful business and have dealt with the loss of my mother on top of helping to keep my family's ranch afloat in my twenty-three years of living. Just because I haven't had children yet doesn't mean I haven't done *anything* with my life.

"I have Kitty," I argue. "She's high-maintenance enough that she counts as a child." She was an impulse decision one weekend after my mom passed. I needed something to focus on besides work, something that made me want to come home. So I got Kitty. My next-door neighbor even helps take care of Kitty on long workdays. She lives the best life for a dog rescued from the streets, but it doesn't make her any less high-maintenance.

Lenora and Rosemary both give me a disappointed look. Damn. They're awfully judgy, considering they're the ones prying into my sex life. "A dog named Kitty doesn't count as a child."

"Shouldn't you be telling me I shouldn't have sex before marriage?" I blurt out. I regret the words the moment they leave my mouth. I didn't mean to bring attention back to the fact that I haven't been properly fucked in a while. The words spilled from my mouth before I could do anything about it.

Rosemary and Lenora share a conspiratorial look. Rosemary is the one who speaks up, but she keeps her voice low and hushed, as if she wasn't just blurting to the entire salon about my sex life. "Listen, Pippa dear," she whispers. I wonder if she can even hear herself over the sound of the dryers. "God will still love you if you test-drive a little."

My eyes close as I realize this will be the moment I die from embarrassment. Right here at the Tame Mane because some old lady told me God will still love me if I don't wait until marriage. I don't tell her that I'm hardly a virgin. I might as well be one, however, because no one can give me as good of an orgasm as I can give myself.

"Noted," I squeak. I'm totally mortified. There's got to be twenty women in here between the hairstylists and customers.

And all of them are here to bear witness to my sex life—or should I say lack thereof.

"Oh!" Rosemary cheers excitedly, slapping her magazine against her lap. "Have you met the man who just moved in right next door to you? He looks like he'd be the *perfect* sin!"

"I think I'd rather be celibate," I mutter under my breath. The only person who hears it is Rhonda. She gives me a questioning look. I don't blame her. Camden looks like the perfect option. I'm sure he's not a two-pump-and-done kind of guy. His jerk of a personality is the problem.

"What's that?" Lenora yells, sitting forward slightly. Her forehead bumps against the bowl of the dryer. She tries to swat it away, but it doesn't work. "You said you and him have already boinked?"

"No!" I screech, sitting forward so quickly I almost fall out of my chair. "Definitely not. Never going to happen."

"You had a hot encounter with the new art owner?" Rosemary asks, equally as loud as her friend.

I didn't think it could get any worse, but it does. It totally does because I know this town, and I know even if I stood on my chair and addressed every single person in here to tell them Camden and I most definitely have never slept together, the rumors would still spread like wildfire, thanks to Rosemary's outlandish question.

This can't be happening. I begin to think of what alias I'll live under when I move halfway across the country. I always wanted to be named after a princess when I was younger. Could I pass as an Ariel? Or maybe Aurora? What was Snow White's name again? Was it just Snow White?

I'm spiraling over names of princesses when the tap on my shoulder by Rhonda brings me back to attention.

I look up to find all of the eyes in the salon pointed right at me. "Sorry, I was thinking about work," I lie. "What'd I miss?"

"I was telling them that the new businessman definitely isn't your type. And that I thought I saw you out at Slopes with Chase not too long ago."

"Right," I answer. I could hug her for rerouting the conversation. While I did enjoy a night out with Chase, the sex definitely wasn't anything to gush over. The night was fun, and I enjoyed flirting after going through everything with losing my mom, but Chase had finished in under a minute. When he'd asked me if I came, I'd lied because at that point, I was over it.

The ladies here don't have to know that, though. I'd much prefer them to think I was sleeping with just about anyone else in this town other than Camden.

"Are the two of you dating, then?"

"Never," I scoff. "Camden is not my type."

Rosemary smirks. "I meant you and Chase."

Shit.

I bite my lip, trying to think of a way to cover my oops. "Obviously." I nervously laugh, well aware that I'm not playing it cool in the slightest. "We're, uh, just friends," I answer, telling the truth. I don't need to elaborate that Chase has called multiple times to go on a date, but I'm not interested. It's not worth my time to get ready and leave my house if my vibrator can get the job done better than he can.

"What a shame," Lenora announces sadly. Her forehead wrinkles, becoming even more pronounced. As if my dating life should matter to her.

"You should go after one of the Livingston boys." This comment comes from Rhonda. Traitor. Everyone might've been ready to move on from my dating life as the topic of conversation until she brought it right back up.

The Livingstons own a majority of this town. They're essentially a founding family of Sutten, and their real estate company, founded by some great-great-grandfather—or maybe there's a few more greats—has helped them own so much of the land and properties here. There are four Livingston boys, but from my understanding, only two are single. I'm not interested in either. The family is slightly intimidating.

Lucky for me, Terri, a server from our local diner, speaks up from a few chairs down. "I wish the oldest would find someone new. His daughter deserves to have a momma. I still can't believe Selena is gone."

My chest feels heavy thinking about Selena Livingston. She was a ray of sunshine in this community. She got in a car accident two months after giving birth to a beautiful baby girl. That was almost two years ago, leaving Dean to care for a newborn all on his own. The Sutten community rallied around the family and helped out, but I still can't imagine how Dean Livingston must feel.

The air around us gets heavy for a moment. Their daughter, Clara, seems happy. He brings her to church every Sunday, and it's cute to watch her talk her daddy into doodling funny things on the program or watch her beg for something sweet when he stops in with her at the bakery.

I get lost in my own thoughts as Rhonda finishes painting the dye on my strands of hair. The only thing that pulls me from my thoughts is hearing Rosemary speak up, now from a chair next to mine.

"I think I might have Harold try out one of the scenes from our naughty book club this week."

Rhonda and I share a look through the mirror. My entire body shakes as I try to hold back a laugh. It's no use—the snort that comes from my body is completely unladylike and probably a little rude.

Rosemary's shrug tells me she doesn't mind. "What, girls?" she asks incredulously. "Surely it isn't a secret that Harold and I go to pound town."

Chapter 13
CAMDEN

I'M SITTING IN MY TINY OFFICE IN THE SUTTEN GALLERY, REVIEWING new pieces I'm having shipped here, when the bell to the gallery chimes. My eyes fall to the time in the corner of my monitor screen. It's barely seven in the morning. We aren't open yet. We aren't open at all today. Almost every piece of art had sold at the opening over the weekend. And anything that didn't sell that night sold on Monday. It's Wednesday, so the gallery is empty, and I won't have new inventory until this weekend.

Sighing, I push my chair away from my desk and head down the hallway. I hadn't bothered locking the door to the gallery because I thought the closed sign on the door and the lack of lights would inform anyone curious enough to wander by that we were closed.

I'm ready to tell the customer I have nothing to sell them when my feet come to a halt. It isn't a customer in the gallery. It's Pippa.

She doesn't notice me, her eyes trained on a piece of art on the far wall that isn't for sale. It was one of the first pieces Margo ever did for me. I'd wanted to keep it because of her take on an artist's life. I'd always displayed it in the Manhattan gallery, but for some reason, it feels more at home here.

Pippa stands a safe distance away from the drawing. I can see her profile, but I'm tucked away in the hallway enough for her to not notice me yet. I welcome the few seconds where I can take her in without either of us having our armor on. I'm sure the moment she notices me, we'll be back to the thing we've created where we throw insults at one another. But for a moment, I forget about all of that.

She holds two coffee cups, one in each hand. The pink lids look out of place in the stark white gallery. She's the one bit of color in here, the white floors and white walls—and muted colors of Margo's painting.

My eyes trace over her hair. It seems lighter than the last time I saw her, but I'm wondering if maybe it's just my eyes playing tricks on me. The first thing I notice after the possible change in color is that her hair looks tame for once. It isn't in her face, and it isn't messily knotted at the top of her head. It's sleek and smooth. If I were any closer, I might be tempted to reach out and run my hand through the locks just to discover what they feel like.

The unwelcome thought has me ripping my eyes away from her because it's Pippa. This is the woman who spilled an entire pitcher of beer on me, who ruined my suit for Beck and Margo's wedding with an array of different-colored icing. The one who isn't shy about making it known her feelings toward me—or lack thereof.

Despite the bad blood between us, as a fan of art, I can't deny that she's a work of art herself. Her skin is effortlessly sun-kissed, like she'd spent a lot of time outside during the summer. I can't help but wonder what she does in her free time, what her hobbies are. The glow of her skin tells me that whatever she was doing, she spent time outdoors. She wears a baby pink shirt that cuts off right above the waistband of her light denim jeans. I can only see the side of her, but the square neckline shows a good amount of her cleavage. There are so many beautiful lines to her body. Her high cheekbones and upturned nose. Her breasts that seem to be a perfect handful. Hips that slightly curve out at her waist and all the way down her legs. My eyes catch on the way the jeans hug her body perfectly. I could spend hours getting to know every slope and curve of her body, beginning with her thighs and getting lost in between them.

I clear my throat, catching her attention. Her features harden, the wistfulness she had in her eyes as she stared at Margo's painting was all but gone.

My eyes blink repeatedly as I attempt to wipe the thoughts I was having of her. It really isn't any use; those dirty thoughts of her are ingrained in my mind forever when they absolutely shouldn't be.

"Why are you looking at me weird?" Pippa questions, coming to a stop in front of me.

I swallow, trying to avert my gaze from the way her breasts almost spill over the top of her shirt. It's her exposed skin above the fucking ruffle catching my attention and tempting me, even though it's the one person in this town I can't tolerate standing right in front of me. At least I didn't *used* to tolerate her. Now, I don't understand why the sight of her doesn't completely ruin my morning. In fact, I think it excited me a little to see her here.

"Nice jeans," I counter, trying to ease the tension between us. It doesn't help.

She smiles, looking down at them. "Funny story. A giant box full of *ten* pairs of my jeans showed up at Wake and Bake."

"I told you I'd replace them."

Her head cocks to the side as her eyes roam over my face. "I looked online. They still say that they're sold out."

"I pulled some strings. It's not a big deal." I clap my hands together, wanting to change the subject. She doesn't need to know how hard it was to track down the brand and get some early stock from their next launch. Trisha spent almost an entire day doing it when I pay her for far more important things. "Why are you in my gallery when we're closed?" I ask, guiding the conversation in a different direction.

"It's weird. I have this very vivid memory of you showing up at my business when I told you *multiple* times we were closed."

My lip twitches, wanting to smile at her response. I fight it tooth and nail, not wanting to show her that maybe she's thawed my icy defenses just a little. "You're not welcome here."

She beams. Her teeth are perfectly straight and white. I could easily reach out and trace the cupid's bow of her top lip. It's pronounced, like a flashing neon light bringing attention to her perfectly kissable lips. "I'm welcome anywhere I want, Camden."

"You sure about that, shortcake?"

She pushes one of the coffee cups my way. "I brought you coffee."

I look down my nose at it. "Is it poisoned?"

Her laugh echoes off the wall. It's sweet and sultry, another jab at the wall I'm trying to build to keep her away. "I'd never ruin my reputation over you." To prove a point, she lifts the coffee to her lips. My gaze is locked on the way they curve along the lid. She tips it back, swallowing dramatically.

There's a lipstick stain on the lid as she pushes it into my chest. "See? Not poisoned."

"What if it's a slow death? I still don't think I can trust you." I want to press the cup to my lips. To place mine on the same spot as hers. And I don't know how fucked up that makes me.

"Well, you're going to have to try something new and trust me for once."

"Trust you? That's pushing it."

"Better get comfortable with it. Because you're going to have to trust me *all* day today."

I take a long drink of the coffee. It's made perfectly. It isn't bitter at all, but the espresso flavor is rich with small hints of the syrup. She makes a damn good coffee. There's something else in here that makes it different from my typical order, but I can't quite place what it is. I'd ask her about it, but I'm too hung up on her idea that we're spending the day together.

"Why would I have to trust you all day?"

"Because I'm here for my *real* payment, obviously. Today's

your lucky day, Camden. You get to spend the entire day with me and the beautiful town of Sutten."

The sigh that escapes my body is long and drawn-out. I'd forgotten all about her silly little stipulation for her assistance during the opening. I'm a man of my word, and no matter how badly I want to tell Pippa to forget about it because I have a thousand things I have to do before returning to Manhattan tomorrow, I try to hold my tongue.

"I have a lot of things to get done today."

She raises one of her tanned shoulders. "I had a lot of things to do when you asked me to slave away for your event—where I was insulted by one of your rich friends, in case you forgot—so excuse me if I don't care if you're busy or not. You're coming with me for the entire day—and maybe even the evening. I've got so many fun things planned for us."

"Your plans were to watch disgusting reality TV. Do you know how much of that shit is actually scripted?"

Her plump bottom lip peeks out in a pout. "Don't ruin it for me. I quite enjoy reality TV.. I'll never be able to look at it the same."

"Maybe we can rain check our little Sutten Mountain adventure?" I ask sarcastically. "And by rain check, I mean never doing it."

Pippa clicks her tongue before taking a drink of her own coffee. "You aren't getting out of this. You have five minutes before you need to meet me outside."

"What about my work?" My argument is futile. I know enough about her to know that this isn't an argument I'll win.

"Work can wait!" she muses. The glee on her face can only be because she knows she's about to torture me for an entire day.

Why did I agree to this again? Surely the guests didn't need food at the opening *this* bad.

Regretting ever saying yes to her, I groan. "You aren't letting me out of this, are you?"

Her eyes twinkle. The light from the floor-to-ceiling windows catches the gold rim around her pupils. "No, I'm not. *Tick tock,* Camden! You now have four minutes until you have to meet me outside."

With that, she pretty much skips out of the gallery. I can't see where she disappeared to, but I'm confident she hasn't traveled very far. She wouldn't miss the opportunity to torture me for a day.

I walk out the door fifteen minutes later just to piss her off, not at all prepared for whatever she's about to put me through in this town.

Chapter 14
PIPPA

CAMDEN LOOKS INCREDIBLY UNCOMFORTABLE SITTING IN THE passenger seat of my old truck. Despite looking completely out of place, he looks pretty freaking good with his dark hair being tousled by the wind. I couldn't resist rolling the windows down, knowing it'd probably piss him off to ride around town with the wind caressing our cheeks.

There's no better feeling than traveling down the winding roads of Sutten with the wind in your hair and the cold air tickling your skin. But I believe that because I grew up here. He grew up with dirty streets and air pollution. He probably never drove around with the windows down in New York. I wonder if he ever drove at all.

"Can you drive?" I blurt, risking a glance over at him. I have to raise my voice to speak over the wind.

He's as far away as he can physically manage in the truck. The look he shoots my way is scathing. "What the hell goes through your brain at all times?"

I can't fight my smile. "I don't think you really want to know that. I've thought about killing you often."

"That makes two of us."

"So?" I continue, turning onto a side street. "Can you drive, or is that not a thing where you're from?"

"You say 'where I'm from' like New York is the worst possible place to live."

"It's not the worst, but I can't say I see the appeal."

From the corner of my eye, I can see his finger running over his top lip. He seems to be deep in thought with the gesture and the slight furrow of his eyebrows. "Tell me why New York doesn't seem appealing to you."

His voice is demanding, leaving no room for questions. Typically that would annoy me, but right now, it doesn't. It intrigues me. I want to know why he cares about my opinion of where he lives.

"It just seems so...crowded." I'm so distracted by his questioning that I almost miss my turn. I try not to, but I have to slam on the brakes before I miss it. Feeling his brooding scowl aimed right at me, I pretend to pay close attention to the road.

Silly mistake.

He shockingly makes no comment, instead choosing to stay focused on our conversation. "Something tells me it gets pretty crowded here during ski season."

He isn't wrong. Once November hits, Sutten gets very packed. But it's just people on vacation. They're happy and carefree. New York City seems like a different kind of packed. Full of people who live there and aren't happy with their lives. They're lost in the hustle of everyday life. It doesn't feel like that here in Sutten—at least to me. I try to think of a way to describe the difference to Camden to make him understand.

I pull into a crowded parking lot and park at the very back. Before I look over at Camden, I feel him already looking at me. He's waiting for an answer, and I guess I'll just have to do my best to put what I'm thinking into words.

"I think there are different kinds of crowded," I begin, turning my body so I face him completely. "In my mind, I think of it this way... You can have a huge group of people who are giddy and ready to begin their vacation. They're away from work and the sorrows of everyday life. They get to just experience life in the moment and not think about anything else. And then you have another group of people. They're having to push themselves every day of their life to make ends meet. They're tired and looking forward to the weekend so they can just take one minute for themselves. Both are groups of people. Both could seem crowded when you're standing in the middle of them. But which group would you rather be in?"

He says nothing. It's silent for so long that I begin to feel stupid because clearly, I'm not making any kind of sense. My fingers play with the loose strings from the hole in my jeans. I twirl the threads of denim around my finger, biting my tongue to not say anything else to make more of a fool of myself.

Why do I suddenly care? I shouldn't. I shouldn't give a damn what he thinks of me, of this town, of anything. But I'm stubborn. And for some terrible reason, I want to prove to him that maybe he shouldn't hate the town of Sutten. If he won't leave, I want to teach him how to embrace the slower-paced lifestyle that comes with the town I've lived in my entire life.

"I've never questioned which group I want to be in," he finally admits.

"And are you now?"

His head cocks to the side. It's with this simple movement that I realize his hair isn't as perfectly styled as every other time I've seen him. It's nowhere near messy, but I don't think Camden is ever unkempt. He strikes me as the kind of guy who wakes up in the morning and immediately gets ready no matter what he has planned for the day.

"I've only ever known the one."

His answer makes me smile. Maybe it's his hesitant tone, so unlike his typical commanding and sure one. Maybe it's because our day hasn't even really started, and I feel like today could change things for him. But mostly, I think it's because Camden is proving to me that he isn't what I thought he was. And I'm curious as hell to find out more about the man who makes a terrible first—and second, and quite honestly third—impression.

"WHAT IS ALL OF THIS?" Camden asks, looking along the community center's gym, which is lined with vendor booths and people.

I take a step forward, trusting that he'll follow me. My instincts are right. I don't have to look over to feel him a step behind me.

"This, Mr. Hunter, is our community art show. Well, more like a vendor fair, but you'll find a lot of art here. And I think it's important for you to see that beautiful art can come from all kinds of places—and that maybe there's a lot of talent for your gallery right here in Sutten."

"Pippa!" a familiar voice calls from a few booths down. I smile at Miss Mary and her booth of handmade soaps. They're my favorite to use, and even though I pretty much have a stockpile of them at home, if she asks if I want to buy one today, I won't be able to say no.

"Hi, Miss Mary," I say with affection as we come to a stop in front of her table.

"I'm shocked you left that bakery of yours to come to the event today." She wraps her arms across her chest, pulling her shawl tighter around her shoulders. "And what handsome man do we have here?"

"I'm not always all work and no play," I answer, eyeing a new scent of soap and lotion I haven't seen from her before. I look over at Camden, who looks incredibly uncomfortable here with his hands tucked in his pockets and his eyes roaming the space. "This right here is Camden Hunter. He bought the Richardsons' gallery. He practically begged me to take him here today. He's been impatiently waiting to check out the local talent."

It's only a small lie. He did pretty much beg me to help him with his opening, which I traded for bringing him here today, but he had no idea the things I had in store. Despite the little white lie, I do think he'll be impressed by what some people here in Sutten have to offer.

Mary clutches her chest as if I just told her Camden saves the lives of babies or volunteers at a homeless shelter. "Wow," she says in awe. "That's so kind and thoughtful of you."

I have to rub my lips together to keep from smiling and blowing my cover. It's just so funny to see her look at him in wonder, knowing that his skin is probably crawling at the fact the attention is on him. "He's a very, *very* kind man," I lie.

Camden Hunter isn't kind. He's a man of power, a man who will do anything to get what he wants, including creating a gallery that goes against all of the small-town values of keeping things local in Sutten.

Miss Mary is completely unaware of the type of man Camden is. She seems to be mesmerized by his charm already, and he hasn't even said anything. It must be nice to have a face so perfect that you don't have to say a word for people to fall at your feet.

"Pippa here is the sweetest girl," Miss Mary admonishes. Now, her bright eyes are pinned on me. "She's as sweet as they come. I've known her since she was in diapers, running around church trying to get naked while Pastor Mark gave a sermon."

My eyes go wide because she's supposed to be on my side. No one except for the people in the church should know about me running around at two without any clothes on in the middle of a service. I blame it on my mom. Dad still to this day loves to tell everyone that my mom found it hilarious and wasn't the least bit embarrassed by my antics. That was my mom. She was vivid and full of life. She could make a joke out of anything, and there are just days that I wish she wasn't ripped out of my life without warning.

"Pippa sure is sweet," Camden drawls. He flashes his straight, white teeth, his incisors slightly sharper than the rest of his teeth. "Kind of reminds me—" He pauses as if he's having to think through his next words. "—of shortcake…"

My eyes turn to slits. His smirk tells me he thinks he's funny, but I don't find it amusing in the slightest.

Meanwhile, Miss Mary is eating up every second of it. She stares at Camden with stars in her eyes. Like she just said, she's known me since I was an infant, and Camden says one complete sentence and she's clearly head over heels for him.

"Shortcake is my least favorite dessert."

Miss Mary whips her head in my direction. I didn't know she could move that fast. "You've won awards with your strawberry shortcakes. I thought you loved it."

She's betrayed me. Camden snickers while my face heats with embarrassment. I'm going to go home and toss out every single one of Miss Mary's soaps because she's supposed to be on *my* side. She wasn't supposed to tell him that the little nickname he's given me isn't as bad as I make it out to be.

"Well, we've got to get going," I lie, pulling on the sleeve of Camden's button-up. "So many vendors to see, so little time."

"Oh, why don't you just get one bar of soap, honey? Or lotion? In the spirit of strawberry shortcake, I do have a few bottles left of my sugar strawberry lotion."

"I'm really o—"

"She'll take it," Camden interrupts. He pulls his wallet from his pocket and thumbs through hundred-dollar bills. I want to laugh when he pulls out two of them, as if one single little bottle of lotion would ever cost that much.

"I hate strawberries," I argue, watching Miss Mary wrap the pink bottle of lotion in white tissue paper.

"Lying is a sin, darling," Miss Mary scolds, looking at me with slight disappointment. "You've bought this lotion from me before."

My cheeks puff out in frustration because I've been caught in a lie. Worse, in front of Camden, who beams so wide I might actually find it charming if I didn't know the smile was at my expense.

Miss Mary gets us all packaged up, and Camden listens to her talk about her five grandchildren. He doesn't strike me as the kind of guy who does small talk with strangers. In fact, his harsh, rude personality strikes me as quite the opposite. I always thought he came off as entitled, meaning he thought he was better than everyone else. Instead, he's showing little glimpses of himself that make me question what I really do and don't know about him.

I reach to grab the little bag from his hand as we walk by a few more additional booths, but he pulls it from my reach. "I'll carry it." His tone makes it seem like there's no further room for discussion.

"I can carry my own bag."

He stops in his tracks, disrupting the flow of traffic for a minute. Shoppers funnel around us as Camden looks down at me. "You can do a lot of things. It doesn't mean you should have to." And with that, he begins to lead the way toward something that's caught his eye.

Chapter 15
CAMDEN

I'VE COME TO THE CONCLUSION THAT ALL THE STEREOTYPES ABOUT small towns are true. Starting with the idea that everyone knows *everyone*.

Pippa is the perfect example of that. We can't walk a few steps without someone stopping to talk to her. Whether it's someone begging for her to finally share her buttercream icing recipe or someone asking how her family is doing, she's always talking with somebody else about something. Some people ask who I am, some of them don't. Most of them don't seem to care who I am; they just want to speak with her.

I don't know if Pippa realizes it or not, but the people in this town love her. Their faces get brighter, their smiles get wider, and they seem captivated by every word she says to them. I was put off by the idea of coming here when she first told me what we were doing, but now I'm almost grateful she brought me. I'm fascinated by how much everyone seems to love her in this town. I'm really just fascinated by *her*.

She talks to every single person like she genuinely cares what they're saying. There was the woman who was telling her that her four-month-old was going through a sleep regression and she felt like she hadn't slept for days, so Pippa offered to come watch the baby sometime so the mom could sleep. Or the old lady who complained about her printer not working, so Pippa offered to come over and fix it. There are countless different instances of this, and as she speaks with yet another person, I focus on one of the questions that keeps being asked.

In one way or another, she keeps getting asked how her family is doing. But it doesn't seem like a polite question in passing conversation. They all seem concerned while asking it. Or that the question is taboo. And her answers give me no clues on what they could be talking about.

And I want to know. I *wish* I knew. I've never cared about being an outsider, but for the first time, I just wish I knew what everyone else knows when it comes to her.

"Yay!" Pippa claps her hands together before she pulls me to a booth with black draping and the words "Tommy Does Art" on a banner across the front of the table. "Camden, you *have* to meet Tommy."

The guy sitting at the table looks like he hasn't even graduated high school yet. Or if he has, it wasn't too long ago. He's got brown hair that's buzzed to the scalp, and he watches me with brown eyes almost the same color as his hair. "Did you bring a friend or something today?" the kid asks, his voice confirming my first thought that he may not even be out of high school yet.

"Or something," Pippa begins, pulling me closer to the table so I stand right next to her. "Tommy, I'd like for you to meet Camden Hunter."

His chair falls backward and hits the gym floor with a loud thump. He wipes his hands on the front of his paint-stained jeans. "Camden Hunter," he rushes out, his words jumbling together making my full name sound like one long name. "Like *the* Camden Hunter?" His tone goes up an octave as he repeatedly wipes his hands on his clothes.

"I don't know how many Camden Hunters there are, but it is my name." I hold out my hand to shake his, but he just stares at my waiting hand in awe.

I freeze, not knowing what I'm supposed to do in this situation. Do I stop the handshake? Wait for this kid to get it together and just look awkward while doing it?

Lucky for me, the kid finally puts his hand in mine and shakes it. "I can't believe I'm meeting Camden Hunter," he breathes.

"I promise you he's not that cool," Pippa pipes up.

Tommy looks at her in disbelief. As if she'd just told him men never walked on the moon or that George Clooney had just retired from acting. "Not that cool?" He looks from Pippa to me. "You're a legend." His eyes bounce around the art displayed around him. "And your eyeballs have landed on my art. Holy shit."

I follow his gaze, looking at the pieces hanging in the booth. "Are these yours?"

"Yes," he squeaks.

"Can I get closer?" I ask, already taking a step around the table to walk behind it.

"You can do anything you want," the kid—Tommy—answers, backing away as if I need that much space to get behind the table.

"Tommy graduated two years ago, and he's been selling his art at shows and conventions and things like that. He even did the mural for me in the shop that leads to the back."

"Are you in school at all?" I let my eyes roam over his different pieces. They're vastly different, but you can still see his style shining through each piece. They are all landscapes. There are mountains, beaches, forests. They seem very traditional, but also, he brings a modern twist to each one. They're very eye-catching. The longer you look at them, the more things you notice. Like how he changes his brushstrokes halfway into painting the beach to make each side look different. Normally such a difference of strokes would make things seem off-balance, but he makes it work.

"He can't see you shaking your head," Pippa says from the other side of the table.

"Right," Tommy states. "No, I'm not in school at all. I'm

hoping if I sell enough art that maybe I'll be able to save enough money to go."

I circle the back of the booth, inspecting all of the pieces he has on display. He's got a lot of talent for someone who seems to have no technical training.

"What's your pricing?" I focus on a landscape of a forest. It's at night, but it still feels warm and inviting. Like everything is asleep around you, and you get to be at peace for once in the calmness of the night.

"That one is one hundred."

"Thousand?"

Pippa sputters behind me. Or maybe it's Tommy because when I look at him, his face is bright red. "No," he whispers, his voice scratchy. "Just one hundred dollars."

I frown. "You're *severely* undercharging for your art."

"I am?"

"Definitely. I already have people in mind who would pay thousands upon thousands of dollars for these pieces."

"What..." The redness from his face is gone. Now he's white as a ghost. "I've never even dreamed about that much money."

Pulling my wallet from my slacks, I fish out my business card. I hold it between my pointer and middle finger as I hand it to him. "I'm going back to Manhattan tomorrow, but here's my card. Email me, and we'll get your art in my gallery. You'll find out what at least half a mil looks like by the end of the month."

"Half a what?" the kid asks. His eyes are so wide with shock that he looks like he's straight out of a cartoon.

"Million," I finish, confident his pieces will sell. The kid will be in for a real treat when he finds out what people will pay if he does custom work for them. I know ten people off the top of my head who'd want a custom piece done for sentimental reasons.

Pippa looks as shocked as Tommy when I finally look at her. Her mouth hangs open, and I hate that the first thing that pops into my mind is how fun it would be to shove my cock in it. Her tongue is a perfect shade of pink. It'd look hot as fuck licking cum from my shaft.

The thought is so abrupt that I almost trip over my own feet. The only reason I don't face-plant is because I'm able to reach out and steady myself on the corner of the table. Luckily, Pippa and Tommy seem to be so swept up in the amount people are willing to pay for art that they don't notice my slip-up.

Straightening my spine, I look around the room to see if anyone else noticed. No one seems to be paying any attention to us. Tucking one hand in my pocket, I slide my other through the crook of Pippa's elbow.

"Any other undiscovered talent here I should know about, shortcake?"

I stop us, turning around so we're almost chest to chest. It isn't lost on me that I could easily drop my hand. She doesn't seem to be going anywhere, so I don't need to keep hold of her. My fingers stay in place. The thrum of her pulse beats underneath my fingertips. Or is it mine?

"You know you just changed his life, don't you?"

"No. That was all you."

Chapter 16
PIPPA

"Should I be concerned that you're going to murder me and hide my body where no one will ever find me?"

I laugh, turning into the long driveway that leads up to my family home. "As tempting as that is, how could I torture you if you're dead?"

"Fair point." He looks out the window, and I wish I knew what he was thinking. What does he see when he looks at the place where I grew up? I don't know how you could look at the rolling hills, the mountains around us, and not fall in love with Sutten Mountain. There's not a better view in this world than the one at the place I called home growing up.

I drive through the gate to the ranch, watching Camden look at the large "Jennings Ranch" sign that hangs over us.

"A ranch?" he questions. "What are we doing here?"

I keep driving, marveling at all the work that's been done already to prep the land for winter. I try and help my dad and my brother, Cade, out as much as possible, but with my own business, I can't be out here as much as I'd like to. After my mom passed, I spent a lot of time here trying to do whatever I could to help my dad and my brother. After some time, I couldn't handle being around them. I couldn't handle being here, being reminded that I lost my mom, so I threw myself into work. All I did was eat, breathe, and sleep the bakery until I realized it was out of control, and I got Kitty to force me to get some work-life balance.

I had no idea what was going on with my brother, my dad was a shell of the man I knew growing up, and I didn't know what to do about it except to distract myself by working.

"Is the guy walking up to us going to help with your murder plot?" Camden teases. He seems looser than when we first started our day, more carefree. That might change once he figures out what I have planned for us.

"The guy walking up to us is my brother. And while he can be a dick, I doubt he has any intention to murder you."

"That's your brother? Is this your family's ranch?" He seems a little shocked as he looks around. It reminds me of how little we know each other. I don't know much about his family dynamic or his life outside of being here at all, actually. It's strange to spend an entire day with someone and not really know anything about them.

"Welcome home," I say with enthusiasm, stopping my truck. Cade holds a saddle over his shoulder, looking at me with a confused expression.

I may have forgotten to mention to him that we were stopping by. He's been a disaster since Mare, my best friend and his girlfriend, left for work. She's currently in Chicago writing a book and in constant meetings. I don't hear from her a lot, and while he might hear from her more than I do, I know he won't get that depressing scowl off his face until she's back here in Sutten. If she comes back to Sutten. It's all up in the air right now.

"I should've known you grew up somewhere like this." Neither one of us makes a move to open the door, even though my brother stands in front of the truck with an even deeper frown on his face than he normally has.

"Should I be offended by that?"

For a fraction of a second, his gaze lingers on my lips. If I blinked, I would've missed it. But I didn't miss it, and I can't help it when my tongue peeks out and traces the spot his focus was just on.

He clears his throat, making both of us jump. "I didn't mean it as an insult."

"I'm shocked."

"I just meant that I should've known we grew up so differently. I grew up being scolded if I had a wrinkle in my clothing. You probably ran around the house with mud on your boots, and no one said a word."

For a moment, I feel sad for the child he must've been. It's only a tiny crumb of information about his life, but it tells me enough. We grew up very differently, and maybe if I got to know him a little more, I'd find out that there's more to him other than just being a grumpy asshole.

Before I can say anything else, the driver's-side door is ripped open. I almost fall out in front of both of them.

"Cade!" I yell, adjusting my butt in the seat. "What was that for?"

"What are you doing here, Pip?"

Camden snickers from the other side of me. "*Pip?*"

I aim a dirty look his way, totally forgetting that ten seconds ago, I was almost feeling sorry for him.

"And who is this?" Cade's tone is not friendly. He definitely isn't rolling out the welcome mat for our new guest. He's acting every bit the overprotective big brother, even though he has no reason to be.

"This," I begin, sliding out of the truck and planting my boots on the ground, "is Camden Hunter. He took over the Richardson gallery."

"The guy you called a prick because he bought the space you wanted?"

Camden's eyebrow arches in curiosity as he rounds around the front of the vehicle. I was too busy gawking at my brother's unnecessary comment to notice Camden even getting out to begin with.

"I didn't want to buy the space," I lie, suddenly embarrassed. For some reason, I don't want Camden to know I wanted the space he now owns. I don't want him to have that to hold against me. Because I'm sure things can't stay neutral between us forever, and even though today he's been friendlier than normal, I know there will be a time when we'll go back to arguing, and when that happens, I'd rather him not know that I'd always dreamed of buying the art gallery to allow myself more space for Wake and Bake.

Cade fixes the ball cap on his head. "What are you talking about? All you ever rattled on about was saving up the money to buy their place and yours and merge them together." He pulls me closer to him, running his gloved hand along my forehead. "Did you get concussed and not tell anyone?"

I shove my brother away, wiping at my skin to see if he got any dirt on me. "Cade, you have no idea what you're talking about."

My brother gives me an odd look, but thankfully, he drops it. I'm sure the next time he gets me alone, he might ask about it, though. I'll answer him when I have to. Right now, I'm more concerned about the inquisitive stare I'm getting from Camden.

Cade pulls a leather glove off his hand and sticks it into the back pocket of his jeans. He extends his hand, waiting for Camden to shake it. "Nice to meet you, Mr. Hunter. I'm Cade."

Camden takes his hand. It's funny to watch the two of them shake hands, knowing how vastly different they are. My brother is a country boy with his worn-in jeans and faded cap on his head. There's dirt on his shirt from working today, and his boots are littered with scuffs. Camden barely has a hair out of place, despite riding around with the windows down with me today. He looks a tad more casual than he normally is by not wearing a suit jacket, but the nice button-up shirt and slacks are no match for the ranch.

I fight a smile at the idea of him on a horse with what he's currently wearing.

"You can just call me Camden."

Cade nods, crossing his arms across his chest. He's tan—too tan. I make a mental note to make sure he and Dad are applying sunscreen every morning. They spend all day out in the sun, and if I find out they aren't taking care of their skin, they're going to get a long lecture.

"What brings you out here, Camden?"

Camden focuses on me. I hate the way that even when he looks so out of place standing in our driveway, he somehow still looks good. He almost looks like he belongs here, even though he's dressed for a business meeting and not a trail ride. "I wish I could tell you, but I'm along for the ride. Your sister is in charge today."

Cade laughs. "Careful giving her that much power."

"I'm already regretting it." His tone is teasing, and it doesn't feel like a jab.

I clap my hands together. I'm ready to put him through it a little so maybe he becomes an asshole again. I can handle Camden being a dick; I'm used to it. What I'm not equipped to deal with are the lingering looks on my lips and the nice things he's saying every now and then. "Camden is here for a trail ride."

"A what?" Camden asks, a scowl appearing on his face once again. *There it is.* This Camden I'm much more familiar with.

"You can't take him on a trail ride wearing that." There's humor in Cade's voice. He was there the night we first met Camden. If you could even call it a meeting. I accidentally ran into this asshole, spilled beer all over him, and he was pissed. Cade was there, but I've since learned he was too busy pining after my best friend to pay attention to what was going on. Probably for the best because he also didn't notice that I was flirting with Chase, one of his good friends.

"I'm not going on a trail ride at all," Camden interjects, looking at me as if I've had the craziest idea in the world to take him out on the trails.

"We're getting you to fall in love with Sutten," I argue, already walking toward the stables. Luckily, it seems like we don't have any guests here right now out on the trails, so we'll have the stables and trails all to ourselves. "And I happen to know the best view in Sutten comes from being in the saddle on the side of the mountain."

"I agree with your brother," Camden yells from behind me. "I don't have the proper clothes to go riding! I don't have any riding boots." I don't bother looking over my shoulder to see if he's following or not. He can follow me or be left alone with my brother. I doubt he picks the latter.

"Riding boots," I call, happy to see my horse, Tonka. I haven't been good about coming out here and giving him attention when I know I should. Life is just busy, and I know that he gets to go on trail rides often. Finally, I turn around, finding Camden following me a few steps behind. "Tell me, Camden, did you ride English saddle growing up? You went to equestrian camps, didn't you?"

"No," he states matter-of-factly. "I'm not really one for... animals. But I once dated a girl who jumped competitively, so I know a little about horses."

"Did you break her heart?"

"Depends on who you ask."

Cade catches up to us, sliding his phone back into his pocket like he'd just gotten off a call.

"Talk to Mare?" I prod. She keeps up with Cade, but she doesn't keep up with me as much. I try not to let it bring me down. She's busy finishing a book, and I'm confident she'll come back once she's done everything she needs to do in Chicago. But I miss my best friend.

"Yeah, she didn't have long—she was about to go to sleep for the day. She was up all night writing."

I hate that I feel Camden staring at me. I'm worried he can read my every thought. That he'll find out something else to use against me.

"How about I go get some clothes and boots of mine to see if they work for you?" Cade offers, sizing up Camden's clothing of choice.

"You couldn't have told me to dress accordingly?" Camden ignores my brother's comment completely, pinning me with a brooding stare.

All I can do is smile and shrug. "And ruin the surprise? Never."

Chapter 17
PIPPA

My cheeks twitch as I try to stifle the laugh threatening to escape. I manage to hold it back for a few seconds before it bubbles out of me, sending me into a fit of laughter.

"I'm glad you find this so amusing," Camden snaps, his lips pressed into a thin line. His tone sends me into hysterics, making me bend at my waist as tears form in my eyes.

"Oh my god," I wheeze, trying to bring air into my lungs. "This is the greatest thing I've ever seen." Reaching into my pocket, I pull my phone from my jeans. "I've got to get a picture to post on the internet."

In the blink of an eye, Camden is across the tack room and ripping my phone from my grasp.

"Hey!" I yell, attempting to snatch it back from him. "Give me my phone back."

Camden clicks his tongue. I'm incredibly uncomfortable watching him swipe through my camera roll, clearly having no boundaries at all.

"I'll give it back when I'm out of this awful outfit and back in clothing that is actually tailored to fit my body."

I almost bust my ass when I attempt to jump up and snag my phone from his grip again. He's too quick for me, holding it above his head so it's way out of reach. His thumb continues to swipe through my camera roll, and he's getting dangerously close to seeing photos on there that weren't meant for his eyes.

So far, we're in the safe zone, and he's mostly seeing photos I've taken of cakes and other pastries to upload to all of Wake and Bake's socials. But if he keeps going...

I lunge one final time, hoping to catch him by surprise. It doesn't work. He pushes against my chest just enough to allow him more room to invade my privacy while he swipes away with his other hand.

Groaning, I take a step back, running right into a saddle stand. I rub at my hip, pinning him with a glare. My only hope is if I stop trying to grab it from him, maybe he'll stop going through my pictures as payback for trying to blackmail him.

When he doesn't stop, I grow anxious. "Okay, fun is over. You can keep my phone until you're back in your rich-guy clothing and not slumming it in my brother's hand-me-downs."

I hate to admit it, but he looks damn good in the outfit, even if the clothes don't fit him as well as his typical clothing does. He's got maybe an inch or two on Cade, making the old pair of Levi's a tad too short on him. His foot was two sizes too big to wear any of Cade's cowboy boots, but we found a pair an old ranch hand used to wear that worked. It's really something to see Camden in a pair of cowboy boots. He looks so out of place I almost laugh all over again at the sight.

He drew a hard line at the cowboy hat, despite my efforts to tell him it was part of the day.

I'd spent too long ogling him that I hadn't realized he never responded to me. I notice his thumb is no longer swiping across my phone screen, but something has still caught his attention by the way he brings the screen closer to his face, staring down at it.

Oh no.

"Camden," I start, my breath hitching. Thank god my brother had to run out to help my dad with a broken fence, or I'd be even more mortified to have him bear witness to this.

Camden's icy-blue eyes find mine. His entire face is stoic, his back ramrod straight as he turns my phone to face me. "Who the hell are you sending this to?" His voice is tight, and even from a few feet away, I can see the muscles along his jaw ticking away angrily.

My stomach drops when I see the picture of me standing in front of the full-length mirror in my closet. "No one," I answer, hating the way my cheeks flush knowing he's seen the photo. I want to say I'm embarrassed, but I don't know if the blood rushing to my cheeks is from embarrassment or excitement— and I think I might like it.

"Pippa." He takes a long, angry breath, air hissing through his nostrils. I always thought the stables were loud and full of life, but as we face each other in the tack room, nothing can be heard but our labored breaths. "Who. Did. You. Send. This. To?"

"That's none of your business. Let's go."

Camden's nostrils flare. It's the only thing that gives his jealousy away, aside from the angry tick of his jaw.

Our angry glares don't falter. Time passes by as we stare at one another. Or maybe it isn't anger in our eyes. It's full of tension, but I don't know what kind, and I know that I need to get out of this room before I do something dumb. Right now, I want to do something foolish and ask him if he liked what he saw.

"You have one more chance to tell me who you sent this photo to before I go through every single one of your text messages to find out."

"That's childish. You hate me, remember? Why does it matter who I'm sending pictures of myself to?"

"Because you're wearing nothing but scraps of fucking lace."

He isn't wrong. I'd found a new website to order lingerie from. I wanted to see how it fit. The lingerie fit perfectly, and I love to do my own little photoshoots when I feel sexy. The pictures weren't taken for anyone but myself. I love the body I have. Strong in some places and soft in others. I liked that this lingerie accentuated my favorite parts of my body. It lay high on the hips, bringing attention to the narrow of my waist. It cut low on my breasts, giving them a needed lift without pushing them up to my chin in a way that is completely unnatural and incredibly uncomfortable. The bra makes my average-sized breasts seem bigger than they actually are, something I really liked about it.

I get so lost in my mind that I don't realize he's closed the distance between us. He's cornered me, the edge of the saddle stand digging into my back. I hardly notice the sting of it because I'm too lost in the way his eyes have darkened.

"One last chance, shortcake. Tell me who you're sending them to."

"Why? So you can laugh with them?"

"No, so I can tell them to lose your fucking number."

My mouth snaps shut. What the hell is happening?

He takes a step forward, fully pressing the fronts of our bodies together. He's warmer than I was expecting, so different from his typical cold personality. He stands over a head taller than me, but the way he crouches down puts us almost nose to nose.

"Camden." My voice betrays me. Gone is the snarky tone I reserve for him and only him. In its place is a breathy tone…and maybe a little lust after feeling his hard body pressed against mine.

He holds the phone in front of me, angling it so both of us can see the screen. He focuses on the dirty picture of me for a few seconds before closing out of it and going to my home screen. The moment he clicks on my text messages, the lust-filled bubble pops, and I'm left with anger.

"You're crossing so many boundaries," I lash out.

His eyes scan over all the text threads I have. "I don't see you trying to stop me."

I frown. Maybe he has a point. "You aren't going to find who I sent the picture to."

His breath tickles my cheeks when he looks back to me. "And why's that? You deleted the conversation?"

"No." I look at where our bodies touch. I should push him

away, but even though fury courses through my veins at the way he's unapologetically crossed so many lines, I can't do it. I don't want to. I'm too lost in the angry fog in his eyes. The way he clenches his jaw so hard that I'm worried he'll chip the teeth his parents clearly spent thousands to perfect. "I took the picture for me."

His head cocks to the side. It seems childish, but I want to reach out and tousle his gelled hair. To make him a little less perfect as revenge for violating my privacy. "Explain," he growls.

Sighing, I finally get in my right mind and push at his chest. It's only haphazardly. He lets me do it, though, only backing up as far as I pushed him—which wasn't far to begin with.

"Yes. For me. Why can't a woman take sexy pictures of herself and keep them just for herself? On days when I'm tired or I'm covered in flour and in a pair of old jeans and a T-shirt, I like to look back at pictures like this and remember the times I felt beautiful and sexy."

He swallows, his Adam's apple slowly moving along his throat. "No one else has this?"

I shake my head. Not that he deserves to know the information in the slightest.

"You're always…" His words drift off. He decides against saying whatever he was going to say as he backs away a few steps, keeping my phone in his grip.

Awkward silence fills the room. He sets the phone down on a shelf before barreling out of the tack room. "Lead me to the beast you're insisting I ride," he clips before disappearing.

Now that I'm alone, I finally take my first deep breath in a while. I grab my phone, noticing that the screen is still illuminated. My entire body flushes when I see a brand-new text thread created, with only one text in it.

The picture we were just looking at. I don't have to ask to know he just sent that picture to himself—and now I'll spend the entire day wondering why.

Chapter 18
CAMDEN

"You know horses can sense fear, right?"

I aim a cutting glare her way, one she doesn't see from slightly in front of me. My fingers grip the reins for dear life as Pippa leads us up the mountain on horseback. I squeeze the horse's haunches with my thighs, trying not to fly off as we climb the mountain.

"I'm not scared," I state, well aware of the hesitant tone in my voice. I'm a man that's all about control in all aspects of my life. There's no one who can do things better than I can. So putting my life in the hands of a horse that could throw me off the side of a mountain isn't exactly my idea of a good time.

It's not the horse I fear. It's giving up control.

"We're almost up to the last part, and then it'll be smooth sailing, *cowboy*." The word *cowboy* is said sarcastically, so sarcastic that she giggles to herself. I'm sure if she wasn't right in front of me, I'd see a satisfied smirk on her face.

"I'll give you a win for the art fair," I yell, white-knuckling what Pippa told me is a "saddle horn" as the horse jumps over a log in its path. "But being in the middle of nowhere on a fucking horse is not making me fall in love with this town. In fact, it reminds me of all the things I don't enjoy about small towns."

Pippa and her midnight horse come to a stop at the beginning of a clearing, the ground underneath us finally flat once again.

"Give me ten more minutes, and you'll see what I mean about the best view."

My horse, whose name is Rebel, doesn't give me ease about putting my life in his hands and leans down to munch on the grass below his hooves. I loosen the reins a fraction, giving him the space to have a snack. It allows my thighs a chance to rest after they just spent forever clutching the sides of him so I didn't tumble down a mountain.

"You know, I'm second-guessing agreeing to your stupid little deal."

"I told you I didn't want to do it. I had to make you miserable if I was going to agree to it."

All I do is grunt, pressing my heel into Rebel's underbelly when Pippa guides her horse forward again. I'm definitely miserable for a multitude of reasons.

Giving up control.

Not working when I have a thousand things to do.

Wearing these stupid hand-me-down clothes that make me feel like I'm wearing a cheap-ass cowboy costume.

Watching Pippa's strong thighs straddle the horse, knowing what she's hiding underneath her jeans. The image of Pippa in nothing but that skimpy lingerie will forever be burned in my mind. I can't get rid of it, no matter how hard I try. I've thought of countless different ways I could rip that lace from her body so every perfect bare inch of her skin would be on display. I'm not proud of imagining what her ass looked like in the lingerie. I'm sure it left little to the imagination, and I can't deny how bad I wish I'd seen the view. There's not a doubt in my mind that seeing the bare curve of her ass would be my undoing. I'd love to see that scrap of fabric settled between her ass cheeks as I put a perfect palm print on them.

My cock stiffens in my jeans. I hate it. It's just another reminder that I've lost control. My body is betraying me by wanting her—but how could I not? She's beautiful—there's no way I could ever deny that—but she drives me insane. She's everything I hate—uncontrollable chaos. Yet, I'm aching to have one little taste of her wild side. She's so incredibly tempting, and she doesn't even know it. At least she doesn't know how tempting she is to *me*. I'm trying to hide it, but seeing her in lingerie, wondering what other man has laid eyes on a body that deserves to be etched into stone, was where all of my careful control snapped.

I didn't care if she knew I was jealous.

But with more space between us, I can't help but hate myself a little for wanting her the way I do—for being so tempted by her. By knowing that if she looks at me with lust instead of anger one more time, I might prove to the both of us that I don't have to like her to worship every inch of her body.

"Hello!" Pippa yells, catching my attention. She's turned around in the saddle, staring at me with expectant eyes.

"What?" I snap, hoping she didn't catch me trying to adjust myself. Having a boner in a saddle is one of the worst things I've experienced. Every time the horse moves, even just by an inch, my straining cock hits the saddle horn. It's safe to say I *don't* see the appeal of horseback riding. This is uncomfortable as hell, and so far, the only view I can focus on is Pippa's round ass in the saddle—something I have no right looking at.

Pippa's sultry smile about does me in. I wonder if she has any idea how much she's fucking with my head. "Are you ready to fall in love with Sutten?"

"No," I bite. I'm ready to get the hell out of Sutten, as a matter of fact. I'm ready to get away from her and all the shit she's doing to my head. I'm not someone who gets distracted, and I refuse to become one when it comes to her.

Pippa shrugs, guiding her horse forward. "I'm going to show you anyway."

She's too far ahead to hear the angry sigh that rips through me. I scowl, training my eyes on the back of her head so I don't get distracted by her body once again. I'm so focused on keeping my gaze in a safe zone that I miss the fact that both of our horses have come to a stop, and in front of us is a view that makes me pause.

"Holy shit," I mutter under my breath, looking at the expansive view in front of us. It's so breathtaking it deserves to be captured in paint forever.

"It's something else, isn't it?" Her voice takes me by surprise. She's no longer ahead of me; instead, she sits on her horse right next to me.

"It's okay," I lie. It's one of the most beautiful views I've ever seen. Some of the leaves on the trees have started to change colors. It's absolutely mesmerizing. I've been all around the world. I've seen a handful of the seven wonders of the world, but fuck, I hate that she's right about the view in front of me.

It's magnificent. A hidden treasure that not many people seem to know about except the people who live here. The trees paint a vibrant picture in hues of red and orange, mixed with a small amount of luscious green from the trees that haven't quite accepted summer changing into fall. There are even mixes of yellows throughout the rolling hills. If I look far enough, there's a large body of water nestled in between the trees. The top of the mountaintop behind it reflects in the water, creating a masterpiece.

If I could have some of my most popular artists come up here, they could create magic. The idea pops into my head without welcome. I shouldn't want to return here. I shouldn't want to bring talented artists here to capture the breathtaking essence in front of me, but I can't stop myself from already imagining it. They'd never come close to capturing how perfect the view is, but damn do I know some really talented people who could try their best.

"What's on your mind?" Pippa's voice is soft, pulling me from all the different plans flying through my head. Even the kid I just met—Tommy, I believe it was—could create a masterpiece if he had the chance to come up here and paint the views.

"I can't imagine what this looks like at dawn." The words

spill from my mouth before I can do anything about stopping them. My jaw snaps together as my head catches up with what I just said. It wasn't at all what I was thinking—or was I? Either way, it wasn't something I wanted to say out loud to her.

I still feel this immense need to act like the view in front of me is ordinary—even though it's anything but. The expanse of land in front of us is everything, but I don't want to let her know that. I don't want her to know she's right.

"It's truly one of a kind." Her eyes soften at the corners a little. It isn't with humor. It's almost as if her features soften with relief. Like she can breathe a little easier knowing I didn't automatically bash something she loves so much.

We've bickered and fought more than I have with any other random stranger in my life. I should have no problem insulting the view she clearly loves—but I can't do it. I've said some shitty things to her, but I can't do it again. Not at this exact moment.

Because I understand what she means. I've seen the incredible craftsmanship in the architecture of Barcelona, the lake at the bottom of the mountains in Hallstatt, Austria, the Amalfi Coast in Italy with water such a vivid turquoise I wondered how it was possible for it to be so vibrant. I've vacationed in the French countryside and walked through rows and rows of blooming cherry blossom trees in Japan. My lifestyle has brought me all around the world, allowing me to see so many beautiful places. Little did I know the one I wanted captured in paint the most was one in a little town I'd never heard of in Colorado. And I never would've heard of it if my best friend and his wife hadn't insisted on getting married here and forcing us all to join them.

"Is this where I say I told you so?" There's sass to her voice as she climbs off her horse.

I roll my eyes at her. She absolutely could say that, but I bite my tongue so I don't admit it to her. Instead, I look at the ground and anxiously wonder how the hell I'm supposed to get off this horse.

As if she can read my mind, she grabs my horse's reins and

holds him steady. She whispers things to him as I climb off—the whole entire process probably being the least graceful thing I've ever done in my life. Sports were never my life like they were some of my friends growing up, but I was good at them, and I did them because it got me away from a house I hated. I was fortunate enough to have been athletic without really having to work at it. But apparently, the years of lacrosse and the swim team at my fancy boarding school did nothing to teach me how to get off a fucking horse.

The moment my feet hit the ground, I almost want to kiss the solid earth beneath the soles of my god-awful boots. I've never been more thankful to be on dirt in my entire life.

"Was he so high-maintenance, Rebel Boy?" Pippa coos to the horse, rubbing between his eyes. "Did he just not know how to ride you properly?"

I grunt, taking a step forward only to find myself a little unsteady on my feet. Even with my feet planted, it feels like I'm still bouncing up and down on the horse. My thighs burn, and my cock finally feels relief to not be rammed against a saddle horn.

"What do we do now?"

If she notices my grouchy tone, she doesn't say anything. Instead, Pippa reaches into a saddlebag on the side of her horse's saddle. She pulls out what looks to be a handmade quilt.

My mind immediately goes to Gran, to the memories of sitting at her feet watching reruns of *The Price is Right* as she dozed off while embroidering quilts.

Pippa also pulls out a bag and a thermos from the saddle bag before she nods ahead of us. "Now, Camden Hunter, we appreciate the view."

Chapter 19
PIPPA

"Can I ask you something?" Camden asks, looking at me from over the top of his coffee mug.

I narrow my eyes on him. "You don't strike me as the kind of guy to ask before doing anything. Just ask whatever you want to ask."

We've been sipping on coffee and snacking on scones while we took in the landscape. It was long enough for both of us to need a refill of the coffee I'd packed in a thermos for us. I'm shocked that we've made it this far without clawing each other's eyes out or at least seriously insulting each other. We've only shared small jabs, but for the most part, conversation between us has been easy.

I hate to admit it, but he's an interesting man. He knows a lot about the world, and I've enjoyed hearing about what he's done in life. I haven't seen much outside of Sutten and Chicago. His stories make me want to take the time one day to see what all the world has to offer.

Camden clears his throat, bringing me back to the fact he wanted to ask me something. He seems nervous about it, which in return makes *me* nervous for whatever's about to come from his mouth. If I know anything about him, it's that he doesn't seem like the type of man to get nervous. He traces a line of thread of the quilt my mom hand-stitched when I was a teenager.

"Why did everyone in town keep asking how your family's doing?"

My eyes go wide as they find his. I'd been staring at the way his long fingers stroked the delicate threading of the quilt that I hadn't been paying attention to his expression. I try not to look at it, in fear I'll stare too long. It's hard to look away with features as chiseled and striking as his.

"It's a small town. People just want to know how everyone's doing."

The straight line of his lips tells me he doesn't believe me. He watches me, heat prickling my skin with the path his eyes trace. "It seemed like more than that."

Because it *is* way more than that. When my mom died, it didn't just hit our family hard; it was something that rattled our entire town. She was the light of this town. Friends with everybody. My mom welcomed everyone she met into her life with open arms, and I don't think I was the only one who kind of imagined her in our lives forever.

"Why do you say that?" My question is meant to stall, and the way he stares me down tells me he knows that. Stupid Camden Hunter. I hate how good he is at reading people, even though I imagine that a huge part of his job is being able to easily read people so he can sell to them—profit off them.

"Because there was pity when they looked at you," he answers softly. His words don't hurt because they're true. It's one of the hardest parts of grieving. You can think you've healed as much as you can from a sudden death, but the people around you never treat you the same. The pity in their eyes doesn't go away with time, and it almost makes you feel guilty for doing the only thing you can do after losing somebody—go on with your life.

I let out a shaky breath. Am I about to tell him about my mom dying? If I do tell him, how much do I tell?

Do I tell him that I feel guilty Cade was the one who found

her? That sometimes I wish it was me who found her because I feel like I could handle the pain better than my brother?

Do I admit that I waited outside the local movie theater the next day because my mom and I had made plans to see the newest rom-com together that afternoon? I hadn't processed that we'd actually lost her, even though Dad had already asked me to begin arranging the funeral and to let everyone know she'd passed because he hadn't faced our new reality yet. I sat on the curb in the theater's parking lot for over an hour weeping because she never showed up.

Do I tell him that I still listen to the old voicemails she left me to pretend she's still here?

Do I admit that sometimes I feel really fucking angry at her for dying? And hate myself for feeling that way because I know in my bones she never would've left us on purpose.

There are so many things I could say that could answer his question. I open my mouth to tell him, but no words come. Words fail me.

I didn't know I was crying until Camden reaches across the quilt, wiping his thumb at my tearstained cheeks.

"You don't have to..." There's a softness to his voice, his words trailing off.

I nod, letting out a shaky breath. I have to tell him. We've made it this far. My tears make it obvious that there's more to what he already knows. I might as well tell him the rest.

"A few months ago," I begin, trying to swallow the lump in my throat that makes my words come out shaky, "my mom passed away all of a sudden. She had a heart attack in the middle of the night."

Camden's body freezes, the rough, calloused pad of his thumb still on my cheekbone. He's silent, and I don't hold it against him. At least he doesn't apologize. That's what I hated most when talking to people after my mom died. I didn't need their apologies. I just needed my mom back.

"We all thought she was healthy. It shattered our world. My

dad had been with her his entire life, and Cade was a total Momma's boy. She was their world, and our family was a mess after."

"And you?"

He lets his thumb stroke along my cheek again, even though I'm confident more tears haven't fallen. "Wasn't she your world, too? How did *you* handle it?"

I pause. His words take me by surprise. "I don't know if anyone really asked about me specifically. It was always 'how's your brother doing...how's your father doing...how's your family doing...'"

"I want to know how *you're* doing."

His eyes are so blue up close. A kind of blue I haven't seen before. It's crystal clear, the pigment so icy that his eyes almost seem gray.

He looks at where his hand still rests on my cheek. I don't think deeply into why I miss his touch the moment he pulls it away like my skin had burned him.

"You don't have to answer that," he insists. His eyes search my face. I want to know what he's looking for, what he's thinking. I'm grateful that he might be the first person to know about my mom and not look at me with pity.

I try to hold back a weak laugh when I realize the first person to really ask me how I'm doing without pitying me happens to be a man that I swore I hated—and one I'd bet money hates me.

I'm well aware how truly pathetic that is.

"If I tell you, are you going to make fun of me later for it?"

He rears back as if I hit him. Of all the insults I've thrown at him, why does he seem most affected by this one?

"I must really have been an asshole to you if you think I'd *ever* make fun of you for how you're dealing with the loss of your mother."

I shrug because I don't know what else to do. We don't have the best track record together, but I really don't think he'd ever use it against me. I just don't like having him know intimate things about me.

"Tell me about her."

I stare at him for a moment, wondering if although he doesn't show it, he feels sorry for me. That could be the only explanation for why he's asking about my mom. It'd make sense why he's acting like he actually gives a damn about me.

"You really want to know?" I shift on the quilt, my knee bumping against his. He doesn't move at all, even though with my new position, our knees barely touch.

"Yeah." He sounds confident but maybe even a little sad. Taking a deep breath, he looks up from his lap, and I find vulnerability in his icy-blue eyes. "I want to know more about her."

"Okay..." I begin, hesitant to tell him much about me. I feel like stuff between us should stay surface level. But I like that he knows nothing about her. I like that I can be the one to tell him how amazing my mother was. Everyone in the town knew her and loved her. I'm excited to be able to talk about my mom and the mark she left on my life without having someone look back at me that pitied me or felt like they lost her, too.

"It's cliché, and I know every kid says this about their mom, but she truly was the best mom ever. She was born to be a mom."

"I wouldn't." The words are said under his breath. Once his eyes go wide, I wonder if he meant to say that out loud at all.

"You wouldn't what?"

He runs a finger along my mother's stitching on the quilt. I'm wondering if it's something he does when he's nervous. I've noticed he's also always stuffing his hands in his pockets once his hands get fidgety. He keeps looking down but clears his throat to speak. "I would never say my mom is the best mom ever. She was not born to be a mother. And she made sure every day of my life I knew that."

I blink, staring at him through a whole new lens. I must admit, the moment he moved into the gallery next door, I googled him. Anyone would've done it. I wanted to know why they sold the business to him and not me. A quick Google search of him brought up a ton of information.

His parents were Russell and Emilia Hunter, both very famous artists who fell in love while on a summer getaway to Venice. Their romance was huge in the art world. They were each other's muses in all aspects. From what I read, they had a tumultuous relationship. There were pictures of them with other people throughout the first few years of dating, but they always seemed to make it back to one another.

There was only one photo of his mom pregnant on the internet. Her husband had an exhibit dedicated to his art, and she shocked everyone by showing up ready to pop. They seemed to do a lot with Camden as a baby all the way up to his teenage years. There were countless photos of them as a family. Photos made them out to be a picture-perfect family. With what Camden had just said, I'm wondering if that's really the case.

"Don't feel bad for me, shortcake. Parents fuck up their kids all the time." He playfully bumps his leg against mine. "Now, tell me what having a mother that loves you feels like."

I don't talk at first because I'm lost in what he's told me, in what I've seen about him and his family on the internet. Everything in me wants to pry further about his life, to figure out why he is the way he is.

"If you aren't ready to talk about her, you don't have to," he offers, his tone gentle.

I shake my head at him. "It isn't that. I just was caught up in hearing about your childhood."

He peels a piece off his scone, popping it into his mouth. "There's a reason I'm a dick. Fucked up childhood. Parents who didn't love me but pretended to when cameras were around. No one in my house to show me love."

"You deserved better," I whisper softly.

"Tell me what I missed out on. Tell me about your mom, shortcake."

"She was my favorite person in the world. My best friend, my mom, my everything. She volunteered in my classroom every year in elementary school. She was the one who taught me to bake, the one who helped me get ready for my first date and held me the first time I had my heart broken. She loved to drink tea and sit on the front porch, and she was always begging for me to make her fresh biscuits to leave with her during the week. Her favorite thing to do was make me laugh during church and would then pretend to scold me when I did. My mom was the life of every party, and people just flocked around her to be in her presence."

Camden watches me carefully, hanging on every single one of my words. He seems to be genuinely interested in everything I say, which takes me by surprise. I didn't expect him to care at all.

Things would be a lot simpler if he didn't seem to care at all.

Chapter 20
CAMDEN

It's mesmerizing to watch Pippa talk about her mom. To see her face light up with love and adoration when talking about her. I'm fascinated by listening to every detail she wants to tell me. I like her better like this. Her cheeks are flushed from talking so fast, her hands moving in every direction from telling a story about how her mom once brought home a box of kittens because she found them on the side of the road and couldn't leave them there.

Earlier, something had hurt inside me to see her cry. I'm not someone who is good at handling other people's emotions. To be honest, I don't do well at handling my *own* emotions—partially due to how I grew up and the verbal lashings I got from my mother if I wasn't acting like a perfect little robot for them to show off to their friends. Partially because I wasn't taught to be compassionate. Other people's feelings have never really been my business. Except right now, I want to know every single feeling she's ever felt, everything she's feeling. I want to know everything about her.

"One time, me and my best friend, Mare, wanted to do a lemonade stand *so* badly. It's all we talked about, even though Cade and my parents kept telling us that we lived on the edge of town, no one was driving by to stop for lemonade. Mare and I would hear none of it," Pippa explains, laughing to herself.

Something about her makes me want to laugh along with her,

as if I was remembering the same memory she is. It's just the two of us, our horses, and the mountains around us. I feel like without the distraction of the real world, I can almost let my guard down with her. At least enough to enjoy hearing what it'd be like to have a parent who cared about you.

"So, come to find out, my mom forced half the town to drive out to the ranch to visit our lemonade stand. Mare and I were so young and naive we truly thought everyone was driving by and wanted to taste our lemonade, but no, it wasn't that. It was because my mom strong-armed half the Sutten population to purchase glasses of overpriced lemonade from us."

"What'd you buy with the hard-earned money?"

"An Easy-Bake Oven," she answers immediately.

"I have no idea what that is."

"Oh my god!" She sits up on her knees, slapping the ground underneath her as she looks at me in shock. "You don't know what an Easy-Bake Oven is?"

I shake my head.

She sighs dramatically, as if the fact I didn't grow up with whatever this appliance is was the reason my childhood sucked. "You're right, you did have a terrible childhood," she mutters, almost reading my mind.

"You're right," I joke. "Not having some fancy oven was the reason my childhood was stolen from me."

Pippa throws her head back with laughter. Her hair falls down her back as her entire body shakes with her laugh. "It's the fact you think the Easy-Bake Oven is fancy." She looks at me once again. There's wetness under her eyes, but this time, it's from laughter. She wipes at her smudged mascara.

The thought occurs to me that I could get used to hearing her laugh more, to seeing her happy tears. And those are both things I shouldn't want to get used to.

"Is it not?"

"No. It's terrible. I don't know how the food that you bake in it is even edible."

"How was I supposed to know that?"

She takes a long, deep breath in an attempt to calm herself. It's quiet between us, but a comfortable kind of quiet. The one without expectations to awkwardly fill it.

Eventually, she takes another drink of her coffee with her eyes trained on the view in front of us. In the back of my mind, I still want to find a way to bring people here. To give some of the landscape artists I know the chance to capture the beauty to the best of their abilities.

"So are you going to tell me more about your childhood?" She doesn't sound timid while asking it. She seems curious, but I also get the sense I could tell her no and she wouldn't keep prying.

"Doubt it," I answer honestly. I have a complicated relationship with my parents. As an adult, I can't fathom treating a child the way they treated me. I could imagine myself having a kid or two if I met the right person, and I can't imagine just discarding a child the way they discarded me. "All there is to say is that I was their trophy child. Paraded around and appreciated when they wanted to show me off to others but hidden away and forgotten about when there was nobody around to brag to."

"Did they encourage you to be an artist?"

I take a drink of coffee because her question is a complicated one. They shoved art down my throat from the moment I could hold a pencil, but even from a young age, I rebelled against them. I didn't want to become them, and every day of my adult life, I wonder if I became everything they hated or everything they wanted me to be.

"Encourage isn't the word I'd use. Forced is more like it."

"Something tells me you don't take well to being forced to do anything."

I chuckle. I appreciate that she seems to always say exactly what's on her mind. "You could say that."

"So you rebelled by becoming an art owner instead of a creator?"

"I rebelled by not ever giving in to their wishes and following in their footsteps. I was supposed to be some nepo baby art prodigy. They wanted me to be that desperately. It's the one thing I refused to become."

"So could you have been an art prodigy? Are you any good?"

My lips twitch as I do my best to fight a smirk. "Remember that statue you liked so much in my office?"

Her face scrunches in confusion. It makes me laugh, a small chuckle rumbling from low in my chest.

"The most beautiful piece of art I've ever seen? Yeah, I remember it."

My teeth run over my bottom lip because she's feeding my ego, and I love it. "The artist who didn't know if they wanted to sell it? That's me."

"Shut up!"

"No one knows it's me."

"Oh my god, I gave you compliments without even knowing it."

"You gave me *so* many compliments," I tease, popping another bite of scone into my mouth. It's my second one. They're just so damn good.

"I want to throw up." She sighs dramatically, falling backward onto the quilt. "How could you let me say such nice things about you and not say anything?"

"Maybe I like it when you say nice things to me."

She looks at me from the corner of her eye. "No you don't."

I shrug because I won't confess to her what I do or don't like. I loved watching her fawn over a piece I spent so long on. It was fun to see my art through somebody else's eyes since I don't allow a lot of people in on my secret. It was even more fun with the knowledge that she had no clue the artist she was complimenting was me.

"Camden," she groans, covering her face with her hands. "You're the actual worst for letting me make a fool of myself."

Leaning forward, I attempt to push her hands from her face,

but she keeps them locked in place. "You didn't make a fool of yourself. I liked hearing what you thought of my work."

She grunts, not giving any indication that she'll move her hands. "I was telling you what I thought that artist was trying to convey when *you* were the artist." Another loud groan comes from her. I try to look away from the skin she's showing between the denim waistband of her jeans and the ruffle at her midriff. So much sun-kissed skin that's begging for attention.

"Stop being dramatic." My fingers wrap around her wrist. I pull again, this time a little harder. Finally, I get one of her hands to move enough to see both her eyes. "Everything you saw was exactly what I wanted the beholder to see. I'll deny this if you ask me again, but to be honest, I was flattered you noticed all the little details I'd hidden in there."

"I can't believe you actually have talent. I thought all there was to you was, well...you being a dick."

"Maybe I like it that way."

She catches her plump bottom lip between her teeth. Without invitation, I wonder what it'd be like to catch her lip between *my* teeth. I imagine myself tugging on it, digging my teeth deeper until she'd moan.

Fuck. What does she sound like moaning?

She seems so untamed. I bet she doesn't hold back in bed. I'd bite and suck before licking across the seam of her lips, hearing the sound of...

"Camden?"

I shake my head once, ridding the imagination from my mind. She looks at me expectantly, her eyes wide with confusion.

"Hm?" My brain's still playing catch-up, trying desperately to wipe the thought of her moaning underneath me, to form anything else coherent at the moment.

"Why would you rather let everyone think there's nothing to you other than being a dick instead of maybe letting yourself be a little more...human?"

I shrug, not wanting to have this conversation with her.

Quite frankly, I don't want to be doing anything with her. I need to get away immediately. I'm not thinking rationally. My libido has taken over, and I can't stop imagining shutting her questions down by having my cock down her throat. "Have you ever thought that maybe I am just a dick? The fact that I don't like to just sell art but I also like to create it doesn't change that."

"If you say so." The sarcastic tone of her voice tells me she doesn't believe me for a second. I want her to think I'm just an asshole. If people think you're a pompous jackass, they have low expectations of you. I don't like expectations—then I feel like I have to live up to them. The thing about other people's expectations is that you're never really able to live up to them. You'll end up disappointing them, and then you feel like shit for doing so.

"Can I ask you one thing?" The words are out of my mouth before I can think better of it.

When I find her eyes again, I'm struck by how close we are. She's now sitting up, bringing us too close together. If I leaned in slightly, I might feel her breath mingle with mine. Her scent would surround me, more than it already is. The idea of it sent my senses into overdrive from the moment we started this stupid day together.

"I won't tell you my secret recipe for chocolate chip cookies," she mutters. I wonder if her half-assed attempt at a joke is a defense. I know it's something I've done when things don't feel like they're under my control and I desperately need to get a grip on the situation.

This seems like one of those situations. We've both leaned in slightly. I can see the slight tinge of pink on her cheeks, despite it being the start of fall. We're so close I can make out her individual eyelashes. Every time she blinks, her long lashes kiss the apples of her cheeks. Her lips have a sheen to them from her licking them with anticipation. Does that mean she's imagining kissing me the way I'm imagining kissing her?

"To be honest, I don't give a damn about your cookie recipe. I don't enjoy baking."

The swells of her breasts almost spill out the top of her shirt. My fingers twitch at my sides, desperate to run along the soft, exposed skin. Would she tremble underneath my touch? All I'd have to do is reach out to find out...

"Ask your question."

I don't ask my question. It's escaped to the back of my mind. At the forefront is the need to lean in closer. Maybe after just one kiss, one swipe of our tongues against one another, I'll be able to get her out of my mind. I'll escape to New York tomorrow and forget all about the woman who drives me mad in more ways than one.

Against my better judgment, I reach up and sweep a stray piece of hair out of her eyes. It didn't seem to be bothering her, but I wanted the excuse to touch her. To finally feel her skin under my touch.

Her chest hitches at the contact. We're both caught in the moment, staring into each other's eyes, wondering who will completely cave first. It's a constant push and pull with us. I'm not a man who likes to lose or a man who gives in to temptation, but for her, right now, I might be.

My thumb skirts along her cheekbone as I memorize the feel of her soft, flushed skin. I won't allow myself to surrender to this again. I need to commit every single moment to memory before I come to my senses all over again.

"Camden," she breathes, leaning into my touch.

God, she's reactive. Her chest heaves, and her lips part, just waiting to press against mine.

"Yes, shortcake?"

"What are you doing?" I wonder if she realizes she's leaned in closer, placing her lips inches from mine.

"I'm thinking of doing something incredibly fucking stupid."

"Like?"

"Like tasting that sharp tongue of yours. I can't help but

wonder if your insults won't bother me as much if I get to taste them."

My pinky and ring finger press into her neck. Her pulse thrums erratically against them, giving away that she's lost control just like I have.

"We shouldn't." There's not an ounce of conviction in her voice, despite her words ringing true. I absolutely shouldn't want to kiss the woman who's driven me mad from the moment I first met her. But lust isn't logical. She's temptation and lust all wrapped into one, and for once, I'm dying to give in to it.

"You're right about that," I say, my voice low.

"I want to."

"Why do I want to give you what you want for once?" My thumb traces over her cupid's bow before running along her top lip. Her lips part even wider. I continue my path down, pushing her bottom lip as her saliva coats the pad of my thumb.

I'm about to trap her mouth with mine when she takes me by surprise. Her mouth opens even wider. I let my thumb slide deeper into her mouth, feeling the scrape of her teeth against my skin.

Her lips close around my thumb. My cock stirs as I imagine her in the exact same position but with my cock between her eager lips.

The moment her tongue runs along the pad of my thumb, I'm pushing off the quilt and getting as far away from her as possible.

Chapter 21
PIPPA

My body freezes as I watch him rush away from me. I can't move. My entire body is flushed, and my lips are still parted as if they were closing around his thick, calloused thumb.

It feels like freezing cold water has been thrown on me, and I don't know how to react.

I was about to let Camden Hunter kiss me. In fact, I think I was close to begging for him to press his lips against mine just once. I lost total control of myself the moment he got too close to me.

The entire day has felt different. Hate was mixing with lust, and when I felt his breath hot on my cheeks, I forgot every reason why I shouldn't let him kiss me and only focused on the one reason he should—because for one moment, there was nothing more I wanted than to know what he tastes like.

I bet he kisses angrily, with a pent-up rage that is all-consuming. I bet he fucks like that, too.

And for just a moment, I was desperate to know what it felt like to feel his anger in a different way. The rushed movement of his lips, the punishing bite of his teeth. I wanted to feel it all.

We were so close, until we weren't. One moment, my thighs were pressing together to try and soothe the ache between my legs; the next moment, all I saw was Camden's back as he got as far away from me as possible.

When I finally get my shit together, he's already disappeared down the hill toward where we'd tied up the horses in a small meadow. I push hair from my face, trying to cool my flushed skin. The sun beating down on me doesn't help, despite the chill in the air thanks to the mountain breeze.

Part of me wants to let Camden go. I want to be glad that he stopped us before anything could have happened. We don't like each other in the slightest. There's no reason we should ever kiss. But no matter how hard I try, there's a tinge of disappointment in my chest because I wanted so badly to know how he kissed, how he tasted, what sounds he'd make if my cheeks hollowed out around his thumb.

It doesn't take long for that disappointment to turn into anger. It must be something he's good at, being such an asshole that it gets my blood boiling. I angrily shove myself off the ground before snatching up the quilt and our coffees. I hold them tightly against my chest as I head in the direction Camden just traveled.

He doesn't get to tell me he wants to kiss me and leave.

"Camden!" I yell. He's got one leg in the stirrup of Rebel's saddle as he swings his other leg over the horse. He doesn't do it with any kind of grace. If anything, he looks incredibly uncomfortable trying to lean forward to grab the reins from where they dangle at Rebel's side.

"Camden," I hiss, now closer to him. I'm well aware of the bite in my tone. I have no reason to hide how furious I am with him for running away without any kind of explanation. My heart hammers against my chest in anger—and maybe still from feeling his touch—and I can hear the angry thrum of my pulse ringing in my ears.

He doesn't bother to look at me when he clears his throat to speak. "I've got to go," he clips, digging his heels into the horse's sides.

"I wouldn't do that," I warn, watching him still try to grab the reins from where they brush in the dirt.

Rebel prances anxiously, tossing his head up and down,

which is never a good sign. He's a great horse, but he doesn't do well in high-stress situations.

I break out in a run, nearing Camden and Rebel to try and calm the horse. Rebel loves it when you run a hand along his neck, telling him to calm with a gentle tone to your voice. Camden doesn't know how to do any of that—not that I think he would right now, even if he did.

Instead, he digs his heels into Rebel's sides once again without having any way to guide the horse with the reins still not in his grip.

"Just wait," I snap, almost to them.

Camden doesn't wait. Instead, he clicks his tongue to tell Rebel to go. The horse does exactly as he's told. It all happens in slow motion. Rebel kicks his back legs out, showing his discomfort with the entire situation. I try to whisper gentle reminders to the horse to soothe him, but it doesn't work. My attempts to grab onto the reins don't go anywhere because of the way Rebel thrashes his body.

He rises on his back legs, letting out a long, angry whinny. I almost take a hoof to the face as he comes back down. The quick movement from Rebel has Camden tumbling to the ground with a loud thud.

I'm too busy watching it happen with horror that I don't notice Rebel coming back down. One of his legs clips me in the shoulder hard enough to have me falling to the ground.

Rebel takes off, galloping away. All Camden and I can do is watch him run down the mountain.

"Great job," I fume, wiping my dirty hands on my jeans. "Now we're down to one horse."

"Are you okay?" Camden's voice sounds concerned as I look up to find him hovering over me. Scoffing, I shove him away from me, not needing his concern.

"No, I'm not, actually. I'm pretty pissed, thanks for asking."

He runs a hand along my forehead. I slap his hand away immediately, ducking under his arm to put distance between us.

We must be a sight for sore eyes. He looks a mess, with dirt covering his jeans and a scrape going down his arm. The skin is red and angry, blood trickling from one of the spots. He must have hit a rock on the way down. He doesn't seem to notice it, his eyes still trained on me.

"Did the horse get you in the head? Maybe you shouldn't be standing."

I roll my eyes, looking at my horse to luckily find Tonka as calm as ever. At least we didn't lose both of them with Camden's stupid idea.

"Maybe you shouldn't have lost one of our horses," I spit. "Rebel will know how to get back to the stables, but he certainly won't come back here."

His nostrils flare as his eyes track my entire body. The lust that was in his eyes earlier is gone. Now, there's concern in them as he thoroughly inspects every inch of my body.

"Anything hurting?"

"I'm not the one who's bleeding," I answer, nodding toward the blood trickling from the wound on his arm. He looks at it, his eyebrows going to his hairline like he didn't even realize it was there.

Maybe if he wasn't so busy worrying about me, he'd notice that his stupidity got him hurt. It can't be bothering him too much if he didn't even notice it to begin with.

"Maybe you should worry about your arm—or the fact we're down to one horse—and stop hovering over me and pretending you give a shit. Now we have to share a horse the entire ride down." I tense up at the thought of having to feel his body pressed against mine for an hour. I'm pissed at him, no longer wanting to kiss him but back to considering strangling him. I don't want to have to be anywhere near him, but he wanted away from me so fast that he lost one of the horses in the process of getting the hell away from me.

Cade is going to go into a tailspin when Rebel returns alone.

Camden's jaw flexes, and I swear I can hear the sound of his teeth grinding against one another. "We'll call for someone to bring us a new one."

I narrow my eyes, trying to stifle the angry laugh bubbling inside my chest. "Good luck getting service. And even if we could, they wouldn't be up here for at least an hour. Is the thought of sharing a horse with me *that* bad?"

"Yes," he answers immediately. His voice is lower, more uncontrolled than what I'm used to with him. It almost sounds strained, like it pains him to imagine sharing a horse on the way down. That would make two of us.

"God, you're so hot and cold." I angrily untie Tonka's reins from a branch. He whinnies at me happily, ready to get going and completely unaware of the tension between Camden and me.

"I'm not getting on the horse with you." He's regained composure in his voice, his cold, calculating demeanor firmly back in place.

I finish stuffing our belongings back in the saddle bags, completely ignoring him. I don't even look in his direction until I'm in the saddle and ready to go.

He scowls as I stare down at him. He looks so out of place up here in the mountains. His hands are shoved into his pockets uncomfortably, blood and dirt still coating his forearm. Camden could look good in anything, but it looks unnatural to see him in a T-shirt and jeans.

"I'm not getting on there with you, shortcake," he repeats, trying to avoid looking me in the eye.

"It's going to be a long walk down, then," I respond, directing Tonka forward.

Chapter 22
CAMDEN

Maybe I could keep walking until I got service. Then I could arrange for someone to pick me up. Or I could just find my way down the mountain on my own. I've watched hiking documentaries before. Surely if I kept walking down, I wouldn't end up lost.

My fingers pinch the bridge of my nose in frustration. I don't have a lot of options but to get on the damn horse with her.

"Fuck," I rant under my breath, watching her and the horse disappear between the thick foliage of the trees. There's no hope of me ever finding my way back to her family's ranch, and I can't bank on finding cell service anytime soon.

Which leads me to only one other option.

"Shortcake!" I shout, defeat clear in my voice. "Wait," I add, jogging toward her. My toes are getting pinched in the tip of my boots. They're probably half a size too small, creating blisters on the back of my heels as well. I ignore the dull ache of the boots and make my way to her, thankful that she at least listened for once and halted.

After stopping what was about to happen between us, it wouldn't surprise me if she abandoned me at the top of the mountain. It might even serve me right.

I couldn't help it. Once reality hit, I knew I couldn't kiss her. I knew that it was the worst idea possible to involve myself with a woman who hates my guts—a woman who keeps trying to prove to me that I'm better than I am when I know I'm not. A kiss would lead to me wanting more of her. More of her past, more of her body, more of her rage. I'd want more and more until I was done with her, and for some reason, I know I wouldn't be able to look at myself if I used her and left like I normally do. The women I involve myself with always know the rules, but some end up hurt anyway.

It occurs to me that I don't want to hurt Pippa—no matter the simple yet complicated past between us when I know I've done just that—hurt her—with the words I've said while lashing out.

Her horse lets out an annoyed sigh, bringing me back to reality. Pippa stares down at me with anger—and hurt—in her eyes. I'm used to the anger. I'm not used to the hurt. It makes my chest feel heavy to see the disappointment. If only she knew how badly I wanted to kiss her. That the reason I stopped wasn't anything to do with her and everything to do with me—as cliché as that sounds.

"Stop staring at me," she insists, not looking me in the eye. "Get on," she adds at the last minute, her tone full of exhaustion.

I don't blame her. She wasn't wrong when she'd called me hot and cold. I'm all over the place when it comes to her—something I'm not used to in the slightest.

My eyes travel the length of the horse. I know little to nothing about horses and the gear you use to ride one, but the saddle perched on the horse's back doesn't look like it's made for two. "Where do I go?"

Pippa inches forward in the saddle, her strong thighs squeezing the sides of the horse. I'd love to feel those same thighs wrapped around me, squeezing my hips as she writhed in pleasure.

The last thing I should want on this planet is to have her body molded to mine. Maybe this was all part of her plan. If she really did hate me, the number one way to torture me would be to have her pressed up against me, her soft, warm body grinding against mine with every move of the horse, her usual smell of strawberries and vanilla taunting me.

Pippa's hand reaches down, her small fingers with lilac-purple fingernails wiggling in the air. I focus on the color of her nails, shocked that something about her isn't pink. Everything I know of her is pink. Her coffee shop. Her work van. The lids of the coffee cups. The T-shirts at work. The neon sign on the wall of Wake and Bake. It seems different for her to choose any other color for her nails.

"Are you going to take my hand and get on, or are we just going to stand here all day?" She doesn't bother hiding her annoyed tone, not that I blame her. I'd be annoyed with me, too. In fact, I *am* annoyed with myself. But only because it will take an act of God to have my body molded to hers and not touch her in all the ways I'd fantasized about.

"I hate this," I mutter, taking a step closer. Completely ignoring her outstretched hand, I grab the back of the saddle to heave myself up. She pulls her leg from the stirrup, allowing me to put the toe of the boot in and mount the horse.

"I hate you," she snaps, attempting to scoot further up the saddle. My thighs straddle hers, my cock pressing up against her perfect, round ass.

"Let's just not talk," I demand. My jaw hurts from clenching it so hard. The sound of my teeth grinding is the thing I'm focusing on to keep myself from moving at all. If I move, my cock brushes her ass. If my cock brushes her ass, I'll get even harder than I already am. If I get even harder than I already am, I might pull her off the horse and fuck her just to see if that'll get rid of the bubbling sexual tension between us.

"You're awfully angry for someone who put us in this situation in the first place." She clicks her tongue, guiding the horse forward.

Fuck me. Every time the horse moves, it shuffles her body

into mine. I'm so horny that even the brush of her against me has me sucking in air, trying to focus on breathing instead of envisioning all the filthy things I want to do to her.

"I said no talking."

She laughs, arching her back way more than necessary. Is she fucking with me?

She rolls her hips again, confirming that she's doing it on purpose.

What the actual fuck.

I sigh, trying not to feed into her little game. I can't even spar with her right now. My focus is on mastering the willpower to not act on every dirty thought running through my mind.

What is wrong with me? I don't even like her. I tolerate her at best because although I hate to admit it, she did show me some redeeming qualities about the town. Yet, all I can think about is threading my fingers through the long hair that falls down her back. I'd tug on it, forcing her to arch her back as far as it could go as I railed into her from behind.

"Hey, Camden?"

"Hm?"

"You don't tell me what to do." Her tone is sweet and innocent. Her hips are anything but. There's no way they need to rock against me in the way that they are. Surely she's doing it on purpose to get back at me. "You're stuck with me. What a perfect time to talk about what the hell just happened earlier. Are you this hot and cold with everyone?"

I grunt. "Unfortunately, just with you." I regret the words the moment they tumble from my mouth, but I can't do anything about it. Hopefully she doesn't read too much into it.

"Lucky me," she says sarcastically. She glances over her shoulder for a moment, bringing her face too close to mine. I lean back, putting the only distance between us I can with us shoved in the saddle.

It's silent for a period of time—thankfully. The only sound

that can be heard is the rustling of the trees in the wind and the clopping sound of hooves against rocks.

My thighs hurt from clenching them so tightly around the horse to keep me on top. It's the only solution besides wrapping my arms around her middle to help me from falling off on either side. I can only do it for so long. When we get to a point where we're at such an incline that I press against her fully from shoulders to groin, I have no choice but to grip the saddle on either side of her hips.

She lets out an exasperated sigh before shoving the reins in one of her hands and pulling my arms around her with the other.

"I'm fine," I argue, trying to pull my arms away.

"Stop being so stubborn. If you fall off the horse and break a leg, I won't be able to get you back on the horse, and then we'll be stuck up here together for even longer than necessary. So just hold on for thirty more minutes, and we'll be back at the stables, and you'll be rid of me since clearly I'm so terrible to be with."

My lips thin out. She isn't terrible to be with, and that's what fucking terrifies me. We don't get along. We fight more than we have a normal conversation, yet I want to spend more time with her. I don't mind bickering with her. In fact, I think I enjoy it, and I hate that. I hate that my body wants her, despite my mind saying anyone but her—anyone but someone in this town that I only came to because I wanted to make more money and stick it to my dad.

"I never said you were terrible."

"So it's just the thought of kissing me, then?"

My arms tighten around her in frustration. "No. It isn't that either."

"Then what is it?"

"It's nothing," I finally answer after a prolonged silence. There's no use getting into it. I'm angry with myself for even thinking about kissing her—for telling her up there that I wanted to. And now I'm having to deal with the consequences.

Pippa shakes her head, letting out a long sigh of disbelief. "You really are just an asshole, Camden Hunter. Why did I think you'd be any different?"

Chapter 23
CAMDEN

"AND THEN THE CAR BLEW UP, AND EVERYONE DIED."

Emma's words catch me by surprise, pulling me from my thoughts of a week ago when I was still in Sutten Mountain. It's been a week since I made a break for it the moment Pippa and I got back to her family's ranch.

And a week of me wondering why I still can't get the feisty brunette out of my mind.

"Who died?" I ask Emma, almost getting lost in my thoughts all over again.

She narrows her eyes at me from across my desk. She'd come to find Margo, her best friend, but Beck and Margo disappeared almost two hours ago and haven't returned, even though we're supposed to be discussing setting up her next show.

"It's my job as your friend to tell you when you're being rude," Emma begins, flipping her blonde hair over her shoulder. "So, Camden," she says sweetly, reminding me of the way my nanny used to speak to me before scolding me. "Stop being rude and listen to me. This is important."

My finger brushes along my top lip. "When did we become friends?" I tease, knowing it'll ruffle her feathers. I wasn't necessarily looking for another friend when Margo first introduced us —I think wanting us to date, which is comical—but Emma strong-armed her way into my life. She's the sister I never had.

Sometimes I enjoy her company, and sometimes she knows how to push every single one of my buttons to drive me nuts.

She sits back in the office chair, putting one of her combat boots on my very expensive desk.

I nod my head toward her muddy shoe, inches away from a stack of very important documents. "Off," I demand, giving her two seconds to remove it herself. She doesn't, so I'm not gentle as I push it off the desk, trying not to laugh at the way her face pinches in faked theatrics.

"We're besties, Camden. Everyone else is busy with their lives. Winnie is off doing I don't know what because she barely answers our calls, and Margo is off in la-la land in newlywed bliss with Beck. They've left us no other option but to be chummy."

"Chummy?"

"It's part of my quarter-life crisis to try out new words. Chummy felt right." She shrugs, picking up a notepad from my desk. There's no such thing as privacy when it comes to Emma. She reads my notes about the quote for new lighting at the Sutten gallery as if she has any idea what she's reading.

"Tell me about this quarter-life crisis," I demand with a big sigh. I know her well enough to know that she won't leave until we've talked about whatever she came here to discuss. Even if she's having to talk about it with me instead of Margo.

She drops the notepad back onto my desk as if she doesn't have a care in the world, narrowly missing the glass of water she insisted she needed the moment she came into my office. "That's so nice of you to ask," she tells me sarcastically. "Now, are you going to listen this time?"

"Sure," I answer with a resigned sigh. "It's not like I have anything else going on."

Emma claps her hands together, straightening her back to prepare to say what I'm sure is a long story that'll put me even more behind on my schedule for the day. "I don't know what I want to do with my life," she admits, chewing on her lip nervously.

"I thought you had a job?" Maybe she was fired, and that's why she's bothering me in the middle of a workday.

She lets out an annoyed sigh. "You really weren't listening, were you?"

I stay silent because I think it's pretty clear—I wasn't listening to her at all. I was too busy thinking about how I can check off everything on my to-do list here so I can go back to Sutten. Why I feel the need to return so quickly is beyond me. I tell myself it's because I'm still trying to get the gallery up and running smoothly, and it isn't because I'm wanting to see the woman at the coffee shop next door who hates me.

"I quit," Emma says with a shrug. I'm a reluctant friend of hers, but since she's given me no option, I feel a tinge of concern for her. She looks sad and defeated, a line creasing across her forehead.

"You quit?"

"Yep. Margo is here. Winnie is...well, I don't know where, but she isn't in California, so I didn't want to be there. I quit."

"And you flew to New York? Where are you staying?"

"God, you suck at paying attention to anything. I've been living at Beck and Margo's old penthouse for a week while I get my shit together."

Damn. Maybe I need to catch up with Beck and Margo. I thought they'd sold the penthouse when they moved to their giant brownstone. I also had no idea that Emma had been back here. "Well, the great thing is that you're in New York. There are so many jobs here."

"What if I don't know if I want to live in New York?"

I frown because sometimes I ask myself the same question. I always thought I loved the city, but now that I'm in my midthirties, I often wonder if I'd rather end up somewhere else.

"Where do you want to live? What do you want to do?"

Emma throws her hands into the air. "That's the problem! I

don't know what I want to do, where I want to be. I'm just now realizing that I've spent the last few years following my best friends around because they're my family—the ones I care about, at least," she adds. I want to pry and ask what she means by that, but unlike her, I respect privacy, so I assume if she wanted to elaborate on her family life, she would.

"And now they both have their own lives, and I have no idea what the hell I want to do with mine."

I stare at Emma for a few seconds because I'm realizing she and I might be more similar than I thought. Maybe the universe has a funny way of bringing a friend into your life right when you need them. She still gets on every bit of my nerves like a little sister, but I do understand where she's coming from. The older I get, the more I don't want to run galleries and instead would rather avoid people and get lost in long days with my hands covered in clay.

"Maybe give yourself some time to figure it out," I offer, knowing I might need to take my own advice. I prefer to just avoid the fact that I don't know if I love it here the way I used to. My life used to be fun and exciting. Now it seems mundane and simple—something I'm beginning to not enjoy.

"I guess." Emma shrugs. "I do love New York," she offers, her eyes catching on my desktop screen. It's a photo of the exterior of the gallery in Sutten. I've hired someone local to help with the curb appeal on the outside. It's something I was told to do, not understanding why there needs to be potted plants on the outside of an art gallery. That type of shit isn't necessary in Manhattan, but apparently, it makes it seem more approachable in Sutten.

"Anyway." She plasters on a smile, even though I can still see the conflict all over her face. "Tell me about Sutten. I would've bet all my money that Sutten Mountain would've been the last place you ever opened a gallery."

"Do you have any money?"

She grabs a pen from the jar on my desk and throws it at me. "Jerk!" she yells. "You don't have to remind me."

I smirk. "Stop hating on my business choices, then."

"It's just you seemed to hate it when we were there for Beck and Margo's wedding."

"Maybe I still do."

"Do you?"

"How could I hate something that's making me a lot of money?"

"Fair point."

The gallery has exceeded my expectations, and it's only going to get better. Tommy has recommended other talented artists in Sutten, and give it a month or two and I'll have a whole section for local talent at the gallery. It was a great idea for Pippa to show me that I didn't have to look far to find people with exceptional talent—not that I'd ever tell that to her. So many tourists are eating it up to buy art from locals. The gallery hasn't even been open a few weeks, and we've already made double what I was expecting, which is a relief.

It felt good to have dinner with my parents and tell them how well it was doing. Especially to my dad. It felt even better when he told me he didn't believe me and to show him the numbers. I did because I feel this stupid need to impress him even when he doesn't deserve it. Even after I gave him the numbers, he told me it wouldn't last. The appeal of the high-end small-town gallery would fade, and I'd be left losing money off my newest endeavor.

I'm ready to prove him wrong, which means I need to go back to Sutten. I need to find more talent. I'm even playing with the idea for the next event to be one fully focused on talent from in and around Sutten.

"Are you going back soon?" Emma's question interrupts me from my thoughts.

I shouldn't. I should avoid Sutten at all costs so I can avoid the temptation that is Pippa, but I know I won't. I've already planned to return under the guise of going back for work. "Yeah. I go back tomorrow."

Her eyebrows rise in surprise. "That's quick."

"Lots of things to get done there." It's kind of the truth. Just add in the fact I need to clear the air with Pippa so maybe my mind will stop thinking of her late at night when my fingers are wrapped around my cock.

"I need to visit sometime. I'm bored. What else do I have to do?"

Emma had the time of her life at Beck and Margo's wedding. Except when she drunkenly cried during the reception that she didn't find a cowboy to "break her back"—her words, not mine. "Not sure if escaping to a small town will solve all your problems, but you can give it a shot."

"Escaping somewhere will. I just have to figure out where that is."

I shrug because it makes no difference to me if she comes to Sutten or not—as long as she doesn't have any unexpected drop-ins like today.

"Just ask Beck and Margo to stay at their place. There's no way in hell you're staying with me."

She laughs. "I wouldn't want to anyway. I don't want to hear anything through the walls when the infamous, dark, and broody Camden Hunter brings some innocent small-town girl home."

I grunt because I'd love to say I've brought a woman home recently, but I haven't. I've tried, but I'm not interested. A certain small-town, opposite of innocent with the way her warm mouth closed around my fingers, always arguing woman has gotten under my skin and made it to where no one else interests me.

Standing up and rounding my desk, I give Emma a squeeze on her shoulder because I don't know what else to do. She has a tiny frown like something is still bothering her, but I don't know how to comfort her. "I leave for Sutten tomorrow. Text me if you decide to come, and we'll have coffee or something. Just find somewhere else to stay."

"I was hoping we'd have sleepovers and gossip about boys with face masks on," she throws out sarcastically.

"Don't expect anything more than coffee, Emma!" I yell as I walk out of my office.

If she does show up in Sutten, it would give me an excuse to go to a certain coffee shop and interact with a certain cafe owner...

"TAKE IT," I DEMAND, ATTEMPTING TO SHOVE A BOX FULL OF cupcakes toward Cade.

My brother pushes it back to me, shaking his head. "I don't need cupcakes, Pippa." His voice is stern as he focuses on the menu board behind me. It's not like he's been at Wake and Bake a thousand times. He knows any food or beverage item you could order from here, yet his focus is on it instead of me. I'd worry he was still mad at me for almost losing Rebel last week, but I know we moved past it after talking about it at a family dinner since then. He was upset because something could've happened to Rebel, but I think it was mostly because he was worried something could've happened to me.

The horse didn't hurt me, but Camden's actions on that mountain did, no matter how much I don't want to admit it.

I shake my head, looking at my brother with a wary look, remembering why I made the cupcakes to begin with. "You absolutely need cupcakes. Why do you think Dad sent you here?"

This gets his attention. He furrows his eyebrows. "How'd you know Dad sent me?"

I laugh, looking around the empty coffee shop. We've been unusually slow today, so slow that I told Lexi she could go home and I'd close alone tonight. We technically closed five minutes ago, but Cade walked in looking like a lost puppy right before I went to lock the doors. "Because he said you needed a pick-me-up and asked if I happened to have some of your favorite cupcakes. Actually, he pretty much begged for me to make some even if I didn't because you've been so miserable lately."

Cade groans, grabbing the hat from his head and running his hands through his hair. "Dad has noticed? Fuck, he shouldn't be worried about me. I don't want to add more to his plate. He's already missing Mom and trying to get everything in order for winter. I hate that he's noticed that I'm really missing Mare lately."

"Let Dad worry about you." I try to keep my tone gentle as I run my hand along my brother's arm. "It helps him not focus on the fact we're getting close to Mom's birthday." I don't mention that it's getting closer to mine, too.

"Maybe I will have a cupcake," Cade mutters. His voice is sad. So sad that I almost call my best friend and tell her to get her ass back to Sutten. She's got to be almost done writing this book at this point, and how many more meetings could one author have? All I know is that one way or another, my brother can't take being away from her much longer. He's different than he used to be, and even though I know they're still trying to figure things out, it's time they're reunited.

Or I'm going to have to double the amount of blueberry lemon cupcakes I'm making.

Lifting the lid of the pastry box, I grab a cupcake and hand it over to him. He gladly takes it, delicately peeling the liner away from the cake before eating half of it with one large bite.

We walk over to a small sitting area with a baby pink, velvet couch. He sits down, letting out a long sigh. "Tell me what's new with you, Pip."

I rest my cheek in my palm, happy to have my brother present, at least for a little bit. Things have been a little off with us since Mom died. Probably because we both grieve very differently. He leaned on Mare; I leaned on working and trying to keep Dad going. But Cade and I have always been close, so I'm relieved for things to go back to how they used to be, at least for a moment.

We spend a long time chatting about life. It feels good to talk to my brother again. To feel close to him. He updates me on how the ranch is doing, how he thinks Dad is doing, and how he and Mare are taking it day by day.

"I know Mom would be happy to see the two of you figuring it out," I tell him softly, taking the last sip of my coffee I'd made an hour ago. After Cade yawned for the fourth time in a ten-minute period, I figured he could use the evening pick-me-up. Hopefully, when he leaves here, he goes home to go to bed instead of trying to get more work done.

"You think?" His voice catches slightly.

I nod. "Yeah." Leaning forward, I wrap my arms around my brother and hug him. His body goes lax, his arms wrapping around me as we stay in the embrace for a moment. His arms shake slightly, making me wonder how much stress and sadness he's hiding underneath his tough exterior.

"I think you should go home and sleep," I coax, pulling away.

He yawns again as if his body agrees with me. "Maybe I will. After I talk to Mare, of course."

I laugh. Even in college, she was always on a totally different schedule than me. I thrive on an early bedtime and waking up before everyone else in the morning. She was the opposite. Mare would sleep all day and work on homework all night, something that was hard to juggle when we were both on completely opposite schedules. We made it work, but I find it funny that even all these years later, she's still working through the night, while I prefer crawling into bed by nine.

"Tell Mare I said hello. And that she should call me."

Cade nods, walking toward the exit. "Thanks for being here, Pip. Sorry if I've been a little MIA lately."

"It's a busy season for you. Once winter comes, I'll force you to spend more time with your little sister. I've got all kinds of recipes you can taste test for me."

I finally get a chuckle from him. He shakes his head at me, opening the door and letting a rush of cold night air in.

"You've got it," he calls over his shoulder.

I watch him get into his truck before I shut the door. With Cade gone, a rush of exhaustion washes over me. I'd thought about getting some things ready for tomorrow, but now, I'm too tired. Instead, my bed and a big bowl of sugary cereal are calling my name.

I've done it so many times that I'm able to rush through getting the cafe closed for the night. It was already fairly ready since we weren't very busy. My eyes roam over the space as I go through a mental closing checklist in my mind. Satisfied I've done everything I'm supposed to do, I flick the lights off and open the door.

Instead of it opening, it runs into something hard with a thud.

"What the h—" My words are cut off as I look up to find Camden gripping the door. His eyes are dark and clouded, his lips pressed into a thin line as his eyes bore into mine.

"Camden?" I ask, shocked to see him standing there. I haven't seen him since he was climbing into the back of a black SUV at my family's house. He'd wanted to get away from me so fast that he couldn't even wait for me to take him back to the gallery. We hadn't spoken since. The time and distance he placed between us has only fueled my anger.

That same fury bubbles inside me at seeing him again. I can't get a read on him. He's hot and then cold, and it's driving me crazy. I should be thankful that between the two of us, he stopped us from doing something drastic like kissing, but I'm really just disappointed I can't describe how he tastes.

"Shortcake." His words are low, coming out almost like a growl. I don't know if it's the fire burning in his icy-blue eyes or the way his shoulders rise and fall in angry breaths, but something about him sends a shiver down my spine.

"Didn't know you were back in Sutten," I breathe, my eyes flicking to the small amount of empty space between us.

He looks down at it, too, before taking a step closer and closing it. I have to take a few steps back so we don't touch. My feet slip on the freshly mopped floor. The only thing that saves me from busting my ass is his strong, thick fingers wrapping around my bicep.

He doesn't let go. I *need* him to let go. We're too close, and I'm thinking that it still wouldn't be terrible to kiss him, even though he gets on my nerves and is constantly acting like an asshole.

"I had unfinished business here," he mutters. I can't help it. When his eyes focus on my lips, my tongue peeks out to wet them. It was involuntary, but the way he stares at my lips with pristine focus makes me want to do it again to keep his gaze like that forever.

"Like what?" I breathe, fully aware that I've slowly leaned closer to him.

All it'd take was for me to move another inch and our foreheads would be touching. I wouldn't know what was his air and what was mine. All I'd know is that we were sharing it and that breathing the same air is so close to tasting him.

My heart hammers against my chest as I wait for him to answer. I'm angry with myself for wanting to kiss him, for knowing with every fiber of my being that if he closed the distance, I'd let him. He has no redeeming qualities except he's so good-looking that it's unfair. He's an asshole, hates this town, and left me wanting more last time he almost kissed me.

None of that matters. Because I think I can deal with him being an asshole if his kisses make up for it.

I just know he's got to be angry in the bedroom. I think I'd like to find out. I know plenty of ways to keep his mouth busy so he wouldn't have to talk.

Starting with having his tongue down my throat.

I swallow, relishing the way he looks at me. I'm confident similar thoughts are running through his head.

"What's the unfinished business, Camden?" I whisper.

He rips his gaze from my body. The moment our eyes collide, I know I'm going to get what I want.

"This," he growls.

Chapter 25
CAMDEN

I COULD TRY AND BE GENTLE WITH HER, BUT I HAVE NO DESIRE TO. I'm so fucking desperate to finally seal our mouths together that my fingers tangle through her hair, giving me the chance to pull her face to mine. My cock stiffens at the small gasp that comes from her lips seconds before our mouths collide.

She tastes better than I could ever dream of. The moment my tongue skirts against the seam of her lips, she gladly opens her mouth for me, allowing our tongues to stroke against one another.

She moans, and I swallow it, yanking on her hair to angle her head even higher. At this point, she must be having to stand on her tiptoes to allow me access to her mouth. Her tiny moans tell me she isn't bothered by the position in the slightest.

Another brush of our tongues, and her palms hit my chest. Her fingers grip my dress shirt so tightly I bet it warps the fabric. I don't give a damn. She could rip it right off me, and I'd thank her for doing it. I think I'd do anything, give anything, to stay locked in the kiss forever. To always have her at my mercy just like this.

I should've known she wouldn't kiss gently. I knew I didn't have it in me to take it slow, to start with a peck before my tongue got involved. But I wasn't expecting her tongue to match every stroke of mine. For her to open her mouth even wider, allowing me even more access.

Her fingers find the back of my neck as she attempts to pull me even lower. One of my hands tangles in the long strands of her hair, keeping her mouth pinned to mine, while the other grabs onto her chin to keep her still. She wants to take control of the kiss, but I won't let her. I've been dreaming of this since the moment I left that mountain, so I'm going to kiss her the way I've vividly imagined for over a week.

There's a sting at the back of my neck from where her fingernails scrape against the exposed skin between my collar and hairline. I groan at the feeling, wanting to feel the bite of her nails all over my body.

Would they dig into my ass as I fucked her as deep as her cunt would allow?

Would they scratch at my scalp as my tongue circled her clit?

God, I need to know. I'm fucking rabid to find out.

My teeth catch her bottom lip. I bite down, wanting to see her reaction. She moans so loudly that my cock aches in my slacks. I want to palm it, to give it some kind of relief, but I can't let go of her. She's allowing me to manhandle her exactly as I want, and I'm relishing every single second of it.

Is she like this in bed? So demanding outside of the bedroom but aching to be dominated while being fucked?

"Fuck," I moan, licking along the spot on her bottom lip that was just between my teeth. "What the hell are you doing to me?"

I could get addicted to the sound of her moans as she throws her head back in pleasure. Her perfect sun-kissed skin is exposed to me, just begging for me to leave a mark. I pull on her hair once again, lost in the way the yelp from the pain turns into a moan when my lips graze the hollow of her throat. Her entire body shudders underneath my touch, only fueling my desire for her further.

"Camden." My name comes out like a plea. I think I could grow obsessed with the sound of it, mixed with her moans. She's so goddamn reactive that it drives me wild.

I kiss along her neck, unable to help myself from biting a spot there, knowing it would be hard for her to hide a hickey. Lost in the moment, I want to claim her for myself, to have something left behind from this moment to remind her how much she drives me crazy. I want her to think of me anytime she feels the throb of the bruise from my teeth. For her to think of us in this very moment every time she looks in the mirror to cover it.

I'm never like this. I'm not territorial, and I've never cared about someone enough to want to claim them. But in the darkness of the night and the heat of the moment, I'm feral at the idea of any other man ever getting to taste her delicate skin.

My lips pepper kisses along her shoulder. This would be so much better if she didn't have a top on. If I could lean down and catch her nipple between my teeth. Would she like it if I nipped at it before soothing the pain with my tongue?

"You've been taking up way too much fucking space in my mind lately," I tell her, feathering kisses along her jaw.

"Good." She lets out a shaky breath when I kiss right behind her ear. If I had more time, I'd kiss every bare inch of her body to find all the spots that make her breath catch the way it just did when my teeth grazed the shell of her ear.

I bring our foreheads together, looking right into her hazel eyes. She stares back at me, at least for the moment not acting like she regrets kissing me. Good, because no matter how terrible of an idea it was, I don't think I could ever really regret swallowing each one of her moans.

"No. It *isn't* good." I don't even attempt to hide the anger in my voice. I'm angry with myself for wanting her this bad. For letting her get under my skin. For somehow letting her go from someone I couldn't stand to someone I desired with everything that I am. "We don't fucking work," I hiss, my jaw clenching. "All we do is argue, but god, we could try never speaking. Let our bodies do the talking."

She steps forward, crowding my space and pressing her body against mine. She fits against me perfectly. Her feet don't stop, but before she can walk me into the glass door behind me, I spin our bodies and press her body into the glass. I'm sure it's cold through the thin fabric of her shirt. I don't really care if it is or isn't. I know exactly how to warm her up.

I click my tongue as I focus on where her chest heaves. With each deep inhale, the fabric of her shirt tightens, and I get a little glimpse of her perky, peaked nipples through the thin cotton of her shirt. Unable to resist, I lean down and blow hot air right over one of them. Her head hits the glass door with a thud as she lets out a loud moan.

"I don't ever want people this desperately," I tell her, licking her nipple through her shirt.

"I don't let men I don't like do dirty things to me," she mutters, her hips bucking when I nip at her breast.

"Maybe you'll change your mind about liking me when I get the chance to kiss your pussy. My tongue can be very persuasive."

My hands drift underneath her shirt, testing out to see if she'll let them roam. She doesn't protest; in fact, she pushes me further, her fingers fisting the fabric of my shirt to keep me close to her.

If only she knew I had no intentions of moving. Not unless she told me to.

"I don't," she pants, her words getting cut off when I shove her shirt up. "I don't typically like it when..." Her words fall short. I lower to my knees, looking up at her to find her cheeks flushed. I hope it's from pleasure, not embarrassment for what-ever she's not saying.

"You don't typically like being tongue fucked?" I pull at the cup of her cotton bra, freeing her breast and eager to finally let my mouth close on her peaked nipple with nothing between us.

"Camden." My name sounds hot as hell falling from her lips. I want to lick every inch of her soft skin to see how many times I can get her to call my name out like a plea.

I take her nipple between my lips, closing my mouth around it. My tongue circles the peak as I soak in every single one of her reactions to what I'm doing. Her back arches, shoving her breast deeper into my mouth. I get so distracted savoring finally getting a front-row view to how perfect she is that I almost forget I'm still waiting for an answer from her.

Pulling away, I look up at her. Her eyes are squeezed shut, like she's trying to fight how good this feels. I'm having the same war with myself. There's no reason for me to want this as bad as I do, but I lose all sense of right and wrong when I'm with her. All I see is her and the desperate need to get as much of her as possible before we start fighting again.

"I'm waiting for an answer," I muse, running my finger along her stomach. Her breath hitches when I trace over the stretch of skin along the waistband of her jeans that's been teasing me.

"To what?"

"If you enjoy coming against someone's tongue as they give your pussy the attention it deserves."

"Oh," she murmurs, clutching the fabric of my collar when I undo the button of her jeans. "I just haven't found someone who could make that happen."

I'm so close to her cunt that I can smell her. It's deliciously sweet, taunting and teasing me being so close but also not close enough.

"You haven't come on someone's tongue?" My voice is full of gravel. I hate the thought of any other man being so close to her pussy, but I hate even more that she seems to have given someone the chance and they couldn't bring her to the brink of pure pleasure.

She shakes her head back and forth, telling me exactly what I want to know. I hook my fingers through the belt loops of her jeans, tugging until I'm pulling both the denim and her panties down her hips.

"You deserve someone who takes the time to get to know your cunt. Who will lick, suck, and do anything to find out what you like and don't like. Who would spend hours with their face buried between your thighs if that's what it took to make you scream their name."

She's finally bared to me, her wet, pink pussy the most perfect view I've ever laid eyes on.

I smirk, pausing for a moment. "Not that I think it'd take me that long. I'll have you coming in no time."

"Don't be so sure."

"I'm quite positive, shortcake. If you don't believe me, you're welcome to time me. Give me two minutes, and you'll be screaming my name."

Her head rocks side to side at the same moment her hips rock back and forth. She wants to fight this. To stop it so I won't have this on her. If only she knew how much I'm giving up by admitting how bad I want her. She thinks by giving me her orgasm that she loses the constant battle between us, but it'll be anything but. If I taste her cum on my tongue, I might let her win every argument between us just so I can have my fill of her as much as I can until she tires of me.

I lean back on my haunches for a moment, needing to capture the sight of her with her guard down and her pussy dripping for me.

Fuck, she's wet. Arousal coats between her thighs, beckoning for me to reach out and spread them open wide to get a better view of her. I won't be able to look for long before I dive in to taste her.

"What are you doing?"

"I'm looking at you."

She tries to squeeze her legs together, but I press my palms into them, stopping her from ruining my fun. "Don't even think about it," I growl.

"Your two minutes have started."

I laugh, leaning in so my breath tickles her inner thighs. "Time doesn't start until I say so. You have to give me a minute to appreciate every perfect inch of your body." I kiss along the curve of her hips. The skin is so soft, a contrast to the way her nails claw at the back of my neck.

My lips lower, hovering along her bikini line. She mewls, clearly dissatisfied that I haven't placed my lips on the place she aches for me the most.

"Don't worry." My tongue peeks out to lick the inside of her thigh. I couldn't resist getting a little glimpse at the taste of her arousal that coats between her legs. "I'll have your hips bucking as you fuck my face very soon. But first—" I pull away, letting my eyes do the exploring for a moment. "—I need to account for every dip and curve of your body."

"Why?" she pants, the word so quiet I almost miss it.

"Because your body is so perfect, one day I'll have to recreate it with clay so I can admire it forever."

Chapter 26
PIPPA

I DON'T THINK I'VE EVER BEEN SO TURNED ON. I DIDN'T KNOW I could ache so much between my thighs. That I'd ever feel wetness pooling from me just from the dirty words a man whispered to me in the dark.

Camden has already shown me so much, and he hasn't even touched the spot where I throb the most. It's infuriating to have my body betray me like this. But even more, I'm relishing in losing control right alongside him. For every betrayal of my body, there's a betrayal of his. There's no way to miss the thick outline of his straining cock through his tailored pants. The lust in his eyes is evident, and I know that I'm not the only one caught up in the heat of the passion. We'll go down together— both of us losing the war with the undeniable chemistry between us.

"Fuck, I'll be thinking about this view for weeks," he rasps. His words catch in his throat, as if the red-hot lust prevents him from speaking clearly.

I moan, rolling my hips to try and get some sort of friction. At least earlier, he was touching me—kissing, licking, exploring my body while he unraveled me little by little.

"Your two minutes are about to start." I try to keep my voice level, but it shakes with how much I want him. My entire body is burning for him, and I feel like the only thing that will help me is for him to ease the ache with the swipe of his tongue along my clit.

His fingertips dig into my thighs. I'm well aware of how much the moonlight illuminates the cafe. He has a perfect view of *all* of me. Maybe if it were somebody else, I'd feel bashful. But not with him. There's no way I could be embarrassed by anything about myself when he's looking at me like he'll starve if he doesn't get a taste.

"You don't start counting until I tell you to," he commands. God, I never thought I'd get so turned on by his demands. I like it when he orders me around. I wonder if this is what he's like behind the scenes. I know why everyone falls at his feet. It's hard to do anything when his voice evens out, going low as he tells me exactly what he wants from me.

He squeezes my inner thighs, forcing them so wide that I'd fall backward if I didn't have the support of the window behind me. It just now occurs to me that the full moon doesn't only allow him to see every inch of my exposed skin, but anyone outside could see us if they were to look in our direction. That realization alone should have me pushing him away.

I don't.

My fingers tangle in the longer strands of his hair at the top of his head, trying to guide him to my throbbing clit. "Anyone could see us here." I don't sound convincing in the slightest, but at least I tried—barely.

He finally gets closer, but his lips hover on my inner thigh instead of the apex of my thighs where I *need* him. He bites down, no doubt leaving another mark on my body.

Why do I like it? Maybe it's because he soothes the pain by licking the skin. I didn't know a tongue could feel so sensual, but the swipe of it along the stinging skin has me aching for more.

"We can move," he says against my skin, slowly moving to where I want him. "But something tells me you like the idea of someone walking by and seeing us." I'd comment on how he

needs to stop dragging this out, but I'm too addicted to the anticipation of it. My entire body trembles, eager for what's to come.

His fingers brush through my wetness, and oh my god,
something's never felt so good than to feel his calloused finger
tracing my clit. At least until he uses another finger to spread me
open, air hitting my most sensitive spot. It'd be cold if his hot
breath wasn't caressing me, warming me up.

I want to protest when I stop feeling the bite of his fingertips
on my thigh, but the feeling doesn't last long. His other hand
joins in, one keeping me spread open while the heel of his other
hand presses against my clit. He slides it up, one finger sliding
into me.

I moan, the sound echoing around us. My eyes flutter open
and shut, the sensations too much. I focus on staying on my feet
—that and the way he achingly slowly pushes his finger deeper
and deeper. The heel of his hand presses harder with each push
of his finger. I'm feeling him everywhere at once. My skin tingles
as my hips buck to meet his rhythm.

His finger slides all the way out of me, leaving me wanting
more of him instantly.

"I bet you love the idea of someone seeing you like this," he
growls. "Everyone in this small town idolizes you. If only they
knew their sweet Pippa was such a dirty slut."

"Camden," I moan when this time he slides two fingers
inside me. Why do I feel so full with only two of his long, thick
fingers?

"I like the idea of someone watching this, too," he mutters,
hooking his fingers. He instantly finds the spot that drives me
wild, making my toes curl inside my shoes with pleasure. "My
cock is so fucking hard at the thought of someone else
witnessing how good I'll make you come. To have you
screaming my name like the dirty girl you are. They'll know that
you're wrecked for me and that I'm the one who knows how to
make you see stars."

"You're down to one minute," I manage to get out, my voice trembling. I have no idea how long it's been. But my body feels like it's engulfed in flames, and I'm trying to get a hold of the situation somehow. Reminding him of his cockiness that he'll make me come when no one else has is my way of trying to take control.

He laughs, his hot breath spreading all over me. "That's fine. A minute is all I really needed."

Before I can boss him around and tell him he better make good on his promises, he seals his mouth to my pussy, and there's not a doubt in my mind that he'll make me come quickly and powerfully.

Maybe it's the confident way in which his tongue enters me. There's nothing timid about him. Just like the way our kiss began, his tongue is angry and determined, moving against me in confident laps.

I have an out-of-body experience. I don't even realize it's me that's making the loud moans and mewls until seconds after they escape from my mouth. His finger pushes in and out of me as he pulls my clit into his mouth. His tongue vibrates against me from his own moans, and I think that might be what has me nearing an orgasm more than anything else.

There's something about knowing that he's so turned on by licking my pussy. I've been with men who made it seem like a chore to go down on me. Camden isn't acting like that at all. He seems to be enjoying every second of it, and I can't fight the building sensation deep in my core.

My entire body freezes when the rubber band snaps. I claw at his hair, yanking at chunks of it as the orgasm takes over my entire body. I might fall—or I thought I was going to, but he keeps me steady.

"Camden," I moan, needing him to stop the angry thrusts of his tongue. He doesn't stop, milking the orgasm for everything it is.

My thighs shake as I ride out the rest of the orgasm.

It's the best I've ever had, but there's no way I can ever tell him that.

It was so good that for a few moments, I can't talk. I can't open my eyes. I can't do anything but get swept up in the way my entire body feels lit with desire.

Nothing has ever felt that intense. It feels even better when my eyes finally flutter open and I find him staring right at me.

I feel powerful knowing I'm the reason Camden looks imperfect right now. He's on his knees, my cum all over his face. His hair sticking out in every direction where my fingers pulled at the dark locks. His wrinkled shirt from where I clung to him, trying to hold him closer. The outline of his large, thick cock. Every messy, out-of-place part of him right now is the most perfect thing I've ever seen.

My chest heaves up and down as I try to recover from the intensity of the orgasm—the intensity of the moment. It was so powerful that for once in my life, I'm speechless.

Camden must be feeling the same way. He stares back at me, his shoulders rising and falling in quick, successive breaths.

Moments ago, the room was filled with our moans. Now, the only sounds are our loud inhales and exhales as we both recover.

I can't look away from his crystal-blue eyes. They've got me in a trance. Or maybe it's because I'm still reeling from what just happened. Either way, he's the first one to look away.

He stands to his full height, giving no indication of what he's thinking when he runs his hand through his hair.

"That was definitely more than two minutes," I tease, knowing damn well he kept his word. My words do nothing to ease the sizzling tension between us. If anything, his fingertips pinching the bridge of his nose throw cold water over us.

I'm about to brave reaching out to touch him, my body aflame with the need to get familiar with him. His cock seems to agree with the way it angrily fights the fabric of his slacks, just begging to join in on the fun.

He beats me to it. Except instead of closing the distance between us, he rips the front door open and bolts.

I stare out at the walking path in front of us, watching his figure disappear, shame creeping over my skin.

Chapter 27
CAMDEN

I can't get away from her fast enough.

I'm completely fucked, and even as I bust into the front doors of the gallery and put distance between Pippa and me, I'm scared that no amount of distance can rid the memory of what just happened.

It was achingly, frustratingly perfect. *She's* perfect—except for the fact I've made an ass of myself to her and she can't stand me unless my tongue is milking an orgasm from her.

I attempt to suck in air, to calm myself from just having one of the best sexual experiences of my life—and she didn't even touch me. All I did was have the chance to make her come all over my tongue, and nothing has ever destroyed me more.

She's exceptional. And I ran away from her, leaving her completely exposed as I escaped her presence. I've already given her enough to make her not like me, leaving her partially naked as I ran out of her shop probably didn't help things.

I couldn't help it. I had to get away before I pushed every boundary and demanded even more from her. Every fiber of my being wants to fuck her, to make her mine and pull orgasm after orgasm from her until I can rewrite the beginning of our story— or at least make her forget all of the messy, heated arguments that have happened between us.

I've never regretted being an asshole until now. I'd do anything to switch our fate by changing our beginning. I wouldn't be a dick when we collided at the stupid bar. I wouldn't call her names when she ran into me. I wouldn't have bought the gallery if I knew she wanted it for her own business.

There are so many things I'd redo if I could, but I can't, and I hate it because no woman has ever gotten underneath my skin the way she has.

"Fuck," I yell, slamming the door behind me. My footsteps echo off the floor as I pace around the gallery.

I bow my head, wondering how the hell I'm going to get myself out of the mess I've created.

I should've never kissed her. Going further back, I should've never asked for her help. Maybe if we hadn't been pushed together by her silly idea to get me to appreciate this small town, I wouldn't be giving in to temptation when it comes to her.

My shoulders stiffen when the front door is pushed open. A smacking sound fills the room moments before the door closes. I don't have to turn around to know who it is.

I can feel her.

"Leave," I plead, knowing my voice doesn't sound convincing. It sounds weak and resigned.

"What the hell was that?" She seethes. I seal my eyes shut when she steps in front of me. I can't look at her. She's fixed her clothes—partially—but her cheeks are still flushed from the orgasm, and there are swollen marks along her neck left by my teeth.

"It was best for me to stop it before anything else happened."

"Best for *who*?"

I open my eyes because I'm weak and want to get a good look at her. "Best for you," I answer quietly. "I'm an asshole and don't deserve to taste you the way I just did. It was perfect and you're perfect and I'm not perfect and fuck, Pippa, why did it have to feel that way with you?"

"I'm tired of this shit, Camden," she fumes, taking a step closer to me. Thankfully, we're all alone here. She can yell at me all she wants. It's what I deserve.

"And I'm not?" I counter. Of course I'm tired of it. I hate how primal I become around her. How much it turns me on to have my way with her and watch her let me.

"If you were tired of it, you wouldn't keep running! You just gave me the best orgasm of my life—something I wouldn't admit except for the fact I'm so freaking pissed at you, words are just tumbling from my mouth—and then you ran like I did something wrong."

"You did everything right," I snap, annoyed she'd ever think it had anything to do with her.

"Then fuck me."

My head rears back in shock at her words. They were the last thing I was expecting. I was prepared for us to argue. I wasn't prepared for her to want to continue.

"No."

"Yes." She takes another step closer to me, pushing her chest against mine.

I shake my head, air hissing through my teeth when her fingers skirt over my cock through my slacks. "It's a terrible idea." Fuck, I might come just from the smallest of touches from her—that's the power she has over me, even though I've unwillingly given it to her.

"Probably. But you have to finish what you started, Camden Hunter."

"You hate me," I protest, trying to get a grip on the situation. I'm losing control quickly at the feeling of her knuckles brushing along my skin as she tucks her hands into my waistband.

"I'll hate you more if you don't fuck me right now."

"Don't say that," I croak. My head falls backward when she pulls my cock free. I hadn't even realized she'd unzipped me and pulled my boxer briefs down.

Her fingers boldly wrap around my cock. There's a satisfied smirk on her lips as she strokes up and down. She knows exactly what she's doing to me. Her eyelashes flutter in mock innocence. God, she's so fucking sexy.

She'd be even sexier if she dropped to her knees and wrapped her mouth around my cock.

"Are you going to fight me on this, too?" she asks sweetly, her thumb running along my tip. I hadn't even noticed the precum until she holds it between us, her skin glistening from the bead of arousal.

My jaw clenches when she licks it from her thumb. Now all I can picture is her swallowing every last drop of my cum as I fill her mouth with me.

"Maybe," I groan, my arms shaking with restraint. I don't think this is a battle I'll win. The desire to shove my cock as far as her throat—or cunt—will allow is too intense. She was supposed to be the one to stop us. To not hunt me down and insist for me to fuck her. "All we seem to do is fight," I add.

"Maybe I like it," she admits, gripping my cock once again, hammering the last nail in our coffin.

I lose all sense of control. My fingers wrap around her neck, yanking her toward me. She gasps as I pull our faces inches apart. Maybe I should kiss her again. Make her taste her cum as punishment for being so goddamn tempting. "We'll fight about this later," I growl. "Right now, the only thing that matters is me burying my cock inside you."

"About time," she muses, a smile on her face.

What the hell am I going to do with her? She fights back, and I'm obsessed with it. It makes me want to punish her, to make her crumble and come apart underneath me.

"I'm going to make you pay for talking back to me." I don't give her the time to respond—my mouth catches hers, and her body goes lax against mine, her arms circling my neck to keep her on her feet. Or maybe I'm the one who keeps her on her feet. All I know is that my cock misses her touch the moment her fingers leave my shaft and wrap around my neck instead.

I tease her a little, getting lost in the kiss. I let her think that maybe she's in control for just a moment until I rip my mouth from hers. Her lips are red and swollen, just begging for my cock to fuck them.

And that's exactly what's going to happen.

I push on her shoulders, giving her no option but to drop to her knees. She yelps, her hands reaching out to brace herself by grabbing onto my thighs.

"You had so much fun teasing me just now." I wrap her hair around my hand, giving me the leverage I need to control her head however I desire. She licks her lips, staring at my cock hungrily before she looks me in the eye. "You clearly want it," I say, wrapping my fingers along my length and stroking up and down. "Be a good little whore and suck my cock," I demand.

She adjusts her position on her knees, giving me no indication if she's going to listen or not. Instead, she rolls her eyes. Actually rolls her eyes at me. Defiant little slut. She still might do as she's told, however, because her fingers wrap around me. Her grip is firm, not timid in the slightest. She pumps up and down achingly slow, so slow that my balls tighten in protest. I need more of her. More of this. More of everything when it comes to her.

"Camden?" My name is said like a question, her breath hot on my cock as she speaks.

"Yes, baby?" I croak.

"You might want to start counting. You'll be coming down my throat in two minutes." Her tongue travels all the way up and down my length, and fuck, I think she might be right. It's all too much.

And then she says the words that have me fucking savage for her. "And I've never swallowed before."

Chapter 28
PIPPA

I'VE NEVER FELT SEXY GIVING A BLOW JOB. IT MUST BE BECAUSE I wasn't blowing the right person because right now, with my mouth hovering over the head of Camden's cock, I've never felt hotter.

My tongue glides around his swollen head. Air hisses through his teeth, his thighs flexing underneath my grip. I let my fingers drift upward, needing to feel his abs. I haven't seen them, but everything about his body is perfect. There's no doubt in my mind that his abdomen is the same.

I let my tongue memorize the feeling of his thick, heavy cock. I lick along the vein that runs from the base to the tip, reveling in the groans that fall from his mouth with every flick. Camden doesn't seem to like to show emotions—I can relate—but it's different in private, with my lips parting to take him down my throat. To the outside world, he's closed off. Right now, his body tells me everything I want to know and more.

I'm enjoying teasing him, punishing him for his hot and cold tendencies. He left me almost naked, pressed up against a window, when he ran away. I'd felt vulnerable and exposed, ruining the euphoria running through my body from the orgasm he pulled from me.

Maybe I want to give him a little payback.

I pull my mouth away, loving the angry set of his jaw when I let go of his cock. It stands at attention, beckoning for me to return to what I was doing. I don't. Instead, both my hands travel underneath the starched fabric of his shirt.

"Off," I demand, trying to pull at the buttons. My fingers don't work quickly enough, so I opt to tug on them instead.

Camden's hand covers mine, his palm sliding over my fingers. "You don't tell me what to do."

I bite my lip, wondering if I should talk back or not. "I want to see you."

He squeezes my hand, the gesture seeming so gentle compared to everything else. I sit back on my heels, watching eagerly when his fingers begin to undo the buttons on his chest. He manages to get two of them undone before he angrily sighs. "Fuck it," he growls, grabbing both sides of the shirt and ripping it open.

Buttons *ping* against the floor as they fall in various directions. I laugh, the sound getting caught in my throat when he looks down at me with fire in his eyes. I'm swept up in the way he looks at me, but from the corner of my eye, I notice him pulling his arms from each side of the shirt.

I don't know where to look. I love the heat in his eyes, the way he watches me like a man watching his last meal. But I want to see his body. I want to commit every single muscle to memory to remember this by. Even though I haven't looked yet, I know the slopes and planes of his muscles are something artists like him could only dream of recreating.

"Look at me." His fingers wrap around my chin. They're firm, nudging my head upward to force me to look at him.

My chest hitches. Everything about him is better than I could've imagined. He's cut perfectly. His muscles are so proportionate, as if his perfectionist personality ensures that every muscle is worked evenly.

His fingers dig into the skin at my jaw, pressing so deeply into my thrumming pulse that he must feel how seeing his taut, rigid muscles affects me.

"You do something to me when you look at me like that," he groans.

I allow my fingers to trace the ripple of his abs. They're so defined. I could've never expected what he was hiding underneath his expensive suits and tailored shirts. I don't know why he bothers with wearing clothes. He could stand in the middle of his art gallery just like this, and every person around would stare at him as if he were the art himself.

"I don't know any other way to look at you," I confess. The list of men I've been with isn't long, but none of them looked the way he does. Staring at him, I can't remember what they looked like at all. The only thing taking up space in my mind is *him*.

Camden grabs me by the chin once again. This time, it's gentle. His thumb caresses my jaw, his eyes roaming over my face. He focuses on my lips. His calloused thumb scrapes my cheek as he runs it over my skin before he places it on my cupid's bow. My lips part as if on command. He smirks, only one side of his lips lifting. His thumb travels slowly, tugging on my bottom lip. My lips feel raw from the ferocity with which he kissed me.

"Your two minutes are running low."

I smile, shifting on my knees to ease the ache from my throbbing clit. He's already paid it attention, but it demands more. My thighs rub together as I attempt to get friction and some kind of relief.

I allow myself one more second of looking into his eyes, of seeing the dark storms of his lust-filled gaze, before I focus on his cock again. My thumb runs through the bead of precum at his tip.

His body jolts with the touch, making me smirk in satisfaction. He's doing it again. Making me feel sexy before I even take him in my mouth.

Using one hand, I push my hair from my shoulders so the pieces fall down my back. I don't want anything in the way when I fully take him. He grunts in approval, his hands sweeping the hair from my back and twisting it around his palm.

I love the feeling of the hair at my roots getting tugged. I like knowing that, at least for right now, he's giving me the control, but with one simple pull, he'd be the one with it.

I wrap my fingers around the base of him. His cock is so large that the tips of my fingers don't even begin to touch. His grip tightens, his short nails raking against my scalp when I use my other hand to cup his balls.

I'm going to have so much fun with this.

Leaning in, I coax his head into my mouth. I speak around his girth, my words muffled due to the tip of him pressing against my tongue. "Remember what I said about swallowing," I tease.

"Fuck," he growls, thrusting his hips so he hits the back of my throat. I moan at his reaction. It's so primal and savage, turning me on as a flush creeps along my skin.

I open my mouth as wide as I can. My cheeks burn from trying to take him, to try and open wide enough to accommodate all of him. He fucks my face savagely. His fingers tangle in my hair to keep my head steady as he pumps in and out, taking everything he wants from me.

Trying to bring him as much pleasure as possible, I keep one hand locked on the end of his shaft, the part that can't fit in my mouth, as the other holds on tight to his balls.

"God." He moans, his pace slowing as he rolls his body into mine. It's sexy as hell. Now I want to feel his hips the same way when he fucks my pussy instead of my throat. "Just like that." His grip tightens, and I don't know if tears threaten to spill from my lids because of the way he yanks my hair or if it's because the tip of him hits the back of my throat with a punishing force.

I blink, letting the tears fall down my cheeks to try and ease the burn from my eyes. I look upward, finding him watching me. He smiles approvingly, using his free hand to reach down and cup my cheek. It's so much more tender than everything else he's doing to me.

"I'm going to keep fucking your face until you gag on me. I won't stop until I've taken your body to its limit." He slams into my throat, proving his point. "You better open that throat, baby."

My eyes flutter shut because everything is too much. My pussy throbs so hard it's painful. I want to reach down and play with my clit, push a finger inside me, *something* to help ease the intense ache between my legs. I know my jeans are in the way, and there's no way I can slip a hand in without him noticing.

For some reason, I'm confident he wouldn't let me touch myself even if I had easier access. Maybe it's the dominating way he thrusts his cock into me, each time his hips try to press deeper and deeper until my body protests. Or maybe it's because he's had a slight smirk to his lips the entire time he's been fucking my face. As if he's satisfied that I'm giving him power over me.

I rub my thighs together, rocking back and forth to try and ease the ache. It doesn't do much. He keeps letting out a low, drawn-out moan each time he hits the back of my throat. If he does enough of those, I might just come without him touching me.

I try to hold back for as long as possible, but he picks up the pace, and each thrust gets harder and harder. I can't take him anymore, my throat gagging as he brings me to my limit.

He pulls out, giving me the briefest moment to breathe before he does it all over again. I gag all over again now that he knows the exact way to pump into me.

"Good girl," he pants. His head falls backward, but I keep my eyes locked on him. I'm fascinated by watching every single reaction. He swallows, the muscles of his throat working hard as he stifles a moan.

He slows, switching to slow, long thrusts instead of quick, punishing ones. It gives me a moment to gather myself as much as possible. Tears still fall from my eyes from the pressure of him. I gag, trying my best to keep my lips over my teeth.

"Maybe I should've fucked your face sooner. You actually listen with my cock shoved down your throat." I moan around him, my eyes fluttering shut.

I'm about to pull away, to beg him to fuck me because my mouth can't take any more, but I feel his balls tighten in my grip. It fuels me, prompting me to keep going to make him finish. I want to taste the proof of his arousal.

"I'm close." He groans, both hands now holding my head to guide it the exact way he wants. I let him, wanting to do whatever I can to bring him to the brink of release.

He keeps the pace until his whole body tenses. His eyes open to meet mine, but he struggles to keep them open. They flutter closed in pleasure. My eyes flick down to how tightly wound his muscles are.

"Get ready to swallow," he demands through a clenched jaw. "Every last fucking drop."

Before I can give any kind of reaction, ropes of cum hit the back of my throat. They don't relent as I try to take as much as I can. He tries to pull back when I can feel some leaking out the sides, but I keep him in my mouth until his body relaxes. He finally gives some relief to my scalp, his grip loosening as the tips of his fingers absentmindedly play with the strands of my hair.

I swallow the last of him when he pulls out of me. He doesn't go far, but enough to give me time to breathe. His gaze focuses on the corner of my mouth. I reach up, wiping at the corner to find his cum. Maintaining eye contact, I slip it into my mouth and lick it from my skin.

He watches me closely, his body freezing for a moment before he pulls me off the ground. Before I can say or do anything, he's smashing his mouth to mine. I've barely swallowed his cum, and he's shoving his tongue in my mouth, kissing me with a type of ferocity I've never felt before.

The kiss slows, his tongue gliding in and out of my mouth until he pulls away. Our foreheads rest against one another as we catch our breath.

"Camden," I whisper, unable to form words at what just happened. I squirm, needing friction between my thighs but also wanting to stay locked in the tender moment between us. I don't want to admit it, but I like the softness of the moment. The way his fingers gently play with my hair, massaging the ache in my scalp from him tugging at it.

I like our matched, heavy breaths as we both try and recover from what just happened.

"What the hell are you doing to me, shortcake?" he says into my hair, pulling me to his chest. He's given me the best orgasm of my life, fucked my face so roughly that I could've come just from how hot it was, and somehow, this is the first time we've ever hugged.

"I'm not doing anything," I admit. Tension still fills the air between us, crackling as if it could explode at any moment.

"This wasn't supposed to happen between us." He pulls away, his head going back so he can look at me. "You weren't supposed to take up so much goddamn space in my mind." The words lash out from his mouth angrily. But it's not like he's mad at me, more like he's upset with himself.

"Have you been thinking about me, Camden Hunter?" I tease, not ready to admit the number of times he's crossed my mind since he left for New York.

"If I tell you yes, are you going to use it against me the next time I piss you off?"

This makes me smile, my teeth digging into my bottom lip in an attempt to fight it. "Try not making me mad for once and you won't have to worry about it."

He pushes hair from my face, tucking it behind my ears. "I'll remember that."

I nod, wondering when things will fall back into place. One heated kiss and a powerful orgasm for each of us isn't enough to settle the angry tension that's constantly between us. Or is it?

"Is this when you fuck me?" I ask eagerly, my body heating with the thought.

"I want to *so* fucking bad. But I told Tommy to stop by tonight, and when I finally get to fuck you, I'm going to take my time."

"Cancel," I offer, well aware it comes out more pleading than I'd intended. I know he shouldn't cancel on Tommy. He's a nice kid, and my night has already taken a turn I wasn't expecting. But I want him, more of him—all of him. Anything he'll give me tonight. "What makes you think that the offer to fuck me isn't only for tonight?"

He aims a wolfish grin my way. "Because your body is terrible at hiding things." He squeezes my hardened nipple as if to prove a point. "And I know that you're in the same boat as me." He traces a finger along the swell of my breast. "And just like me, you'll be counting down the seconds until I'm buried inside you once again, except this time, it'll be your pussy that's full of me."

He buttons his slacks, looking down at the ground where his ripped shirt lies.

I laugh. "Tommy might think it's a little odd for you to be holding a late-night meeting with him shirtless."

"I've got a spare in my office."

I nod, stepping away from his grasp. It feels cold without the warmth of his body pressed against mine. The thought pops into my mind that we've never really said goodbye to one another. He ran away the time we almost kissed on the mountain. He wouldn't have said goodbye to me tonight if I hadn't angrily chased him.

"Last chance to fuck me," I say, backing away toward the entrance.

"It won't be the last," he responds confidently, tucking his hands into his pockets. He looks hot as hell, standing in nothing but a pair of dress pants.

"You're going to have to work for it, then."

His eyes roam down my body. "I plan on it."

And right before I walk out the door, he closes the distance between us and lays a chaste kiss to my lips.

"Goodbye, shortcake."

I press my fingers to my lips, watching him back away as my mind reels with what just happened.

Chapter 29
CAMDEN

I STARE AT MY COMPUTER SCREEN, WATCHING THE MINUTES TURN AS one of my buyers on the other line drones on about something I should be paying attention to.

It's been two days since the walls came crashing down between Pippa and me. Our encounter in her cafe, in the gallery, has been playing over and over again in my head, despite the mountain of work I'm supposed to be getting done.

"How does that sound?" Leo asks, pulling me from my thoughts. I sit up in my chair, running a hand down my face because I have no fucking clue what he's talking about.

"Run it by me again," I clip.

If Leo suspects I haven't paid attention to a word he's saying, he doesn't say so. Instead, he takes a deep breath and rehashes everything I've missed while I've been daydreaming about the sounds Pippa made while coming undone under my tongue.

"So to sum it up, I think the best plan of action would be to move the Franklin piece to a later show at the Sutten location—or wait until winter and do it in Manhattan—and we add these new pieces from the inn owner to the Sutten Collection. An entire show dedicated to the people of Sutten. It's a genius marketing move, Mr. Hunter."

I grunt. I wish the idea was my own and not Pippa's.

"How soon can we get it all together?" I push all thoughts of Pippa to the back of my mind, needing to have this conversation with Leo. He's been my best buyer from the moment I could afford someone else seeking out new talent other than myself. He's a loyal guy—something I appreciate immensely—and he has a superb eye for spotting the next big thing.

I manage to keep her from my thoughts long enough to iron out some details for the next show. I'm surprised by how excited I am for this one. It is panning out to be the most unique exhibit I've ever done. It's new and fresh and something I hope pushes this new venture to the next step.

With Leo no longer on the other line and Trisha back in Manhattan, I'm left in the silence of my office. It's too quiet here. In New York, you can hear the bustle outside the windows. Even into the early hours of the morning, you can hear the thrum of bass from the clubs down the street. You can hear laughter from the sidewalks as people walk home. The sound of honking taxis. None of that is here in Sutten. It's truly silent. Maybe it isn't like that during tourist season, but right now, you can hear every-thing—and that everything leaves me alone with my thoughts.

Suddenly, I'm really wanting a coffee. I look at my coffee cup from earlier, the hot pink lid taunting me. It's barely noon. I don't need another coffee, but Pippa hadn't been at her shop this morning. And I hate to admit it, but I need an excuse to stop by to see her. I've been thinking about her leaving the gallery. She told me I had to work for it—and it's the only thing I can think about.

I *want* to work for it, a realization I don't care to dwell on.

It wouldn't hurt to stop by the coffee shop again. We are next-door neighbors, and she makes the best coffee in this town. It makes total sense for me to drop in. It's better than texting her, something I've thought about doing numerous times as I look at the one text we've shared in our thread. The photo of her in the lingerie. The photo that sent me spiraling from the moment I saw her. Even though I didn't want to admit it then, I knew I wouldn't be able to get her from my mind after that. And after tasting her, I know I'll do anything to experience more with her. I wasn't lying when I said I'd work for her. I look forward to biding my time and winning her over.

I sigh, scrubbing my hand along the stubble on my chin. It's out of character for me to chase a woman, but I can't help it with her. She gets on every one of my nerves, but I can't stop.

It's the very reason I find myself stepping through the hot pink door of her cafe. My eyes immediately travel around the space, looking for her in the group of people. It's busy, some eyes catching mine as I search for her familiar gaze. I don't find her at the tables, and when I look at the counter, she isn't there either.

"Here for another?" the girl behind the register asks. She'd been the one to help me this morning right when the cafe opened.

I clear my throat, stepping up to the counter. "I was working late last night."

"Same thing from this morning?"

Movement catches my attention from the corner of my eye. Looking over, I hope to find Pippa walking out of the swinging doors to the kitchen but instead find another face that isn't her.

"Sir?" the barista pushes.

I focus back on her. "Yeah. That'd be perfect." I scratch my chin, trying to think of a nonobvious way to ask where the hell Pippa is. "So." I clear my throat, making things more awkward and obvious. "Where is the owner? Pippa?"

The girl smiles—Lexi from her name tag. She grasps the counter, leaning over it slightly. "Why are you asking?"

"I'm just used to seeing her every day."

She nods her head, her eyes narrowing on me. "*Right.* No other reason at all you want to know?"

"Nope." I cough, looking around to try and avoid her knowing stare. It's hot against my skin, even as I pretend to look at a prepacked bag of coffee beans to avoid it as long as possible.

"She's always complaining about you," she states, humor in her voice.

My eyes snap to her. "Why do you say that like it's a compliment?"

"Because I think she likes you."

I bite the inside of my cheek, fighting the urge to say the first thing that popped into my head—she definitely seemed to like me when her fingernails were scraping my scalp, her moans echoing off the walls of this very shop as she screamed my name. I want to look back at the door, to close my eyes and remember having her pinned against the windows. What it felt like to spread her thighs open and have her completely bared to me.

"You good?" Lexi asks. Her eyes are lit with mischief as she beams at me. She's clearly having too much fun pestering me about Pippa.

"Yeah." I clear my throat again, looking over my shoulder to see if there's anyone behind me in line. There isn't, giving me time to aim more questions in her employee's direction.

"Her complaining about me makes you think she likes me?" I feel like I'm in middle school again. I want to ask *does she like me or like* like *me* like a goddamn twelve-year-old. "That doesn't make very much sense."

"It does if you know Pippa. She gets bored easily, needing..." She pauses, her eyes traveling to the ceiling as she thinks for a moment. "Well, she needs fire, you could say. Something that keeps things interesting."

"Complaining about me keeps things interesting?"

"Yesterday, I opened the cafe for Pippa. She'd texted me saying she'd been out late and needed help."

My eyebrows draw in because this conversation has taken a turn I wasn't expecting. "Okay?"

"The front door was unlocked. Which was unusual because Pippa *always* locks it when she closes. She sometimes forgets to do other things, but locking the door is never one of them."

The girl points to a security camera in the corner. It looks down at me, a light flickering.

My cheeks heat. Shit. Am I about to blush? Prickling sensations run down the back of my neck as I pray that this conversation isn't going where I think it's going.

"I checked the camera, wanting to make sure no one had broken in. It didn't look like anyone had, but I wanted to be sure."

Holy fuck. Did this girl, who can't be much older than eighteen, see me feasting on her boss's pussy?

I've never blushed in my life, but I think I might actually be blushing from embarrassment. My entire face feels hot, the feeling running down my neck as well.

"Oh," I mumble, having no idea what I'm supposed to say in this situation. I'm a grown-ass adult—I shouldn't be fumbling over words right now—but I'm stuck visualizing all the dirty things this girl could've seen.

"Don't worry. I figured out pretty early what was going to happen. I stopped it before I saw too much."

I let out a sigh of relief. Thank god.

"So where is she?" I ask, changing the subject. Now that I know she hasn't seen anything, I want to never speak of this moment again. It'll haunt me wondering what she did see and at what point she stopped the replay.

Maybe I need to find a way to get that security footage. I don't want anyone else getting a hold of it. It'd also be hot as hell to go back and rewatch.

"She's sick today."

"Sick?" I don't like the thought of her being sick. Is she alone without anyone to take care of her?

"Yep. Which she must really be feeling like shit because she never calls out of work. Even when her mom passed, she showed up to work most days."

My skin prickles with the need to show up at her house just so she'd have someone there for her. This girl has a point. Pippa doesn't seem like the kind of person who'd miss work unless she really wasn't feeling well. What if something bad has happened and no one is there to help?

It doesn't take long for me to decide the right thing is to go check on her. I have no idea where she lives, but I bet Lexi knows.

"Where does she live?" I ask, pulling my phone out so I can plug the address into a maps app.

This makes Lexi smile. I'm tired of all her knowing smiles. It's like she knows too much. Which maybe she does, depending on how far she got into the security footage.

"How do I know that you aren't going to stalk my fun and amazing boss?"

I roll my eyes. "I'm not the stalker type."

"Tall, dark, handsome with a mysterious and arrogant air to him? I think that's the dictionary definition of stalker."

"Pippa and I haven't quite had the time to exchange addresses yet, but I can assure you she wouldn't consider me a stalker."

"What if she doesn't want me to give you her address?"

Does everyone in this town like to argue?

"Fine," I clip, looking back at the menu. "I'll take the same thing as this morning, and then I'd like to add a specialty drink that helps with sickness."

"That's on our secret menu."

"Make it a large, please." Pulling my card out, I hold it between us. "And maybe add whatever food item you have here Pippa likes best."

She stares me down, but I don't back down under her gaze. Eventually, she must deem me trustworthy because she shrugs and pulls an additional cup from next to her. I'm waiting for her to finish writing on the cup and let me pay when she grabs a napkin and begins to write Pippa's address. With a sigh, she slides it across the counter.

"If I get fired, you owe me a new job."

I laugh. "You won't get fired. Thank you."

She snatches my card from me and runs it through their machine. "Don't mess it up with her. She's just now smiling after her mom." Her tone got serious quickly. The joking tone to it is completely gone.

"I have no intentions of hurting her." My intentions are exactly the opposite. I want to make her feel good by plucking orgasm after orgasm from her until her body is completely spent from pleasure.

Chapter 30
PIPPA

A KNOCK ON MY DOOR PULLS ME FROM MY SLEEP. I WIPE AT THE corner of my mouth, finding drool all over my chin. I took NyQuil late last night after I couldn't get to sleep from my head feeling so full, and apparently, it really knocked me out. I have no idea what time it is.

Reaching for my phone on my nightstand, I find it dead, not helping me to figure out what time it is. It's late enough in the morning that the sun fully beats through my bedroom curtains.

I rub at my eyes, wondering if I'd dreamed the loud knocking sound when I hear it again. Groaning, I rub my eyes again, trying to adjust to the light that pours in. I slide off the bed and slip my feet into my favorite pair of slippers. Kitty's tail thumps enthusiastically at the end of the bed, clearly unfazed by whoever is at the door. I look down at my outfit, forgetting what I went to sleep in last night. I should probably change before answering the door in an old sweatshirt and only a pair of underwear underneath, but the sweatshirt is long enough that I should be good. I don't plan on chatting long with whoever is on the other side of the door.

I'm expecting to find my neighbor Francine. Sometimes she pops by to give me fresh eggs from her chickens. She also enjoys watching Kitty for me when I need help or feel like Kitty needs extra attention. Sometimes she even stops by to ask if she can take Kitty for a walk. Because of that, I swing the door open without looking through the window.

Francine isn't standing on my doormat. Instead, I come face-to-face with a smirking Camden. My mind immediately goes to the time his full lips were covered with me the other night.

"Camden?" I look over his shoulder to see if anyone is with him or if he's alone.

He takes a step toward me, pushing a Wake and Bake coffee between us. "I heard you weren't feeling well, so I brought you this."

Why does he have to look so good? My hair has to be a rat's nest, and there's a good chance there's drool drying on my chin as he stands in front of me dressed like he could grace the cover of a business magazine while I look like Gollum from *Lord of the Rings*.

"You brought me coffee?" I ask slowly.

He holds up his own cup. "No, I brought myself coffee. I brought you some sort of special drink from your cafe that is good when you're sick."

My heart squeezes in my chest that he remembered about the drink. It wasn't something I'd expected him to think twice about.

He pushes the drink out a little further, gesturing for me to take it. "Is that okay? I can go back if you want something different."

I prop a hip against my doorframe as I take the drink from him. I tentatively take a sip, savoring how the warm liquid soothes my throat. "It's perfect," I mutter.

He swallows, stuffing his free hand in his pocket. I fight a smile as he uncomfortably shifts from one foot to the next, not knowing what to do.

"I'd offer for you to come in, but I don't want to get you sick."

"My tongue was down your throat—among other places—just a couple of days ago. I'll risk it."

I'm staring at him in disbelief as he shoves his way into my house, not bothering to wait for an invitation.

Kitty wags her tail enthusiastically as she weaves between his legs. She's a terrible guard dog.

"Kitty, attack," I instruct, pointing my finger at her.

She doesn't even look at me, too content at getting back scratches from Camden to follow directions.

"That's a good girl," Camden coos, bending down to pet Kitty's stomach as she rolls over for him.

I try not to react, my mind remembering when he was calling *me* a good girl for *very* different reasons.

"You're cute but useless," I scold Kitty, trying not to laugh at her tongue hanging out the side of her mouth.

She's in heaven. Camden takes me off guard with how sweet he is with her.

My hands find my hips. "You didn't strike me as a dog person."

He gives her attention for a few more seconds before he stands back up, earning a dissatisfied sigh from her. "And why's that?" he asks.

"Well, for starters, you're extremely uptight."

"So because I'm uptight, I don't like dogs?"

I shrug. "Dogs are messy. You don't seem to like messy."

Camden holds my stare, the two of us standing across from one another in my entryway. I'm about to say something else to fill the silence when he opens his mouth. "Maybe I'm starting to like things a bit messy."

Our gazes stay locked, and the only sound is Kitty's paws moving over the hardwood as she tries to get Camden's attention.

His eyes move from mine, but they stay on my body, taking their time raking over my bare legs. I cross my ankles, becoming aware of how little the oversized hoodie hides.

"How are you feeling?"

I run my fingers through my hair, the thought just occurring to me how rough I must look. I'd taken a shower with the little bit of energy I had but hadn't taken the time to blow-dry my hair. I fell asleep with it soaking wet, and I don't have to look in a mirror to know it's probably a tangled mess.

Taking me by surprise, he takes a step closer and presses his palm to my forehead. His hand feels cold against my skin. When he slides it down my face and presses it to my cheek, I can't help but lean into the feeling of his cool skin against mine.

"You're warm," he clips, his voice gruff. He sounds upset. Like he's angry that I'm running a fever.

"I probably need to take more meds," I offer, walking toward my room.

My eyes scan my place. It's kind of a mess right now because I haven't had the energy to clean up. My shoes are haphazardly strewn through the hallway. I have to step around a pair of heels before I fall flat on my face over them.

I want to apologize for how messy things are, but I'm focused on his words from moments ago. What did he mean by them? There was a hidden meaning behind his words, and I can't help but wonder—maybe even hope—that his comment has something to do with me. Compared to his pristine life, I'm chaotically messy. But I like that about myself—and now I'm left wondering if he's starting to appreciate that about me.

"This wasn't the way I first envisioned you in my room," I joke, walking to my nightstand. There are four different kinds of medications lined across the top. I inspect them, deciding which one I want to take. As tired as I am, I'm going to pass on the NyQuil since it's morning and I'd like to be awake for some of the day at least.

Camden grabs my ruffled comforter, holding it up and nodding toward it. "Get in," he demands, his voice stern, making me break out in goose bumps despite my feverish skin.

"Now demanding me to get in bed? Is this why you came today, Camden?"

His lips press into a thin line. He's clearly not amused by my taunting. "You can get in bed, or I can pick you up and throw you in bed. Either way, you'll give your body the rest it deserves."

I stare at him wide-eyed. Why does he have to be so hot when he's bossing me around?

I tell myself I only listen because my body aches, and I'm starting to feel a little light-headed from moving around. I climb in between the sheets, trying not to let out a satisfied sigh when he begins to tuck my blankets in around me.

"You don't have to do this." My eyes stay trained on him as he reads the labels of each of the medicines on my nightstand.

"I don't have to do what?" His eyes don't move from inspecting each label.

"Come over and take care of me because I'm sick."

Camden pins me with a stare, a slight smirk to his lips. His large hands grip one of the pill bottles as he shakes his head at me. "If you haven't learned this already, I don't do anything I don't want to do. I heard you were sick, and I wanted to be here." He pops the lid off and empties a couple of the pills into his large palm. He holds it out, wagging his fingers at me. "Take these."

"What if you're poisoning me?"

He rolls his eyes. "You saw me take them out of the bottle. Open your mouth."

The look on his face leaves no room for argument. My mouth parts, my tongue peeking out to take the pills. He places them on my tongue, handing over my water from the nightstand.

"Swallow," he commands. And I do, my body heating even more from the way he looks at me. It wasn't long ago he was telling me the same thing, and I did exactly as I was told, just like I am now. His mind must be going to the same place because his eyelids get heavy.

"Now, drink some more water and lay down. I'm going to go grab the food I brought. I forgot it in the car."

I watch his tall, athletic body storm out of the open doorway, giving me time to appreciate him from the back. He's dressed as if he could have a meeting at any moment—while I don't even have on pants because I was so tired when I got out of the shower last night—and I miss his cocky smirk the moment he walks out the door.

I stare at the empty doorway for a few moments before I take a few more gulps of water. Kitty whines from her dog bed, making me apparently not the *only* one missing Camden.

When he comes back in, he's carrying food from the bakery. He hands it to me, and I can't hide the smile when I look inside. "My favorite."

I take a bite of the pastry, my eyes closing because I hadn't realized how starved I'd been.

Camden watches me scarf the food down, taking the trash from me and setting it down on the nightstand as soon as I'm done. We stare at each other for a few moments before he sighs.

"Scoot over. I'm going to lay with you to make sure nothing happens."

"I've got a fever. What do you think is going to happen to me?"

He doesn't wait for permission. His long legs are pushing against mine as he forces his way into my bed.

"Camden!" I scold, shoving against his hip. "This is *my* bed and *my* sick day. You can't just barge in."

"Sure I can." He slides an arm underneath my body, pulling me into his chest. The movement stuns me.

I'm pretty sure Camden Hunter is cuddling me. And I'm fairly confident I love it.

"Any more arguments?" he quips, reaching across the bed for the discarded remote. He begins to flip through Netflix as I stare up at him, my cheek still pressed into his chest.

"Uh…" I don't know what to say. I like feeling his body pressed against mine. I like the comforting way his fingers play with my hair. It's tender, making my heart leap inside my chest. I don't know if he even realizes he's doing it.

His chest rises and falls with a deep breath, moving me with it. "Look, shortcake. I think you and I are a lot alike in some ways when it comes to the way we run our businesses. I know you must've felt terrible to take a day off work, so just let me stay here and take care of you, okay? Please?"

All I can do is nod because the emotion clogging my throat is overwhelming. His words mean too much to me, and it terrifies me.

I think between all of the arguments, I've started to develop feelings for him. At first, I thought it was sexual attraction, but there's nothing sexual happening between us right now, and he has my pulse racing.

Before I can think too much into it, my eyes flutter shut as I fall into the best sleep of my life—nestling deeper into the chest of a man I have no business developing feelings for.

Chapter 31
CAMDEN

I'M DEEP INTO REORGANIZING MY EMAIL INBOX WHEN PIPPA FINALLY stirs against me. I look down, finding her eyes still closed as she gets more comfortable, draping a leg over me.

We've been in this same position for two hours. I've watched two complete episodes of *Supermarket Stakeout* and am well into a third episode, and she's barely moved a muscle during all of it.

My arm tingles, needing to move to get some blood flow, but I don't want to risk waking her up. Her body clearly needs rest, and I'd sit here all day feeling like my arm might fall off if it meant she'd stay sound asleep.

I don't know if I've ever held still for so long. It isn't in my nature to sit on my phone and do nothing. Every now and then, my gaze drifts to her as I allowed my eyes to drink her in without her knowing.

She's breathtaking, in a way that's both quiet and loud. She doesn't have any makeup on, yet her features are striking. The upturned nose, full, slightly parted lips. Her eyelashes dance along the apples of her cheeks. Every time I look, I want to run my thumb along her cheekbone, but I fight the urge so I don't wake her.

She's stunningly beautiful in a way that makes my chest hurt. I want to capture her features forever so I can carve them into stone later. People would stare in awe at it, marveling at how the closer they get, the more she'll steal the air from their lungs.

I keep lying to myself that I'm here because it's the decent thing to do. But I'm not a decent man. I've done ruthless things in my life if it worked out best for me. But when it comes to her, I can't stay away. It isn't because I'm a nice guy. It's because she has a magnetic pull that I can't deny, not that I've been any good at attempting to fight it.

It's a catastrophic thought to think that the pull I feel toward Pippa isn't just surface level. I'd love to blame it on the way it felt to have my cock down her throat, my fingers buried in her pussy, the anticipation of finally sliding into her and pushing her body's limits.

But it's much more dangerous than that.

Pippa Jennings—the woman I yelled at the moment we met —is stealing pieces of my cold, black heart. She's breathing life back into it, and I don't have it in me to fight, even when I know it can't end well. I didn't come here today because I wanted something from her. I wanted to be around her. I wanted to take care of her. And I can't think too deeply into what all of that means.

My phone vibrates in my hand. I look down to find a text from Beck.

BECK
Call me

CAMDEN
Can't. I'm busy.

BECK
Are you on another call?

CAMDEN
No.

BECK
In a meeting?

CAMDEN

No.

BECK

When have you ever declined a business call?
What could you possibly be doing?

HIS CALLER ID pops up on my phone. I decline it immediately, not wanting to wake Pippa up. My phone vibrates immediately with another new text.

BECK

You're being weird. I'm trying to talk business.
Answer your phone.

CAMDEN

I'll call later. Busy.

BECK

I need proof of life. Is this even you?

I SNAP a picture of my middle finger against the sheets to not give myself away and send it to him.

BECK

I know cheap sheets when I see them. I know
the place you're renting doesn't have those
sheets, or if they did, Trisha's replaced them.

CAMDEN

I'm living like a local.

BECK

I call bullshit.

HE CALLS AGAIN. The fucker is relentless. I don't remember prying so much into his life when he disappeared into a bubble when Margo first moved in with him.

CAMDEN

Leave me alone.

BECK

We'll talk about this later. I have to know what townie has lured you into their bed.

Are you cuddling at two in the afternoon on a weekday?

CAMDEN

Fuck off. Shouldn't you be galavanting with your new wife?

BECK

She's ignoring me, busy painting shit for your gallery. I'm lonely and wanted to talk about a new business venture.

CAMDEN

Tell her she can have an extension if you'll leave me the hell alone.

BECK

Can't wait to get all the juicy details later.

I ROLL MY EYES, placing my phone next to me so I'm not tempted to respond back to my nosy friend. I glance at Pippa, not expecting to see her eyes fluttering open.

"Did I wake you up?" I whisper, pushing pieces of hair from her face.

She gives me a sleepy smile, and fuck, it disarms me. I almost push her off my chest, not wanting her to feel my rapid heartbeat against her cheek, but I can't bring myself to do it. I just pray that she doesn't feel the way my pulse spikes at the sheer beauty of her sleepy smile.

"I'm sorry if I did," I add as she stretches her legs underneath the blankets. Her foot brushes against my leg. I want to tangle my limbs with hers, to hold her against my chest as we both get lost in sleep.

"I should probably get up anyway." Her voice is throatier than normal as she tries to wake up.

My thumb traces over her cheekbone, over the same place I wanted to caress while she slept peacefully on my chest. "Go back to sleep for a bit. I'm going to go make some food for when you wake up."

She doesn't argue, the medicine getting the best of her as her eyes flutter closed once again. I take a few moments to watch her again before I carefully slide out from underneath her. I miss her body the moment we're no longer connected, but I want her to have more to eat than just the pastry I bought from the cafe, so I break the connection and walk in the direction I think her kitchen is.

My stomach growls. Watching episode after episode on the Food Network is making me hungry as well.

Her dog—named Kitty, which is such a Pippa thing to do—follows closely behind me. It isn't hard to find the kitchen in her small one-story house. I like how homey it feels here. Even with the limited amount of space on the quiet, small-town street, she's made the space she has feel like a home, not a house. As I look around, making my way to the kitchen, I realize how cold and empty my penthouse in Manhattan must feel.

I stop on pictures that line the wall in her living room. There are so many of them, and I can't help but look closely at each photograph. There's some with Pippa and who I now know as her brother and who must be their parents. I look at the woman who has to be her mother because of the resemblance between the two. My heart feels heavy when I look at Pippa's arm wrapped around her. I haven't had to mourn a parent—not that mine were really ever parents at all—but I can't imagine what it'd feel like to lose one who was as amazing as Pippa made her mom out to be.

I continue to look at all the photos, marveling at the life Pippa's lived. There are pictures of her on horses, at her bakery, and some with a blonde that seem to be from college. I fight the urge to want to know everything about her. I want to know the backstory for every photo. It isn't lost on me that I searched for men in them, wondering if a man has ever stolen her heart or what her past must look like.

Moving from the photos on her wall, I look around her living room. She has a large white sectional that covers an entire wall and cuts across the open floor plan. There are throw pillows on almost every inch of the couch. They're bright and fun colors, something I appreciate. I paid thousands upon thousands of dollars to have my place decorated back in Manhattan, and the most color there is the little bit of navy in certain rooms.

I finally walk into her kitchen, laughing because, like everything else about her, it's a little messy. There are cups lined by the sink and a few dishes in it. It isn't dirty, but the keys and mail strewn about the counter are far more disorganized than my own space. I like that about her, which is something I never imagined myself saying. I like that she's always moving to the beat of her own drum, moving from one thing to the next without ever taking things too seriously.

I open her fridge to find it relatively empty. Trisha has made sure my fridge at my rental stays stocked, so even if I wanted to leave Pippa's to get her some groceries—which I don't—I wouldn't even know what to get.

She has one pack of chicken in there. I check the expiration date, finding that it still has a few days until it goes bad. Pulling the chicken out, I set it on the counter and continue to rifle through the contents of the fridge until I feel like I have enough to make her some soup.

As the skillet heats, I pull my phone out and call Trisha to ask her to send some groceries. I might not be able to run out and get Pippa some, but I want her to have options without having to worry about going grocery shopping. Trisha doesn't ask any questions, even when I give an address for the delivery she knows isn't my rental.

I'm busy adding some last-minute salt and pepper to the simmering pot of chicken noodle soup when Pippa ambles into the kitchen. The entire right side of her face is red, imprints from the sheets pressed into her skin.

I look up, trying to fight a smile at the way her hair sticks out in every direction. It's cute as hell. An unwelcome thought creeps into my mind. I think I could get used to being here when Pippa wakes up. I wouldn't complain about being on the receiving end of many more sleepy smiles from her.

"Good morning," I tease, looking out her kitchen window. "Or should I say afternoon?"

She stops next to me, peeking inside the pot. "Did you make this?"

I give it one more stir before I place the lid over the pot. My hip rests against the counter as I lazily cross my arms across my chest. "I did."

"You cook?"

"If I want to."

"It smells edible."

I reach out and grab her by the hips, pulling her body against mine before I can think too deeply about it. She smiles at me, the color back in her face after being pale and clammy when I first arrived.

"I can't believe you made me homemade soup." She sounds shocked, rising to her tiptoes to loop her arms around my neck.

It feels natural to be in this position with her. It feels like something we've been doing for years and not some new foreign thing to the both of us.

"I actually made it for myself," I joke. "You can fend for yourself."

Her bottom lip juts out in a pout. "But it smells delicious."

My head rears back. "Did you just give me a compliment, shortcake?"

"Don't get used to it."

"But it felt good."

"You'll have to earn them."

"I think I'll have fun earning more from you."

Red tinges her cheeks, spreading down the skin of her neck before the flush disappears into the fabric of her hoodie. "You could've had a lot more of them if you weren't a humongous dick to me the first time we met."

"I'll just have to make up for lost time." I fight a smirk, remembering the insults she threw at me the second time we met. "At least now you know I wasn't an asshole to compensate for my cock," I add.

Her eyes get wide. She reaches up and holds a hand over her mouth, trying to hide a smile.

"You've got me there."

I cup her face in my hands, fighting every instinct of mine to lean down and kiss her. I know I shouldn't do it. She's sick, and I have no idea what the hell is happening between us. But there isn't a part of me that doesn't want to claim her mouth with mine. To kiss along her cheeks and down her neck.

Groaning, I let my forehead fall against hers. I take a deep breath to calm myself before I pull away and turn back to the stove. "Let's get you some food."

She doesn't move for a moment, her gaze hot on me.

Did she want me to kiss her? Is her mind reeling from thoughts of all the tempting potential for us, or am I alone in this?

"Let's see if you can actually cook," she quips, reaching around me to grab a bowl.

Chapter 32
PIPPA

CAMDEN HUNTER IS INFURIATING.

He has a perfect face. A perfect body. Is rich as hell. One of the most talented people I've ever met. And the asshole can cook, too.

His eyes are trained on me as I blow on the spoonful of soup, cooling the hot liquid down before taking a bite. My mom used to make the best soup ever, spending Sundays throwing everything in the fridge into a pot and somehow making it delicious. But damn, this chicken noodle soup almost compares to what she used to make.

It's delicious, which is annoying as hell.

I can't even say he's lacking in personality anymore because the more I get to know him, the more I think the whole asshole thing is a front. Sure, he still has his moments where he can be a dick, but he's not as bad as I first thought.

And I don't like that at all. Because now he's doing things like taking off work to come take care of me and make me soup, and it doesn't feel like we're enemies who might have sex anymore. It feels like I might have actual feelings for the art dealer next door, and I have no idea if it will hurt me in the end.

I try to push any negative thoughts out of my mind. One day, I might come to regret letting Camden into my life little by little, but right now, I want to soak it in. I want to feel special, like maybe him taking care of me is out of character for him and that he may be feeling the attraction between us, too. For me, it isn't just the sexual tension. There are feelings, and it's terrifying and exhilarating to wonder what might happen.

"So are you just going to leave me hanging, or are you going to confess that my soup blew you away?"

I slurp the liquid from the soup with a casual shrug. "It's okay."

He narrows his eyes on me. "You're lying."

I like the casual way he sits in his chair, his long legs slightly parted. He holds himself so confidently, even while sitting in my tiny kitchen, watching me eat soup. He's got the sleeves of his shirt rolled up, showing off his perfect forearms. The muscles along the top ripple with his movements, beckoning me to reach out and touch them.

"You're watching me awfully close, shortcake." His voice is low and taunting.

I meet his blue eyes, trying to play it cool like I wasn't just imagining gripping his strong biceps as he railed into me.

What kind of medicine did he give me?

"I have no idea what you're talking about," I lie. He and I both know I just got caught ogling him, but it's fine. I'll distract him by telling him he makes mediocre soup when in reality, I think it's the best chicken noodle soup I've ever had.

"Mhm," he hums, sitting back in his chair. He knows exactly what he's doing when he brings his fingers to his mouth and runs his thumb along his bottom lip.

The asshole is bringing attention to those perfectly chiseled forearms. He's trying to tempt me, tease me, and if I didn't feel foggy from the sleep—or the medicine—I might just crawl across this table so he could finally fuck me.

"Careful with the speed at which you inhale the soup." He nods toward my bowl of soup, which is already halfway gone. "You might have me believing you're actually enjoying it."

"It's because I'm starving, and I have no other options."

"You have a pantry and fridge full of food. If my soup is so terrible, I can find you something else."

My spine straightens, the spoon clanging into the bowl as I look at him in confusion. "Did you buy me groceries?"

His lips pick up in a cocky smirk. "I did. Would you like me to make you something different?"

I don't answer him at first. All I can do is stare, trying to figure him out. He's constantly shocking me. His thoughtfulness takes me by surprise. He didn't have to bring me herbal tea and food this morning. He didn't have to hold me while I slept. And he certainly didn't have to make me soup and buy me groceries.

He's so different today than all the other days I've known him. It can't only be because we hooked up.

"Shortcake?"

"Hm?"

He aims a knowing smirk my way. His eyebrows rise as his thumb still teases me by tracing his bottom lip. "Would you like me to make you something different?"

"The soup is fine." I take another bite. It warms every part of me, comforting me in a way I didn't know I needed.

It reminds me of being with my mom, of the days I stayed home sick from school and she took care of me and made me soup. We'd watch game shows on TV, and she'd hold me while I napped. He probably doesn't realize he's done it, but he's given me a little piece of my mom back. A little reminder of her. And it means the world to me.

"Thank you," I begin, suddenly feeling overcome with emotion. "For making this. For all of it."

"You don't have to thank me."

I set the spoon down and sit back in my chair. When my eyes meet his, I feel the burning sensation from fighting back tears. If he notices, he doesn't say anything. He just watches me carefully, as if he's ready to round the table and comfort me at any moment.

"I do, though. I'm sure you've missed a lot of work to be here today, and you spent money on groceries—which I'll pay you back for, by the way—and yeah...just thank you for it all. No one's ever really done this for me. No one but my mom."

His eyes soften. He sits up, placing his hands in his lap. "The fact you even offered to pay me back is insulting. I will never take your money, Pippa." The use of my actual name and not the nickname he's given me makes it seem like he's scolding me—maybe he is.

"And I don't care about missing work today. It can wait. What I care about is that you feel better. I can't believe I'm saying this out loud, but I like taking care of you."

Neither one of us looks away. His breath gets faster, but his gaze stays steady. If he regrets giving me that little slice of vulnerability, he doesn't show it.

"I don't need anyone taking care of me." My words come out crueler than I'd intended, but I can't help it. I don't want to let my walls down completely. To tell him that today means the world to me.

"I think you do." He doesn't seem deterred by me lashing out in the slightest. In fact, he angrily shoves out of his chair, the legs making a scraping sound against the hardwood. Before I can ask him what he's doing, he's rounding the table and crouching in front of me.

"I haven't been here very long, but from what I've seen, you're always taking care of other people."

I don't say anything. I'm too lost in the way his fingertips dance along my inner thigh in a comforting motion.

"But after your mom, who's been taking care of you?"

All I can do is swallow, trying to fight the feelings bubbling out of me. I hate letting people know how I feel. I don't want people to know their words and actions have power over me. But I can't help myself at the moment. His words have split me wide open, my vulnerability on full display for him. Now all I can do is hope that we don't go back to the place where he'd use that vulnerability against me.

"You give so much to your business. Your family. This town. But I think it's time someone gives something to you. And today, I'm making it me."

"And tomorrow?" My voice shakes. Maybe it's because my entire body slightly trembles from his tender words and the gentle caress of his fingertips.

"Well, I'd like to take care of you tomorrow, too, if you'll let me."

His piercing blue eyes bore into mine, unraveling every single defense I've put up against him. I'm supposed to hate the man who wants to change some of the things I love most about Sutten, but instead, I find myself developing feelings for him. It was a lot easier when there was hate in my heart for Camden Hunter. The feelings that are blossoming deep inside seem like ones that'll last far longer than any hate.

He looks like he wants to say something else, but he doesn't. Maybe he doesn't have to. By the way he squeezes my inner thigh and the way his eyes travel to my lips for a fraction of a second, I'm confident he's thinking about kissing me. If I wasn't worried about making him sick, I'd already be closing the distance between us.

"You done?" He nods his head toward the almost empty bowl of soup.

"Yeah." My voice is hoarse, but it isn't because of my throat hurting. It's because emotion clogs my throat as an unwelcome guest.

I watch him clean up, portioning the soup into small dishes so I can just heat them up in the microwave and eat. He wasn't wrong about getting groceries. The leftover soup containers barely fit in the fridge with everything else that's in there.

As I look around my kitchen, I realize not only did he cook and order my groceries, but he's cleaned it as well. The stainless steel fridge gleams, so clean that if I walked up to it, I'd be able to see my reflection. The counters shine underneath the lights.

Did I get sick and enter some parallel universe? Why's he being so nice?

When he's got the pot cleaned and drying on my drying rack, he wipes his hands on a towel and turns toward me. "Time for you to lie back down."

"I have a fever—I'm not dying. I don't have to lie down."

"Do you have to argue with me about everything?" This time, there's a slight smile on his lips. Like his question is playful.

"Well, we made it a couple of hours without fighting. At least we set a new record for ourselves."

"You were sleeping for most of it."

I shake my head at him, not bothering to hide my grin. God. I think I really like this guy.

"Come on, Kitty," I call, tapping my thigh to get her to follow me. "Let's leave him behind and go lie down."

"So you actually *do* follow directions." His voice comes from right behind me as he follows me back to my room.

I climb into bed, watching Camden scratch at Kitty's ears as she looks up at him like he's her favorite person ever.

"You know, it's annoying that I rescued her and have taken care of her for months now, and you give her one belly rub and she's completely in love with you."

He sits down on the floor with her, a sight I never expected to see, and lets her climb into his lap. "I've heard I have impeccable charm."

I scoff, pulling the blankets to my chin. "You're the least charming person I know."

He holds a hand to his chest, pretending that my words hurt him. "I'm going to change your mind about me, shortcake."

"I'd like to see you try."

Chapter 33
CAMDEN

"WHAT DID YOU WANT TO BE WHEN YOU GREW UP?" PIPPA ASKS, sitting back and leaning her body against her sectional. Her legs are outstretched, her fuzzy socks with bright pink hearts resting against my thigh. We sit on her living room floor, *Supermarket Stakeout* playing in the background as we eat straight from an open pizza box between us.

"Do you really want to know my answer to that?" I take another bite of my own slice. I had to slip away for two hours when Pippa took her second nap of the day to finish some work at the gallery, but before I left, she requested I pick up pizza from a place named Crusty's Pizza Parlor. When I asked why she wanted it from this specific place, she'd answered it was something her family used to do when someone was recovering from being sick. They'd order pizza when they were on the mend. It was her mom's way of making sure the kids didn't milk their sickness for all its worth and try to get extra sick days from school.

"Of course I want to know the answer. Did you want to be an astronaut, or were you dead set on selling other people's art from a young age?"

I chew the pizza. Despite the cheesy—no pun intended—name for the pizza place, the pizza is actually phenomenal. It's far greasier than I typically choose to eat, but I like indulging. I like breaking my own rules for her—even if it's just in the form of opting for something not high in nutritional value for the night because pizza excited her, and I like to see her happy.

"My answer might be far more depressing than you like, shortcake," I answer honestly. My childhood wasn't terrible in the way that some others deal with. But it wasn't happy. I didn't know a parent's love. And even though I got every material thing I could've ever wanted, I didn't get the one thing I needed —for my parents to actually love and care about me.

"Tell me anyway?" She sets her pizza slice down and leans forward, hanging on to whatever I'm about to say.

"To be honest, I didn't look to my future imagining a career. I just pictured myself away from my parents, doing something that would upset them because I felt like that was just a little slice of karma."

"So you never had an outrageous childhood aspiration? Like becoming a marine biologist or a knight or something?"

I shake my head, running my palms along her shins. She changed into a pair of leggings, creating a thin barrier of fabric between us. "I was forced to be a tiny adult as a child. I didn't have a childhood. I was dressed in tuxes by the time I was two and was scolded if I got something like paint or a splatter of ketchup on the expensive fabric. I was placed in art classes from the moment I could hold a pencil. My tutors didn't believe in childhood play. I didn't know what it was like to have adolescent dreams."

A tiny line appears on her forehead as her face develops into a frown. "That's so incredibly depressing."

"If it wasn't for my gran, I truly don't think I would've known what love was at a young age."

"Then tell me about her."

My head falls against the cushions behind me. I don't realize I'm doing it, but my thumbs work the muscles of her calves as I try to think of what to tell Pippa. Before I made friends in school, the only person I knew actually cared about me was my gran. She's my everything, and I don't know how to explain to someone who doesn't know her how incredible of a human she is.

"You'd love her," I toss out, imagining the trouble the two of them would cause. The things I find endearing about Pippa are the same qualities Gran has. "She's incredibly sassy, always speaking her mind, even if no one asked."

Pippa laughs. "I already love her."

"I've always looked up to the way she doesn't take shit from anyone. She's unbothered by other people's opinions of her, and it's something I admire."

"Is she your mom's mom or father's mom?"

"She's my father's mother, even though she isn't proud to say it. As I've gotten older, she's told me how her only regret in life is feeling like she didn't do enough to prepare my dad for being a good father."

Pippa nods. I like that she really listens to me. Her entire body is facing mine, and even though she looks at the ceiling instead of making eye contact, I know it's just because she's thinking deeply about what I'm saying.

"I'm sorry you didn't know the love you deserved from a mother. But I'm glad your gran was there for you."

"She's pretty incredible. One time, she brought a stray cat into my parents' brownstone and let it loose during one of their fancy parties because she thought it'd be hilarious."

Pippa gasps. "No she didn't."

"She sure did." The look of horror on the crowd's faces will forever be ingrained in my mind. I think it was because I'd told Gran how my dad had yelled at me for breaking a dish an hour before the party. I was trying to make myself useful—trying to get the favor of my parents—and thought I could help set up. Instead, my little hands couldn't hold all the plates I'd tried to grab, one of them tumbling to the ground and shattering all over the formal dining room's floor.

"She let the cat loose in the house, pretending to have no idea how it got there. As the cat was wreaking havoc on the party, she'd told my parents she was taking me for the week, and then she let me stay with her for *two* weeks before I'd told her it was time I probably went home."

"I'd love to meet her one day," Pippa confesses, pulling her eyes from mine like she's embarrassed by saying that.

I squeeze her leg, wanting to reassure her. "I'm terrified of the trouble the two of you could cause, but I'd love for you to meet her."

All I want to do is kiss her. I don't need anything else but to feel the press of her lips against mine. To feel the fireworks throughout my entire body as I taste her little moans and sighs as my tongue coaxes her lips open. I wouldn't need to do anything else, knowing she must not feel good from being sick. I've been a good man today. I've shown far more restraint than I ever have in my life, but the restraint is running out.

There's nothing more I want for myself than to claim Pippa's lips again.

"Camden?"

I can't focus on anything but her lips. They're a beacon. A lighthouse in the dead of night, just begging me to head right to it. "I'm feeling much better," she says, her voice breathy.

"Okay," I answer, only half paying attention because I'm so lost in the primal need to kiss her. It's like middle school all over again. I'd be satiated just by making out. I think just a peck might be my undoing. I want to feel her lips so badly.

"In fact, I think I feel one hundred percent again. I could go to work if I wanted to."

"Why are you telling me all of this?"

"Because I really need you to kiss me."

I pause for one second. For *one* second, I try to be a good guy and give her body the rest it deserves. I don't want her to think I came over today to get anything from her. But that only lasts for a second before I'm pulling on her thighs, almost pulling her on top of the pizza box between us in the process of molding her body to mine.

She lets out the smallest of yelps, her hands finding the fabric of my shirt the moment I pull her within reach. I'd changed at the gallery, opting for a quarter-zip sweater and a pair of dark jeans.

Her thighs straddle one of mine as I pull her even closer to me, lining her face up with mine.

"I don't want to get you sick, though," she mutters, her eyes trained on my lips. Both our chests are heavy as we gulp in air, lost in the moment together.

"Does it look like I give a shit about being sick?"

"I'll take care of you if you do get sick. Please just kiss me."

"I didn't come here to kiss you."

"I'd be okay with it if you did," she admits, leaning in even closer until our lips brush against one another, achingly close to fully closing the distance between us.

Chapter 34
PIPPA

I WAKE UP WITH A WARM BODY PRESSED AGAINST MINE. AN ARM IS thrown over my middle, fingertips barely tucked in the waist-band of my pants.

Camden stayed all night. I remember waking up multiple times throughout the night with his palm pressed to my fore-head. As if he'd woken worrying if I had a fever or not. I haven't had a fever since he first showed up yesterday morning, but the fact he spent his night ensuring I didn't spike another one means more to me than I care to admit.

He slept with me all night. We'd spent so much of the evening kissing, making out like a pair of teenagers. Anytime I'd try to push it further, he'd stop me with promises of more when my body was ready for him.

It only thrilled me more, despite the aggravation that coursed through my veins at not being able to have him at that very moment. The night was perfect anyway. We spent it talking about my mom, his gran, and everything that led us to where we are now.

He's far more fascinating than I thought he'd be. I carefully roll over, finding his eyes shut and the muscles of his face relaxed as he sleeps soundly. I think about everything I learned about the man holding me.

I learned that our birthdays are only a week apart. Except I'll be turning twenty-four, and he'll be turning thirty-seven. I look at him and can't believe he's closer to forty than he is thirty. Every part of me wants to reach out and trace his sharp cheekbones, straight nose, his chiseled jaw. I fight the urge, not wanting to wake him. I'm enjoying being able to look at him—soak this moment in—without him knowing. I'm sure women pay tons of money to have skin as flawless as his. There's not a single wrinkle on his face as he sleeps, which is shocking; with the amount he frowns, he should have prominent frown lines. It's unfair men don't have to take care of their skin the way women do and their skin remains flawless.

One thing does take me by surprise. It's a jagged scar that's right behind his ear and travels to his jaw. It's long, but the line is so thin that it's hard to notice until you're this close to him. My fingers itch to trace it. To wake him up and find out what it's from.

I want to know everything about Camden Hunter. And while I learned last night that he spent his life looking forward to school because he was shipped off to boarding school, where he got away from his parents, and that he graduated top of his class, I still want to know more. He did fill me in that he would've been valedictorian, but his best friend beat him to it. I laughed, hearing about the stories of him and his closest friend, Beckham Sinclair. I remember him from Slopes the night Camden and I first met, but more from the time I dropped off cupcakes for Beckham's wedding, where Camden was the best man—and a complete asshole.

I learned that Camden wouldn't take any money from his family to start his gallery. And at first, he started online because he didn't have the money to rent a space until a year after opening. He didn't say it out loud, but I could tell that he wasn't proud of his last name. That he still dwells on the fact he thinks some of his success was because of it.

Not realizing I'm doing it, I reach out and run my palm along his jaw. His facial hair scratches against my palm. His eyelids flutter open, the crystal-clear color of his eyes taking me by surprise. I'd never seen a blue so clear. I think I'd told him that last night as we drifted off to sleep, staring into each other's eyes. They remind me of the clear waters I see in the movies from all the places I hope to visit one day.

"Hi." His voice is rough and gravelly, the sexiest sound I've ever heard.

"Good morning," I whisper, running my thumb along his cheek.

"You sleep okay?" I want to ask him question after question to keep him talking. I'm far too enthralled with hearing his morning voice.

I nod, my teeth digging into my bottom lip. "I slept great. You?"

"I've never slept better." He grins, turning his face toward the pillow as if he's embarrassed by admitting that. His arms tighten around me, pulling me to his chest so I can't see his face.

"I wouldn't have guessed that," I mumble against his strong chest. "I swear I remember you checking my forehead throughout the night."

He puts his jaw over my head, fitting our bodies together like perfect puzzle pieces. "I did. But I still slept great. Except for your little snores."

I gasp. "I *don't* snore."

He chuckles, his chest vibrating against my cheek. "Oh yes you do. It's adorable, shortcake."

Groaning, I pull away from him so I can look him in the eye. He's grinning ear to ear, embarrassment prickling my cheeks as blood rushes to them from finding out I snored all night.

"I can't help it that I'm sick! My throat hurt. That's the *only* reason I was snoring."

"I guess I'll have to sleep next to you again to find out. I'll have to test it over multiple nights until I make a final conclusion if you snore or not."

My heart flutters in my chest as if I'm a silly schoolgirl again and my crush just looked my way. The more time we spend together, the more giddy I get around him.

"Should I take your silence as you telling me that I won't get to test my theory? Am I not allowed back in your bed, shortcake?"

He spins us, his body rolling on top of mine, his weight pushing me into my mattress. "Think about your answer *very* carefully." He grinds his hips into me, bringing attention to his morning wood.

I suck a shaky breath in, getting more and more turned on by the second by the way his hips rock against mine.

"That depends," I manage to get out, trying not to moan when he peppers kisses along my neck.

"Depends on what?"

His hair is a perfect, tousled mess. It falls into his eyes, making him seem boyish. I like this non-perfect, more raw version of him. I could get used to seeing what he looks like every morning before he puts on a suit and gels his hair.

"It depends if you stay on my good side or not."

His grin is wolfish as he holds eye contact with me for a moment before bringing his lips to the other side of my body.

Groaning, I look at the time on my phone. I should already be making a smoothie for the morning and heading out to the cafe. Since I wasn't there yesterday, I don't know what still needs to be prepared and what doesn't. My employees are great, but I'm sure there's still a lot more for me to do before opening this morning compared to other mornings.

Which means I can't let Camden continue on the path his lips are moving. If I do, I might end up in bed with him all day.

"I have to get up," I tell him, my fingernails skirting down his shirtless back. I like feeling his muscles against me. Having him in just a pair of boxer briefs as we greet each other in the morning. It seems so mundane. And definitely something I'd never expected. He was only supposed to be the grumpy asshole art dealer next door. Now, he's the man with his lips pressed against my pulse, sending shivers down my spine.

"Stay in bed with me," he counters, nipping at my ear.

"I have to work. *You* have to work."

"Who cares about work? I'd much rather work your body all. Day. Long." He punctuates every word with a kiss.

I squeeze my eyes shut, almost giving in to the temptation. My mind fills with all the possibilities for the day. We'd barely have to leave this bed. He could worship my body, let me worship his, until we finally felt what it was like for him to push inside me.

I'm busy thinking if I can call in sick again when I push against his chest. I don't push hard, but my palms against his defined pecs make his lips pause, his head lifting.

"So you're going to be the responsible one today?"

I laugh, nodding my head. "Apparently, someone has to be. Aren't you a workaholic? I can't believe you're trying to get me to play hooky with you so we can have sex."

Damn. He looks good with a grin. He's so cocky and sure of himself, the smile making me squeeze my thighs together because of how much I love seeing the upturn of his lips and the gleam in his eyes.

"Fucking you all damn day seems like the perfect excuse to play hooky."

I roll off the bed to get away from him, my feet barely catching me before I fall on my ass. His body is too defined—too hard in all the right places—to allow it to stay pressed against me. If I feel the ripple of his abs against mine or his cock grind against my inner thigh again, I might just close the shop down unexpectedly today and spend the daylight hours wrapped in bedsheets with him.

"You're no fun, shortcake."

I toss him a look over my shoulder, loving the heated way he stares at my body. "Never in my life did I think Camden Hunter would be telling me *I'm* no fun. People look at you and fall ill with boredom you're so...well, boring," I tease. I try to take a mental picture of what he looks like at this exact moment. The sheets are pulled down from me rolling out of the bed. They gather around his hips, giving me the perfect view of his shirtless body. He props himself up on his elbow, a few pieces of dark hair falling into his eyes as he aims a lopsided smile in my direction.

"I'll punish you later for calling me boring. You won't think that of me when you can't walk straight because I fucked you so good. You'll be reminded of the fun we had for days."

My entire body heats because I think he means it. And I think I'm eager for it.

He must find my gawking amusing because he laughs, running his hand through his hair in an attempt to tame it. "You better get ready for work, shortcake. You can't ogle me all day."

"You know, for you to fu..." My words fall short because I don't know if I can say the word out loud to him.

"Fuck you?"

I quickly nod my head up and down again. "Yeah. That. For you to do that, I meant it when I said you have to work for it."

He swings his legs over the bed, placing his feet on my fluffy, pink rug. His palm runs along his very obvious erection. "Let me take you on a date, then."

I almost drop the hairbrush I'd just picked up from the shock of his words. "Date?"

He stands to his full height, reaching his hands over his head to stretch. My eyes get stuck on the trail of dark hair that runs into his briefs. I remember my fingers sliding over it the other night, leading me right to his awaiting cock.

"Yes. A date. You, me, and wherever you think we should go in this town."

"You have to earn it, but I'm the one planning the date?"

He closes the distance between us, watching me closely as I run the brush through my tangled hair. "I have no problem planning the date, but I figured you'd want to decide. You know what's best here in Sutten."

It's the way he says Sutten instead of saying this town or putting some kind of negative connotation on it. He says it casually. I could get used to him saying Sutten in conversation.

"Am I right?" he presses.

"I have some ideas." There are so many places we could go. My mind runs rampant with ideas, trying to decide where I'd like to take him.

"I knew you would. Is this part of your ploy to get me to see the beauty in Sutten?" He says "beauty" sarcastically but not in a condescending way. It's more playful.

"I guess you'll have to find out."

"I think I'm already seeing the appeal." His voice is gruff, his eyes boring into mine with what I think—or maybe hope—is affection.

"Yeah?"

He grabs me by the neck, pulling our lips together. He lazily kisses me, like he has all the time in the world. The kiss stops, but he only pulls away slightly. "I could get used to this town. This place. *You*." The last word is said quieter, like he's unsure if he should be adding it or not.

I rise to my tiptoes, planting another kiss on his lips, giving him the only answer I can at the moment. "I've got to get ready now, or my new boy toy is going to make me late," I joke, my lips moving against his.

"*Boy toy?*"

"Yep."

He pulls my lip between his teeth, biting down to create the slightest tinge of pain. "You better start getting ready for work." He spins me by my shoulder, pushing me into my en suite bathroom. I let out a loud yelp when he slaps my ass. "Our date is tonight. As soon as you're off, you're mine."

"Are you leaving now?" I ask, keeping eye contact with him

through the bathroom mirror, watching him pull on his shirt from last night.

"No. We're going to ride to work together, you're going to make me a coffee, and then we're going to both do our jobs before I get you after the workday ends. You decide what we'll do for our date."

"And then what?"

He slides his legs into his jeans, looking up at me with a sly smile. "By then, I'll have earned your pussy, baby. After our date, I'm going to fuck you all night—making good on the punishments you've earned."

Chapter 35
CAMDEN

THE DAY DRAGS BY ACHINGLY SLOW. TOO FUCKING SLOW. IT'S A shame I actually have to get work done because all I really want to do is walk next door and see Pippa. I want to steal her—even if she's kicking and screaming—and pull her all the way back to her house. Or she can come to my place. I just need to be near her again. I want to feel her soft, warm body sleeping next to mine. I want to run my fingers along her bare skin, further exploring every single inch of her exquisite body.

I want to hear her soft moans in her sleep when my fingers play with the waistband of her pj's. I want to see how many orgasms I can get from her until she's begging for a break, her body too spent to take any more.

I want to sit on the living room floor and talk about life with her. I want to know about her childhood, to hear the silly stories of the trouble she got into. She seemed to be a rebellious teenager, and I want to know every detail from every day of her life from her very first memory to the moment she met me. I'm obsessed with knowing everything there is to know about her, and I'm afraid of what that could mean for me.

I've never been like this with a woman. Quite frankly, I've never cared about women. I've ended up in mutually agreed-upon relationships that were based on sex alone. The expectations were clear from the very beginning. Feelings weren't supposed to get involved at any point in time. And if I ever felt like someone wasn't holding up their end of the bargain by not developing feelings, I'd simply leave.

Now, it's a terrifying realization that I *want* to stay. I don't want to book a flight back to New York. I don't want to run away from Pippa, even when her eyes soften and she looks at me like I couldn't do a single thing wrong. I'm not terrified of asking her on a date. Usually, the thought of a date would put me off. This morning, I found myself holding my breath, waiting for Pippa to answer me. I wanted her to agree to it. I want to take her out, to show her off, to have people know she's with *me*. That she's mine.

And that's never happened to me before. I don't know how to handle it.

One thing I do know is I'd spend every second with her if I could, and that's unlike me. I like my personal space. I like to be alone. I spent entire days and nights alone without someone talking to me as a child. I got used to it. As I've gotten older, I've found myself having to reset my social battery, getting overstimulated by being around others. It's not like that with her. I'd be in a better mood if she was right next to me, not an entire building away.

The thought of her used to irritate me. She used to get under my skin in a way that I wanted to put states between us. Things have changed. Quickly and dramatically, in a way that I can't keep up with.

I think I have actual feelings for this woman.

I don't do feelings.

But I *want* to do feelings if they're for her.

Speaking of feelings, I look down at my vibrating phone, finding Beck's caller ID on it.

"Fuck," I mutter under my breath. He's texted me upward of ten times since our chat yesterday, which isn't typical of him. He's the friend that gives me space. He doesn't send dumb memes all day and night or send weird-ass videos he found on different apps like some of our friends.

But he's still apparently a nosy motherfucker regardless because even though I ignored his first call, he's calling again.

He's going to ask about Pippa. Which means he's going to know about my goddamn feelings for her because why else would I be in a woman's bed in the middle of the afternoon? We used to be cut from the same cloth until he met Margo. He knows the importance of what he stumbled upon yesterday.

I angrily swipe to answer it, annoyed he's intuitive. "What?" I spit, already wanting to hang up the call.

"Someone's grumpy this morning. Were you up late last night with that local friend of yours?"

"Fuck off, Sinclair," I growl, angrily clicking my computer mouse to give myself something to do.

Beck chuckles on the other line. "You knew I'd bother you until you gave me details."

"I don't remember prying into your love life when you were pining after Margo like a goddamn lost puppy. Even when you talked about her all the time, although she was dating your brother."

"We don't need to bring Carter into this. Plus, I didn't talk about her *that* much."

"You talked about her all the damn time."

"I don't know why the conversation got pointed in my direction, but we're going to circle back and talk about you, my friend. Don't think I didn't miss the fact you said love life. Is *the* Camden Hunter in love?"

I grunt. I'm not in love with Pippa. I haven't known her long enough to love her—I think. I have no prior history to know what it'd even feel like to be in love. But I do believe I've developed feelings for her. Weird, foreign feelings I've never felt before.

"No, I haven't fallen in love," I snap. "I don't know what you're talking about."

"I'm talking about the fact that you were willingly lying on a pair of sheets that seemed to have a lower thread count than your IQ."

"I told you, it was the rental."

"Margo is still ignoring me for your damn project, which means I have all the time in the world right now. So I can keep asking you questions until you eventually stop dodging them, or you could just answer me now, and we don't have to keep going back and forth."

My finger and thumb pinch the bridge of my nose. Screw him and the fact he can read me like an open book. "Do you remember when we first all came to Sutten?"

"You mean the time I got married there? Yeah, you could say I still remember it."

"Has anyone ever told you you're a dick?"

Beck laughs on the other line. "Takes one to know one. Keep going. But yes, I do, in fact, remember my wedding, thank you for asking."

"Well, remember when someone spilled beer all over me at the stupid tourist bar?"

"Yes."

"And remember when your dessert caterer ran into me and spilled cupcakes all over me?"

"I do remember hearing about that, yes."

"Turns out the woman in both those scenarios owns the neighboring business to mine. She owns the cafe next to the gallery."

"And you're seeing her? I swore I remembered Margo saying how much of an asshole you were to her."

I swallow because I do regret how awful I was to Pippa. Looking back, I don't know what my problem was, but I definitely wasn't kind to her. It's a miracle she still wants to speak to me—is allowing me to take her on a date. "Yeah, I was," I finally answer, remembering Beck waiting on the other line.

"I've got to know more about how this happened."

So for the next ten minutes, I relay everything to Beck like a couple of gossiping teenagers. He asks questions the entire time, seemingly interested in the story of me and Pippa.

At the end of it, Beck lets out a long whistle. "Damn. Never did I think I'd see the day where this happened. Your crush is cute."

If he was here in person, I'd flip him off. I do it regardless, even though he can't see me. I lean back in my office chair, staring up at the white ceiling. Even after filling Beck in on everything and talking about it out loud, I have no idea what to call what's happening.

"Fuck off, man. I'm a grown adult. I don't have a crush. I don't know what it is, but I can't get her out of my mind."

"They're called feelings, Camden. Have fun with them."

I grunt. I don't want to have feelings for Pippa, but I don't *not* want to have feelings for her either. It's a terrible situation. One I can't wrap my mind around.

"I'm going to take her on our first real date tonight," I blurt. God, I really am a little lovesick teenager. Now I'm talking about first dates at almost forty years old. This woman is too far in my head—my skin—my everything.

"Please tell me you have something romantic planned."

"She's planning it, actually."

Beck lets out a disappointed sigh. "You're making her plan the date? What the hell, man."

"She loves this town and all the little local secrets about it. I wouldn't know where to start here when planning a nice date. So yeah, asshole, I told her she could pick where, and she seemed very excited about it, thank you very much."

"If you say so." He laughs, managing to irritate me more.

"I actually don't remember asking your opinion."

"What a shame for you, then, because I'm still going to give it to you."

"Not if I hang up on you." I spin a pen in my hand, needing something to do with my hands. I'm getting anxious because the only thing I really want to do is forget about everything I need to do today and give Pippa a visit next door.

"All jokes aside, I'm happy for you. Maybe you've always needed someone who will talk back to you and isn't scared of you. I hope things work out between the two of you." He laughs again. The asshole needs to stop finding my life so comical. "I can't quite picture you settling down in Sutten, though. Are you going to get yourself a nice pair of cowboy boots? Finally ride that bull at that damn bar?"

"Oh, fuck off. We haven't been on a date yet. No one's talked about moving."

"Mhm," he hums, clearly not believing a word I'm saying. "Anyway. Care to hear my next idea?"

Beck gives me a welcome distraction by laying out the logistics for a new idea he has. It isn't terrible. Not like any of his ideas are really ever bad. I hate to admit it, but he's too smart for his own good.

He manages to distract me for almost an hour before we hang up and I'm left alone with my thoughts again. My fingers twitch at my sides as I stare at my computer screen. I'm supposed to be going through the portfolio of a new talent Leo found, but I'm not in the mood. Instead, my fingers itch to get dirty. I want to get them covered in clay. To feel the weight of a carving tool in my palm. I have a few bases ready to go at my Manhattan studio, but that's too far away. I'd never thought I'd be here long enough to need supplies.

But now, I'd do anything to have everything here to get lost in making some art. That might be the one thing that'd keep my mind from Pippa.

I'm not so lucky. But I do get a reprieve from Trisha calling me, wanting to discuss the monthly budget.

Chapter 36
PIPPA

Rosemary needs to leave. We're supposed to be closing in ten minutes, and she's sitting at a table with a basket of knitting supplies in front of her, gossiping about everything that's been happening in Sutten.

Normally, I love it when she comes in and talks with me while I close the cafe. She's hilarious, and I love to get the inside scoop on who I went to high school with, about my parents' friends, and everything else. I'm not too proud to admit that I'm an extremely nosy person. It's not my fault I feel the need to know everything about everyone at any given time.

I like gossip. Sue me.

It's just really unfortunate timing that she chose *today* of all freaking days to plant her butt in one of the chairs, expecting to stay well after closing.

"I heard that Timothy and Marietta are getting a divorce," Rosemary comments, staring at the knitting needles in her hand. She's working on some hideous sweater for one of her grandchildren—not that I'd ever tell her the mustard yellow with neon green stripes is horrid. If she asks, I'll tell her it's the most beautiful sweater in the world.

"I don't believe that," I reply anxiously, wiping down the front counter for the third time. Everything is ready for Camden to come by—except the fact that Rosemary is lingering.

Even her coffee sits only half drunk in front of her. I don't know how she drinks coffee this late and still manages to sleep, but it's none of my business. She can do whatever she wants as long as she pours that coffee in a to-go cup and skedaddles.

"I heard it on very good authority that they were. Apparently, she had an affair with someone from out of town." Rosemary's good authority is useless. I love Sutten. I love living in a small town. But the rumors can get out of hand quickly.

"I guess we'll have to wait and see," I answer, my eyes looking toward the door. Any moment, Camden could walk through them.

Talking about rumors flying, if Rosemary sees him come in here, then Camden and I will be outed to this entire town before we even get the chance to start our first date.

I don't really mind if people know. But I don't want them asking questions because I can't give any answers. Camden and I aren't boyfriend and girlfriend. But we aren't enemies anymore either. We never were really friends. Where does that leave us? I'd like to figure it out before Rosemary blabs about it to every single person in this town.

"How's your brother doing? He still sulking about our sweet Marigold being in Chicago?"

I nod while wiping down the espresso machine. "Oh, that I can actually answer on good authority. He's a mess."

"He's always loved her hard. I remember when you girls left for college. Boy oh boy, was he a fiery disaster with you both gone."

"Yeah," I mutter under my breath. Looking back, I should've known something was going on between Cade and Mare. She'd always had a crush on him, that I knew. I just really didn't think about it being possible he'd fall for her, too. When Mare and I moved to Chicago, she was so quiet at first. Quieter than normal. I thought it was because she missed her dad. Missed Sutten. But now I know it was because she and Cade were going through a breakup.

I've been asked a lot if I knew they were together, and I really didn't know. Looking back, I don't know how I didn't, but I also trusted both of them. It was my brother and my best friend. I'd figured they'd tell me if something was happening. But I don't blame them for not telling me. Sometimes you just want to keep things private. There's nothing wrong with that.

"When will Miss Marigold be coming back?" Her knitting needles click against one another as she works hard on a row of the ugly sweater.

"Hopefully soon. I don't think she'll be able to stay away from Sutten for too long this time." She'd texted me last night to check in before going back into her writing cave. The way she was talking, I'd be shocked if she didn't have the first flight back to Colorado booked the moment she turns in her manuscript and finishes whatever meetings they need her at.

"That's really for the be—" Rosemary stops midsentence. I follow her gaze until we're both gaping at Camden opening the door to the cafe.

He looks hot as hell, dressed in a button-down shirt and a pair of khakis. But that isn't what catches my attention. It's the enormous bouquet of roses in his arms. It's the most massive bouquet I've ever seen—and they're for me.

Rosemary gasps as the door shuts behind him. "I knew it!" She gawks, staring at Camden in shock. "You're getting freaky with him!"

I close my eyes, wanting to disappear from the face of the planet. This isn't happening. This can't be happening. I groan, letting one eye pop open to find Camden looking between Rosemary and me, his eyebrows drawn together in confusion.

"Excuse me?" He coughs.

"You're penetrating our dear, sweet Pippa, aren't you?"

Jesus. I don't know what's worse. Her saying "getting freaky with it" or using the word *penetrating*. They're both terrible—horrific—and the pink tinge to Camden's cheeks tells me he agrees.

Rosemary's words are so out of pocket that she's even making cool, calm, and collected Camden blush.

"Well, are you going to answer me?" Rosemary asks. She pulls her glasses down her nose, her eyebrows raised on her wrinkled forehead, waiting for Camden to answer.

He looks at me, clearly not knowing what to do in this situation. Too bad I have nothing for him. This is what nightmares are made of. I take back every single thing I ever said about loving living in a small town. This part is mortifying. Having people invested enough in your life to pry into it even when it's none of their business.

Maybe this is my karma for being nosy.

Maybe it's hearing Rosemary continue to fire questions at Camden in rapid succession—using words from the human language that should never ever be used to describe sex.

"How long have the two of you been fornicating?"

"Are you making sure to wrap your willy?"

It keeps getting worse and worse until I hold my hands in the air. "Rosemary! Can we not?"

She places her knitting supplies in her lap, pinning me with a disappointed-grandmother-type look. "I'm just asking some questions, dear."

I look at the clock above the door. "Looks like we're closed now. How about I help you gather your things? I bet Harold is waiting for you at home!"

She gives me an incredulous look. "No. You know darn well he's sleeping in his recliner, pretending to watch TV." She looks back to Camden. "You listen very closely, young man." Camden's eyes widen at the way Rosemary's voice turns stern. "If you hurt Pippa, I might just kill you. I'm old enough I could handle a few years in prison before dying there. She's gone through too much, and I don't know much about you New Yorkers. You hear me?"

"Yes, ma'am." His voice catches for a second. Is he actually scared of her?

I try to hide a grin despite the mortification seeping through my veins. This is too funny. I think sweet, old Rosemary terrifies Camden.

"I won't hurt her," he promises, his eyes finding mine for a split second.

Damn. I really like him. He's cute right now, fumbling over words under the scrutiny of Rosemary, and I'm eating it up. I like seeing this vulnerable side of him.

I'm starting to like a lot of things about him. A lot.

"I best be going now," Rosemary mutters, acting as if it was her idea to leave, as if I wasn't just begging her to disappear two minutes ago.

I try to help her, but she swats my hand away. Camden stays frozen in place. These kinds of encounters probably don't happen where he's from. Everyone is too busy with their own life to worry about yours. That isn't the case here in Sutten. Not even close.

Rosemary stops halfway to the door, her wise eyes bouncing between Camden and me. "One more thing before I go. You make sure to use that condom, you got it? Or I can ask Dr. Boone if you're on birth control, Pippa?"

A blush creeps over my cheeks just when I thought I'd gotten rid of the flush from the last outlandish thing she said. This is another terrible thing about a small town. We all share the same doctor, who hopefully wouldn't share details about my health—like my current birth control status.

"You have a great night," I squeak, pretty much pushing Rosemary out the door. I'd much prefer to forget this encounter ever happened—and for Camden to wipe it from his memory as well.

"Good night, dear," Rosemary calls over her shoulder, completely unbothered.

When the door shuts behind her, Camden looks at me, his eyes wide. "Well, that was an experience I never thought I'd have."

I let out a long, controlled breath. "Can we pretend that never happened?"

His nice shoes make a smacking sound against the floor as he walks to me, holding the flowers out between us. "Happy first date." He says the words with a hint of a smile on his lips.

They're stunning. There are too many of them to even count. When I try to hold them, it takes two hands to even grab them because the bouquet is so massive.

"No one's ever gotten me flowers," I whisper, regretting it the moment the words leave my lips. He doesn't need to know that although I've dated, no one has really even attempted to sweep me off my feet. I once had a boy give me a dandelion in the fourth grade, but other than that, there haven't been any surprise flower deliveries or flowers on the first date.

"I'd have bought you more if the florist had any left."

"Did you buy Ms. Lori out of roses?"

"I did."

"You didn't have to."

He reaches out and traces my jaw with his thumb. "I wanted to."

My heart thumps erratically in my chest, like it wants to jump right out of it and nestle right into his. It's happened so fast that I don't think too deeply into it. Things have moved quickly as we've run straight from arguing all the time to flowers on a first date. But I'm happy at this very moment, so I don't want to dwell on thinking of moments that haven't passed yet or even focus on moments that have already come to pass.

I want to think about right here and right now and whatever unexpected thing is happening with Camden.

"I love them," I tell him, leaning into his touch.

"I thought about you all fucking day," he admits, running his thumb along my bottom lip.

"Good."

"Did you think about me?" He tries to lean in, but the flowers get in the way. He lets out a grunt of disapproval, swiping the flowers from my hand and holding them at his side so nothing stands between us any longer.

"Maybe I did. Maybe I didn't."

"My guess is you did." He leans in and places a quick, chaste kiss against my lips. It seems more special than the long, heated ones we've shared for some reason.

"I guess you'll never know," I tease, running my hands up his back. His muscles tighten underneath his shirt from my touch.

"God, you're so frustrating." He kisses me again, this time swiping his tongue along the seam of my lips. "I fucking love it."

His tongue caresses mine, and suddenly, I'm melting into him. My fingers clutch his shirt to stay steady, the power from his kiss making me light-headed. He knows how to kiss. Expertly. So good that I wouldn't tell him this, but I dreamed about kissing him all day. I thought about all the things that could happen tonight. I'd messed up multiple coffee orders because I couldn't think of anything but him.

Finally, we both pull back to get some air. It feels hot in the cafe, despite me keeping the AC at a low temp. Maybe it's because my mind flashes with the memories of what happened here the other night—right up against the window behind him.

The hand of his not holding the flowers reaches down to hold my hand in his. "So what did you have planned for us?"

Chapter 37
CAMDEN

Pippa gives me a nervous smile. She shouldn't be nervous—I'd be excited about anything she planned. I just want to spend time with her. To get to know her a little bit more. To try and wrap my head around what it is about this girl that drives me fucking wild. She's always driven me wild. At first, with anger; now, it's with something else. I can't put a finger on what exactly, but there's something about her. Something different. Something special. And because of that, she could plan a date with the two of us in the middle of a cornfield, and I'd be ecstatic about it.

Although I don't know if there are cornfields in Colorado. The temperatures don't seem conducive to it, but I don't have a fucking clue.

"I thought we'd start the night here."

"Here?"

She nods. "Yes. I want to bake something together. Pasta with some other things I have planned. And then I want to take you to Pop's for dessert after."

"Funny because I think I'd much rather make *you* dessert."

She rolls her eyes at me, playfully swatting at my chest. "In case you've forgotten, you have to work for that, Mr. Hunter. You better get to it."

I kiss her cheek, gesturing for her to lead the way. She tugs on my hand, pulling me toward the back kitchen. "I really thought the roses would work in my favor. I made your Ms. Lori search her entire stockroom to make sure I got every red rose in the place. I'd actually asked for pink ones since it seems, you know..." I look around her cafe, which has pink in every direction. "You really like pink."

When we get to the back room, I find a little table placed in the corner. There's a candle at the top with the table already set.

"I could've done all this," I note, missing her touch the moment she lets go of my hand. It falls awkwardly to my side as she heads to a cabinet. I look back to the table, upset that she had to do all of this. That wasn't my intention when I told her to pick. I just thought she might want to choose the location—not set up and plan out an entire meal.

"You could've, but I wanted to. To start the night, I didn't want to share you with anyone. There's still so much I don't know about you, and I don't want to go somewhere public where everyone will be stopping at our table to snoop every two seconds."

"I was wildly unprepared for how interested people are. That Rosemary was something else earlier."

She laughs. "A little advice for you. Everyone here knows everything about anyone. If you take it public—and even sometimes when you don't—people will find out. If you wanted to keep us a secret, it's too late. Rosemary has already called up her bunco friends, book club ladies, and probably half her bible study."

"Do you think I want to keep this a secret?"

She places the flowers on a large, narrow table on the far side of the room, getting them out of the way for whatever she has planned. My heart races in my chest, anxious to hear her answer. Is she stalling? I don't want to keep it a secret. At least, I don't want to go out of my way to hide anything. I'm sure men fall at her feet in this town. I want them to know to look away. She's mine.

Is she, though? It's still too fresh to say that, but I don't give a damn. I've tasted her, gotten to know the parts of her she doesn't share with the world, and I want her as my own.

I feel awkward, standing in the middle of her small kitchen, waiting for her to answer me. Maybe I've misinterpreted things. We haven't had any conversations about what we are, but it might sting a little to find out she'd rather keep whatever is developing between us a secret from this town that she loves. I'd be proud for them to know we're seeing each other.

Are we seeing each other?

"Do you want to keep this a secret?" I press. Fuck. My heart beats so fast. Why am I so anxious? Why do I care? This hasn't ever happened. It feels like everything hangs in the balance as I watch her with bated breath, fully realizing that I might care about her far more than I'd anticipated.

"I'm not sure what this is."

"I'm not either," I confess, scratching at my chin. Do I lay it all out on the line now or keep my cards close to my chest? I never want to be the one to admit how I feel first. I like to watch people, read them, to see where their head is at before giving them any indication of what's going on in my own head. It's something I've done with work for years. I've never had to do it with a relationship because I've never cared enough. Taking a deep breath, I make my decision. And if it backfires, I'll just do the simple thing and pack up and head back to Manhattan, never to return to Sutten again. Maybe avoid Colorado altogether. "But I want more of this. More of you. More of us. And unless you want to, I don't have anything to hide. I want you, shortcake. In an intense, ferocious way I've never wanted anyone else." Another deep breath in. "And it's actually really fucking unnerving."

"Good," she whispers, her voice so soft I almost miss it.

"Good?"

She rubs her lips together. "Yes. *Good*. I want to unnerve you, Camden. I want to rip away the cold and collected front you put on for everyone else and see what you hide underneath. That way, I can find out what parts you save just for me."

I shake my head, staring at her for a few drawn-out seconds before rushing to close the distance between us. She helps me close it, her body catapulting into mine as our lips meet in a heated rush of desperation.

Our hands cling and clutch at clothes, limbs, hair, everything. We can't get enough of one another.

I'll never have enough of her.

Pippa grabs at the lapels of my shirt, her fingers fumbling with the buttons. She gets the first few undone, pressing her hand against my exposed chest. My heart beats erratically underneath her touch, further proving the words I just confessed.

"Your heart is racing so fast," she says against my lips, pressing harder.

"It always does that when I'm with you."

"Good," she repeats, smiling before leaning in to kiss me again.

I roughly grab her hips. "You think you're pretty cute saying that word, don't you?" I'm not gentle as I pull her lip between my teeth and pull, stretching it out slightly.

"Maybe." Her hands drift lower.

Her yelp echoes off the walls when I spin her, pushing her hips into the lip of the island. "I tell you that you're driving me fucking mad—stitching yourself to every single one of my thoughts—and your response is *good*?"

I reach around her, undoing the button and zipper of her jeans. I don't take my time pulling the fabric down her hips, down her legs, coaxing her to step out of each pant leg before I toss the jeans to the side.

She wears a red thong, the same color as the roses I got her. It's so goddamn sexy, cutting through her ass cheeks, teasing me as the perfect globes just ache for attention. I kiss above the high-rise fabric on her hips, kissing along the path the thong travels.

"I tell you that my heart skips a beat, completely against my will, every time I'm near you, and you have the nerve to say *good*."

I nip at her soft skin, earning a moan from her. "I'm beginning to hate that word," I mutter against. "I want more from you, shortcake. I want it all."

Her hips arch as I trail my hand up between her thighs. She steps apart of her own accord, widening her stance so I have better access to her sweet cunt. "Good." She moans when my fingers pull at the fabric between her round, perfect ass cheeks.

I smack her ass, the sound of my skin against hers ringing loud in the small space. "Two can play this game," I say, admiring the red mark I just put on her skin. I do it again, my cock stiffening at the loud moan from Pippa. She jolts, knocking over a bowl full of flour, which falls to the ground in a cloud of white powder until it covers both of us.

The mess doesn't bother me. I wipe away the flour on her ass, annoyed by it obstructing my view of the red marks I've left on her ass cheeks.

"Camden," she moans as I kiss the slightly raised skin, wanting to ease the sting.

"You like that, don't you?" I note, letting my hand drift between her legs. The fabric of her thong is soaked through. "Being punished for being a defiant little slut."

Her head falls forward, her fingertips going white from gripping the island so hard. "I—" Her words cut off when I sneak a finger underneath the triangle of fabric, running it through her wetness.

Goddamn. She's soaking wet.

"I, I—" she stammers, her back arching further from my touch. "I'm so wet," she finishes.

She can't see me, but I smirk. "Good." My finger slips inside her, inching in achingly slow.

"I know you're feeling what I'm feeling, baby." I slide another finger in, relishing in the way she tightens around my two fingers. "You can feel proud giving me one-word answers, thinking you have all the power. I'll let you have your fun." I nip at the meaty part of her ass, leaving a love bite next to my palm print. "Because your body speaks to me. It gives you away. We're in this together."

"I don't know what you're talking about," she bites, pushing her ass into me.

I shake my head. Fuck. I like it when she talks back. "Keep talking back to me, baby. It turns me on." I slide my fingers out of her, a small punishment for having the nerve to do it despite how hard it makes me.

She moans in annoyance, looking over her shoulder with anger in her eyes. "Don't stop."

Reaching around her, I grab her by the throat and bring her body flush against mine. My straining cock pushes into her ass cheeks, trying to fit itself in the seam of them. I feel her moan against my palm, the sound vibrating against my fingertips.

"Want to know why I stopped?" I force her chin up, my lips dancing across her jawline.

"Why?"

"Because I want to hear you say it." My palms run along her body, her skin raised with goose bumps, traveling to the bottom of her shirt. I lift the fabric over her head, throwing it behind me.

I like having her nearly naked with my clothes still fully on. It's hot as hell to see the difference between us.

"Hear me say what?" Her body shakes with anticipation. She jumps when my hands find her again, my fingers slipping underneath the band of her bra.

"That I drive you wild. That you think of me all damn day. That you don't hate me anymore."

"Hate's a strong word. I don't know if I ever hated you," she confesses.

"Then tell me that you feel something stronger for me now. And that it isn't hate."

She doesn't answer. In fact, she even seems to fight it so hard that her top teeth rake against her bottom lip as if she's trying to force the words from spilling from her mouth.

"I'm waiting." I slide the straps of her bra down her arms, getting rid of the fabric as soon as I can so I can feel her perfect, perky tits without anything in between us.

When she still stays silent, I pinch her nipple between my fingers, grinding my cock against her ass at the same time she lets out a loud, uncontrolled moan.

"Camden." She tries to arch into me, but I roughly push between her shoulders until her cheek is pressed against the cold counter of the island.

"Be that way," I mutter, letting one fingertip drift down her spine. She's covered in goose bumps. I don't know if it's from the press of her skin against the cold island or if it's from me. Maybe it's both.

My finger stops at the small triangle nestled right between the dimples of her back. I pull at the fabric, pulling it down her legs. She's fully bared to me now, ready for my taking.

I let my fingertip drift along the seam of her ass cheeks. She shudders.

"Has anyone ever touched you here?"

"Where?"

I apply more pressure, trailing the path again, ending in her wetness. I push inside her again, getting it nice and wet before it travels up again. "Right here," I say, pushing against a place I haven't explored on her yet.

Her face rolls against the counter, her forehead pressing into it as she stifles a moan. "No," she confesses. I don't think she realizes that she pushes her ass against me, allowing my finger a fraction of an inch inside the tight hole.

"Good." I fling the word back at her, pleased with myself.

She doesn't argue. Instead, she moans again. I lay my palm flat against her skin. One finger drifts to play with her clit while the other pushes a little deeper inside her.

"It'll be too much."

"Good," I repeat. "You've taken too much of me. It's time I take more of you." I fall to my knees, lining my face up with her perfect ass. I'll think about it in my dreams, remembering how good it looked covered in flour except for the red handprint on her delicate skin.

"Spread your legs," I demand. "Wide."

She does as she's told, spreading them, but not wide enough. I slap the inside of her thigh with the back of my hand. "More," I continue, pushing her feet even further apart.

I grab both her wrists, forcing her to grip the corner of each side of the island to keep herself steady. It's a beautiful sight having her ass on display, her cunt wet and begging for my complete attention. She watches over her shoulder with hooded eyelids, waiting for my next move.

With her in the exact position I want her in, I bring myself to her sweet cunt once again. My tongue circles her clit, my eyes closing with how good she tastes.

She tastes like mine. Like no other man should ever have the right to have her again.

While my tongue caresses her pretty cunt, my hands find either side of her ass cheeks, spreading them slightly to expose her. She moans when I let my fingertip drift over it again.

"You dirty girl," I muse, coating my finger in her wetness. "You like it when I play with your ass?"

She doesn't answer me, but I wasn't expecting her to. I've learned enough about her to know not to expect an answer. Once I feel like my finger is nice and wet, my mouth seals to her clit once again. My tongue and finger play with her, making her hips buck with pleasure.

I don't let up until her legs shake. The nice thing would be to have her come against my tongue. But I'm not a nice man. So right when I feel like she's close to coming, I pull away and stand up. She moans in protest, her head rocking back and forth.

"No," she pleads, trying to find friction by pushing her ass against me.

I step back, marveling at the sight of her. She's wet between her legs from her own pleasure and my mouth. I admire the view, finishing unbuttoning my shirt and pulling my arms from the sleeves. She waits for me to touch her again as I fold the shirt nicely and place it on the counter nearest to me.

"Don't move," I command when she begins to push the top half of her body off the island. "Let me keep looking at you."

She does as she's told, but not without a defiant rock of her hips against the lip of the counter.

I take my time undoing my belt, pulling it from my belt loops and rolling it up nicely before placing it on top of my folded shirt. I strip from my shoes, pants, and boxer briefs, finally as naked as she is.

I fist my cock, needing the relief immediately as I take a few extra moments to gaze at her. She's fucking perfect. She looks vulnerable, watching me through hooded eyelids as she antici-pates what's to come.

"Your cunt is dripping," I tell her, looking at the wetness coating between her thighs. "Does that mean I've worked hard enough for it, baby?"

She nods. I knew she wouldn't be able to resist this thing between us. I've had her since the moment we shared in this very building, but I don't tell her that. I let her believe she's the one in control.

"Good," I get out, taking a step closer. My cock jerks eagerly when it runs along the line of her ass.

I give her a small smack on her ass again, nowhere near the amount of pressure I had used before, but it's still hard enough for flour to fly in the air around us from it.

"Now, stand exactly like this as I fuck you until I get the answers I want. That you're gone for me like I am for you."

Chapter 38
PIPPA

My entire body shakes with anticipation. My arms are stretched as far as they can go in a wide wingspan, my fingers clutching the corners of the counter to keep myself up.

All I want to do is turn around and pull Camden into me. I want to feel his body flush against mine. To wrap my legs around him and dig my heels into the muscles right above his hips as he rocks into me. But I don't because I'm turned on by the way he tells me what to do. He's incredibly commanding, and it fuels my desire further. When he runs the tip of his cock through my wetness, I let out a loud moan, eager to feel him slip inside.

He teases me, circling my clit with his cock but never quite pushing in where I need him.

"Camden," I moan, needing more of him. Needing to finally feel him inside me.

"I want to feel all of you." His voice comes out forced, as if he's speaking through a locked jaw. Maybe it's taking all of him to show the restraint he is. "Tell me you're on the pill. I will wear a condom otherwise, but I don't want to put a barrier between us."

"I am. I don't either." I pant, arching into him to try and coax him inside me. It doesn't work, but I do hear him suck in a breath from the feeling.

At least I'm not alone in the pure lust and desperation I feel right now.

"Good." He pushes a little further, already stretching me when only the head of his cock is inside me. "Fuck, baby, you're squeezing me so hard."

I moan, my eyes squeezing shut from the overwhelming sense of him. He's everywhere all at once, with his cock pushing into me, his fingers digging into my hips, keeping me right where he wants me. His weight falls on me, his front pushing into my back as he slips inside.

He curses under his breath again. It's too much. He's too big. "I can't," I pant, even though my body does the opposite, pushing against him to push him deeper inside. "You're too big," I finish.

His palm smacks against my ass again. I feel myself clench around him in pleasure from it. I've never had someone be rough with me in the bedroom. My sex life has always been as vanilla as it comes. This isn't vanilla—and I've never been more aroused. I love the bite of his skin against mine as he strikes the delicate skin as a punishment. The careful way he watches me after, his palm soothing the pain as he makes sure he's not doing anything I don't want him to do.

"You will take me like the good little whore you are. You got that?" To prove a point, he shoves all the way inside me, no longer letting me adjust around him slowly.

I take a deep breath in, using the slight stall of his movements to my advantage to take a breath. It hurts. He's far larger than anything I've ever had, but it feels incredibly good. When he slowly pulls back, I can't help but moan.

"You're doing such a good job taking my cock, baby." He slides in and out a few more times before he shocks me by ripping his body away from mine. He doesn't leave me any time to complain. Before I can do anything, he's lifting my body, turning me in midair and setting me on the island. It's cold against my bare ass, but I love being face-to-face with him again.

He dives in for a kiss, kissing me with so much desperation and passion that for a moment, it takes my breath away. I don't know how to exhale the air in my lungs. All my body can do is think of the way his kiss owns me. I've never felt the red-hot passion that I feel with him. It's been seconds since he's been inside me, and I already miss him. Luckily, he must feel the same way because he's forcing my legs open and fitting his narrow hips between my thighs.

"You come around my cock when I tell you to," he commands, pushing into me once again. "And you save your energy because I have so much planned for you."

"What about the date I planned?"

"I'll make sure it still happens. But not until you've come again and again and I say you're done."

He pulls me across the island until I'm seated on the very edge of it. His hands grab at my hips, keeping me steady as he picks up the pace. He's too big, and it feels like too much. Between my thighs stings from how wide he stretches me, how deep he pushes in.

It's all too much, but at the same time, it isn't nearly enough. I'm not sure anything would ever be enough. Our first time isn't even over yet, and I know he's laid claim to my body forever. There's no way another person will ever fit as perfectly as he does.

He picks up speed until it's a punishing pace. I'm lost in watching his every reaction. He's fucking me like he's lost all sense of control. Like he can't get ahold of any of his actions, and it's his body doing all of the talking.

I love it.

My head falls backward as a satisfied smile spreads over my lips. I've made Camden Hunter lose control. I've never felt more powerful from the realization, even if I'm losing just as much control as he is. The difference is I'm always a person who loses control. I find it fun to let loose. Camden isn't the same. It feels even more special to see him unravel like this. To lose himself completely to the magic our bodies are creating.

"Fuck, shortcake." He buries his face in the crook of my neck. His breath is hot along my skin, his kisses against it warm and tender. "You're taking my cock so well. You're molding around me, your body proving that your pussy is meant for me and only me." His teeth rake along my skin, but he doesn't sink them into the tender flesh. His mouth is sweet and gentle along my neck. His hips are the opposite. The sound of smacking skin fills the room.

He catches my mouth with his, plunging his tongue inside. We taste each other's moans, my hands circling his neck to try and keep my body steady. He fucks me so hard I'm close to falling off the counter. Not that I think he'd actually let that happen.

His fingers tangle in my hair, pulling on it to force my back to arch. "In case I haven't made it clear," he adds, slowing down. This new pace overwhelms me. It's slow and passionate, firing off so many nerve endings in my body.

I'm about to come. The pressure builds low in my core, threatening to spill over in pure ecstasy.

"Camden," I plead, remembering what he said about waiting until he told me to. I don't think I can stop it from happening. It feels too good and too intense to stop.

"You're squeezing me so hard. It's greedy and sexy as hell."

I moan again, my skin prickling with pleasure from the building orgasm. "I'm going to—"

He pauses, making my eyes pop open because this is the second time he's brought me right to the edge, only to yank me away from it.

His cocky smile is almost enough to send me over the edge anyway. Sweat beads at his brow from the exertion. He's so incredibly beautiful. So sexy. But he'd be a lot hotter if he let me come.

"You're an asshole," I moan, bucking my hips to try and get friction. He holds steady inside me, not giving me what I want.

"Ask for it nicely." The cocky smirk doesn't leave his lips. He does pick up pace, but barely. Just enough to tease me even further.

"I need to come," I beg, circling my hips.

Air hisses through his teeth, his jaw tightening with restraint. "You'll come, baby. Multiple times. But not until you ask me nicely to make my cock all messy from your cum."

Jesus. His mouth is dirty. I feel like I need to go to church after this to wash the filthy words from my mind. I'd never do it. I want to remember the naughty words he uttered. Even the dirty words are another reminder of how perfect, put-together Camden can lose control.

"Please, I need to come," I pant, my fingers tangling in his hair to pull his face to mine.

All it earns me is another satisfied smirk, the upturned corners of his mouth only an inch from my lips. "Yes, my girl needs to come. Good job asking for it nicely." He seats himself completely in me, stealing my surprised yelp straight from my mouth. He pulls away slightly, choosing a pace that easily has the pressure building all over again. "Come all over my cock. Let me feel it."

His words send me over the edge. Even with his tongue in my mouth, my moans still echo between us. There are so many sensations that tears prick my eyes. It's the most intense orgasm I've ever felt, and it isn't even over yet.

Camden milks the orgasm for all it's worth, his pace never relenting.

When my eyes finally drift open, I find him watching me closely. "That was the sexiest thing I've ever seen," he mutters. "I want to see it again."

Chapter 39
CAMDEN

Pippa's cunt spasms around me. It hugs me tight, keeping me locked inside pure heaven. Her moans are loud and powerful as she comes down from her orgasm. I think I've become addicted to making her come. I could do it again and again until the entire day has gone by with me between her legs.

My hand snakes up her body until I wrap my fingers around her throat. I press my palm against the hollow it, wanting to feel every single one of her breaths and moans against my skin.

I slow my hips, circling them slightly as a change of pace. She must like it because her moan vibrates against my calloused fingers.

"Like that," she pants, lifting her hips to try and guide me.

"You don't tell me what to do," I growl, circling my hips again despite my words.

Her head falls backward, giving me more of her smooth skin. I want to squeeze, to see how deep she lets me push my fingertips until it's too much for her.

Our bodies move against one another. It's sticky and sweaty. Flour is now coating both of us. All it'd take is for me to pick up the pace and pound into her, and I know I'd be coming in seconds. She feels too fucking good.

"You were made for me." My lips move against her skin, not knowing where to go. I want all of her at once. I want everything.

My grip on her throat tightens slightly, testing to see her reaction. She moans louder, only prompting me to grip even tighter. My hand seems so large compared to her slender neck. It wraps around her so easily, giving me so much power as my fingertips dig into her skin.

She watches me, her eyes telling me she's enjoying this as much as I am.

"If only everyone knew that sweet Pippa likes to be fucked rough and dirty. That she is such a little slut that when I choke her, her pussy clutches me so tight it's almost painful."

Her face turns red, but I know from her breath that tickles my cheeks that she's still able to get some air, no matter how small it is. I'd stop if she wasn't moaning so loudly, her pussy taking me so greedily that I know she gets off by this.

When I'm not fucking her, she's mouthy and defiant, constantly pushing my buttons. But when we're like this, she likes to give up the power. To have her limits tested.

"Cam—" Her words get cut off when I roughly push inside her.

"You're so fucking sexy with my hand around your throat and my cock deep in your pussy. You like feeling me everywhere, baby?"

Tears prick her eyes, her pulse jumping underneath my fingertips. This thrills her, which makes me go wild. All I can think about is fucking her harder, filling her with more of me, marking her body—and maybe even her heart—so there's no way she could ever forget what it's like between us.

"Just wait until I fill you with my cum. Then you'll really be full of me. And you'll love it, won't you?"

Her eyes flutter closed with a loud moan. Fuck, I'd prefer to pull more orgasms from her before I come, but I'm too close. I've never been as turned on as I am at this moment. She has that pull on me. I'm intoxicated with every single facet of her existence. No matter how hard I fight it, I feel the tightening of my balls, the prickles down my spine. I'm going to come, and there's no way I'll let it happen without feeling her spasm around me one more time.

"It's time for you to come again," I demand, pulling her lips to mine. I still squeeze hard enough that she has to gasp for air, but I give it to her from my own lungs instead. I pound into her with a punishing rhythm. The sound of skin slapping fills the tiny kitchen. It's so fucking sexy to hear our bodies jolting against one another, to hear her moans mixed with mine. Even the kiss is so heated and sloppy that you can hear it fill the room.

Will I ever get enough of her? I don't think so. No other feeling in the world could ever compare to this.

I shove my tongue in her mouth, reveling in how she greedily opens up for me. I'm always wanting more from her, but she's wanting more from me, too. She's greedy and needy, and I fucking love it.

"Be a good girl and come on my cock," I persist. "I want to feel you come so hard that you make *me* come." Sweat drips down my back as I pick up speed, circling my hips slightly because I know that's what she likes. She hangs off the counter at this point, relying on my body pressing into hers to keep her from sliding off.

"And I want you to moan so loud I not only hear it, I feel it against my fingertips."

Another pump in and out of her, the muscles in my back tightening from the upcoming orgasm. "Now," I grit out, knowing I'll be coming in seconds.

I know she's close when her thighs begin to quiver around my waist. Moments later, she tightens around me, a low moan coming from deep in her throat.

"Good girl," I growl before going in for a deep kiss.

My skin heats as I come with her, filling her completely. My tongue in her mouth, my hand around her throat, my cock deep inside her, filling her full of my cum.

It's the hottest moment of my life. The only thing hotter is when our foreheads crash against one another, the two of us trying to catch our breaths from the intensity of what just happened.

I click my tongue, pulling my cock free and finding my cum spilling from her. "I said you'd be full of me," I note, pushing my cum back inside her. "And you'll *stay* full of me." She jumps when my fingers run over her clit. God, even though she just came, I wonder if I brushed against it again, would she let me? Could I get her to come again with just my fingers?

It's tempting. Incredibly tempting. I'm about to try when she finally speaks, her hands rubbing at her throat where my hand just was. "I need a minute," she rasps. Her shoulders rise and fall in rapid succession. Mine do the same. That was the greatest workout of my life. I wouldn't have to meet with my trainer ever again if I could just do cardio by fucking Pippa for the rest of my life.

Her body goes limp as her head falls against my shoulder. She wraps her arms around me, pulling me close. There are probably a thousand different health code violations we're breaking, but I lean into her despite the mess between us.

"That was..." Her words trail off as she presses a kiss right on top of my racing heart. It races because that was the best sex of my life—but also because I'm imagining myself doing that with her for the rest of my life, and that's a dangerous fantasy for two people who started out despising one another.

"Incredible. Mind-blowing..." I brush my hands through her hair as she presses another kiss to my beating heart. "Catastrophic," I whisper.

She looks up at me with wide, curious eyes. My eyes can't help it when they drift to the red mark around her throat for a moment. "Why catastrophic?" she asks.

I pull her into me, tugging her off the counter. She gladly wraps her legs around me. We're perfectly lined up against one another again, the head of my cock brushing against her clit.

My hands cup her ass cheeks, keeping her in place as she rakes her eyes over my face. I want to know what she sees. Is it a different man than she first thought I was? Or deep down, does she have the same opinions of me that have always been there?

"Because I think I want to do that a lot more, for a long time, and I don't even know if you like me, shortcake."

Her thighs wrap tighter around me. "I think I'm starting to like you more," she answers playfully, a wry smile on her lips.

"Are you only saying that because my cum is leaking out of you?"

She smiles even wider at my question. *Dirty girl.* I fucking love it. "No. I was thinking it before tonight, but the *great* sex did help your case."

I playfully nip at her, clutching her to my chest. I want to keep her in my arms forever, to never let go. Maybe then, the real world would never catch up with us and remind us why a sweet small-town girl like her and a cold city guy like me aren't meant to last. "I think a better adjective is needed. *Great* isn't doing it for me."

She slides down my body, and I hold on to her until her feet are firmly planted on the ground. Even then, she keeps her arms wrapped around my middle. I like it—too much. "What would you like to hear, then?"

"That it was the best sex of your life. That you'll never let another man have you that way. That the rush of emotions coursing through you right now are as intense for you as they are for me."

I like how comfortable she is standing in front of me, completely naked. She takes a step back, playing with strands of her hair as she watches me closely. "All of the above," she whispers.

I don't know if I've ever smiled as wide as I do at this very moment. It's probably goofy and takes up too much of my face, but I can't help it. I'm captivated by her, and I need to know it isn't just me feeling this way.

My mind races with a million different things I could say back to her, but only one word comes to mind as I take a step closer to her and press a kiss to her forehead.

"Good."

Chapter 40
PIPPA

I'm busy plating our dinner when Camden casually looks up at me from across the island. I haven't told him this, but he's got a smear of flour across his forehead from when we were making the noodles. It's too cute to have him wipe it away. I like the little imperfection across his face. It makes him look less cold and intimidating and more boyish.

He couldn't look cold to me right now either way. Not with the way he's looking at me. Everything about the way he's watched me cook has been lit with passion. His stare isn't cold. It's hot, burning my skin even from across the room. I almost asked him to fuck me right in the middle of rolling out the dough for the noodles because the ripples of his forearms were turning me on too much. Even when I'd asked him to try the pasta sauce, his lips had sucked the sauce into his mouth so seductively that I'd imagined the other places his mouth had been. All the places along my skin he's licked, kissed…bit.

A small laugh from deep in his throat pulls me from my dirty thoughts. I look down to find a little too much cheese grated on the dish in front of me.

"Shit," I mutter, trying to pinch some of the cheese from this plate and putting it on the noodles from the other. It doesn't look as good as it was supposed to, but it'll do.

"You were licking your lips like you were having dirty thoughts about me, shortcake."

"Maybe I was."

He raises his eyebrows, pouring more wine into my glass at the table. We haven't even eaten dinner yet, and tonight has been the best date of my life. The sex before the date really even started helped. But it was also the easy conversation as we prepared the three courses I'd planned for the night. He'd listened intently as I told him how to help prepare a salad and crab cakes. He was an excellent student as I taught him how to roll out the noodles and feed them through the noodle attachment on my mixer.

I thought things would get awkward after we finally had sex. Like maybe we'd both learn that our intense connection was only physical. Tonight taught us it isn't. The more I've learned about him, and the more random conversations we had on what NFL team is the best—the Broncos, obviously—and what the best Adam Sandler movie is—his answer of *Click* shocked me— the more compatible we seem.

All of it is adding up to me falling for him little by little. I can easily imagine making him coffee in the morning before he lays me out and has *me* for breakfast.

"Are there security cameras in here?" Camden's question brings me back from my daydream.

I cock my head, wiping a smear of sauce from the corner of the plate. "What?"

His eyes look to the ceiling, scanning the place. "Are there cameras in here?"

"How did you know we had cameras anywhere?"

"Because your employee, Lexi, caught me enjoying that perfect pussy of yours on camera."

My hand drops in shock, hitting the corner of the plate and sending smears of pasta sauce all over. "Excuse me, what?" I shriek.

There's no way Lexi saw us. Right? Oh my god. Has she seen my vagina?

The asshole doesn't look embarrassed by it in the slightest. If anything, he looks proud as he continues to look around the room. "Yeah, I forgot to mention it to you. Figured it was best you didn't know. But after tonight, I just needed to know if we just accidentally made an amateur porno."

"Camden!" I yell, my face heating with embarrassment. Thank god there aren't any cameras in here. I haven't found it necessary —and haven't really wanted to put the funds into getting an additional camera—so this and my office, which used to be a closet, don't have cameras. "This isn't funny," I continue, thinking about whether I should text Lexi to apologize for whatever she saw.

He shrugs, his shoulders rising and falling. "I'm not laughing." He coughs, totally lying because he's absolutely laughing.

"Yes you are. My employee saw my bits! This is terrible. Is there some kind of law against this? Am I going to get sued?"

He brings my glass of wine over, handing it to me. I suck down a large gulp of it to try and ease my mortification. "She stopped it before she saw anything. She was only looking because you'd forgotten to lock the door, and she wanted to make sure no one broke in."

I take another drink, squeezing my eyes shut as I pray to god that I didn't ruin Lexi forever. I'm going to have to have a very awkward conversation with her and apologize for whatever she did end up seeing.

"God, I can't believe you didn't tell me that. I'll never be able to look at her the same."

"It's okay. She didn't see anything. And even if she did, I bet my face covered anything intimate, anyway. I was very dedicated to making you…"

"Okay, that's enough," I interrupt, not wanting to picture it again. I don't want to think too hard about everything she could've seen.

"So are there cameras in here?"

"No."

He whistles, watching as I take another drink of my wine. At this point, I've almost sucked down the entire glass in under a minute. "What a shame."

I almost spit my wine out at his words. "What?" I wipe at the corner of my mouth from where the wine drips from my lips from the shock.

"I look at that little photo of you often, the one of you in the hot-as-fuck lingerie—which you'll have to wear for me soon, by the way." He says it so nonchalantly as he grabs both our dinner plates and walks them over to the small table in the corner of the kitchen. "I was kind of hoping we caught all of that on tape. I wouldn't mind fucking you while us fucking played in the background."

My jaw hangs open. There's too much to process at once. "You look at that photo of me?" I question, needing that answered first.

He pulls out one of the chairs, standing behind it and gesturing for me to take a seat. I untie my apron, pulling the top loop over my head and placing it on the counter. I'm still waiting for him to answer, even as I take a seat and let him push my chair in.

His eyes are pinned on mine as he takes the seat across from me, pouring more wine into my glass but a little less this time. He doesn't look embarrassed by what he's told me. "Why else do you think I sent it to myself?"

"I don't know. To blackmail me?"

He sighs loudly, clearly not amused by my answer. "No. That was *never* my intention. It was because I felt pure, jealous rage at the idea of anyone else seeing you like that. And I fought it, but I think even then, I wanted you more than I'd cared to admit."

"I would've let you kiss me that day. On the mountain at my family's ranch. I thought it was going to happen."

His dark eyebrows are pulled in on his forehead. He stares at me silently for so long I wonder if he's not going to acknowledge what I said. His finger traces over his top lip as he thinks his words through.

"I wanted to, but I thought I'd hate myself if I did."

His words sting a little, but it doesn't mean I don't understand them. It would've been the same for me. There was still so much uncertainty between us—there still kind of is, but in a different way—it's best we didn't kiss that day.

"It hurt. To have you leave like that."

I don't know how I once thought that Camden was a cold, emotionless man. Sitting across from me right now, he wears so much emotion on his face. It's clear how well he's trained himself to hide it. He's hurt me before, and there's a good chance he'll hurt me again, but I'll always remember that for some amount of time—however long that may be—he let his guard down for me. That I got to see the real Camden Hunter and not the one he wants the world to see. Not the son of two of the most famous artists of our time. Not one of the wealthiest art dealers in the world. Just Camden. The man who takes care of me when I'm sick and brings me flowers on our first date. The one who complains about how cold my feet are against his in the middle of the night but still presses his against mine to keep them warm. The one who woke up and let Kitty out early in the morning because she was whining, and he wanted me to get more rest.

I like this version of him. A lot. And all I can do is keep letting myself feel these emotions and hope I don't get burned in the end. Or if I do, that it'll be worth it.

"What are you thinking?" I whisper. He hasn't responded to what I admitted. I didn't tell it to him to make him feel bad. I just wanted him to know that even then, he had more of a pull on me than I wanted to admit, even to myself.

"That it fucking guts me to know I've hurt you."

There's no way he doesn't hear me gasp. His words catch me

off guard. They're sweet and vulnerable and most of all raw. All things I never imagined Camden being.

"It's okay. It was silly of me to feel hurt after that."

"Your feelings are never silly, shortcake." His voice breaks slightly. It does things to me. I feel the impact of his words deep in my chest.

Chapter 41
CAMDEN

I'VE BEEN TO SOME OF THE MOST EXTRAVAGANT PLACES IN THE world. I've had a casual date at a cafe in front of the Eiffel Tower and dined late into the night at a table on a cobblestone street with a view of the Amalfi Coast. No date has ever compared to the night I'm having with Pippa.

She licks eagerly at the ice cream cone in her hand, trying to keep up with the drips of melted ice cream running down her fingers. It's the most adorable thing seeing her do it, but it also makes me incredibly horny. Her tongue peeks out to get a drip that runs down her hand. She can't eat the ice cream cone fast enough, even after she'd sworn that she wanted two scoops on top of the cone instead of one. Rainbow sprinkles keep falling off the top, unable to stick to the melting cookies-and-cream ice cream.

I can't help but laugh when a glob drips off the top, landing on top of her thumb.

She gives me an evil glare, licking it. "This isn't funny."

I grab her wrist, pulling her closer. I maintain eye contact as I lean down and lick from her forearm all the way up her hand.

Her eyes go wide, darting around to look at the people around us as I do it again on the opposite side of her arm, getting her nice and clean.

"Camden," she scolds, trying to pull from my grasp.

My fingers tighten. I make sure to wait until she looks back at me, her cheeks pink with embarrassment, as I stick my tongue out and lick the top of the ice cream before it melts over again. Her gaze heats when I repeat it, knowing *exactly* where her head is at. It's the same place mine is—thinking of the dirty, delicious things I could do to her instead of this ice cream cone.

"People are staring," she whisper-shouts. Her eyes dart around our surroundings again. I smirk because there are tons of people around us. Apparently, tonight is the night to grab ice cream at the small little shop in town. We waited twenty minutes in line just to get our ice cream. And now, we mill around the town square with what seems like the rest of the town.

"Let them stare," I answer lowly, licking a small drip running down the back of her hand.

"They're going to know we—" I cut off her words by catching her lips with mine. She tastes sweet, like ice cream and cookies. When her tongue eagerly meets mine—despite her argument of people watching us—it's cold and sweet.

We get lost in the moment, making out like a couple of teenagers, not caring who is around us.

Pippa lets out a squeak, pulling away and looking down at her arm. Ice cream drips all the way down it. I wish I could bottle up her giggle and keep it forever. "Oh my god," she mutters, attempting to use the one napkin they gave her to wipe up the mess.

She walks a few steps, throwing the ice cream cone into the trash. She continues to try and use the napkin to clean herself up before I reach into my pocket and hand her a pile I took from the counter. "I grabbed some extras. I figured that extra scoop you told the man you had to have could make things messy."

Her smile is bright and radiant as she snatches them from my hand, wiping her arm and cleaning up the mess. "What would I do without you?" she teases.

I hope you never find out.

I keep my lips pressed together so I don't say the words out loud. I've admitted enough tonight. More than I ever imagined I would. Before I say anything else, I need to figure out what's going on in my head when it comes to her—and maybe even my stupid heart, something I didn't even know I had.

We pass by groups of people, all of them stopping Pippa to try and talk to her. She politely answers their questions, but she's good at ending the conversation early and moving forward. It's not lost on me that I don't love how she introduces me as her friend. I've never been her friend, and she's acting like everyone here doesn't have eyes and just didn't see us with our tongues down the other's throat.

I keep my mouth shut because there's not much I could really say. We're not boyfriend and girlfriend. We'd need to be more serious for that, and I don't know if that's what she wants. I know I don't plan on even breathing in the same direction as another woman—it'd be no use. They'd never compare to the grip Pippa has on me. But does she feel the same way? Is there some man in this town who's pining over her, just waiting for her to look their way? Is there someone here who's broken her heart before? That she's desperately waiting for him to look at her?

These are the thoughts that plague me as we walk along the dimly lit sidewalk. The gallery and cafe aren't too far from us, but they're in the opposite direction. I don't know where she's taking me, but I just follow her lead, too caught up in wondering if it's too soon to ask her to be my girlfriend.

She must feel me go silent because she weaves her arm through mine and places her head against my shoulder. "Aren't you going to ask where we're going?"

I stare ahead, not really caring where we go. I'm too lost in thinking about what happens next for us. What do I want? What's realistic? Most importantly…what does *she* want?

Pippa stops, turning to face me with her eyebrows raised.

"You're quiet. And not in the normal *I'm Camden Hunter, and I'm broody* kind of way," she mocks, her voice going deep in a terrible impression of me. "But more like you're in your head kind of way."

I need to touch her and feel her skin against mine. Without any excuse, I reach out and brush my thumb along her cheek. She leans into it almost immediately. "I just got lost for a minute." I look around us. "Where are you taking me, shortcake?"

She gives me a questioning glare for a few seconds before her face lights up with a smile. God, my heartbeat picks up at the sight of her smile. It's radiant. I want to pull out my phone and capture it forever, wanting to always remember her looking at me this way.

"I'm taking you for a redo," she states matter-of-factly.

My head cocks to the side. "A redo?"

I should be scared of the mischievous gleam in her eye. It can't be good for me. She stuffs her hands in the pocket of my jacket, pulling me by the fabric to her. "Yeah, a redo. At Slopes. You're going to make a better first impression on me."

"I think first impressions are long gone. I've felt you come against my tongue."

Her eyes bulge, her hand coming up and slapping against my mouth as she looks around us. There isn't anyone within earshot, but she checks just in case. I smirk underneath her touch. God, it's so fun ruffling her feathers and making her blush.

"Do it for me," she pleads, looking at me with puppy dog eyes. I think I'd give her anything she wanted if she kept looking at me with those wide, adorable eyes. "I want to go up to the bar alone and have you slip behind me minutes later. I want you to buy me a beer—one that doesn't get spilled. And then, if you're lucky, I'll say yes to a dance with you."

"What if I don't dance?"

"You will for me."

"You aren't wrong."

She beams at me, breathing life into my chest. I used to think it was cold, dark, and empty where my heart should be. The only person I ever really truly loved is Gran—and maybe Beck. But I thought it'd forever be desolate for a woman. It turns out I think it was just waiting for Pippa.

Before anything else is said, she loops her fingers through mine and pulls me toward the last place I want to be. I tried getting out of coming here the first time for hours. Beck wouldn't hear any of it—more like Margo wouldn't. It was their joint bachelor and bachelorette party, and Margo was determined to come to the country tourist bar. If anyone ever wanted to interrogate me, they could probably lock me in the bar for days, and I'd lose my mind. I don't do country music, and I don't do people in cheesy cowboy hats. Yet here I am, letting Pippa pull me toward the bar without any complaints.

If she wants a redo, I'll give her one. It'd be good for us. I wish all the time I could take back the things I said to her in annoyance the first time we met. I was being an ass because I didn't want to be there, and I took it out on her. This time, I'll do better. I'll buy her the cheap, nasty beer because she wants me to. I'll pull her onto the dance floor, even though the classical technique I was taught as a child isn't anything like the goofy line dancing that was happening last time we were here. I'll let her teach me how to do the dances with all the cowboy wannabes. Then I'll pull her off the dance floor and back her into a dark corner and show her how our first meeting should've gone.

Pippa eagerly jumps up and down as we wait in a small line to get in. "We need to get you a cowboy hat!" she declares.

I groan, shaking my head violently. "I draw the line at a cowboy hat."

She sticks out her bottom lip in a pout. "You can't go to Slopes without a cowboy hat."

"Sure you can. I've done it before. Plus, I don't see you wearing one."

She rolls her eyes, smiling at someone in front of us who says her name.

The cowboy hat argument is dropped for a moment as we're let inside. It's busy, but not as busy as it was when I came for Beck's bachelor party.

Beck can *never* find out I came back. He'd never let me hear the end of it. This will be a secret I take to my grave.

The smile on Pippa's face as she leads me deeper into the bustle of the night makes me forget how much I hate this place. If she's happy, then I'm happy. Even if it smells way too much like BO and cheap beer. I'd much rather be back at one of our houses with my face buried between her thighs.

She spins to look at me, eagerness on her face. "Okay, I'm going to go to the bar. In five minutes, you're going to pretend we're strangers and ask to get me a drink."

"If another man tries to talk to you in that time frame, I'll kill them."

She pushes against my chest, rolling her eyes dramatically. "No one's going to come up to me, Camden. Just you."

I let out a low growl, but I don't know if she hears it. I don't think she realizes how stunning she is. Of course a man is going to try and speak to her. Just look at her.

She leaves me standing there alone, watching her shimmy her way to the bar. I stand against the wall, not taking my eyes off her. She's too sexy for her own good. She's far too dressed up for the bar tonight—we both are—which brings even more attention to her. I eye everyone around, and my fist clenches at my side when I notice a man staring her down from across the bar. He's paying far too much attention to my girl for my liking. I try to ignore it because when I look back at her, she hasn't noticed him. She's lost in her own world, chatting with the bartender. They look friendly, but the man behind the bar she speaks to looks safe. He looks at her with fondness, not attraction.

I peek at my watch, finding it's only been one minute since she went to the bar. How the hell am I supposed to stand here for four more minutes? Maybe I can go there now. Surely she doesn't know the exact time I'm supposed to meet her at the bar.

I'm telling myself I'll give it two more minutes when a man slides in next to her.

Oh, hell no. This man doesn't look safe. He lets his hand brush down her back, pulling her into a hug that's way too fucking friendly for my liking. I push myself off the wall, heading in their direction. Fuck the five minutes.

I force myself in between them, leaning over the bar in both of their views.

"What do we have here?" I growl, my eyes boring into Pippa's.

"Hey, man, we're busy," the asshat trying to talk to Pippa says.

I let out a disapproving hum, not looking away from Pippa. "She's not interested."

The guy gawks, a weird sound coming from his throat. "Do you know this guy, Pip?"

Does she know me? "I'd say so. She was coming around my co—"

"No, Chase, I don't know him," Pippa interrupts, giving the guy an apologetic smile.

You've got to be kidding me. My blood boils with jealous rage. She'd told me she wanted to play this little game and pretend we didn't know each other, but that was before some country prick started looking at her like he was imagining her naked.

"Maybe we should go somewhere else," the guy—Chase, apparently—offers, brave enough to put his hand over Pippa's.

I see red. Wrapping my hand around her middle, I pull her closer to me. "Let me buy you a beer," I growl. The words are angry, sending a shiver down Pippa's back.

"What the hell," Chase calls, trying to wrap his fingers around Pippa once again. She drops her hand from his, fighting his attempts.

Good girl.

"Who are you?" I bite.

"Her ex. Who are you?"

My eyebrows rise as I look back at Pippa. "Ex?" My words come out cool and full of venom.

This just got a lot more interesting.

Chapter 42
PIPPA

"FUNNY. SHE NEVER REALLY MENTIONED HER EXES. EXCEPT FOR THE fact they couldn't make her c—"

"Alright, well, I'm going to order a beer," I interrupt Camden, not wanting to hurt Chase's feelings. He's sweet; he just wasn't for me. Not that I'd ever consider him an ex. No matter what, I don't want him to be bullied by Camden because he's jealous.

He's really freaking hot when he's jealous. A vein has popped up on the middle of his forehead. He's tense all over, his jaw muscles showing off with ripples every time he clenches his jaw.

"A Miller?" Chase asks, trying to get the attention of the bartender.

I feel Camden's deep growl against my back. I try to hide the shiver that runs down my body with excitement.

Damn. Why do I love jealous Camden so much?

Before I can answer, Camden has already gotten the attention of another bartender and is ordering. "Two Stellas," he clips, handing over a hundred-dollar bill.

"I'll get you your change," Linna responds. She was two grades older than me in high school and one of my favorite bartenders here at Slopes. She knows how to make a mean limoncello shot. Good enough to make me hungover for days after a few.

"Don't worry about it. Keep it."

She looks at him wide-eyed. That's a hefty tip, but I keep my mouth shut. Even when Chase lets out an annoyed sigh from my other side.

"You don't even like Stella," he mutters under his breath.

I actually love Stella. I just always order the cheap shit because I could have two beers for the price of one. I'm all about saving money. Beer is beer. But I'll never turn down a more flavorful, expensive beverage.

"You can go now," Camden drawls, his hand tightening around my waist again. "She's not interested."

His hand around my waist is possessive. I feel bad because I've lied to Chase and made it out like Camden and I are strangers when we're anything but. I don't change my story because I want to pretend that Camden and I don't know each other so we can get that redo. Chase is just a casualty of it.

Chase stares at me, probably waiting for me to tell Camden off. I don't. Instead, I give him a friendly smile. "I'll call you later?" I offer politely.

"She won't," Camden counters from behind me. I give him a dirty look. Jealous Camden is something else.

Chase holds eye contact for a few moments longer before he backs away with his arms in the air. I groan, knowing he's probably already texting my brother and telling him about this encounter. I don't think Cade will say anything, however. He's too busy killing himself getting things ready for the winter and pining over Mare. But it might be an interesting conversation if somehow he does pay attention and asks me what's happening between me and the guy I brought to the ranch.

As soon as Chase disappears, Camden is pulling on my hip and facing me toward him. Jealousy is written all over his face. The clench of his jaw, his straight lips, and narrowed eyes.

"Did you have your fun?" he clips, nodding to Linna when she hands over our beers.

I avoid his question for a moment, taking a long pull of the beer. It's delicious. No wonder it's more expensive. It tastes so much better.

"This is amazing," I mumble, my lips moving against the top of the bottle.

"Answer my question."

"Thanks for the beer," I say, knocking it against the one he hasn't touched in his hand. "Since you've bought me a beer, I think I should at least know your name."

He stares me down, no hint of amusement on his face. This is kind of fun.

"Are you jealous?" I tease.

He holds out his free hand between us. "Camden," he gets out, moving his fingers, gesturing for me to shake his.

I place my hand in his, squeaking when he pulls me against his body. He lines his mouth up next to my ear. I get shivers down my body when his breath hits the spot behind my ear that drives me wild.

"Yours. That's what I am," he whispers. "And you don't have to tell me your name. It's *mine*."

I moan when he kisses the spot under my ear. My skin breaks out in goose bumps. His lips are tender yet possessive. "Oh, am I now?"

He nods. "Yes. And I hated every fucking second of him looking at you."

"He doesn't matter," I admit, my back arching as his lips move down my neck.

"Damn right he doesn't."

"Hey, Camden?"

"Yes, baby?"

"Can we forget all about that dance? I want you to take me to bed. I'm really freaking turned on after watching you go all caveman." He rips his lips from my neck, staring me down as if he's trying to figure out if I'm serious or not. "We can always come back here, right? I'll do it properly and force you to wear a cowboy hat and boots and everything."

"Not happening."

I smile, taking a long drink of my beer. I'm not wasting the good beer. "It's absolutely happening. But I'm really wet right now, and I need you to take care of it."

He gives me a wolfish grin. Reaching out, he knocks his full beer against mine, a loud clinking sound filling the space between us. "Chug your beer, shortcake. We're leaving."

I do as I'm told, drinking every last drop as quickly as I can before letting him pull me from the bar. My heart races in anticipation as he leads me out the door. People try to stop and talk to me, but I don't pay attention to any of them. Between my thighs is getting more and more wet as I dream of all the ways he'll punish me for that little thing with Chase.

Maybe that's why I let it happen. Maybe I wanted to make him jealous so I could see how he acted. I won't admit that to him, but as my feet hurry to try and keep up with him, I know all of that was done on purpose.

He doesn't say a word as he pulls me down the sidewalk. I must not be quick enough for him because eventually, he stops in his tracks. I'm opening my mouth to ask him why he's stopping when I'm soaking wet and need him immediately when he sweeps me off my feet and clutches my body to his chest.

"Whoa!" I yell, wrapping my arms around his neck. "What are you doing?"

"You're too slow, and since I don't think you'll let me eat your pussy on one of these side streets where anyone in your precious town can find you, I'm carrying you to your house."

"Oh," I whisper, clutching my thighs together because damn, that's hot.

We had sex only hours ago, and I'm already ready for it to happen again. I'm eager to see what he has in store for me. Will he still be angry when we get to my house, which is a few blocks away? Will he take it out on me? Punish me a little before finally letting me come? Or will I see the soft side of Camden again? One where he slowly pushes in and out of me with his eyes locked on mine.

"Quit squirming," he says through clenched teeth.

"Sorry," I mumble.

"No you aren't. You love knowing that I'm hard as a goddamn rock, imagining how soaked your panties must be right now."

I groan. Why do I have to have morals? Surely no one would see us if we just slipped in between two buildings...

"Fuck it," Camden comments, veering a hard right and taking us between a tourist shop full of T-shirts and trinkets and the local deli.

He leads us deep into the alley, roughly pushing me against the brick wall when he places me on my feet.

"What are you doing?" I ask, already knowing exactly what he's got planned by the way he shoves the fabric of the dress I'd changed into up my thighs.

"Eating your pussy," he states casually, as if the words aren't naughty and dirty and anybody could be walking along the sidewalk a few feet away from us.

"My house isn't too far from here." I anxiously look toward the street. It's illuminated by the streetlights, the occasional car passing by. So far, no one walks along it, but that doesn't mean someone won't.

"It's too far. The cafe is too far. Everything is too far. I need you right now."

I'm getting far too used to seeing this man drop to his knees for me. The gravel underneath him can't be comfortable, but he doesn't act like it's uncomfortable. He's too busy pulling my panties down, hungrily looking between my legs.

"What if someone catches us?"

"Then they catch us," he answers, placing his palms inside my thighs to spread my legs.

I shouldn't be doing this. I'd be horrified if someone were to see. But I need him more than anything. That fit of jealousy has me desperate for him. And I can't lie that the thrill of him eating me out right here, where anyone could find us, turns me on even more.

"I'll make it quick but fucking phenomenal, baby. Just please, let me taste you."

My head falls against the brick after hearing the desperation in his voice. "Did you just beg to eat me out?" I tease, gripping the skirt of my dress so it doesn't cover me for him.

"I did." He doesn't look at me, his focus staying between my thighs. Before him, I hated being eaten out—not that it happened often. Now I think I could get used to feeling his mouth against my clit and having him tease me with his tongue while his fingers push in and out of me. "Now can I make you come? Please?"

"Yes," I pant because holy shit, that *please* might've been the sexiest word that's ever come from his mouth.

He doesn't warm me up or tease me. He seals his mouth to my tender flesh, his tongue flicking against my clit immediately. He must not be satisfied with my position because he hooks one of my legs over his shoulder, allowing him to bury his face deeper between my thighs.

One of my hands finds his defined shoulder, feeling his sculpted muscles even below his fancy jacket and shirt. The other tangles through his hair, gripping it so tight, making sure he doesn't come up for air until I've come against his tongue.

He moans as I pin him to me, which in return has me moaning along with him. It's how much he gets off on getting me off. It doesn't take long at all for him to make good on his word. I don't know if he ever comes up for a breath before I'm moaning his name up to the night sky, my fingers fisting his hair as I grind against his mouth.

My moans are amplified by the two brick buildings on either side of us. They echo off them, making my moans of pleasure seem way louder than they are.

Camden doesn't move his mouth until he's made sure I've gotten everything possible out of the orgasm. He pulls away, his mouth wet with me. It's even hotter when his lips, coated in my arousal, spread into a grin.

"You're so fucking sexy, shortcake," he muses, picking up my panties and tucking them into his pocket. He'd tossed them onto the ground—there was no way I was going to put them back on. I make a mental note to make sure I get them back from him. They're one of my nicest pairs.

I brace myself on his shoulders as he fixes my dress before he stands to his full height. I just came, but I want more of him. More of that, but not with the adrenaline of getting caught.

"Take me home," I whisper, biting my lip playfully. He tugs my lips from between my teeth, replacing them with his lips.

"Gladly." He kisses me, slowly and deliberately. His hands find my hips. I'm about to remind him we need to hurry when a bright light illuminates both of us.

"Kids!" someone barks. "This is not the place to fool around. Get on with it."

I squint, holding my hand up to try and see past the light shining in my face. The figure comes into view right as I step away from Camden.

"Pippa?" a voice asks in shock. "Is that you?"

I groan, plastering a fake smile on my face. "Hi, Sheriff Phillips."

He frowns underneath his handlebar mustache. "What are you doing?" His words are careful but accusing as he looks between Camden and me.

Shit. Between Rosemary, the little show at Pop's, Chase, and being caught by Sheriff Phillips, I'm bound to be the talk of the town tomorrow.

Great.

"I had, uh—" I look around to try and think of a good enough excuse to give the man whose wife used to teach my bible school. "A splinter," I rush out to say, closing my eyes the moment the words leave my mouth because they're not believable in the slightest.

"A splinter?" He narrows his already small eyes on me.

I risk an anxious glance in Camden's direction, finding an eyebrow raised as he looks at me.

"Yep," I say, committing to this story because I don't have any other choice.

"In your mouth?"

"A terrible accident," Camden offers before trying to hide a laugh with a cough.

Sheriff Phillips doesn't seem to believe me. I try to give him an innocent smile as he looks between the two of us.

"I heard moans. I thought someone was injured."

I close my eyes, trying to fight the smile wanting to bloom on my face. This shouldn't be funny at all, but I've always laughed in uncomfortable situations—something I got from my mom—and right now, I can't help myself.

"All good. Just a deep splinter," I answer, my voice tight because I'm trying so damn hard not to laugh. There's no way I can tell this man that instead of Camden helping me with a splinter, he was eating me out and no one was injured. The orgasm was just that good.

Sheriff Phillips doesn't seem to believe me, but he doesn't say anything. He just holds his flashlight between Camden and me and takes a step back.

"Well, fix your splinter in the privacy of your own home," he scolds.

"Yes, sir," I answer, my cheeks hurting from trying to fight the smile.

He turns around and walks away. I'm able to hold the laugh in for two more seconds before it bubbles from deep inside my chest.

I double over, laughing so hard because I was just moments away from the sheriff catching me with Camden between my thighs.

"Glad you find this hilarious. I just had to talk to that man with a goddamn boner," Camden gripes.

Chapter 43
PIPPA

My phone vibrating against my nightstand wakes me up. I groan, scolding myself for not putting it on do not disturb last night. I swore I had before Camden and I went in for round three for the night, but he might've distracted me before I could do it.

I ignore my phone, letting one eye pop open to find Camden fast asleep next to me. He lies on his back, the sheet barely shielding his naked body. It drapes low on his hips, giving me a perfect view of his chiseled abs. I remember paying close attention to them last night, tracing the crevices with my tongue between the muscles he must work hard to maintain.

Well, now that I'm awake...

I do have the day off. I could technically start the morning with Camden's cock down my throat, seeing how long I could touch him until he woke up. I'm licking my lips, getting ready to slide my hand down his muscles, when my phone rings again.

I pull it from the nightstand, finding my brother's name on the screen. I swipe to answer, trying to keep my voice down so as not to wake Camden.

"Everything okay?" I ask, my voice cracking from not being used this morning. Or maybe it's because I spent half the night moaning Camden's name, making my throat feel hoarse this morning.

"I'm going to the airport," Cade says, his words making me shoot straight up in bed.

"What?" I ask, shocked.

"I'm going to Chicago to see Mare. To tell her I'll move there or do whatever I need to be with her. I miss her, Pip. I have to see her."

I take a deep breath. "Okay, well, for starters, about damn time."

He must not find it funny because he doesn't respond.

"Is she excited to see you?" I ask, happy that maybe finally he'll see her and stop moping. I'm ready to have the normal Cade back. He's always been broody, but he's more tolerable when Mare's around.

"That's the thing. I'm surprising her."

"Oh," I answer, knowing Mare isn't the best with surprises. I don't tell him that because I'm just glad he's going out there and doing some big gesture for her. It's cute.

"Is it a dumb idea?" he asks, his voice nervous.

"Not at all. It's romantic. She'll love it."

"I just have to see her, Pip. Everything aches because I miss her so much."

"Then it's good you're going to see her. Girls like big, romantic gestures," I add, looking over to a sleeping Camden. Except he isn't sleeping anymore. He's awake and looking right at me.

"Dad and I talked last night. I'm not making any rash decisions right now other than going to see her. But I'll do whatever it takes to be with her. Even if that means moving to Chicago if that's what she needs."

I swallow because I can't imagine what it'd be like not to have Cade or Mare here. I'd miss them both too much. So much of my life has interwoven with theirs over the years. But I don't say anything because more than anything, I want them to be happy. Plus, if I know anything about Mare, I know her heart truly belongs to Sutten.

"Is that okay?" He sounds so unsure it makes my heart hurt.

"Of course, Cade," I answer, not wanting to imagine what Sutten looks like without him, Mare, or Mom. "Go get our girl," I add, trying to lighten the mood.

He laughs. "Hopefully she doesn't see me again and question why she ever fell in love with me."

"As if," I say, shaking my head, even though he can't see anything. "She's been obsessed with you since we were kids. She loves you, Cade. I'm excited for the two of you to be back together. You were getting a little too moody...even by your standards."

I don't have to see him to know he's rolling his eyes at me right now. I smile, excited to hear how it goes.

"Let me know when you get there, okay? Keep me updated."

"I will. Love ya, Pip."

"Love you," I respond before hanging up the phone and placing it back on the nightstand once again.

Camden gives me a sleepy smile, opening his arms wide. "Come lie with me." His voice is raspy and sexy. I listen, placing my cheek to his chest and enjoying the way he wraps me up in a warm embrace.

"I vote we go back to sleep for a bit," he mutters against my hair. "Let's get a little more rest before I give you a proper good morning."

I smile into his chest. "Or I give *you* a proper good morning," I tease, snuggling deeper into him.

He pulls the blanket over both of us. "I wouldn't mind that either. But first, you need more sleep."

"And why is that?"

"Because I kept you up late, baby. No regrets. But get some more sleep." He softly brushes his fingers through my hair. I close my eyes, loving the way it feels. He easily puts me back to sleep.

I WAKE up to the sun beating against my face. My legs stretch underneath the blanket, softly brushing against Camden's. I open my eyes, finding him already awake.

"Sleep good?" he asks, cupping my cheek.

"You were right. That extra sleep was needed," I admit. I don't even remember what time Cade called, but I know it was early in the morning by the time Camden and I even fell asleep to begin with.

You could say it was a *really* good first date.

"Did you sleep?" I ask, letting my fingers drift along his abs. They tighten underneath my touch. He really is as perfect as the art he creates. Over time, I want to memorize the way every single one of his muscles ripple under my kiss.

"No, but I'm used to not sleeping much. All part of the gig."

I nod, letting my fingers trace his thick, pronounced oblique muscles. "I'm sorry for keeping you up late."

He smirks, placing a small kiss to my nose. "It was all your fault that I had to spend so much time punishing—and pleasuring you—for that little stunt you pulled at Skis."

"Slopes," I correct with a laugh.

"My point still stands." He sucks in a breath when the backs of my fingers drift against his already hard cock. "I know one way you can apologize to me."

"Lie flat," I instruct, pushing my palm against his chest and using the leverage to push my body off his.

He watches me carefully, fire burning in his eyes. I'm wet from seeing him look at me like this. My eyes leave his, traveling down his body.

"I've got a lot of apologizing to do," I suggest, leaning down to kiss along his abs. I lick at them, wanting to memorize how they feel against my tongue.

My lips continue to travel down his body, taking their time. I push the sheet away, wanting to see all of him. He's ready, his cock thick and hard, waiting for attention. I grab it, fitting my fingers around his girth.

"Fuck," he breathes, moving his hips slightly.

"I haven't even done anything yet," I tease, talking right next to the tip of him.

"It doesn't matter. Everything you do undoes me, shortcake. Don't you see that?" He groans when my tongue peeks out and licks along his thick vein lightly.

His words fuel my desire to make him feel good. To continue to undo him until he has no choice but to shatter—and that he needs me there to put the pieces back together.

"Good," I offer before wrapping my mouth around him and coaxing his hard length deep inside.

"Holy shit." His fingers find my hair, but this time, he lets me have my fun. He just keeps them there lightly, letting them tighten in my tangled hair just enough to give him something to hold on to.

"It's so hard to fit you in my mouth," I note, putting my hand at the base of him to try and make as much of him as possible feel good.

"You can do it," he encourages.

I try, opening my mouth wider as I push more of him into my throat this time. His moans guide me, even when my cheeks burn from opening so wide.

I'm busy going up and down, loving the way he moans my name when my phone vibrates on my nightstand. I don't pay it any attention at first, too busy wanting to have him come down my throat again. We've been together multiple times from that first night at Wake and Bake and then at his gallery, but I haven't been able to have him like this since then, and I'm eager to feel him tighten between my lips all over again. To feel him come down my throat, to hold eye contact as I swallow every last drop of him.

My phone vibrates again, catching my attention a little more this time. Camden must hear it, too, because once it starts vibrating for a third time, he lets out an annoyed growl. "Ignore it," he demands.

I pull off, climbing up the bed. "I just need to make sure everything's okay with my brother," I explain. "What if something happened?"

I look at my caller ID, finding Mare's face there instead. I'm about to ignore it, thinking maybe she's calling to tell me she found out about the surprise, when I see she texted me, telling me to call her immediately.

"Don't you dare do what I think you're doing," Camden warns, fisting his cock.

"One second," I tell him, holding a finger up before swiping to answer.

His head falls back into the pillow with a soft thud. "You've got to be fucking kidding me."

Chapter 44
CAMDEN

"You can't be serious." My hands rest on my hips as Pippa throws my pants from last night on the bed.

"I said I'm sorry!" Pippa says, shoving her arms through the sleeves of her sweatshirt. "If it was anything else, I would've said I couldn't help. But this is my brother and best friend, Camden."

My cock throbs. I try to run my hands along it to get some sort of relief, but it's no use. I'm going to be blue-balled, and there's nothing I can say. She's determined to help the people she loves—something I'd admire if I wasn't hard as a goddamn rock for her, my cock still wet with her saliva.

"You don't have to come with me. You can stay here and wait, and I'll come back and…" Her eyes drift to my cock. "Finish what I started."

"Damn straight we'll finish this later," I growl, angrily stepping into my boxer briefs.

"Don't you have people you love? People you'd drop things for?"

I'd drop anything for you.

I seal my lips shut, not ready to admit that. All I do is pull clothes on and aim a dirty look in her direction whenever she looks at me. I hate that she's a good person. I don't, not really. But it's really inconvenient at the moment.

"This wouldn't be happening if they could just communicate better," I spit, following her into the bathroom.

She laughs, running a brush through her hair. It's a tangled mess from last night, from having my fingers weave through it as I fucked her. I was really looking forward to pulling the long strands of her hair while I fucked her face. Instead, I get to play goddamn cupid with her for her brother and best friend, who apparently don't know how to use a phone.

"Probably," she quips. "But they're both stubborn as hell. They wanted to surprise one another. I think it's cute, even if it failed on both their ends."

"Why don't I just book a private jet for your friend to get a flight back to Chicago? I could pull some strings and get it there quickly."

"You'd charter a private jet for my best friend so I can go back to giving you a blow job?"

My frown turns into a smile. "Yes."

She closes the distance between us, wrapping her arms around my middle and looking up at me with a smile. "That's the sweetest thing you've ever said to me," she teases.

I roll my eyes because I know I've said things far more romantic. Things I've wondered if I should've admitted or not. "Is that a yes?" I pull out my phone and hold it up between us. "I'll make the call right now."

She pushes against my phone. "No. I'm leaving in two minutes. If you're coming with me, you need to be ready."

"What happens if I don't come?" I've already decided I'll come with her. In my mind, I had her to myself all day. I don't want to miss out on more time with her, even if a lot of it is tragically spent with other people.

"Then I'll consider you not a hopeless romantic. It'll make you way less attractive. A mini road trip will be fun," she adds on, squeezing through her bathroom door.

"One more minute, Camden!" she calls from her hallway. I

look over at Kitty, who stares up at me with big puppy dog eyes. Her tail wags enthusiastically, making a thumping sound as it hits the bathroom door.

I don't have hair gel here, which is unfortunate because my hair is a mess. I wet my hands, trying to tame it as best as possible. I'm due for a haircut, but I won't get it done in Sutten. Next time I'm back in Manhattan, I'll have to book something with my barber. The water doesn't work as effectively as I thought it would. My eyes scan over her bathroom counter, trying to see if she has anything I could use. I land on a giant red can of hair spray. Shrugging, I pull the lid off and spray my hair, almost hitting myself in the eyes in the process.

"What are you doing?" Pippa asks from behind me, a smile playing on her lips.

The can drops to the sink, making a loud clanking sound as it hits the marble. "I have no idea what you're talking about." I'm sure I look guilty as fuck, my hands crossed over my chest as I try to act inconspicuous.

She giggles, keys jangling in her hand as she attempts to cover her smile. "I'm never going to let you live that down. Just so you know, that was dry shampoo. *Not* hair spray."

I let out a disgruntled sigh, pushing past her and walking toward her kitchen. Her footsteps follow me through the hallway. I open the door, letting Kitty out into the backyard before we leave.

When I turn around, I find Pippa still beaming at me. "My hair looked like shit because *someone* tugged on it all night. You had no gel. Water didn't do shit. It was my only option."

Her lips twitch. "You're pretty cute when you're flustered."

I roll my eyes. "Perfect. Instead of coming down your throat this morning, I get to hear you call me cute. This is exactly how I wanted the morning to go," I grumble, opening the back door and letting Kitty back in. I give her a few scratches on her ear before Pippa claps her hands together.

"Okay! We've got to go. I forgot my truck needed gas, so we're going to have to take the van, but it should be fun. I just might have to speed a little so we don't miss Cade."

"Kitty, all of this could be solved if people just knew how to text," I tell the dog, giving her one last chin scratch. I think I'm even getting attached to Pippa's dog.

I follow Pippa out the front door, waiting for her to lock it before I follow her down the driveway. We walk past her truck and stop at her bright pink van. I remember it vividly from Beck and Margo's wedding, the memory of icing splattered all over the suit that cost me three grand.

"This is the most *you thing* I've ever seen," I clip, climbing into the passenger seat. I close the door a little too hard, making my thoughts on our current little field trip obvious.

I'd much rather have my cock in her perfect, warm mouth right now. Or at this point, I'd already have been pounding into her from behind as she watched me fuck her through the mirror on her dresser.

Or I could be making her breakfast in bed, doing something sweet because she makes me want to do shit like that. Instead, we get to play matchmaker for two people who could solve all their problems with a simple phone call.

Pippa climbs into the driver's seat, turning the car on and backing out of her driveway too fast for me to feel safe. I grip the handle above my head for dear life.

She looks over at me, shaking her head. "That's a *tad* bit dramatic."

It turns out I'm not being overdramatic because she has to slam on the brake before almost running right into the poor mailman.

She waves her hand out the window at him. "I'm so sorry, Joel! We're in a rush!"

He gives her a dismissive wave. She doesn't wait long for anything else, stepping on the pedal and rushing out of her quiet neighborhood. I close my eyes. I'm not a religious man by any means, but I say a prayer that she doesn't get us killed before we even make it to her friend.

"Okay, so I tried just focusing on getting to Cade, but I have to ask. How did this happen?" Mare asks, looking at me with an unreadable look on her face. She keeps looking over her shoulder at Camden, as if she's checking to see if he's real or not.

I meet Camden's eyes through my rearview mirror. It's been silent for a majority of the car ride, but we still have some time until we make it to the airport. Apparently, Mare wants to spend that time talking about me, even when she's the one doing a big, elaborate gesture of love.

"Pip, are you dating the asshole tourist?" Mare presses, her voice full of shock. She bites her lip anxiously, her eyes darting from Camden to me and back again.

"Yeah, Pip, are you dating the asshole tourist?" Camden asks sarcastically from his tiny seat in the back. It'd be way more funny seeing his tall, athletic body squeezed into the seat way too small for him if I wasn't getting the third degree from my best friend.

I sigh, risking a glance over at Mare. "You're asking an awful lot of questions. Can't we just talk about what you're going to say to Cade when we get to the airport?"

She shakes her head, a small smile blooming on her face. *Bitch.* I'm not prying into what's been happening between her and Cade, even though I have plenty of questions.

"I already know what I'm going to say to him. We're talking

about you." She looks back over her shoulder again. "And how you ended up hooking up with this asshole."

Camden whistles. "Kind of harsh, considering you haven't even met me until today."

"Technically, I met you at your friend's wedding."

"I'd hardly call that meeting."

Mare hums. "It doesn't matter. I know things."

"And what kind of things are those?"

"Things." She huffs, looking to me for help. I don't say anything because I don't know what to say. I wasn't prepared for my best friend to meet my...Camden. I don't know what else to call him. Boyfriend? Lover? Maybe it is time for me and Camden to talk about what this is.

"Well, those things you were told were wrong. In fact, if you see her walking a little funny today, it's from me."

"Camden!" I yell, wanting to disappear. Mare just gawks, her jaw hanging open.

My cheeks have to be as red as the tomatoes Mom used to grow in her garden. I'm not cut out for this. My only saving grace is the fact that Cade isn't here, too. Then I actually would die from embarrassment.

"She started it," Camden gripes from the back. I don't have the nerve to meet his eyes through the mirror, even though I can feel him watching me. He's going to be pissed when we drop Mare off, I already know it. I squirm, thinking about what that can mean for me later.

"So you're just hooking up?" Mare prods. "What are you even doing in Sutten anyway?" she asks, turning back to Camden.

"I own the gallery next door to her bakery."

"The one the Richardsons used to own," I add. At least that's an answer I can give at the moment.

Mare blinks, clearly still confused. "Okay, so you bought the gallery next door, and that led to the two of you...you know..."

"Fucking?" Camden finishes.

I don't have to look over to know that Mare is blushing as well. Camden and that mouth of his.

I laugh. "You know, Mare, you write *really* dirty books to not be able to say the word *fucking*."

"Shut up," she warns. "We aren't talking about me. We're talking about you."

"Well, I don't want to talk about me either," I counter.

"Maybe I want to talk about us," Camden pipes up from the back seat. *Traitor.*

"Probably not the time," I suggest, risking a glance at him through the mirror.

He smirks, but there's no humor in his face. I know for a fact he's simmering back there, just waiting for Mare to be gone. Maybe this was all a big mistake. I shouldn't have brought him with us.

Or I shouldn't have answered my phone at all.

I'm one hundred percent going to regret this.

"Tell her what we are, shortcake," he pushes, leaning forward to put his arms around both of our seats. His breath tickles my neck, making me shift in my seat.

"Shortcake? What kind of nickname is that?"

I shoot her a look. "Funny you're saying that, *Goldie*," I emphasize, raising my eyebrows when I briefly look over at her.

"I don't have to explain the meaning behind it to you," Camden drawls, his body still right next to mine.

"There's meaning?" I ask, unable to resist.

He kisses my cheek. He can't be that pissed off at me if he's doing that. Right?

"I have no words," Mare admonishes.

Trying to change the subject, I smack Camden in the chest. "Sit back. And buckle your seat belt."

"There isn't a seat belt," he counters.

Good point.

It's silent for a minute or two. My mind races with what I could say. I don't feel like I have to explain everything to Mare.

It's not like she's made me privy to her entire dating life before—not that I'd want to know every detail because, ew, it's my brother—but I'm also excited to have her back and don't want to act like I'm keeping secrets from her. I just truly don't know what Camden and I are. It's been fun and nice to not put pressure on it. To just see what happens.

"I wanted to prove to Camden how great Sutten was. How we had talent right here in our lovable town and he didn't have to bring in rich assholes from New York. One thing led to another, and now we're here. He's kind of a softie underneath that asshole persona."

Camden laughs. "I'm not a softie."

I smile. "You totally are."

When Mare doesn't say anything, I look over at her. I find her looking right at me, a slight smile playing on her lips. Normally, Mare isn't one to ask other people's business. She's quiet and reserved. I don't know why she chose today to dig into my life. Maybe it's to distract herself from thinking about if she'll make it to the airport in time.

It's quiet for a while before Mare speaks up. "Just don't hurt my best friend, okay? I don't want to have to get away with murder."

I snort, almost missing Camden's deep sigh with the sound.

"What is up with people in Sutten and murder?"

Mare gives me a look.

I smile. "Rosemary already got to him," I explain.

This makes her bust out in laughter. "My god. I miss that woman."

"The whole town misses you, Mare. Do you think you'll be back for a while?"

"I'm hoping I'll be back forever," she answers immediately.

I press down on the gas, sending Camden flying backward. I try not to laugh at the stream of curses from him. "Oops," I manage to get out before cracking up.

Mare joins in. He grumbles in the back while I speed to the airport.

"Alright, Mare, let's go get your man!" I yell, turning my blinker on and flying into the right lane before I miss my exit.

"That's if you don't get us all killed first," Camden quips.

Chapter 46
CAMDEN

"Good morning, shortcake," I say, walking into Wake and Bake on a Friday morning. I just got off a conference call that lasted over two hours, and I'm ready to see my girl. As if I hadn't spent my morning between her thighs, eating her out at the breakfast table as she attempted to eat her Cheerios.

I've spent every morning with my mouth on some part of her for the past week. It's been a week since our date—and our little adventure to get her brother and his girl together—and it's been the most mundane, incredible week of my life.

I like mornings with her. I like watching her take her first sip of coffee every morning, watching her fuss with doing her hair to ultimately throw it up on the top of her head. I like walking or carpooling to work with her. Doing normal things together. We take our lunch break together whenever we can and return back to her place hand in hand every night.

It's amazing. I love it. And I'd never imagined myself doing this every day for the rest of my life—especially in a small town I'd never heard of in Colorado—until her.

Pippa looks up at me, the light not reaching her eyes as she focuses on a piece of paper in her hand. "Isn't it afternoon at this point?" she asks, her heart not really in it. Her focus is still on whatever she holds.

I shrug, closing the distance between us and pressing a kiss to her hair. "Well, good whatever it is, shortcake," I correct. "What's this?" I point to the piece of paper she won't stop looking at.

She finally looks at me. "A letter we just got in the mail. It's a warning that the rent might be raised here, by over a thousand a month." She sounds stressed, and I hate it.

"May I?" I ask, gesturing to the paper. She hands it over, and I let my eyes scan over it. It's from the same realty group that I bought my space from. I thought they'd just owned that space, but apparently, it is more than just what I purchased.

"I thought you owned the space?" I ask, my eyes still tracking over the letter. I don't know who this realty group is, but they're saying the strip is at risk of being sold to a new, interested third-party buyer.

"No, I wish. I rent it. I'd own it if someone let me, but I've never been able to."

"I can look into it for you," I offer. There's no reason her rent should go up by a grand each month. There's no reason she shouldn't just own the place to begin with if she wants.

"You don't have to do that," she argues, her voice exhausted. She presses her palms to her forehead, sucking in a long, shaky breath.

"I want to."

She lets the breath out slowly. "It's just not me, you know? It's everyone on the block. We'll all be put in jeopardy because someone from out of town who knows nothing about Sutten is coming in and getting greedy. Maybe I need to speak with the Livingstons."

I ignore the jab at her opinions on people from out of town, even though at one point, that's exactly what I did. "Who are they?" I ask, not wanting to approach the first part of her sentence.

"They're one of the oldest families in Sutten. I think I might remember that their great-great, maybe even a few more, great-grandfather was one of the founding fathers of this town. They own a lot of the real estate here. A lot of the residential land is theirs, but I know they own commercial properties, too. I've just somehow got the shit end of the stick and rented on the *one* block of town somehow not owned by them."

"We'll fix it," I promise, cupping her face in my hands. My thumbs brush along her cheeks as I try to think of a way to comfort her.

"Hopefully." She sighs, turning her head to press a kiss to one of my palms. "Anyway. How was your morning?"

"Well, I was actually coming here to ask you something."

"You didn't show up just to be around my amazing personality?"

I shake my head. "That's a given. I came here to ask if you've ever been to New York."

Her eyes narrow on me. I don't let go of her cheeks, loving feeling her skin pressed against my fingertips. "I haven't. Why?"

"Would you want to come to Manhattan with me?" My heart races underneath my sweater. It's gotten colder here in Sutten. The temperature seemed to really drop over the last week, proving that summer has drifted away and fall is creeping in.

"When?"

"Right now." I want her to say yes so bad. I want to take her to the place I grew up, to the only city I've ever really called home. I imagined having her in my space, showing her my gallery—my own personal art studio. It's easy to imagine us on a double date with Beck and Margo. Hell, I can even see her getting along with Emma, even though that thought terrifies me.

"Yeah, let me just snap my fingers and end up in New York with you," she answers sarcastically.

"Well, it wouldn't be that easy. But I have a jet waiting at the small airport not too far from here. There's a gala tomorrow night. I'd love to bring you as my date."

"Me? Your date?"

"I'm sure as hell not bringing anyone else."

This makes her smile. Her teeth dig into her lip as she shakes her head at me. "I can't go to New York with you, Camden. I have nothing to wear. I can't leave Wake and Bake for the weekend. And I have no one to watch Kitty."

"I'll buy you a hundred options until you find something perfect for tomorrow. Your employees are amazing and can handle things themselves here. And I've already spoken with Marigold. She and your brother will watch Kitty."

Her eyes turn to slits. "I thought you and Mare hated one another."

"She's pretty cool now that she isn't interrogating me like she's in the FBI. She even said she and Cade could stop by tomorrow to make sure everything is running smoothly here. Come to New York with me, shortcake. Let me show you my world."

"What if I don't fit in?" she asks nervously.

"Is that what this is about?" I press a kiss to her lips, just now remembering I hadn't kissed her when I first walked in.

She shrugs, looking up at the ceiling as if she doesn't want to admit it.

"Shortcake, you shine brighter than any other person I've ever met. You don't have to fit in because you outshine everyone else. It's a remarkable thing."

"If someone would've told me months ago that you say such sweet things, I would've told them they've lost their mind."

A small laugh erupts from my chest.

She grabs the collar of my shirt, bringing my face down closer to hers. "No, really," she continues. "Who knew this cold, ruthless man isn't all that cold at all."

"I'm only like that because I'm with *you*. No one else gets this side of me."

She smiles, standing on her tiptoes to place a kiss against my lips. I try to deepen it, but she pulls away before I can.

"This idea is crazy," she points out, her eyes scanning my face. "You don't seem like the spur-of-the-moment kind of guy, yet here you are."

"What can I say? You bring out the worst in me, shortcake."

"I think it's the best."

I kiss the tip of her nose. "Yeah, I do, too."

I feather kisses along her cheeks, pulling her body fully against mine, trapping her arms between us. "So is that a yes?" I ask against her cheek before moving my lips to her forehead. I don't stop peppering kisses along her face until she finally answers.

"Okay, I'll do it!" she yells, trying to push me away. "Camden, you have to stop. What if a customer walks in?"

"There have been times they could've found us in far more compromising positions," I point out.

She snakes her arms around my waist, sliding her cold hands into the waistband of my pants. "Did you hear me say I'd go?"

I smirk. "I did. But I'd like to hear you say it again."

"I'll go to New York with you."

"Good." I slap her ass just before Lexi walks out of the back room, carrying a large pan of pastries. "Time to go get packed."

Chapter 47
PIPPA

"THIS IS ALL FOR ME TO TRY ON?" I ASK, STARING AT FIVE RACKS OF clothing that fill one of Camden's guest bedrooms.

He stands behind me, his hands on my arms and his lips pressing into my shoulder. "It sure is. I told the stylist I wasn't sure what kind of look you were going for, so I wanted you to have options."

I stare at the mountain of sequins, tassels, and silk in front of me. It's overwhelming. We landed in New York a few hours ago, and my head has been spinning ever since. I went to school in Chicago, and while it's not Manhattan, it's still busy and totally opposite of Sutten. This has been a whole different world. I should've known from the moment the private jet picked us up that nothing could've prepared me for the world Camden lives in.

He has drivers, a private chef, and house staff who greeted us upon our arrival at his penthouse. And apparently, he has things like stylists who show up with dresses that probably cost more than my mortgage.

"I don't know what to say," I whisper.

"Don't freak out." He presses his lips to my neck, as if he can tell I'm getting overwhelmed.

"I knew our lives were different," I begin. "I'm not dumb. But this is just…a lot."

"If it's too much, we can skip the gala altogether tomorrow. We can hang out here or go somewhere low-key in the city."

I shake my head, turning around to face him. "No, I wanted to come and experience your world. I want to see your gallery tomorrow, and I want to go to the gala. I want to see everything about your life here. I just didn't really know people had personal stylists, is all."

"She only helps me with elaborate events."

I sigh, leaning into his touch. "That's no pressure at all."

"You're radiant, remember? You could wear what you have on right now, and you'd still capture everyone's attention tomorrow night. Don't worry about a dress. If it's too much, we can just go shopping tomorrow."

"I just wish I had Mare or a girlfriend here to help me."

"About that…" He looks off to the side as if he's nervous about what he's about to say.

"What?" I press, shivering because his penthouse is far colder than I imagined it would be.

"I may have invited Beck and Margo over. I figured Margo could help you out. She's been doing this stuff for a while now with Beck. But they'll understand if I tell them never mind."

I purse my lips. I've only briefly spoken to Margo on her wedding day; most of my conversations were with her planner. We didn't get the chance to speak at Camden's gallery opening. But she seems nice. And if she knows more about this fancy New York life, I could use her help.

"I think I'd like that." I nod, further deciding. "Plus, if she's going to be there tomorrow night, it'd be nice to have another familiar face."

"Is my face not good enough?"

I trace over his cheekbones. "Your face is perfect."

He nips at my fingers. "Good girl." He presses a kiss to my lips. "And I'm glad you said yes because I think they're on their way up."

"You were very confident I'd say yes."

"Margo is persistent. She wanted to officially meet you. Beck did as well. He doesn't believe any woman would put up with me this long."

"It really is a chore," I tease, completely lying. It's easy being with him. Almost too easy. I'm waiting for the ball to drop, to find out where this goes wrong.

"I'm going to warn you right now, there's a good chance Margo brought Emma. And maybe even Winnie. The three of them are often a package deal."

I feel a little nervous if it's more than Margo. If the three of them are so close, will they even talk to me? I already feel out of place. This might even make it worse. Or maybe they'll make it better. I need to try and be optimistic.

I suck a breath in, feeling incredibly overwhelmed. When he asked me to come to New York with him, I imagined us visiting Times Square together. Maybe stopping by a booth to buy an "I <3 NYC" shirt. He'd take me to his gallery before we had to get ready for the gala. I wasn't anticipating stylists and groups of friends and galas so fancy that it takes an evening gown to attend.

The nicest dress I've ever worn was my slutty prom dress that I got at a department store. I'm not used to things this nice. We grew up with money compared to others in our small town. The ranch was profitable. But it was nowhere near the Livingstons. Or anything close to the world that Camden lives in.

"Asshole," a voice calls from somewhere else in the penthouse. It's so much open space that the voice echoes off the marble floors and walls. "Yoohooooo," it calls again. "Looking for Mr. Cranky Asshole."

Camden's head falls backward, his throat bobbing with a long swallow. "Please don't listen to anything she says, okay?"

"Is that Margo?"

"No. *That* would be Emma."

A head pops into the doorway. She's gorgeous. Her hair is a

perfect blonde. I truly can't tell if it's natural or if she dyes it that color. "Oh my god, you're here!" the girl shrieks, running into the room and scooping me into a hug.

My eyes go wide as I look to Camden from over her shoulder. She's shorter than me, giving me a perfect view of a smirking Camden. He looks from us to two more figures that appear in the doorway.

"Okay, Emma, let her go. You're going to scare her away before we even get to spend time with her," a voice I don't recognize says.

The blonde gives me one final squeeze before she pulls away. "I'm sorry. I'm a total hugger, and to be honest, I was wondering if Camden was making you up when he kept talking about you."

"Hi," I get out, giving her a friendly smile. "He talks about me a lot?" I push, looking to him with a wink.

He gives me a playful smirk with a shrug.

The girl—Emma—lets out a long sigh. "All the time, really. I thought for sure he had to be making you up. I mean, who would want to put up with him?" She gives him a look, one to which he flips her off.

"I'm Margo," a girl with dark hair says. "And I'm also a total hugger, but we can shake hands, too, if Emma just overwhelmed you."

I can't help but laugh, holding my arms out for a hug. "I'm Pippa. I kind of saw you in Sutten at the gallery opening. My cafe did the food."

Margo's eyes go wide, and she looks over to Emma, who must come to the same realization as her because she gasps. "Camden! You're dating the poor woman you were an absolute ass to at my wedding?"

"That would be me," I admit, finishing the hug with Margo.

"Tell me you gave him a lot of hell before he got into your good graces," Margo muses.

"Oh, I *really* had to work to get in her good graces," Camden pipes up from behind Emma and Margo.

"I'm sure you did," a man comments from next to him. I know it's Beckham Sinclair—or Beck as Camden calls him—because there are many photos of them together on the internet.

"I'm Beck," the man offers, holding his hand out in a very businesslike handshake. "And what Emma said. I've heard a lot about you."

"I can't believe it was you who did the dessert at our wedding. We still have people talking about how delicious it all was! God, I feel like a bitch I didn't recognize you to begin with," Margo adds.

I swat at the air. "It's fine, really. I'm terrible with names and faces, so I totally get it. It's great to meet all of you. Or officially meet you, I should say."

Emma shakes her head, looking at me like I'm a ghost. "I remember how much of a tool he was to you. He must have really had to work for it."

All I do is smile because there's no way I'm going to tell them every single way he made up for it. A lot of it is far too intimate for me to tell people who are basically strangers to me.

"Let's just say a *lot* has changed since then," I answer.

"I'm shocked you don't have your third wheel with you," Camden notes, walking up to me and pulling me into his chest. I like that even with his friends around, he seems comfortable with public affection. "Where's Winnie?"

Emma rolls her eyes, walking over to the racks of clothes and searching through the dresses. "She's late and not answering my calls. Which is unfortunate because she has more gala experience than all of us combined." She looks over at Beck and Camden. "Well, most of us. These two also grew up with that nice silver spoon in their mouths."

"Winnie will be here soon, Em," Margo offers, walking to where Emma stands. "But we don't need her to have Pippa start trying on dresses." She turns to me, a huge smile on her face. I remember thinking when we briefly spoke at her wedding that she was one of the most beautiful people I'd ever met. It was her striking green eyes and the way she really looked at you when she was talking to you. "Is that okay with you?" Margo adds at the last minute.

I nod. "I'm going to be honest. I grew up on a ranch. I don't really do fancy." My eyes scan over all the dresses. "I don't even know where to begin with all of this."

"That's why we're here," Emma says energetically, pulling a clementine-orange dress from the racks. "Okay, well, this is an immediate no," she notes, shoving it back into the mountain of silk and tulle.

Margo turns to the guys. "Okay, you two can go. Make yourself useful and make us some dinner."

Camden cocks his head to the side. "I'd envisioned taking Pippa out somewhere tonight. There's a few places I want to show her."

Margo shakes her head. "No. She traveled all day; there's an event tomorrow. Give the girl some peace and let her chill here tonight. There's plenty of time to show her around the best city in the world tomorrow."

"Now, go make us some food. The both of you, shoo!" Emma claps her hands together, dismissing them without any kind of afterthought as she turns back to the rack of clothes. Margo joins her, looking at the dresses on the one next to her.

"You good?" Camden asks, leaning down to place a kiss to my lips.

I nod. "We're good in here. Go make me food."

"See you in a bit, shortcake," he says lowly, giving me a wink before following Beck out the door.

When I turn to face Margo and Emma, I find them both grinning ear to ear, looking at me.

"What?" I ask, confused as to why they're both staring at me.

"Oh, he's *so* gone for you," Emma teases.

Chapter 48
CAMDEN

"How do you feel about surprises?" I ask Pippa as I lead her into the elevator. We landed in New York yesterday, and I want to show her as much as I can before we fly back to Sutten tomorrow.

She gives me a sweet smile, tucking a strand of curled hair behind her ear. "It depends on what the surprise is," she answers, molding her body to mine the moment the penthouse elevator doors close.

I wrap my hands around the back of her neck, savoring the moment with her. I liked waking up with her in my bed. I liked both of us sitting at my kitchen island as Kiley, one of my personal chefs, made us breakfast. I liked lounging around the table late into the night last night as we spent time with my friends. Pippa fit in perfectly with them, and I went to bed thinking how easy it was to imagine her in my life here. How simple it'd be to go back and forth together between our two homes, how amazing that life together would be.

Pippa's eyes travel over my face as my thumbs brush along her cheeks. She waits for me to respond, but for a moment, I'm too swept up in wanting to ask her what we are. The words to ask her to be my girlfriend are at the tip of my tongue, but I want to do it in some romantic way and not in an empty elevator on a Saturday morning.

"There's someone I'd like you to meet," I confess.

"And who is that?"

I play with one of her curled tendrils of hair. I'd never seen her take so long to get ready in the morning, but she'd spent almost an hour carefully curling her hair and applying makeup. It's something I hadn't seen her do before. I sat on the edge of the tub, responding to work emails as she got ready, not wanting to be too far from her. The entire time, I wanted to tell her she didn't have to change anything about her to fit in here. There was no need for her to put on more makeup than normal or do her hair differently than she normally would, but I kept my mouth shut. If she wanted to wake up and get ready before our day, then I'd wait as long as she needed.

"Camden?" she presses, reaching up to run her fingers through my hair. "You there?" she laughs.

I nod, pressing a kiss against the inside of her wrist. "I'd love to introduce you to my gran."

Her features soften, a timid smile forming on her lips. "I would love to meet her."

"Yeah?" My heart pounds inside my chest, loud as a drum. In the quiet of the elevator, I'm sure she can hear it. It doesn't matter to me if she does. I want her to know how excited I am for the two most important people in my life to meet one another.

"I mean, if you want me to, but I don't want you to feel like I have to meet her. I can always wait if it's not something—"

I cut her off by placing my lips against hers. She eagerly kisses me back, allowing me to steal whatever she was about to say. Once the kiss slows, I pull away far enough to be able to speak. "There's nothing I want more," I answer, a small laugh escaping my throat. "Although it terrifies me for you to meet her."

The door chimes before opening, revealing the lobby of my building. Pippa wraps her hand in mine, her cold fingers squeezing my own. "I'm more than ready."

HAVING Pippa meet Gran was a *terrible* idea. The two of them giggle like a bunch of gossiping schoolgirls, casting looks my way as they whisper to one another from across the sitting room.

"Should I be concerned about what you two are talking about?" I ask, looking at both of them from the top of a newspaper. I tried engaging in a conversation with them for almost an hour before it felt like it was no use. They're two peas in a pod, and I'm just an outsider whose presence they don't need.

"She's just telling me about the time you cried at the top of the Statue of Liberty."

My eyes narrow on a completely unfazed Gran. She gives me a sly smile, feeling content about spilling all my childhood secrets. "He was petrified up there. I couldn't peel the kid off me to even attempt to take us back to the ground."

I turn the page of my newspaper, unamused by what they're talking about. "No one tells you about how it sways," I note, remembering the first and the last time I ever went to the tourist attraction.

"You cried for an hour even after our feet were firmly planted on the ground."

"I was a child. It was scary."

"You were thirteen."

I place the newspaper in my lap, leaning forward to look at Pippa. "I think Gran is getting rather tired. You ready to leave, shortcake?" The nickname tumbles from my mouth before I can think better of it. Which makes Gran break out in a huge smile.

"*Shortcake?*" she muses, giving me a knowing look.

My cheeks begin to heat. "You look exhausted," I hurriedly say, standing up and closing the distance to her.

Gran swats at my arm. "I'm not tired at all. Stop hovering." I try to grab her again, but she pushes me away. Even in old age, she's stubborn as hell.

"Camden, are you blushing?" Pippa chimes in, reaching up and pressing her hand to my flushed cheek.

"No," I clip, fully confident that I am, in fact, blushing.

Gran looks at Pippa, a serious look developing on her face. "Does he call you shortcake often?" she asks quietly.

This was a *horrible* idea. I don't know what I was thinking.

Pippa's eyes bounce between both Gran and me. "He's been calling me that since we first met."

I close my eyes because I know what's going to happen. I know Gran is onto me.

"He has?"

"Yeah," Pippa answers, her tone unsure. "Am I missing something here?"

"Strawberry shortcake was his favorite as a child," Gran offers, totally outing me. "He'd beg me to make it for him all the time. It was the one dessert he actually liked. Everything else he wouldn't bother with. But shortcake? The kid loved it. Even when he'd visit from college, he'd beg me to make it for him. Every birthday and celebration always had strawberry shortcake."

Pippa holds my eyes. I wish I could climb into her mind and discover every thought running through it. Gran isn't lying. Strawberry shortcake has always been my weakness, an indulgence I couldn't deny. When Pippa came barreling back into my life that day at the gallery, the name slipped from my mouth, and it felt right.

Gran digs a bony elbow into Pippa's side. "I know he's all tough on the outside and terrible to put up with sometimes, but don't let him fool you, sweet girl. I think he might be crazy about you."

I didn't think it was possible for my grandmother to embarrass me when I'm a grown-ass adult, but leave it to Gran to find a way. I should disappear and pretend Gran hadn't just outed the nickname that stuck for Pippa, but to do that, I'd have to break eye contact with Pippa, something I can't seem to do.

"I happen to make an amazing strawberry shortcake. It's even better as a cupcake. My favorite cupcake to make," Pippa admits, her voice quiet. She doesn't break eye contact with me, and I'd give just about anything to climb into that beautiful mind of hers and figure out if she thinks any differently of me now.

From the corner of my eye, I see Gran cross her arms over her chest with a satisfied sigh. "Seems like you two are a match made in heaven."

Chapter 49
PIPPA

I HOLD GRAN TIGHT, SAVORING THE SMELL OF HER EXPENSIVE perfume. I've had the best morning getting to know the one person who showed Camden love as a child.

"You make sure to come back and visit me, you got that?" Gran says into the crook of my neck. I give her a big squeeze, trying not to hold her bony shoulders too tight. I feel like one too-intense hug could break her straight in half.

Pulling away, I nod at her, feeling emotional at leaving this woman, even if we just met. Maybe it's because her fiery personality reminded me of my mom. Maybe it's the knowledge that she's the one positive memory Camden has of his childhood, or maybe it's something I can't put a finger on. Whatever it is, I feel like Gran is someone I want as a constant figure in my life. "Maybe you'll come visit Sutten?" I offer, grabbing her hands in mine because I don't want to lose contact with her. "I want to know your strawberry shortcake recipe," I add, a large smile on my face.

Knowing the meaning behind the nickname Camden gave me has done something to me. It might be silly, but after knowing what Gran told me, I can't help but rethink everything that's happened between Camden and me. Was he thinking about me sooner than I thought? Did he feel the pull between us from the moment we met again at his gallery?

I have so many questions, ones I want to ask him the moment we're alone. For now, he's off on an important call. He'd tried ignoring his ringing phone a few times as we exchanged our goodbyes, but after the third phone call from Daly, he had to excuse himself for a moment.

"Maybe I'll come up for Camden's birthday," she offers. "Camden told me your birthdays are close. I'd love to come celebrate the both of you if you don't mind."

"He told you that?"

She smiles, giving me a nod. "Oh, he's told me a *lot* about you, darling. I never thought I'd see the day, but I believe my sweet boy is in love with you."

My eyes go wide. I shake my head, looking over my shoulder to make sure he isn't eavesdropping. "No," I insist, my throat feeling clogged. The moment I saw his entire demeanor change when he said hello to his grandma, I realized I was falling in love with him. It was the way he crouched down to hug her tiny frame, fussing about it being too cold in her house before he threw a blanket over her lap as she argued with him. It was sweet—tender even—and as I watched from the side, awkwardly not knowing if I should introduce myself or let them argue for a moment, I realized I was giving my heart to him. It was a kind of feeling I'd never felt before. It felt heavy in my chest, telling me that it'd be a feeling that'd settle deep in my bones.

I'd tried pushing the realization away. Camden and I are still so new—so different. I shouldn't fall for him. We haven't even discussed what to officially call us, but none of that matters.

At some point between the heated arguments, the passionate nights, and the tender moments, I started falling for a man I swore I couldn't stand.

"You look like you've seen a ghost." Gran's voice pulls me from my thoughts.

"I just don't know what—"

She swats at the air. "You don't have to say anything. I'd prefer you didn't so I can get out what I want to say before Camden comes back."

I nod, eager to hear whatever has made her turn serious.

"To the world, Camden had a beautiful childhood filled with love and adventure, but that's the furthest thing from the truth. He was born to two incredibly selfish people. Ones who kept him locked away from the world until they deemed him useful. I tried doing what I could for him, but even I know I failed him. I should've never let him return to that cold and empty home. You'd walk inside and know it was void of love."

"He loves you dearly," I interrupt, needing her to know that he idolizes her. "He's told me plenty of times that your love was the one thing that got him through that."

Her eyes gloss over—something I feel mine do at picturing a sad and lonely Camden as a child. "I could've done more. I *should've* done more. But I didn't. And I've always been scared of what kind of person Camden would turn into. At times, he felt just like his father, something I never told him. He seemed cold and unattached to the world. I was worried no one would be able to see past the mask he put up in fear of being rejected the way he was by his parents. And then you came along."

I swallow because I don't know how to respond. She doesn't give me the chance to say anything anyway. "He called me one day to tell me about how this *infuriating* woman—" She laughs at the word. "—his exact word, by the way—how this infuriating woman had made him an herbal tea that morning. The man spent two minutes telling me about it when it made no difference to me what kind of tea he was drinking. But I could tell it was important to him. And let me tell you something. Not much is important to Camden."

"It was nothing."

"To him, it was something. In fact, I think it was the start of everything. You're the most important person in his life. He loves you, even though I know he probably hasn't told you that. I can see it written all over his face."

All I can do is shrug because I don't really know how to respond. "I'm not sure," I answer honestly, because I truly don't know how Camden feels. He's hard to read. It's hard to know where his head's at.

"Now, I have to tell you something you might not want to hear," Gran admits, her voice sad.

My stomach drops because I don't like the look on her face.

"Camden doesn't know how to be loved. He doesn't know how to love. And since he was a child, he's had to face the cruel world alone. He'll probably push you away. He might even shut down because he's terrified of loving someone the way he loved his parents and not having love given back to him. His parents rejected him, and I think he'll spend the rest of his life wondering if anyone else he loves will, too."

Tears fall down my cheeks. I'm sad for Camden as a child. The one who just needed to be shown love. I cry for the man that child turned into. The one who believes no one could ever actually love him.

I wipe at the tears immediately, using the sleeve of my sweater to dab at my cheeks. I'd meticulously applied makeup this morning—something I don't normally do—and now I'm ruining it as I cry in his poor grandma's arms.

Gran grabs both my cheeks lovingly, her eyes crinkling at the corners as she smiles at me. I don't tell her that her hands are cold or that I want to cry all over again because my mom used to do the same thing to comfort me. All I do is lay my hands over hers and try to blink the tears away.

"Be good to him, sweet girl. I hope he lets you love him the way I know you want to."

"Me too," I croak, trying to let out a shaky breath.

"Now, let's both stop crying before he comes in here and catches us?"

I laugh, nodding before I pull her in for one last hug.

Things have never been so clear. Once we're done with the gala and back in Sutten, I have to tell Camden I'm falling for him. He needs to know he's loved. It'll be up to him to decide what to do with that information.

Chapter 50
CAMDEN

"YOU'RE QUIET," PIPPA NOTES AS WE COME TO A STOP IN FRONT OF my gallery.

"I could say the same thing to you," I respond, thinking about our walk here. I'd bought Gran a place close to my gallery on purpose years ago. She didn't want to live anywhere near my penthouse, but she didn't mind a spot closer to the gallery. It worked out in my favor anyway since I'm not home much. The building looming in front of us is more of a home to me.

From the moment I got off the phone—suddenly in a terrible mood from the conversation I had with Daly—and said goodbye to Gran, Pippa's been quiet. But she isn't wrong—I've also been quiet, too in my head about the shit Daly just piled on me to hold much of a conversation.

"So this is it." Pippa turns to the gallery building, looking up at the iridescent structure. "Camden Hunter's gallery. The one the rich and famous visit."

I shake my head. "Are you making fun of my work?"

She rubs her lips together in an attempt to hide a smile. "No. I just thought it'd be bigger."

I scoop her in my arms, all of the drama from the phone call being pushed to the back of my mind as I squeeze her sides and tickle her. "I know you didn't just say that," I warn, digging my fingertips into the spot that has her squealing with laughter.

She doubles over, her small hands trying to push mine away

as her body shakes with laughter. "It's kind of small," she gets out in between fits of giggles.

I spin her body, forcing her to face me and giving her a break. Her entire face is red from laughter, her neatly curled hair sticking in her lip gloss. I push the pieces of hair from her lips, earning me a smile.

"I'll have you know it has the most square feet of any independently owned gallery in the area."

"Is that supposed to impress me?" she teases, standing on her tiptoes to get her lips closer to mine.

I lean down, trapping her lips with mine for a moment. She tastes like strawberries, reminding me of our earlier conversation with Gran. Her soap, her hair, her lips have always tasted like strawberries and vanilla. Now she knows why that's driven me wild from the moment she was catapulted back into my life.

"Yeah," I answer with our lips still pressed against each other. "It was supposed to impress you."

"Why don't you take me inside? I want to see this secret studio where you create magic. Now, *that's* something that'll impress me."

I shake my head, taking her hand to lead her inside. The gallery is empty today, something I planned on purpose. There was a private client early this morning, but Leo handled it. I wanted to be able to show Pippa something I've poured my heart and soul into without anyone else around.

I selfishly need all to myself for a little while. I shared her with Gran this morning, and I'll have to share her at the gala tonight. For the afternoon, I want it to just be the two of us.

And then there's the looming thing I have to tell her after my phone call with Daly.

It can wait. I want to enjoy today and give myself time to figure things out. For the first time in my life, I want to share with someone what I'm truly passionate about—my art. Not other people's art. Not my gallery. But the thing hidden in the back with the art I've spent hours on.

I lean against the white wall in one of the rooms of the gallery, my hands tucked in my pockets. Pippa stands right in the middle of the exhibit, her head spinning as she takes in the framed art on the walls.

"Margo did all of this?" she asks in awe, stepping closer to a piece Margo created.

"Yeah," I answer, standing still. I like watching her here. She pays close attention to detail of everything on display. She's an artist's dream, completely enamored with every piece and giving them the attention they deserve.

"I can't believe you found her. She's so talented."

"She found me," I admit. "Showed up one day and convinced me to let her show me her work."

"Is that not how it normally works?"

I bark out a laugh. "Not at all. But I'm glad it did."

"I've loved seeing all of this," Pippa begins, walking toward me. "But I want to see *your* space. Show me your work, Camden."

I grab her by the hand, fighting the urge to tell her I'll show her anything she wants if she just keeps her hand firmly planted in mine.

She's quiet as I lead her through the back to the door I keep locked at all times. I type in the key code, holding the door open as she takes a step inside.

She gasps the moment she steps fully in. I let the door close behind us as her eyes go wide. Her perfect mouth hangs open slightly.

My skin prickles with heat, the nerves of her seeing my hard work spreading throughout my body. I feel the intense need for her to love the sculptures neatly organized on the shelves. For her to see them and think I'm talented the same way she thought Margo was.

I want to prove myself to her. And I've never wanted to prove myself to anyone when it comes to my art.

"Tell me what you think," I say, my tone pleading. I'd get on my knees if she asked me, if that's what it took to know every single one of her thoughts.

She turns toward me, her eyes finding mine. She looks at me so deeply it feels like she's looking inside me and uncovering every single thing I keep hidden. Taking a deep breath, she gives me a timid smile. "I think you're the most talented person I know."

I think I'm in love with you.

My eyes go wide at the thought. It crept into my mind unexpectedly, but at the same time, it feels like something I already knew. It's almost like my head was just accepting what my heart already knew—I'm in love with Pippa Jennings. My shortcake. *Mine.*

"Don't lie to me," I croak, my voice going hoarse with emotion. I desperately want her words to be true, but I'm riddled with self-doubt, making me believe that there's no way she's telling me the truth.

Pippa runs her fingers along one of my pieces. "I'm not, Camden. These are enchanting."

"*You're* enchanting."

Her eyes immediately find mine. She continues to walk through the shelves, taking her time looking at all the pieces I store here.

"There are so many," she mutters.

"It's years and years' worth of work," I admit, my hands finding my pockets.

"They deserve to be on display."

I lift a shoulder. She's right. As someone who has to have an eye for art, I know they're good. But there's something that stops me from giving them to the world. It's scary putting your hard work on display for other people to criticize. I don't need the money to sell them. But eventually, I think I'd like for them to be appreciated.

I follow Pippa through the shelves after she disappears from sight. When I find her in the next row over, she's stripped out of the sweater she was wearing.

She wears a wide smile as I give her a questioning look. "Isn't it cold in here?"

"It's incredibly cold," she answers, pulling at a tie at her waist. When she gets the knot undone, the sides of her dress come all the way open, exposing her perfect body.

I swallow slowly, appreciating the view in front of me. "What are you doing?"

"Showing you my body. Maybe you'll get inspired to carve mine into clay if I show you every inch of me."

She playfully bites her lip, walking backward as she reaches behind her back to unclasp her bra.

"I'd first need to get a rough sketch of you so I can create a base for the piece."

Pippa's eyes travel to the corner of my studio space. There's a table with supplies lined up along the top, with one chair placed next to it in case I want to sit. "It looks to me like you have a sketch pad. I bet you can find a pencil somewhere."

She maintains eye contact as she bends over, pulling her thong down her legs until she's completely naked in my workspace.

I'm so fucking turned on. My cock strains in my jeans, aching to be touched by her. I hadn't shown her this part of the gallery thinking to fuck her back here, but goddamn I'd love to fuck her on top of my drafting table.

"Pippa…" Her name comes out as a warning.

"Draw me, Camden," she suggests, knowing exactly what she's doing by running a hand along her naked skin. Her fingers pinch her nipples as she palms her full breasts.

"I don't enjoy drawing."

"You just said you have to before doing anything with clay."

"I do," I answer, letting my eyes rake along her body. Her legs cross at her ankles, not giving me a view of her pussy. I don't have to see her to know she's already wet for me. It's something I love about her, how reactive she is to me.

Pippa looks around, her eyes lighting up when she focuses on the table. Her hips swing in a sexy rhythm as she makes her way to the large wood table. I want to ask her what she's doing, but I follow her lead, watching her with hungry eyes as she climbs up onto the table.

Fuck the sketch. I want to skip to the part when I spread her legs wide open and taste her sweet, perfect cunt.

Pippa adjusts her body on the table, keeping her eyes pinned on me the entire time.

"Sit," she instructs, her eyes motioning to my chair. She picks up a sketchpad and a pencil from one of my utensil cups, sliding them across the table for me.

"We've talked about this before," I growl, making my way to her. "You don't tell me what to do."

"Take charge, then," she suggests, shifting to her knees. She runs her hands along her body, tracing the curves my fingers itch to bring to life on paper and then in clay.

"It takes time to get a sketch developed." I take a seat, the chair groaning underneath my weight.

She pushes her thighs open, her knees gliding along the wood as she flips her hair over her shoulder. "I can be patient."

I grab the sketchpad, placing it in my lap before I reach for the pencil she laid out. "Since when have you ever been patient, shortcake?"

Her teeth dig into her bottom lip as she fights a smile. "I can learn." Her fingers brush along her clit. She's showing restraint by not playing with herself in an effort to continue to taunt me.

Sighing, I open to a blank page of the book. I always hate this process of development. The moment I hold a pencil in my hand, I'm transported to the times my mother would crash my tutoring sessions. She'd hover over my assignments, watching every single pencil stroke of mine to see if I amounted to anything.

I'd mess up on purpose, not wanting to give my parents the satisfaction of knowing I was exactly who they wanted me to be.

Even in adulthood, this part is always my least favorite. I know I have talent, and I hate it. But with Pippa's hooded eyes watching me begin, I wonder if she can make me appreciate this step of the process.

"Get to work," she demands, letting her thighs open a little wider.

I can see all of her.

Her clit, pink and swollen with pleasure. Her arousal, already making her pussy glisten. I can even see bite marks on her inner thighs from last night.

"You're not the one making demands," I snap, getting comfortable in my chair.

"I kind of think I am."

I look at her from over the sketchpad, holding her stare.

"Touch yourself," I demand.

Her eyes go wide, her fingers skirting along the sensitive skin between her thighs. "But you're..."

"I'm drawing you, baby. Keep yourself busy as I do so. It's going to be a while."

Her hips rock back and forth. I don't know if she even realizes she's doing it, but as she rocks forward, she lets her fingers drift over her clit.

"Just like that." I groan, wishing it was my fingers running through her wetness. "Finger fuck yourself, baby."

Her eyes flutter shut as she slides one of her fingers into her waiting pussy. She lets out a long moan as she picks up speed, fully leaning in to what I'm telling her to do.

"Two fingers." My voice doesn't leave any room for argument. It's loud and commanding, the passion I feel for her taking control.

My right hand moves quickly along the piece of paper as I begin to lay out the base for my sketch. The point of these drawings is just so I can get the wiring right for the base. It doesn't have to be vividly detailed, but I could be persuaded to make it as detailed as possible if I get to watch her touch herself the entire time.

When I look up, I find Pippa coaxing two fingers into her cunt, just like I told her. "Good fucking girl," I praise, running a hand along my straining cock. I could easily toss my sketchpad to the side and replace Pippa's hand with my tongue, but I fight the urge.

She's sexy as hell getting herself off. I want to sit back and watch her make herself come. I'll study every single movement of hers so I can learn new things about what brings her pleasure.

"God, look how greedily you fuck yourself. You're shoving your fingers as far as they will go, baby. Are you missing my cock?"

"Yes." She moans. "I'm imagining it's you."

"What part of me?"

Her thumb runs over her clit as her fingers push in and out of her. "Any part of you," she answers.

"Imagine your fingers are my cock. Ride them hard, like you'd ride me."

She bounces up and down, her tits jiggling. She does exactly as she's told, riding her hand as if she was riding my cock.

I let her have her fun, savoring every moan that falls from her lips as I trace the curve of her spine on the paper. I want to remember her just like this. Her back arched, her thighs open, and her head thrown back in pleasure.

I already know without a doubt in my mind that I'll be bringing this picture to life. I'll spend countless hours forming her perfect, round breasts from clay. I'll put in the time to create a piece that attempts to do her majestic body justice.

I take a deep breath, trying to fight my aching cock and balls. All my body wants to do is close the distance between us and shove into her soaking wet pussy.

"Are you close to coming?"

She nods up and down, her curled pieces of hair dancing along the top of the table from how far her head is thrown back.

"Come for me like a good little slut. Let me see your cum drip out of you, and then maybe I'll fill you with mine."

I've never heard her moan so loud, her fingers working faster.

I set the sketch pad down. I've got what I needed. I wouldn't miss watching this for anything. Sitting forward, I let one hand work at unbuttoning my jeans while the other clutches the armrest to keep myself seated.

"Let your cum drip over the table," I demand, my voice hoarse with lust. "That way, I can think of you every single time I'm here."

If she hears me, she doesn't give any indication of it. She's too busy riding her hand, grinding her hips back and forth until her moans are loudly ringing throughout the room. I can't resist pulling my cock free, letting my fingers wrap around my length as I stroke myself up and down.

"You're exquisite when you come," I muse, my voice mixing with her moans. "You with your cheeks flushed and your thighs spread open for me is the greatest masterpiece I've ever seen."

"God..." she moans, her fingers still pushing in and out of her.

I click my tongue, standing up and walking to her. "God's not here, baby. You're not his dirty whore—you're mine."

Her eyes pop open as she finds me standing right in front of her. "Fuck me," she pleads, pulling her fingers from herself. She goes to wipe them off on her thigh, but I grab her wrist before she can do it. I keep it in my grasp, guiding her wet fingers to me. We keep eye contact as I coax her cum-coated fingers into my mouth. My tongue circles them, my eyes fluttering shut with the taste of her pussy filling my mouth.

I let my teeth scrape against the pads of her fingers, earning myself another moan from her. It mixes with my own moan at tasting her. My cheeks hollow out, cleaning her fingers of her arousal.

"Camden," she pleads, trying to reach out and grab my cock. "Fuck me. Right now."

I take a step back, quickly stripping myself of my clothes. "Only because you said *my* name."

She smiles, her white teeth biting her bottom lip. "Or because you're dying to fuck me." She gestures to my straining cock, the tip already wet with precum.

"Don't get mouthy with me," I demand.

"Then fuck me."

I roughly grab at her ankle, pulling her to the edge of the table. She yelps, her hands smacking against the wood to steady herself. My arm wraps around her, spinning her so she's on her hands and knees. With her position on the table, I'm met with a view of her soaking wet pussy and her tight asshole. I run my finger from her clit and travel up, circling the puckered hole. She moans loudly, the top of her body falling to rest on the table. With her back arched at me, I'm tempted to feast on her pussy—and her ass.

I do just that, getting her warmed up and ready all over again. My tongue swipes up and down, caressing the most intimate parts of her.

"You said you'd fuck me." She groans, pushing her ass against my face despite her words.

"I'm going to, baby," I say in between licks. "But one taste of your pussy and I couldn't help but feel you come against my tongue." With my words distracting her, I push my finger into her puckered hole, my cock twitching with the loud moan she lets out.

"You're so fucking dirty," I muse, my tongue flicking her clit. "My dirty girl likes her pussy licked and her ass fingered."

"Camden," she pleads. I push my finger deeper inside her, waiting for her to lose control and come all over again.

"I know you want me to fuck you, baby, and I will. But first, you're going to come against my mouth. I want to taste it. After you've done that, you'll have earned my cock."

She spasms around me, her body shaking as an orgasm takes over her entire body. I don't stop until I'm confident I've milked the orgasm for everything it's worth. Once her body relaxes, I flip her over, not being gentle with her.

I pull her down the table until her ass hangs off the edge, putting her in the perfect position to take my cock. Her chest rises and falls in quick breaths as she recovers from the orgasm.

"Is this what you wanted?" I ask, running the tip of my cock through her wetness.

"Yes," she answers, her body jolting when I begin to inch myself inside.

"Good. Now, take this cock like the dirty slut that you are."

I NEVER IMAGINED GOING TO MY FIRST EXTRAVAGANT EVENT WITH cum leaking from me. I cross my legs in the back of a limousine, well aware that the scrap of lace between my legs is soaked with both my cum and Camden's.

When we finally left his gallery, running a little late after breaking in his workspace, we had to rush to get back to his penthouse to get ready for the event. I'd intended on just taking a quick shower to get myself clean, but then I discovered soap from Miss Mary in Camden's shower, and I was turned on all over again.

Lips meet the shell of my ear, moving against my sensitive skin as I break out in goose bumps. "What are you thinking about, shortcake?" Camden's voice is low and sexy, his fingers trailing up my leg from the slit in my dress.

"Soap," I answer honestly, my mind going to discovering that Camden's been using the same soap as me.

"You're never going to let me live that down, are you?" His lips move to my neck. I'm suddenly thankful he'd denied riding to the event with Beck and Margo so we could have some time for just the two of us.

I smile, turning my face to his so we're eye to eye. "I was thinking how much it turned me on to know you took the soap all the way from Sutten to Manhattan."

His teeth rake against my throat. "I hated myself for buying it. For packing it in my bags. But it reminded me of you. Every time I showered with it, I pictured you were there with me. I'd fist my cock, thinking of you."

His fingers drift dangerously close to the wetness between my legs. I squeeze my thighs together. The hair and makeup team had spent two hours getting me ready for tonight; I'm not going to let him mess it up. Even though it is tempting…

"Camden," I moan as he squeezes my inner thigh. "Your cum literally still leaks from me from when you interrupted my shower while the glam team waited for me. Wait until tonight."

He laughs, the sound sending tingles down my spine. "If I remember correctly, you're the one who dropped to your knees for me the moment I stepped into the shower. I was just trying to get clean for the event."

My cheeks flush because he's right. I couldn't help myself. He'd fucked me until my legs were numb at the gallery, but seeing the soap, knowing what it meant, I needed him all over again.

I worry that I'll always feel like this, no matter what happens between us. Camden Hunter is a force of nature, and I don't think I'll ever get enough of him.

"Not going to say anything to that?" he continues, his tongue caressing the base of my neck.

"Can you blame me? It was sexy to know even when you were gone, you were thinking of me."

"Thoughts of you have plagued my mind for far too long. I'm always thinking of you. I've got the soap at my place in Sutten, too. And the lotion," he adds.

The limo slows. I try to look out the window, but it's far too tinted to see anything. I can make out headlights behind us, almost like we're in a line of waiting cars.

"I'd much prefer to ditch them," Camden continues, his fingers finding my chin. He guides my face to look at his. "And just have you with me at all times instead."

My heart pounds in my chest from the mix of not only his

words but the intense way he looks at me. "You have to take me on at least four more dates before you ask me to spend every night with you."

"I need to know you're mine. Just mine." His words come out hurried, like he didn't even have time to second-guess them before they left his lips.

My back straightens, my fingers tightening on the lapels of his black tux. "That sounded like a demand and not a question."

He smiles, his thumb brushing over my lip. "It's a demand but also a plea. You're already my everything, shortcake. Now I just need to know you're all mine. *Please.*"

If I didn't already know I was falling for him, I'd be positive by the sheer vulnerability in his tone. In the way his eyes roam my face, trying to get a read on my reaction. In fact, this might be the time I realize I'm past falling for him. I've fallen.

"Words," Camden croaks. "I need words to know where your head's at."

I'm too busy thinking if I should blurt that I've fallen in love with him. It's at the tip of my tongue, desperate to be put out in the open. But I'm too terrified that my feelings have developed too fast and they'll scare him away. That his gran was wrong when she told me he was in love with me. So I keep them locked inside, instead fusing my lips to his to distract myself.

He greedily kisses me back for a moment before he pulls away. His fingers stay locked on my cheeks as his icy-blue gaze stares at me deeply. "I'm yours. All yours. Are *you* mine?"

"Yes," I immediately answer, glancing at his lips.

"Really?" His voice is laced with vulnerability and excitement, doing something to my heart.

I nuzzle my nose against his. "Is that even a question? You're rich, give phenomenal orgasms, and are a softie underneath that grumpy facade. Of course I'm yours."

"I can't wait to introduce you on the red carpet as mine."

My head rears back. "Red carpet?"

His lips twitch as a smile plays on his lips. "Yes. This gala is huge. There will be celebrities and people of power from various industries in attendance tonight. And every single one of them will know you're *mine*."

I look down at the dress Emma and Margo helped me pick out. The blush-pink color was one that I couldn't say no to. When Emma convinced me to try it on, I knew immediately it was the one. The corset top hugged my body perfectly, accentuating my breasts and the narrow of my waist. At the waist, it pleats before the silk fabric falls all the way to my feet. It's sexy but in a classy way, with a slit that runs up my leg and off-the-shoulder sleeves.

I've never felt so beautiful as I did when I stepped out of the room I got ready in and found Camden staring right at me. His shoulders had stilled, as if I'd actually taken his breath away with the formfitting dress and the pristine curls that fell down my back.

Now I'm second-guessing everything, knowing we'll have to walk a red carpet.

"Will there be cameras?" I ask anxiously, gripping him tighter when the car comes to a stop.

"Yes. A lot of them. But I'll be with you the entire time."

"I don't know if I can do this," I admit.

His hand finds mine at the same moment his door opens. "I've got you, shortcake."

And before I can say anything else, he slides out. The moment he's out of the car, he turns toward me and holds out his hand. I grab it, taking a deep breath and letting him lead me into his world.

Chapter 52
CAMDEN

"I think my cheeks hurt from smiling," Pippa whines next to me before taking a large gulp from the champagne flute in her hand. We stand off to the side of the dance floor, waiting for Beck and Margo to meet us before finding our table.

My eyes scan the room, looking for familiar faces. There's an uneasy feeling in my stomach as I search for Daly. We need to have a conversation, but I have to find a way to do it without Pippa hearing. The pit in my stomach could also be from the idea of my parents being here. It depends on their mood if they show up to these events, and I hope tonight is a night where I get to avoid them.

I don't want to introduce them to Pippa. They don't deserve to meet the woman I love.

"If one more person asks if I'm pregnant, I might actually punch them in the throat," Margo rants, walking up to us with Beck and Emma following closely behind.

"Want this?" Pippa offers, holding out her half-drank champagne glass.

Margo snatches it from her hand. "Thanks. I'll need about five of these to dodge the baby questions all night."

"Next time someone asks you if you're pregnant, you should aim the question back at them," Pippa suggests, a mischievous smile on her face.

Margo and Beck both laugh as Emma walks away to flag down a server with a tray full of more champagne.

"I might actually do that next time." Her smile falters for a moment as she looks back at Beck. "There's nothing I want more than to tell people we're having a baby, but it hasn't happened yet. And even if we were, I don't feel comfortable telling people until we're out of the first trimester."

Pippa reaches out and squeezes Margo's hand. "You don't owe anyone an explanation. It's nobody's business. I'm sorry they're asking you."

"I told you we could avoid the press," Beck offers, wrapping his arm around his wife.

Margo smiles up at him. "I don't mind the press when they're asking about our work or how much money we think will be raised for charity tonight. I just feel like the baby questions are out of hand."

"Hold the champagne all night and people will stop asking," Pippa adds.

Emma returns, her hands full of multiple champagne flutes. She holds them out to our little circle, each of us taking one. "Maybe we should just have you chugging from a bottle in front of everyone. That'll make them stop."

Everyone laughs. I hold up my champagne flute to declare a toast. "To the assholes who think they're entitled to our business."

"And to my rich friends who get me into these types of things," Emma adds with a laugh. "Cheers!"

It's quiet for a moment as each of us takes a drink. The champagne is bubbly and sweet as it goes down my throat.

Margo finishes her drink, turning to face her body toward Pippa and me. "Speaking of questions, how did your first red carpet go, Pippa?"

Pippa's eyes widen as she lets out a slow breath. The exposed skin of her breasts moves with the breath, making me want to reach out and pop one of her perfect nipples free. Too bad there are too many people, and she's making me wait to devour her until this night is over.

"It was actually terrifying," Pippa answers with a resigned sigh. "They kept asking for my restaurant's name as if any of them would have a clue about Wake and Bake."

"Holy shit!" Emma calls, the back of her hand hitting Beck in the stomach with her sudden movement.

"What the hell, Emma," Beck rants, giving her a look. She doesn't notice it; she's too busy looking at the grand staircase that leads down into the ballroom.

I follow her sight, catching on to what she sees at the same moment as everyone else.

"Is that *Winnie*?" Margo asks, completely shocked.

I squint my eyes, looking from the girls' friend to Beck. "Is that Archer Moore?"

Beck watches the two of them with his eyebrows drawn in on his forehead. "It definitely is."

We stare wide-eyed at Winnie, arm in arm with Archer Moore—someone Beck and I went to school with. And someone I thought Winnie's family hated.

Pippa shifts next to me, leaning in close. "I recognize your friend Winnie. Did we not know she had a boyfriend?"

Emma lets out a low, long whistle. "I knew she had one. Just last time she confided in me, she was not with *him*."

"I didn't know she was with anyone at all," Margo notes, staring at her best friend.

The word on the street is decades ago, there was a business deal that went wrong between the Moores and the Bishops. They were supposed to be business partners before Winnie's grandfather pulled out, stabbing Archer's family in the back in the process.

We all stare at them as they head in our direction. Archer seems to almost be dragging Winnie over to us. Her fingers are wrapped so tightly around his bicep I can see the little indentations on his suit from the pressure.

Archer stops in front of us, giving Beck and me a cold smile. "Sinclair. Hunter. Good to see you two."

He shakes both of our hands, his handshake firm.

"I thought events like this were never your thing," Beck comments, giving Archer and Winnie a polite smile. Archer was a year younger than us in school, but he was always avoiding parties at all costs. Even after we all graduated and moved on with our lives, he rarely showed up to functions hosted by New York's elite.

"I had to come to celebrate," Archer answers, his eyes flicking to Winnie at his side.

She's always been quiet when I've seen her with Margo and Emma, but she seems unusually quiet tonight.

Emma tries to get Winnie's attention, but she doesn't say anything. She looks at Archer's profile as if her life depended on it.

"Celebrate what, exactly?" Beck asks, looking at me, confused.

Archer lifts Winnie's hand, a giant diamond ring on her gloved hand sparkling underneath the chandeliers.

"What?" Emma shrieks, ripping Winnie's hand from Archer's grip. Margo leans in close as well, inspecting what appears to be an engagement ring.

My head cocks for a moment, but before I can ask the questions running through my mind, Archer pulls Winnie's hand from Emma's grasp and plants a kiss to the glistening diamond on Winnie's finger. "We couldn't pass up the opportunity for our first event as husband and wife."

"I think I might pass out," Emma comments, her words coming out shaky.

"What is he talking about?" Margo presses, taking a step closer to Winnie.

Winnie looks up with a soft smile. "We've got some things to catch up on."

Margo wraps her arm through Pippa's, something I appreciate because I don't want Pippa to feel left out, even though she clearly has no idea the impact of what's transpiring in front of us.

"I need to go to the ladies' room," Margo chimes, pulling Pippa with her. She uses her other hand to grab Winnie, having to pretty much rip Winnie from Archer's grasp. "You're coming, too, Win."

Winnie doesn't argue, even though Archer's lips press into a straight line of displeasure.

"You okay with that?" I ask Pippa, wanting to make sure she feels comfortable.

She smiles. "Yes."

Margo doesn't waste any more time. She pulls on Pippa and Winnie, gesturing for Emma to follow.

The three of us watch them leave, no one speaking until their bodies disappear into the group of partygoers.

After they're gone, I turn to face Archer. "It appears congratulations are in order."

Archer gives a curt nod. "Thanks, Hunter."

"Did we miss an invite?" My eyes fly to Beck. Normally, I'm the one who is an asshole between the two of us.

"She wanted something small," Archer answers, his eyes searching the room.

Beck and I share a look. Something seems different about this, but it's not my place to say anything. My eyes catch on Daly talking in a group of people across the room.

"I'll be back," I tell the two of them, dismissing myself. As fun as it'd be to hear all about how Winnie ended up married to him, there are more pressing things for me to handle.

I weave in and out of the bodies of people until I find Daly. His eyes find mine immediately. He excuses himself from the conversation and stops in front of me.

I don't waste time cutting to the chase. "Tell me you have more answers."

Just by the way his face pinches together, I know he doesn't have good news for me.

"The paperwork hasn't fully gone through, but the real estate group said the sale is under contract."

"Did they say with who?"

Daly shakes his head. "No. All they said was that it was all the properties on your block but yours and that it was a New York buyer."

"Fuck." I seethe, my mind racing with who it could be.

I'd asked Daly to help me get to the bottom of the notice Pippa was given. If the real estate group was wanting to sell, I'd gladly purchase all of the properties so the rent didn't go up or wasn't sold to someone else. Or at least give Pippa the opportunity to buy herself out like she said she wanted. It makes no sense why all of a sudden, someone from out of town has come in to buy Sutten real estate. It was a shock to most that I did. I don't understand what business anyone has with those properties.

"At this point, we might just have to wait until the sale is final, and then if you choose, you could go to whoever purchased it and give them a number."

I run a hand over my mouth, my eyes scanning the room to see if Pippa and the girls have returned yet. "Do you think we know them?"

Daly sighs. "It seems too coincidental for us not to, but I don't know. I'm trying to think of anyone who could profit off those spaces."

I frown, looking through the crowd of people, wondering if they're here now. "I need to find out before it goes through. I can't let Pippa know that the business location she's worked so hard for might've been purchased from right underneath her."

"Can she get a different space? I haven't looked around."

I shoot him a scathing look. "I'm not even going to put energy into your stupid question."

His cheeks puff out as he looks at anything but me. He's

done with the conversation, which is fine. He's not useful to me at the moment anyway.

Instead, I look out at the crowd of the wealthiest people in New York. Someone here has to have answers. I just have to find them.

Chapter 53
PIPPA

I EXCUSE MYSELF FROM THE CONVERSATION BETWEEN MARGO, Winnie, and Emma. They were very nice to include me, but as they huddle together in the fanciest bathroom I've ever seen in my life, I realize I'm just a bystander to what seems to be a *very* private conversation.

I sneak away as Emma fires question after question at Winnie, not even giving her time to respond before asking another. None of them notice me leaving, which I prefer. I'll find them later tonight after they've ironed out their conversation.

It takes me a few moments to stumble back to the elegant ballroom. I keep getting lost in small rooms full of people mingling. When I'd agreed to come to the gala, I imagined something completely different than what it actually is. I knew Camden had money, but I just didn't imagine him in this lavish of situations.

I'm trying to squeeze next to a group of women deep in conversation when I pick up Camden's name from one of their mouths. "Did you see who Camden Hunter brought tonight?"

My steps pause for a moment. I know I shouldn't listen, but I can't help it. I want to know what else they'll say.

"I don't get it. He's dated far prettier. Why bring *her*?"

"Because he probably found it funny," one woman offers with a high-pitched laugh. "Or thought it'd be great publicity for his newest gallery if he brought someone from that tiny, shitty town.

He'll use her and then discard her when he grows bored." There's a pause for a moment, or maybe it's the blood rushing through my ears that makes me unable to hear anything else. Regardless, I don't hear anything until the same voice adds, "That's what he does to every woman. This country nobody will be no different."

My face flushes with embarrassment. Part of me wants to walk up to them and tell them to not be so careless with their words. To tell them I'm a human with feelings and that Sutten is actually an amazing town and doesn't deserve the hate they're giving it. The other part of me focuses on what they said about Camden, letting doubt creep into my mind when I know they shouldn't be.

I hurry away before I can say something I'll regret. Camden made it clear to anyone who asked on the red carpet that I was his. He doesn't seem to be hiding anything, but we still haven't truly defined what we are. As I make my way to the ballroom, searching for Camden, I can't help but wonder if their words ring true. What were his reasons for wanting me to come tonight?

I can't find him anywhere at first, completely circling the room, looking for his familiar broad shoulders and icy gaze. Finally, I spot him, seeming to be in a heated discussion with the asshole I spilled a drink on from his gallery opening. Jack, I think? Or maybe Jason?

Camden stands with his back straight as a board, his hands crossed over his chest in an almost defensive position. I stop, wondering what I should do. If I take a few steps closer, I might be able to hear their conversation, but I don't know if it's something he'd want me to join in on or not.

Someone bumps into me, pushing me slightly closer to them, allowing me to now overhear bits of their conversation.

"I don't see a reason for any of this." Camden seethes, the venom in his voice making me pause. I've never heard him that angry, even if his anger has been aimed at me before.

"That's a silly comment, considering you're the one who gave me the idea in the first place," Jason responds. "Without you, none of this would be possible."

"I don't understand."

"If you hadn't bought the Sutten gallery and invited us all, I wouldn't have been introduced to the lucrative real estate market in Sutten Mountain."

"My space was actually up for sale when I purchased it," Camden hisses.

"Mine was, too, once I gave the right price and talked to the right people. Why are you acting this way, Hunter? That country broad giving you such good sex she's got you not thinking clearly?"

"You're a goddamn disgrace," Camden spits.

I'm so stunned by the conversation that I can't move, my mind trying to piece together what they could possibly be talking about.

"Jason, tell me the price, and I'll buy it from you."

I can only see a sliver of Jason's face, but I see a smile form. "I'd have to like you to do that, and I haven't forgotten how you embarrassed me. I'd much rather raise the rent for the existing tenants higher and higher until they can't afford it any longer. Then they'll have no choice but to leave, and I can bring in people we know to rent the spaces. We'll take over that shithole town that tourists seem to love, and it'll all be because *you* started it."

I can't stand back any longer. I walk until my fingers are wrapping around Camden's bicep, pulling on him until I'm forcing him to look at me. "What's going on?" I ask, my eyes desperately searching his face to figure out what's happening.

Jason gives me a sinister smile. It makes my skin crawl. I hate that Camden knows people like him. One look at the man and it's evident that he's a terrible person. "Look who it is, the little bitch who wasn't taught manners."

"Watch your fucking mouth," Camden snaps, his voice booming. It's so loud it catches the attention of others around us.

I don't even care what Jason called me; I'm still trying to process what he'd said before.

"Camden?" I ask, my voice trembling, even though I hate it. "What's going on?"

"I think he wanted to hide it from you, but I can cut to the chase and tell you I'm your new landlord."

My heart sinks. It hurts even worse when Camden's eyes don't meet mine. Instead, his jaw clenches as he stares down at his shoes. I want him to look up, to look at me and explain what's happening.

He does neither.

Instead, I'm left with the sneering Jason, his beady eyes gleefully staring at me like his entire night has been made by sharing this information.

"I'm confused," I stammer, trying to have my mind play catch-up. None of this makes sense. Why would he be my landlord? Why would he have anything to do with Sutten?

"I'm buying your business location, along with the others on the block. They'll all be mine once everything goes through. And then, you'll pay me or get out to make room for people who can actually afford it."

I feel sick. The world seems to get fuzzy around me as I think through what he's just said.

"Why?" I squeak, my voice sounding meek and timid. I hate everything about it.

He looks over at Camden, and I do the same thing, finding his eyes finally on me. All I can see is regret in them. It hurts my heart because I don't even fully understand why he's looking at me like that.

Jason lets out a low laugh. It sends goose bumps down my skin because it's weird and creepy, and I'm uncomfortable even being in his presence.

"Because Camden showed me how booming the market is in

your tiny town. People flock to it, and I didn't even visit during your busy season. Imagine the profits we could make from specific stores during the ski season. It isn't personal." He looks over at Camden, who refuses to look away from me. "Or maybe it is. Either way, you'll find a way to pay me big, or I'll replace your store with someone who will."

"The owners weren't selling," I note, looking to Camden for clarification.

"Jason swooped in and convinced them." He reaches to grab me, but I put my hands up to stop him. I can't have him touch me right now, not when he might be the very reason everything I've worked for goes up in flames.

"I'll fix it," Camden adds, his voice low enough for just me to hear. "I just need time. I've had Daly on it all day."

My eyes widen as a lump forms in my throat. This can't be happening. "You...you knew?" I hate how my shaky voice betrays every single one of my emotions.

I look weak right now, and I can't even begin to care because mostly, I feel betrayed by the man I've fallen in love with. The guilt is written all over his face. In the way he frowns, a crease appearing on his forehead as his eyes move from mine for just a fraction of a second in pretty much an admission of guilt.

"I found out earlier, but I didn't want to tell you until I knew more."

"Why wouldn't you tell me the moment you found out this asshole was trying to get rid of everything I've ever worked for?"

"I didn't know it was him," Camden counters. "I just knew the block was under contract, and I've done enough business to know the intentions when big real estate groups buy up smaller real estate."

"Because you're one of them." Everything comes crashing down all at once. My reality gets messed up as I realize Camden is exactly who I originally thought he was—not who I hoped he was. Which unfortunately means he belongs in their world—not mine.

Camden winces like my words actually hurt him. "Don't say that," he rasps. "I'm going to fix it."

I shake my head back and forth slowly, my eyes stinging with unshed tears.

Before I can say anything else, Jason speaks up. "I'll let the two of you handle this. I look forward to speaking with you more, Pippy. The deal should be final soon. Keep an eye out for the rent increase."

"It's Pippa," Camden fumes, cutting a glare in Jason's direction. "And you'll be speaking to *me* sooner because this isn't over."

Jason gives a satisfied smile. "Give it up, Hunter. You should thank me. This can only lead to you getting higher-paying customers."

He leaves, and everything I want to say to him gets stuck in my throat. I'm in shock and dealing with too much hurt to speak. Not with my world crashing down around me with the realization that Camden's and my worlds are too vastly different to work.

"I'll fix this," Camden promises, trying to reach for my hand. I pull mine back, not wanting to feel his skin against mine. If I let him touch me, my head will become foggy all over again, and I can't have that right now. I need to think clearly. I have to figure out a way to stop this.

"Can we talk somewhere private?" I ask, looking around at the partygoers who are eyeing us over their shoulders.

"We can talk wherever you want to talk. Just please don't shut down on me. I'm going to fix it."

All I can do is nod because the lump in my throat is too big. I want to believe him with every part of me, but for him to fix this, he'd have to go against the only world he's ever known.

He places his hand on my back, steering me through the

people until we step out to the cold breeze of the night. There's a chill to the fall air, making my skin break out in goose bumps.

Camden begins to shrug out of his jacket. "Take my jacket," he insists, pulling his second arm free.

I shake my head. "I'm fine."

His eyes darken, his icy-blue irises turning dark and stormy. "You're rubbing your arms like you're cold. Take it. Now."

I don't argue when he places it on my shoulders, even though I know it is a bad idea. I'm engulfed in his smell, a scent that's become too comforting to me. A scent I've grown far too accustomed to when I knew in the back of my mind one day I'd have to let it go.

I hate it, but I can't help but wonder if today is that day.

Camden doesn't take a step back. His hands stay on my shoulders as his eyes search my face. "I need you to talk to me. I need to know that we'll figure this out together."

I cut my gaze from his, unable to look him in the eye. It hurts too much. "Maybe it's best we don't."

His body jerks like I've hit him. "Nothing will ever be the best for me if it isn't with you."

My legs shake, and I realize that maybe it isn't the cold air making me shiver. Maybe it's the heaviness of the reality of our ending finally hitting me. "My entire world is that cafe, Camden." My voice quakes, but I keep talking because I don't care if he sees me break down. "It's all I've ever wanted. Everything I've worked hard for."

Tears pour down my face. He tries to reach out and wipe them away, but I turn my head to avoid him. "My mom helped me pick out everything there. We spent hours at the hardware store, selecting the perfect shade of pink. She helped me design a logo and went to countless thrift stores with me to help decorate the place. I walk into that building every morning and feel her with me. She's everywhere in it. And some rich asshole in a suit wants to take that from me." My head rocks back and forth as my eyes close. I can't see anything through the tears. "I can't lose this one thing I still have of hers."

He tentatively grabs my chin. When he tries to coax it up, I fight him, not wanting to look at him. He sighs, not forcing my head up, even though I know he wants to.

"I told you I'll fix it. I stick to my word. You won't lose it, baby. Let me fix this for you."

I let out a shaky breath. "You wouldn't have to fix it if you hadn't tried to fix Sutten in the first place." I know my words are harsh, that he doesn't deserve them, but there's an irrational part of me that thinks they're true. If he hadn't tried making Sutten something it wasn't, then businessmen like Jason wouldn't have ever threatened everything I've worked for.

"I never could've imagined he'd do this." His voice catches with emotion. "You have to believe me on that."

I finally look at him. I can't help myself, and I regret it the moment our eyes connect. Because I know he means that, and I hate myself for ever even having the thought to blame him for this. It isn't his fault, but I'm lost and scared, and I hate that I'm lashing out at him.

"I need to go back to Sutten," I tell him, my voice quaking.

"We'll go together."

I shake my head. "I think I should go home alone."

Chapter 54
CAMDEN

It feels like my heart is being ripped in half. Pippa looks up at me with a blank expression. There used to be light—and maybe even love—in her eyes when her eyes met mine. Now, there's nothing but tears. I want to rip apart the world after seeing her like this, seeing her so upset.

"You don't have to do this alone," I tell her, wiping a tear from her cheek. There's no use doing it; seconds after I've wiped it away, another one follows suit.

"What are we doing here?" Pippa asks. Even her voice is void of emotion. She's pulling away from me. I can feel it, and I don't know what to do. I've never had to fight for someone. I've never cared about someone enough to be in this position.

"We're here because I wanted to show you my world. I've seen so much of yours in Sutten, I just wanted to have you here and show you off to everyone. But we can go back home if you want. I'll just—"

Pippa places a hand to my chest. "No, not here physically. But here in general." Her eyes look to the building next to us. "I wanted to love this part of your life, Camden. I really did. But this isn't me. I don't want this, and I'll never fit into this life."

My heart hammers inside my chest from the panic of losing her. "Until Jason, I thought you were having fun."

She lets out a sad laugh. "Did you know when I was looking for you, I overheard these women talking about you? I think one of them was someone you used to see. They were also talking about me. About how I don't belong. About how we don't belong together and that there's no reason you'd bring me here unless you were using me."

My pulse hammers through my ears with rage. I tighten my jaw, trying to fight the anger coursing through my veins. "You don't think I'm using you, do you?"

She shakes her head. "No. I don't think you're using me." I feel the smallest moment of relief until she keeps talking. "But it made me think they might have a point. We don't work, Camden. Our lives are different. Too different. No part of me wants to fit in here. Not when women talk nasty about each other behind their backs and men with money purchase businesses with the intent to drive out the good people who have worked their asses off to be there. I don't want to fit in here, and you don't want to fit in in Sutten." She takes another breath. "So what are we doing here?"

I stare at her as it feels like my world is crashing all around me at once. I had no idea she'd felt this way. I truly thought before Jason ruined the night that she was enjoying herself. Was it all pretend? Or was I just too blind to see that she wasn't comfortable?

"What are you saying?" The feeling in my chest is the reason people never fall in love. It's the reason I've never allowed myself to care about another human this way because it hurts too fucking much to put your heart in someone else's hands and have them hand it back to you.

"I think reality finally caught up to us. Our lives are too different to make this work."

My jaw clenches as I try to think about what to say to her. I'm angry. Angry at Jason. Angry at our circumstances. And angry at her for wanting to give up so easily.

"I love you." My voice trembles, doing nothing to hide the vulnerability in it.

She sobs, streaks of black running down her face with tears.

She's silent. I'm used to her speaking her mind. Her silence is unnerving. Or maybe it's the defeated look on her face. I've never told a woman I was in love with them. I've never been in love, but I didn't imagine saying the words and having the woman who owns my heart look at me like she wished I'd never said them at all.

I take a deep breath, collecting my thoughts before speaking up. "I didn't know love until I knew you. And I'm trying to figure it out because I want to do better—be better—for you. But I can't do that if you won't let me. There's nothing I can say if you want to give up the second things get hard. But I do love you. I love you in a way that consumes me. You're my every thought, every dream, my entire being. I love you so much that it fucking hurts you think I wouldn't do anything, give up *anything*, to make us work."

Her bottom lip trembles. I hate seeing it. I hate all of this. I want to go back to this morning when we woke up and were happy. When things didn't feel like they were falling apart.

"I love you." Her three words do something to calm my racing heart. I can figure anything out from here as long as I know she loves me. "And I'm scared."

I nod, pulling her body into mine. She melts against me, her body molding to mine. I take in a deep breath, clutching the back of her head to my chest. I hold on to her for dear life, fearing if I let go for even a second, she'll leave. "I'm fucking terrified," I croak. "I've never felt like this. But please let me figure things out. Let *us* figure this out. There's nothing I wouldn't do to make you happy. To keep you. Jason won't get Wake and Bake. I promise."

She nods against my chest, her shoulders shaking as she weeps into my dress shirt. I hold her as she cries, her cheek pressed against my racing heart. People walk by us, probably finding us quite the show. I don't pay any of them attention; all I do is clutch her to me, only letting go long enough to lead her into the back of the limo and take her home.

She doesn't talk to me the entire ride home. After ten minutes of silence, no matter the questions I ask her, I resort to calling whoever I can. It doesn't feel like we both confessed our love. Nothing feels happy, and I know the sinking feeling in my stomach was warranted when I wake up early in the morning and find her side of the bed empty. The only thing left in her place is a neatly folded note.

Camden,

I couldn't sleep. Even after you stopped tossing and turning, I lay awake staring at the ceiling, a pit deep in my stomach as I thought about everything that is in jeopardy in Sutten.

As I felt hopeless about what to do, my mind went to you. To thoughts of you. To thoughts of us and what a life could look like between the two of us. I tried picturing myself here, in this world that you love, and I couldn't do it. I'd never fit in here. And I don't want to make you choose between this life and me. I know you don't picture yourself in Sutten. If I've learned anything about you, it's that Sutten will never have your heart like it has mine.

I want us to work. I stayed awake for hours trying to come up with a solution that doesn't end up with both our hearts broken, and I came up with nothing.

I won't allow you to choose me because to choose me would be to choose Sutten, and I know that isn't a choice you can make. The people in your world are the very reason I might lose what's most important to me in mine. I can't ask for you to go against them and jeopardize everything you've worked hard for.

I'm sorry for leaving. But I'm weak and knew if I looked you in the eye, there's no way I'd ever leave.

Please know this has nothing to do with you. You were the easiest person to fall in love with. You're deserving of a beautiful love story, Camden Hunter. I want it to be me and you, but I can't completely give my heart to you until I know I haven't lost the one last piece I have of my mom.

I have to go back to Sutten. I have to find a way to keep Wake and Bake. Please forgive me for leaving. I have to fix this, and I can't ask you to put everything on the line for me.

I love you. Don't ever forget that. I'll cherish your love forever. It was fun tempting fate with you, even if our fate isn't what we'd hoped for.

If you love me, give me time to fix this.

Yours,
Pippa

I READ it so many times that it becomes permanently etched into my mind, and once I've angrily committed it to memory, I toss it to the side.

For once in my life, I'm going to put someone else before myself. I'm going to prove to Pippa there's nothing I wouldn't do to keep her in my life forever.

Chapter 55
PIPPA

"I THINK MY FINGERS MIGHT FALL OFF," LEXI COMPLAINS FROM MY side as she twists the top of another piping bag.

"We just have six dozen more to ice, and we'll be done."

Mare whines from my other side, accidentally squeezing her bag too tight, and icing plops down onto the cupcake in one giant glob. "I never want to look at another cupcake again," she announces, trying to cover the glob of icing with even more icing.

"Same," Cade pipes up from across the counter. He proved to be terrible at icing cupcakes dozens and dozens of cupcakes ago, so instead, he's been given the job of neatly arranging them in boxes for presentation. "And I normally love Pip's cupcakes," he adds.

"We're almost done," I assure them, taking a moment to appreciate all of them showing up to help me. I'd arrived in Sutten early in the morning yesterday, and the only time I slept was on the way back from the airport when Cade and Mare picked me up.

I'd spent the entire plane ride coming up with ways to try and save not only Wake and Bake but our entire block. It started with a bake sale to raise the funds to come up with as much money as possible to take it to the people selling our block. But one thing led to another, and eventually, it ended in all of us coming together to create one huge fundraiser with everyone donating items to sell and simply donating money to the cause. People from all over town have donated items and services, trying to help in any way to help us raise as much money as possible.

Our town has been brought together in ways I never imagined. Everyone in Sutten really rallied around us when Mom died, but they've done it all over again with this.

My eyes get glossy when I think about all of the hard work everybody's put in for the last day. The vendor fair is tomorrow, and we're hoping that we'll get a lot of people to visit from the rodeo that's happening two towns over.

The bell chimes to Wake and Bake. Lexi pops up with the sound, letting her icing bag drop next to the rack of cooled cupcakes. "I'll go see who it is!" she cheers, trying to use any excuse to get a break.

She's gone for a moment before she's pushing the door open, the outline of a man in an expensive suit appearing behind her.

My heart skips as I wonder if it's Camden. I know I'd told him not to come back, but for a small moment, I was hopeful he did and he'd somehow come up with a solution that ended with us both happy and together.

It isn't Camden, and I hate the way my stomach drops with disappointment. I should've known better than to get involved. I should've thought about how different we were and never let him kiss me. Because the moment his lips hit mine, my heart was destined to be his. There was no use fighting it. It didn't care that we weren't compatible, that we were as opposite as two people could get. It wanted him regardless. And now we're both left with an ache in our chests because of it.

Maybe once I know I'm not going to lose this company I worked so hard to create, I'll be able to figure things out with Camden. But until I'm not threatened by someone from his world, I can't even think about it. It's no use.

"Mr. Livingston is here for you," Lexi announces, taking a step to the side to reveal Dean Livingston. He's still tall, dark, and handsome. But it's the wrong figure, the wrong face. The wrong man. And disappointment runs through my bones when I realize how badly I'd hoped for it to be Camden.

The toddler holding Dean's hand would've been my next clue that it wasn't Camden here to see me. Clara pops her head around the doorway, her eyes lighting up when she sees the rainbow of cupcakes lining my entire kitchen.

"Daddy! Cupcakes!" she squeals, trying to make a run for it. He keeps a hold of her hand, not letting her get very far.

"Hi, everyone," he says as he reaches down to lift his daughter. She has his same dark hair and brown eyes. Her eyes are wide with glee as she pays none of us attention and looks around at all of the cupcakes. "Clara wasn't supposed to work with me today, but Ma couldn't watch her, and I'm in between nannies." His eyes meet mine for a moment. "I hope you don't mind."

I smile wide, putting my piping bag down for a moment so I can say hi. "I'd never mind. I love seeing sweet Clara," I assure him, walking up to take her from his arms.

He gives a forced smile. There are bags under his eyes and not a lot of color in his face. He looks exhausted, but I can't say much else because I probably look the same. "I'm here because I have what can seem like good news."

My arms tighten around Clara, propping her on my hip. "Yeah?" I'm well aware of how hopeful my voice sounds.

"There's going to be an auction for the properties."

I gasp, looking around at everyone else in the room. For the first time since speaking with Jason in New York, I feel hopeful, and for the moment, that's good enough for me.

"So that means the contract fell through?"

Dean nods. "Sort of. I had some help, but I managed to convince the realty group that they could get far more if they took it to auction."

"Thank you." I look down at Clara, finding her still eyeing

the cupcakes. "Your daddy might have just saved the day. We'll owe him big-time."

Dean smooths out Clara's hair, looking at her affectionately. "It wasn't just me. And it won't be cheap. I don't think this Jason Vincent guy will go down without a fight. But there's a chance. I'm trying to speak with Dad to see if we could get in on the auction. He's trying to go more residential, but there's nothing he loves more than this town. We've got a chance, Pippa."

My eyes drift shut in relief. All I need is a chance—no matter how small it may be. That's enough.

"I don't know how to say thank you," I begin, setting Clara on the ground when she starts to wiggle her legs.

He keeps his eyes on her. "Don't thank me yet. We don't know what will happen. But between the town rallying together for the fundraiser tomorrow and the auction in two days, we might just make this happen."

"I want one," Clara declares, pointing her chubby finger at a box full of pink and purple cupcakes. Her brown eyes find her dad's. "Daddy, please?"

He sighs. "You haven't even had lunch yet."

"We've got sandwiches in the fridge. I can take her to have one before a cupcake if that's okay with you?" Lexi offers.

Dean looks nervous about it for a few seconds. His eyes bounce from Lexi to Clara and back. "I don't want to make you watch her. She can hang out with me while Pippa and I talk a bit longer."

I smile. "Lexi's amazing with the kids that always come in. Plus, I think she's looking for an excuse to get out of icing cupcakes."

Lexi laughs, shrugging. "You caught me."

"Please, Daddy?" Clara asks, pulling at Dean's pant leg. "I want to play with someone new."

"Are you tired of me?" he jokes to his daughter.

Except she smiles up at him and gives him a confident grin. "Yes."

Cade busts out with laughter behind us. It doesn't take long for all of us to double over in a fit of laughter, thanks to Clara.

"On that note, if it's okay with you, I'll take Clara out front." Lexi takes Clara's hand and walks her to the door.

Dean doesn't say anything, but he does keep his eyes pinned on Lexi and Clara until they're out of sight. Finally, he turns back to me. "I can trust her, right?" His voice is cautious. It's cute. I never would've expected the face of Livingston Realty to seem so vulnerable, but he's always been that way when it comes to his daughter.

"She's great. Clara's in great hands, I promise."

Mare claps her hands together excitedly, licking icing from her finger once she finishes her last cupcake. "Everyone get their heads back in the game. We have a small town to save!"

Chapter 56
CAMDEN

THE LAST COUPLE OF DAYS HAVE BEEN THE LONGEST ONES OF MY life. Being in Sutten and not being around the woman I love has been torture, but the next time I see her, I'm going to make damn sure I'm in the position to give her anything and everything she's ever dreamed of. Starting with making sure she and the people she loves don't lose their hard work to an asshole like Jason Vincent.

I've been hiding out in my rental, afraid that if I spent too much time at the gallery, I'd run into Pippa. I didn't want her to know I was back. I didn't want her to know I was doing everything in my power to fix this before I'd actually fixed it. She doesn't deserve empty promises. She deserves grand gestures and facts. And I'm determined to give her that.

"You've got a visitor," Trisha tells me, walking in with a Starbucks cup. The coffee is shit. Pippa's is far better, but I didn't want Trisha to blow our cover by going into Wake and Bake, so I've settled with coffee that always tastes like it's burnt. And it sucks. What's even worse is waking up in an empty bed. I've become far too accustomed to waking up with her body draped across mine. Once I've righted this wrong, I'll be telling her that she'll be sleeping next to me every night for the rest of our lives. There's no other option. I don't give a damn where the bed is; I just have to be with her.

"Camden?" Trisha prods, taking a step deeper into the room in my rental that has become my office.

I shake my head, sitting straighter in my chair. "Sorry." I gladly take the cup of coffee from her outstretched hand, even when I know it sucks. I hold it up to her. "Clearly, I need this."

Trisha smiles, looking over her shoulder. "Can I send Mr. Livingston your way?"

I take a sip of the coffee. "Which one?"

I hear a low chuckle from behind Trisha, Dean appearing in the doorway. "The best one," he insists, giving a confident smile to Trisha. "The one that comes with good news."

"Yeah?" I ask, gesturing for him to take a seat. I thought it was a long shot to reach out to him the morning I discovered Pippa gone from my bed, but to my surprise, he'd responded. Well, his secretary did, but shortly after, I got Dean himself. Come to find out, Pippa had already contacted him asking for help.

Dean unbuttons his suit jacket and takes a seat across from my desk. "I don't have long. My daughter is with Pippa and her crew, having the time of her life while I told them I had a meeting. If I'm gone too long, I fear they may feed my daughter enough cupcakes that she'll be bouncing off the walls all night."

I laugh. I met his daughter briefly last night. She was as cute as can be. It was comical to see how wrapped around her finger he was. We'd only met long enough for Dean and me to go over some paperwork to take to the real estate group selling the properties before he had to go. "She's probably had three cupcakes in the ten minutes it took for you to drive here."

He grunts, picking a pen up from my desk and twisting it between his fingers. "Hopefully I don't regret leaving her with them. I feel bad—she doesn't get a lot of time with women. My mom watches her some, but she spends way too much time with me. I couldn't say no to her tears when they offered to watch her as I had my next meeting."

"How's Pippa?" The question falls from my mouth before I

can think better of it. It's almost instinct, my desire to know how she's doing. I know she must be hurting and tired and worried, and I hate it. Hopefully in two days, all of this will be in our past, and she'll take my word for it when I tell her I'm all in with her—for the rest of my life.

Dean watches me closely. I barely know the guy, only enough to know he was kind enough to help me pull some strings to try and get the block of properties to go up for auction. We've discussed ways it can help him, too, of course. He's still a businessman. But he also seems like a decent human. One who cares about the town he grew up in, and I respect him for that. Finally, he sighs, still turning the pen between his fingers. "She seems tired but hopeful. She lit up when I told her I got confirmation that they're taking the block to auction."

I almost choke on the sip of coffee I was taking. "It went through?" I croak, trying to speak through the burning in my throat.

Dean nods. "Our plan worked. I told them they'd be foolish if they didn't hear other offers."

"This isn't hearing other offers. This is just an auction, correct?"

He smiles. "Exactly. I made them feel like it was *their* idea to go to auction. Why hear offers when people can battle it out with money? Your idea was genius. It'll go for far more than your uppity asshole friend offered."

"He's not a friend."

"Either way, what's stopping me from outbidding both of you at auction? My family owns most of the developments in Sutten anyway. Pippa's block was the one part that went to a partner of my grandfather's years and years ago."

I swallow. I like the guy, but I don't want him or anyone else to own Pippa's space. I want Pippa and Pippa alone to own it. "Because Pippa deserves to own the space. I'll buy it and immediately put it in her name."

"And the other properties? There are good people with businesses that are their livelihood that are also in jeopardy."

"I have no desire to deal with tenants and all of that. They can purchase their locations. Or you can take them over—I'll do whatever they prefer. I just want Pippa to own what she's worked so hard for, and I don't want the others to be taken advantage of."

Dean watches me closely, his lips perfectly straight as he thinks through my words. I don't cower under his gaze. I have nothing to hide—I mean every single word I'm telling him.

"And I'm supposed to just believe you on this?"

"Yes, but if you still don't think I'm a man of my word, you're welcome to join the bidding war."

He cracks another smile, his brown eyes roaming my face. "I knew I liked you."

"Why's that?"

"Because you don't beat around the bush. You're straight to the point. It's refreshing."

"People here don't speak their mind?"

"Not like you. There's a lot more behind-the-back deals and backhanded jabs. You're a good addition to Sutten, Hunter."

"You're tolerable," I tease, fiddling with my coffee cup. "And I don't say that about many people."

He sits forward, tapping the notepad in front of me. "Let's review the plan for the auction. I want to make damn sure that the good people of my town don't have to deal with this bullshit any longer than necessary. You're prepared to spend a lot of money? It won't be cheap."

"I'd gladly spend every last dime of mine for her."

He whistles. "Hope you've got the pockets to back this."

This makes me laugh. He's used to old money. People with old money don't understand new money. My family may have made a name for themselves, but there isn't a long line of Hunters with prestigious money like there is for his family. But I'm good at what I do. I've made a lot of money, much more than

Jason ever has. There's no way Jason will ever outbid me. "Don't worry about that part, Livingston. You just keep your ear out to make sure this goes through. And tell me if you hear anything from Pippa."

"You could just go talk to her. Tell her your plan."

I shake my head. "No. I'm respecting her boundaries until this problem is solved."

"She and this entire town think they can raise enough money to buy back the block."

I frown. I don't want her to be disappointed when she realizes there's no way they could raise enough to outbid Jason. He's narcissistic and rich—a horrible combination. He won't go down without a fight. A fundraiser could never raise the money needed, but I fall even more in love with her for trying. My stubborn, magnificent woman. I can't wait to have her in my arms again.

"Let them have hope," I speak up. "It's good for them."

Dean holds my gaze for a bit longer before he pushes his chair out and stands up. "I'll see you at the auction, then."

"Thanks for helping. I appreciate it."

Dean stares at my outstretched hand, taking it in his. "I helped you for Pippa and for the rest of the good people in this town. I don't normally like out-of-towners. You'll be the exception."

"I appreciate the help, regardless."

"Yeah, well, when this is all said and done, I'm going to make damn sure you do right by the other people on the block."

Both our hands drop, but I give him a nod. "You have my word."

Chapter 57
PIPPA

I'M SICK TO MY STOMACH WITH NERVES. I'VE ANXIOUSLY REAPPLIED lip gloss so many times that my lips practically stick together from the number of coats I've put on them.

"Breathe," Mare tells me, reaching over to grab my hand. She gives it a big squeeze, keeping it firm in her grasp. "This is going to work," she reaffirms, looking at my brother.

Cade nods. "We won't let you down, Pip. We're going to figure this out today. Just take a deep breath."

I close my eyes, wanting to find something to wipe my lips off with. We're sitting in a row of fold-up chairs, waiting for the auction to start. My senior prom and sixteenth birthday party both took place in this rec room. Never did I imagine I'd also be fighting for the chance to keep my business here, too.

"What if we didn't raise enough?" I whisper, my stomach feeling heavy with nerves. I truly haven't slept the past few days. Between preparing for the fundraiser and preparing for today, there was no way I could sleep peacefully. At least that's what I keep telling myself instead of admitting my bed felt far too empty without Camden's warm body next to mine.

"Open your eyes," my dad instructs from my side. I don't listen, afraid that if I open my eyes, I might cry from worry. I've tried keeping a brave face since the moment I returned to Sutten, but I'm nearing the end of my rope. I won't be able to handle it if I lose Wake and Bake today. Because losing to Jason will be that

—he's said it himself. There's no way I can pay the rent he expects. He'll force me out, and the dream I've worked on for years will go up in smoke.

"Pippa Linda Jennings," my father all but growls. "Open your eyes."

I'm a grown adult, but my eyes have never popped open so fast. His booming voice scared me as a child, even though he never raised it to Cade and me. Right now isn't any different.

"This is going to work out," he assures me, his voice confident. He reaches out and smooths my hair.

"You don't know that, Dad." My voice trembles, the tears pooling in my eyelids threatening to spill over.

"I do. I can feel it."

I let out a sad laugh, rolling my eyes. "You can't feel this sort of thing."

He scowls at me. "Don't tell me what I feel, darling. Your momma is here with us. She won't let you lose the shop. I can assure you of that."

At the mention of Mom, I can't fight the tears another second. They freely run down my cheeks, ruining the little bit of makeup I managed to put on this morning.

"She'd be so disappointed if I lost Wake and Bake," I croak.

"She could *never* be disappointed in you," he answers, his voice full of conviction.

Mare squeezes my hand, reminding me that she never let go. I don't look at her, but knowing she's right there next to me is enough to have me taking a deep breath in an attempt to settle my nerves.

"She was so proud of me when I got the place. And now I might lose it."

People start to fill in next to us, taking me by surprise. I see so many familiar faces, the people of Sutten showing up to support us. Tears spill all over again, my stomach turning in knots.

Now, I could disappoint all of them if we aren't able to bid the highest number for the block.

I look away from Rosemary, carrying her grandson in the terrible sweater she knitted, and look back to my dad. Everything is foggy through the tears in my eyes, but even through the tears, I can see his features soften. He pulls me into him.

"Your momma was proud of *anything* you did, Pippa. You could do no wrong in her eyes. I can feel her with me right now —with us—and I know with everything that I am that she's incredibly proud of you. You hear me?"

I nod against his chest, taking in a shaky breath.

"Then you also know that if she were here right now, she'd tell you to take a deep breath and compose yourself. Believe in yourself, Pippa. Because if you believe in yourself only half the amount she believed in you, I know that this will all work out, and the cafe will remain yours."

A hand covers Mare's and my intertwined fingers. When I pull away, I find Cade's overlapping ours.

"That Jack guy should be fucking terrified of you, Pip," Cade says, trying to lighten the mood.

It works—I let out a laugh, wiping underneath my eyes. "It's Jason, and if he should be scared of anyone, it's Rosemary back there. She's a loose cannon."

All of us laugh, and it does something to my soul. It soothes it. And as I let my eyes drift shut, for a moment, I feel my mom. I feel her calming presence. It gives me the confidence to straighten my spine and grab my auction paddle from the ground. I grip it tightly, waiting for everyone to show up so this can get started.

I don't have to wait long. Only a few more anxious coats of lip gloss later, a representative from the realty group is standing at the podium, covering how the process will work.

I risk a glance over at Jason. He's got two men sitting in the row with him, but other than that, everyone else in the room are all Sutten locals. It's all of the people who have worked tirelessly with me the last few days to even give me the chance to fight for my business.

"Good morning," the man comments, clearing his throat. His eyes anxiously roam over all of us seated in the crowd. He doesn't hold eye contact for long before he looks down at the piece of paper in front of him.

"Today, we're here to auction off the five properties along the block of Main and Birch. Each business is about a thousand square feet. We've opted to sell the properties together instead of individually. All properties have tenants who pay rent. It's the entire block except for one building."

My mind goes to Camden. The one person who owns his space. The one person not being threatened by Jason and his terrible plan to force locals out.

"The starting bid will be at one million."

Dean had prepared me for where it'd likely start out, but it still makes my stomach turn. That number is already so much of what we raised from the fundraiser. We had numerous donors who donated large sums of money, but I'm still scared it won't be enough. Even with the check my dad cut me this morning—money I knew he should use for the ranch—the creeping feeling of nothing being enough to compete with Jason creeps over me.

The man takes a step away from the podium, and Clyde takes his place. I've seen Clyde stand at this podium on multiple occasions. I was constantly coming to auctions with my dad as a kid. We'd buy horses, hay, feed, so many things from the man standing in front of me. Never did I think he'd be auctioning off what I've worked hardest for in life.

"I'm going to get right to it," Clyde announces, running a hand over his mouth. He looks incredibly uncomfortable up there, and by the hug he gave me at the fundraiser yesterday, I know this is the last thing he wants to be doing right now.

"Do I have one million and one?" Jason and I both raise our paddles.

"One million and three?"

My paddle stays in the air, no matter the dread coursing

through my veins. We're getting dangerously close to the point we'll have nothing left.

"Two million," Jason calls out, even though it wasn't time for that amount yet.

I swallow, risking a glance at my dad. He watches me, wrinkles creasing his entire forehead. His eyes look sad, and I hate the disappointment that's written all over his features.

"I can't," I mutter to my dad. "We don't have it."

My eyes sting with unshed tears. I hate this. I hate the feeling of knowing I tried everything I could do to not only keep Wake and Bake but the businesses next door, and it still wasn't enough.

"Two million," a voice calls from behind me. I look three rows back to where Dean Livingston sits with a raised paddle. His dad sits on the other side of him, looking at his son with wide eyes.

"Two million and one," Jason counters, angrily looking back at Dean.

"Two million and two," Dean continues, glaring daggers at Jason.

Rosemary grabs my shoulder, leaning forward in her chair. "Do we have anything else?"

I shake my head. "I can't compete with that," I answer sadly. "It's in Dean's hands now."

"Two and a half." Jason seethes.

"Three," Dean immediately counters.

I watch Dean hopefully, my heart thumping in my chest. It isn't up to me anymore; it's up to Dean. And I'm petrified even Dean will have a number he won't go to for five simple properties that shouldn't cost this much.

Dean and Jason go back and forth a few times, and the numbers are so high it makes me want to throw up. The world around me starts to get fuzzy and black at the catastrophic realization our plan is falling through. Everything I've worked for is slipping through my fingers, and there's nothing I can do.

I look at the row behind me, where Ms. Lori sits with her

husband. They'd put in all of their savings to try and buy back her flower shop, and it still wasn't enough. Or Ty who owns BlueBird Bookstore, who sits on her other side and volunteered his retirement money to help us have funds to try today. Everyone on the block has offered up everything they have. And even those who have nothing to gain and don't own businesses gave more than we could've ever expected.

And it's all going up in flames right now. Everything we've worked for is disappearing in a cloud of smoke.

"Ten million," a voice thunders from the very back of the room.

My entire body breaks out in shivers. I'd know the voice anywhere. At any place, in any crowd, I'd recognize it.

Chapter 58
CAMDEN

My hand not holding the bidding paddle stays firmly in my pocket. I'm scared if I pull it out, people might see it shaking with nerves. It's not about the money or the attention; it's the fact that I'm here to lay my heart out on the line, with no idea if Pippa will even speak to me.

It's terrifying. Nothing has ever scared me more than seeing her again with the fear of wondering if she'll allow me to love her the way I dream about.

I wish I could look into her mind or that she'd wear her emotions on her sleeve so I could know what she was thinking. Is she angry I'm here? Happy? Relieved? I can't figure it out from the look in her eyes.

The only hope I have is the fact she doesn't look away from me. Her chest rises in heavy breaths as her eyes travel my face.

"Hi," I mouth, well aware that there are too many eyes on us for me to be comfortable. I block all of them out, only focusing on the woman who owns my heart.

"Okay," the auctioneer says from behind Pippa. He clears his throat awkwardly. "I've got ten million. Going once…"

"We can't go from three to ten," Jason sputters. The anger in his voice takes me by surprise, my gaze ripping away from Pippa to find Jason angrily pushing out of his chair. His face is beet red as he looks between Clyde and me.

"Do you have a counterbid?" Clyde asks. It isn't exactly protocol, but I don't say anything. I know Jason won't meet my bid.

"I'm out," Dean announces, sticking to our plan. We'd give Jason hope for a moment before I showed up with a number he'd never be able to beat.

It seems to work because his eyes almost bulge out of his head as he yells at the auctioneer. "That price for five properties is ridiculous!"

"Ten million going once..."

Jason's beady eyes focus on me. He kicks his chair, almost hitting one of his associates as he barrels over to me. "You'll regret this, Hunter," he hisses, jabbing his finger into my chest.

I don't react. It isn't in my nature to show any kind of reaction. He doesn't deserve another second of my time.

"Going twice..."

"This isn't the end of this," Jason snaps. I don't bother to hide my laugh. He's already told everyone in Manhattan the sale had gone through. He'd promised his friends to rent out the spaces to their businesses. He'll return to Manhattan embarrassed, having to admit that he didn't have the funds to close the deal.

"Sold!" the auctioneer yells.

Jason doesn't move. I let out a long, annoyed sigh. Men like him will just never understand when to cut their losses. They'll forever embarrass themselves further instead of walking out with at least a little composure intact.

I take a step closer to him, letting my shoulder bump against his. I angle my head down due to the sheer height difference between us. "I'm going to say this once, so listen fucking closely." My voice is lethal. I don't bother to hide the disdain I feel toward this pathetic excuse of a man. "You will leave this town on the first flight back, and you will never return. You lost. It's embarrassing. If I hear you even mutter the word Sutten, I'll have no problem telling every single person I know how shallow your pockets actually are."

The entire room breaks out into cheers.

Jason's eyes go wide. Last night, I had my people deep dive into his finances. It all made sense why he was trying to buy these properties for cheap. He's about to go bankrupt, and this was his last hope to try and get some cash flow. He attempts to walk away, but I grab him by the bicep, keeping him in place.

"I wasn't finished," I grit out.

He doesn't say anything, but he doesn't need to. I keep going, wanting to make my point vastly clear. "Say one bad thing about Pippa or anyone else in this town again and I'll buy your companies right out from underneath you just because I can. Don't talk about *my* girl, and don't talk about this town. Understood?"

My fingers loosen around his arm. He doesn't linger for another second. He rushes out of the doors, his two associates following closely after him.

There's no way Jason will return to Sutten Mountain. But if he does try, I'm fully prepared to take him down for everything he's done. I won't be generous twice. I don't want to deal with him now because my biggest goal is making Pippa happy. But if he reappears, I'll end him.

My eyes find Pippa again, but she's too busy hugging her dad, her face tucked into his chest, to find me watching her. If she'd just look at me again, maybe she'd give some sort of indi-cation of how she felt about me being here. Will she be mad I purchased the properties? I only did it so she'd never have to fear someone taking it from her again.

I did it because I'm madly in love with her, and I'd do anything she ever asked of me.

A hand claps my shoulder. Dean steps in front of me, a cocky smile on his lips. "Ten million? I thought we decided on five."

"I wanted to end it. There was no way he'd ever be able to compete with that number."

Dean whistles, shaking his head with humor. "You're something else. I was worried for a moment there that I'd be the one shelling out the money for the properties."

"You know I wouldn't have let you. Pippa won't be paying anyone for her space. It's hers."

"And everyone else?"

"It's theirs."

He stares at me, silently assessing what I said. He must know at this point I'm a man of my word. After a few seconds, he reaches his hand out. I shake it, grabbing his forearm.

"I look forward to seeing you around, Hunter."

"Thanks for helping." He nods, walking away to join a group of locals chatting in a circle.

With his body gone, I'm able to see Pippa walking to me, her arm looped through her father's.

They stop in front of me, and I worry for a second that they might be able to hear my racing heartbeat. I'm so anxious. She's so close I could reach out and touch her. Would she let me? I don't try. It can't be a good sign she brought her dad with her. If she wasn't still upset, she'd come here alone and give me the time to tell her how I've fallen in love with this small town because I've fallen in love with *her*.

"Camden," Pippa begins. My heart skips a beat at hearing my name come from her lips.

"Hi," I croak. *Hi?* There's a million and one things I want to say to her, and the only thing that comes from my mouth is fucking *hi*.

I wince, looking over to her dad to see if he's privy to how anxious I am right now.

"I'd like for you to meet my dad, Jasper Jennings."

He reaches his hand out. I take it, not sure where this is going.

"Dad, this is my boyfriend, Camden Hunter."

"Nice to meet—" My words fall off when my mind registers what exactly she just said.

Boyfriend?

I must look hilarious, my eyes wide and mouth agape as I tear my eyes from her dad and look to Pippa.

Her dad clapping his hand over mine is the only thing that brings me back to the fact that he and I are still shaking hands. His eyebrows are raised as he looks between Pippa and me. If he has any questions, he doesn't ask them. I almost wish he would; that way, I could also get clarity on what's happening.

Something that feels a lot like hope develops in my chest. It's a dangerous feeling, knowing at any moment, she could crush me with one sentence.

"Nice to meet you, son," Jasper says, pulling his hand from mine.

I shake my head, trying to get my shit together. Pippa's introducing me to her dad, and here I am fumbling with my thoughts. "Pleasure, sir," I rasp, shoving my hands back in my pockets because I don't know what else to do with them.

"Thanks for what you did back there. I hope your intentions are pure for what you're going to do with those properties."

"They are." I clear my throat. "I'm not trying to do anything shady."

He assesses me for a few moments before he turns to Pippa. He pulls her in for another hug, whispering something against her hair that I can't quite hear. Once they're done, he turns to me once again. "We'll talk more."

And then he walks away, leaving me standing at the back of the room alone with Pippa.

She's the most stunning thing I've ever laid eyes on. I know without a shadow of a doubt that I'd do anything in my power to make it work with her. I need her more than I need money, art, anything. She's become my everything, and as my heart hammers against my chest, I make a silent plea she feels the same way.

"Boyfriend?" I ask, my voice coming out far more unsure than I envisioned.

She stands in front of me in a white skirt with ruffles, a tan shirt, and a pair of cowboy boots. She's breathtaking, her sun-kissed strands of hair falling down her shoulders. I know even if she tells me things could never work between us, I'd never get over her. I try not to think about it, focusing on her introducing me to her father as her boyfriend instead.

"Can we talk outside?" she asks, a blush creeping on her cheeks as she looks down at her boots.

"Yes," I answer, reaching out my hand to take hers. There's probably paperwork I have to sign and things to do now that I've won the auction, but they can wait.

First, there are some things I need to tell her.

Chapter 59
PIPPA

I've missed his touch. I'd forgotten how perfectly my hand fit in his. How much I love the confident way he moves and the way his thumb traces over the top of my hand, even when I don't think he realizes he's doing it.

He leads me through the building with self-assured ease, even though I'm fairly positive this is the first time he's ever been here. Instead of taking us out the main front doors, he leads us in the opposite direction, out the back doors.

At the back, there's a slab of concrete with trees planted along the perimeter. The leaves have turned into vibrant hues of gold and red, painting a stunning picture as we step into the cold air.

The chill to the air brushes along my skin, leaving a trail of goose bumps. I shudder, cold for only a few seconds before Camden is placing his jacket over my shoulders.

"Thank you," I mumble, suddenly nervous to be standing in front of him. Memories of the last time we spoke run through my mind. I remember the sight of him lying in bed, sleeping peacefully as I cried next to him, writing a note that shattered my heart into pieces.

"I didn't want you to be cold," he answers, his eyes roaming my face. It's only been a few days since I've seen him, and I've missed his icy gaze. The way his long, dark eyelashes flutter against his strong cheekbones every time he blinks.

I've really just missed *him*, and I realized when I saw him at the auction, I didn't think about all the ways we were different or all the things we still have to figure out. All I thought about was how much I loved him and how much I missed him and how I really wanted to fling myself across the room and into his arms.

"I wasn't talking about the jacket." I tug at the sides, pulling the fabric closer to me. I don't hide the way I take a deep breath in, inhaling the warm, comforting smell of him. "Thank you for standing up to Jason. For getting our properties back. For saving the day."

He clears his throat, reaching out to run his knuckle along my cheek. I lean into his touch, welcoming the feeling of his skin against mine.

God, I've missed this man. Now that the stress of having to fight Jason to keep Wake and Bake has passed, I'm hit with the realization that I'm willing to try anything to make this work between us. He's become too important for me to let go.

"I told you I'd fix it." His voice is deep and raspy, sending tingles down my spine.

"You did," I answer. "I should've believed you. I was just so worried about losing everything, about losing the only piece I still had of my mom, I took it out on you. I'm so sorry for leaving. I wasn't thinking straight. I wasn't thinking of anything but finding a way to save Wake and Bake."

He nods. "I'm sorry for everything I've ever done to make you think I wouldn't put you above anything or anyone else. I know there are scars from our past and that I haven't always been a man deserving of your love. But you make me better, Pippa. I know little to nothing about love. Everything I know about it, you've taught me. But I'm an excellent student, and I want to spend the rest of my life learning new ways to love you the way you deserve."

I told myself I wouldn't cry. That I've cried enough in the last few days than I have in a lifetime, but a tear falls down my cheek of its own accord. I can't control it, and I don't even try to stop it. I allow it to fall, my heart swelling with the intense love I feel for the man standing in front of me.

"I love you," I get out, my voice trembling with emotion. "I love you, and I'm sorry for ever believing for a second this love wasn't enough to overcome any differences or distance between us."

His silence unnerves me. It seems like forever that he doesn't say a single thing. It's long enough that my pulse spikes with nerves. Eventually, he takes a step forward, pressing our bodies together. His large hands rise to gently cup my face.

"Do you remember when you forced me to spend the day with you in Sutten?"

I smile. There's no way I could ever forget the day that shifted the balance between us. It was easy to slip from hating him to feeling for him. "How could I forget?"

"There was something you asked me that day that's really stuck with me."

"What was that?"

"You asked me what group of people I'd want to be in. It was something I couldn't stop thinking about. I'd find myself lying in bed in the middle of the night with answers to the question plaguing me by keeping me up all night. You see, until you asked me that, I thought I'd always want to be in the only crowd I've ever known. Never did I imagine myself in a place like Sutten. Until you. And the more I thought about it—the more I still think about it—I've realized I don't care what crowd I'm in. As long as it's the same crowd as you."

"Camden," I breathe, no other words coming to mind. He's taken me by complete surprise.

"I love you, shortcake," he continues, seemingly unaware of what his words have done to me. "I was so busy falling in love with you I didn't even realize I'd fallen in love with this town, too. I'd never ask for you to give up your life in Sutten. All I'm asking is for you to welcome me into your life so we can create a life here together."

A loud sob comes from my throat. My hand comes to my mouth as I look at him in disbelief. "You mean it? You'd be here with me?"

He leans in, his lips moving against mine. "I'd be anywhere with you. What else do I have to do to prove to you that I'm nothing without you?"

"Nothing," I whisper, needing to kiss him for a moment before continuing. "I love you, Camden Hunter."

"Not as much as I love you."

"Are we going to argue about this, too?"

"Probably." His lips tug up in a cocky smile. "But I've always loved fighting with you."

"I know something else we're going to fight about," I offer, wrapping my hands around his middle.

"And what is that?"

"I have to pay you back for what you did today. I don't have *that* much money, but we did raise some, and I want to give it to you."

His lips press into a hard line, the muscle in his jaw angrily ticking away. He doesn't have to say a word for me to know he's upset.

"We won't fight about this."

My head cocks to the side. "You'll let me?"

He laughs. "Absolutely not. The first moment I can, the ownership will be transferred to you the way it was always supposed to be. I'm going to transfer the gallery to you, too, so you can expand like you'd always imagined."

My jaw hangs open. "We can't. What about the gallery?"

He nips at my nose playfully. "I'd much prefer Wake and Bake to have more space. I only want to showcase local talent. I think it'd be really special to create something together where people can celebrate art and drink coffee."

It takes a moment for me to form words. My throat feels

clogged, completely overwhelming me. How is he so perfect? How do I make sure I keep him forever?

"It's too much," I finally get out.

"Too much would never be enough for you, shortcake."

And then he kisses me. It's long and sweet, as if he knows he has the rest of our lives to kiss me exactly like this. I kiss him back the same way. Months ago, I thought this man would be the bane of my existence. I wanted him out of Sutten as quickly as possible.

Now, my mind is filled with all of the possibilities of having him here with me.

I thought I'd always hate Camden Hunter, and I definitely never imagined myself falling for him. But I've always been a bit of a rebel, and as his hands drift up my leg, his fingers drifting underneath the hem of my dress, I'm looking forward to showing him more of Sutten.

I want to take him to the top of Peak Four during ski season and point to where you can see the ranch from the top. I want to take him to the Christmas Light Show that takes place in the Town Square. I want to test out my new recipes on him and make him enter the Annual Sutten Chili Cook-Off with me.

"I love you," I tell him, pulling away because I need him to know. I don't think I'll ever grow tired of saying those three words to him. "And I'll spend every day making sure you know how easy it is to love you. And how cherished I feel to have your love."

His body shudders, making me want to wrap my body around his. I do just that, holding the beautiful, broken man who owns my heart. I'll never understand why he was never shown the love he deserves, but from now until forever, I'll make sure he knows how effortless it is to love him.

Epilogue
CAMDEN

"I can't believe the day is finally here," Pippa says from the passenger side of our SUV. She presses her forehead to the window, trying to get an early glimpse of the event.

"You've not so patiently been waiting for it," I tease, flicking the blinker on to turn into the parking lot. It's already full, even though the event doesn't start for another hour. I search the lot, finally finding a spot that happens to be right next to a Jennings Ranch truck.

Good. Mare told me she'd make sure she and Cade and Jasper would be here early. I've been working on this surprise for Pippa for months, and now that the day is finally here, I'm incredibly nervous.

"I still can't believe this is real," she mutters, looking at the space in the distance.

"It's about to become a lot more real," I tell her, putting the car in park. My hand reaches into the pocket of my suit, making sure the little box tucked into the inside pocket is still there.

"Wait," Pippa says when I open the passenger door. She twists in the seat, looking at me with anxious eyes. "Before we go in there, I just want to say thank you again for this. I know I'm about to be a sobbing mess, and before I see the completed project I need you to know how much this means to not only me

I push her legs open, letting my fingers trail up the skirt of her sundress. There are little blue flowers all over it. I itch to push it up and get a better view of her tan thighs. We're in the middle of summer, nearing a year since I first opened the gallery in Sutten, and I've gotten attached to the golden glow of her skin from spending so much time outside.

When I feel like she's close enough, I grab her by the hips and pull her just a little closer to me because I can.

She speaks up before I respond to her. "I know there's so much we could've done with the money, but it means the world to me you decided to do this."

We argued a lot about the money Pippa and the rest of the town raised from their fundraiser. All of the owners on the block wanted me to keep the money in an effort to repay me for buying it. I wouldn't hear it. The moment I could, I put all of the properties in their respective names. I wasn't lying when I said it was never my intention to rent it out to them. I've gotten to know every single one of them in the months since I permanently moved to Sutten. They're all incredibly hardworking and deserve to own the space they've dedicated their lives to.

It didn't sit well with any of them—including Pippa. After enough fights about it, we decided to put the money toward something for the town.

It was my idea to create a space for the community to gather. And thus, the Linda Jennings Community Center was formed. It's been a labor of love to create and bring to fruition, but its opening today has been something we've been looking forward to.

In more ways than one.

"You scare me when you're quiet," Pippa teases, fiddling with my tie. "You're not second-guessing this, are you?"

I scoff, my hands trailing up her bare skin underneath her dress. I grab at her ass, rocking her hips back and forth. "I should punish you for even thinking that," I hiss. "This is one of the most special things I've ever been a part of. I'm excited to see it all come together. My only regret is that I never got to meet the woman it's honoring."

She smiles.

I nip at her neck, wondering if we could spare five minutes to climb into the back seat of the SUV so I could make good on my threats. We don't have the time, and I'm anxious with the way her hands travel over my body that she's about to brush along the box hidden away in my jacket.

"She would've loved you, Camden," Pippa mutters as I take a step away. I hold my hand out, assisting her out of her seat.

"I hope," I answer honestly. I'll forever wish I could've met the woman who made Pippa who she is. I've heard countless stories about Linda from not only Pippa but Jasper, Cade, and Mare and the rest of the town. I know she would've been a person I loved immediately. I just hope this community center ends up being a positive reminder to the community of the incredible human Linda Jennings seemed to be.

Pippa and I walk hand in hand toward the building. It isn't massive, but the indoor space is large enough to have four basketball courts, a gymnasium, and five large rooms that'll host weekly classes for the community. One of them being sculpture, taught by myself now that I have a lot more time on my hands. The gallery pretty much runs itself in Manhattan. And I help fill spots with the art at the now expanded Wake and Bake, but I mostly have time to create my own art.

We reach a fork in the sidewalk. One path leads to the front doors of the community center, while the other leads to the outdoor space of the center. I tug on Pippa's hand, leading her to the back of the building, where a surprise waits for us.

"Why are we going this way?" she asks, letting me lead the way.

My heart begins to hammer in my chest as I realize she's about to see what I've spent hours and hours on the last few months. It's been the hardest secret of my life to keep from her, and I just hope she loves it when she sees it.

We walk to the community garden. There are rows of garden boxes for anyone to use to harvest. And behind that is a space full of beautiful flowers, with rocking chairs pointed to the mountain view. Pippa and her family were always talking about how much Linda loved to sit in a rocking chair and look at the mountains at night. We wanted to bring her love for that here, creating a space where anyone could gather and spend time together.

Pippa aims a hesitant glance my way when we round the corner, the crowd of people waiting outside coming into view.

"What is this?" Pippa asks, her eyes traveling over everyone smiling at us. I make eye contact with the people who have welcomed me with open arms in the last year. I never thought I'd be someone to form attachments with so many people, but as I look at them as we make our way to the end of the path, I think about how much happier my life is now that I have all of them in it.

"Keep walking," I tell her, my eyes landing at the end, where Jasper, Cade, and Mare all stand in front of a large piece of cardboard as tall as Cade.

"What's going on?" she presses, her hand tightening around mine. If she can feel my hands begin to shake, she doesn't say anything.

"There's one more surprise," I say, stopping in front of her family and the piece of cardboard. I pull her back to my front, wrapping my arms around her middle. Leaning down, I line my mouth up next to her ear. "I've been keeping a bit of a secret from you, shortcake. And it's time for me to come clean."

She looks over her shoulder at me with a hesitant smile. "Camden…" she begins, looking at everyone surrounding us. "I don't know what's happening."

I never thought I'd do this with so many eyes on us, but it didn't feel right for us to be alone at this moment. So much of our story is tangled in the lives of the people around us it felt right to have them all here to share in the moment.

I press a kiss to her cheek before nodding to Cade. He looks at his dad, the both of them taking the hint and grabbing either side of the cardboard.

She must feel my rapid heartbeat against her back as I place my chin on her shoulder, cuddling her close as I take a deep breath. "I've learned so many wonderful, incredible things about your mother from countless people," I begin, for the moment speaking to her and only her. "And I'll always wish I could've met the woman who raised you. But even though I never got the chance to meet her, I love her. I love her for who she helped you become and who she was to every single person in this town. When planning this place of community in honor of her, one thing always seemed to be missing."

I nod. Cade begins to walk backward, his dad following his lead as they pull the piece of cardboard to the side.

Pippa gasps, her hands going to her mouth as she bends over with a sob when her eyes land on what's behind.

I follow her, crouching down with her and holding her as powerful sobs overtake her body. "I wanted to memorialize your mom forever. I know she did that herself in the hearts of everyone in Sutten—including my own through the stories people have told—but it felt right to create this, too."

I give her a moment, looking at the real-life statue in front of us. I'd spent countless hours perfecting the frame and features of her mom in stone. I'd pored over image after image of her, wanting to make sure I made this tribute to her absolutely perfect.

"Oh my god," Pippa weeps, one hand reaching out to the ground to steady herself. "I can't believe you did this." I let her soak it in, even allowing her to take a few steps closer and trace the features of her mother I replicated.

"How'd I do?" I ask anxiously.

All I can see is her back as she pays close attention to every detail of the statue. I use the opportunity to drop to one knee, pulling the velvet box from my suit jacket.

For a few moments, I'm stuck in the position as she doesn't turn to face me. Everyone around us goes quiet until finally she turns around.

There are streaks of mascara on her cheeks. "What?" she gasps, letting out a loud sob.

Her legs seem to shake as she takes the two steps back to me.

"Pippa Jennings, I always thought I was a man who needed structure and order in my life," I begin. She wraps her hands around my outstretched hand holding the ring box, stopping it from shaking with nerves. "But it turns out the structure I thought I craved was all kinds of wrong for me. You chaotically entered my life and threw me for a loop at every single turn of our story. Even when I thought I hated you, I was giving you pieces of myself. And it didn't take long for me to realize the feeling in my heart I had for you was love."

"Camden," she cries. I want to reach out and wipe the tears away, but I can't move. I'm too caught up in the moment between us. I need to get these words off my chest.

I need my ring on her finger, to solidify that she's mine forever.

"You taught me everything I know about love, and every single day, I wake up wanting to be a better man for you. You've turned me into the man I want to become, not the shell of the man I used to be. I've known from the moment I told you I loved you that I wanted you to be my wife, but I wanted to give you time. I wanted to give *us* time. And while I wish with everything in me your mom was here with us to watch me ask you to be my wife, I thought maybe if I did it here, with all the people who loved her surrounding us, that it'd be the next best thing."

She lets out another sob, closing her eyes for a moment before opening them back up. "She's here. I can feel it."

I nod. "I know, baby. I can feel it, too." I just now realize that I'm getting choked up. My tears well up at the sheer over-whelming emotion in the moment.

"I've never been so sure of anything in my life that I want to be your husband. I want you to be my wife. I want to have some big, elaborate wedding here if that's what you want and then take you on a honeymoon to France and go to every single French pâtisserie we can find. I want to share coffee with you every morning and have kids with you and really just grow old with you. I will spend the rest of my life proving to you that I'm the man you think I am."

I open the box, letting her look at the custom ring I'd spent hours designing with the jeweler. She gasps, her eyes widening at the cushion-cut pink diamond on a band of smaller diamonds.

"Pippa Jennings, will you marry me?" The words are barely out of my mouth before she's catapulting her body into mine, her arms wrapping around my neck.

"Yes!" she screams, crying into my neck. "Yes, yes, yes," she continues, her entire body shaking.

An overwhelming sense of peace settles over us. I wrap my arms around her even tighter.

"You feel that?" Pippa says into the crook of my neck.

"Yes," I answer.

"It's my mom. I just know it is. She approves," she whispers.

I laugh. "Thank god."

People around us cheer as I clutch the love of my life to my chest. It seems like everything slows down as we both embrace the moment. She cries, and I think I might cry, too, from the sheer magnitude of happiness overcoming me.

For the rest of my life, I'll be thankful that this small little town brought me and Pippa together. And that both of us opened up enough to each other to tempt our fate.

WANT MORE
Kat Singleton?

It's the end for Camden and Pippa...but the start of something new for...

Dean and .... in
Chase Our Forever (Sutten Mountain Book Three): https://amzn. to/3PIj85V

Winnie and Archer in
Pretty Rings and Broken Things (Black Tie Billionaires Book Two): https://amzn.to/3Ponrlc

To read the extended epilogue for Camden and Pippa, make sure to subscribe to Kat's newsletter. You can do that here: https:// bit.ly/3pgnbM1

Acknowledgments

Writing a book isn't easy, but there were so many people who kept me going every step of the way while I was writing Pippa and Camden's story. I'll never be able to put into words how much I appreciate their constant love and support, but I'm going to try my best.

First, to *you*, the reader. I wish I could eloquently put into words how much I appreciate you, but every single thing I've typed doesn't even begin to share how much I love and appreciate you. It is you who is the lifeblood of this community. It is you that shows me endless support. You're the reason I get to wake up every single day and work my dream job, and for that, I'm so freaking grateful. Thank you for choosing my words to read. Thank you for supporting me. You've given me the greatest gift by choosing *my* book to read. I love you so much.

To my husband, AKA Kat Singleton's husband (iykyk), A-A-ron. I'd be lost without you. You're behind so many things Kat Singleton. Thank you for always supporting my dream, even when it means working late nights every single night. I wouldn't be here if it wasn't for your love and support and having you always in my corner. You're a real-life book husband and I'm so thankful my sixteen-year-old self locked you down. I love you. Here's to many more books (and late nights) together.

Selene, thank you for keeping organized and running all things Kat Singleton. Your help allows me to do what I love— bringing new books to readers. I'm so grateful you chose me to work with. Thank you for keeping me organized! I know it isn't an easy job.

Ashlee, thank you for always bringing my cover dreams to life. You create magic with your designs and I'm in awe of everything you create. I'm so happy this industry brought us together. I love you forever.

Kate, thank you for making this book so stunning. Every page is a work of art and I'm so thankful to work with you. Thank you for putting up with me as I list off idea after idea for things to go with this book. It was an honor to work with you on this book and I'm looking forward to many more.

Melanie, thank you for organizing the most stunning cover photo shoot for Tempt Our Fate. Your talent shines through all of the photos we got. Ashley and Zach, thank you for not thinking I was crazy when you were asked to model for the cover. You brought these characters to life and I'm forever grateful you both said yes.

To my soul sisters who spend every day writing with me, encouraging me and cheering me on. I love you three with my entire heart.

To Salma and Sandra. Thank you for breathing life into this book and helping me perfectly share Pippa and Camden's love story. Your feedback is so important to me and I'm so grateful to work with the both of you. Thank you for helping making *Tempt Our Fate* ready to be released to readers.

To my alphas. You ladies were the first people to read this book and you got it in its most raw and real form and you loved it anyway. Thank you for helping make this book what it is. Thank you for believing in me and encouraging me when writing felt hard and I wanted to scrap the entire story. I'm so fortunate to have you ladies in my life. Please never leave me. I love you.

To my betas. Thank you for all of your vital feedback that made this book what it is. I wouldn't be able to do this without you and I appreciate your help in making Tempt Our Fate as perfect as possible. I love you forever.

To the content creators and people in this community that share my books. I'm so eternally grateful for you. I've connected with so many amazing people since I started this author adventure and it means the world to me to have all of you to connect with. I'm appreciative of the fact that you take the time to talk about my stories on your platform. I notice every single one of your posts, videos, pictures, etc. It means the world to me that you share about my characters and stories. You make this community such a special place. Thank you for everything you do.

To Valentine and everyone with VPR. Thank you for everything you do to keep me in check. It's not a secret that I'm a constant hot mess, and all of you are the reason I'm able to function. Thank you for making all things Kat Singleton run smoothly and amazing. I'm so thankful to call VPR home and for your help in getting *Tempt Our Fate* out to the world.

I have the privilege of having a growing group of people I can run to on Facebook for anything—Kat Singleton's Sweethearts. The members there are always there for me, and I'm so fortunate to have them in my corner. I owe all of them so much gratitude for being there on the hard days and on the good days. Sweethearts, y'all are my people.

Links

SPOTIFY PLAYLIST:
https://spoti.fi/480MfZ5

PINTEREST BOARD:
https://bit.ly/3EpdG1e

WANT
Bonus Content?

To read the extended epilogue for Camden and Pippa, make sure to subscribe to Kat's newsletter. You can do that here: https://bit.ly/3pgnbM1

ABOUT THE
author

Kat Singleton is an Amazon top 5 bestselling author best known for writing *Black Ties and White Lies*. She specializes in writing elite banter and angst mixed with a heavy dose of spice. Kat strives to write an authentically raw love story for her characters and feels that no book is complete without some emotional turmoil before a happily ever after.

She lives in Kansas with her husband, her two kids, and her two doodles. In her spare time, you can find her surviving off iced coffee and sneaking in a few pages of her current read.

ALSO BY
Kat Singleton

BLACK TIE BILLIONAIRES:

Black Ties and White Lies: https://amzn.to/40POdqu

Pretty Rings and Broken Things: https://amzn.to/3Ponrlc

SUTTEN MOUNTAIN SERIES

Rewrite Our Story: https://amzn.to/3KNni8W

Tempt Our Fate: https://amzn.to/3W0K2XW

Chase Our Forever: https://amzn.to/3PIj85V

THE MIXTAPE SERIES

Founded on Goodbye

https://amzn.to/3nkbovl

Founded on Temptation

https://amzn.to/3HpSudl

Founded on Deception

https://amzn.to/3nbppvs

Founded on Rejection

https://amzn.to/44cYVKz

THE AFTERSHOCK SERIES

The Consequence of Loving Me

https://amzn.to/44d4jgK

The Road to Finding Us

https://amzn.to/44eIs8E

Printed in the USA
CPSIA information can be obtained
at www.ICGtesting.com
LVHW092014101023
760741LV00005B/49